THE QUEENSLAND FILE

Recent Titles by Julian Jay Savarin from Severn House

MACALLISTER'S RUN

MACALLISTER'S TASK

NORWEGIAN FIRE

PALE FLYER

STRIKE EAGLE

TARGET DOWN

TYPHOON STRIKE

THE QUEENSLAND FILE

Julian Jay Savarin

Severn House

This title first published in Great Britain 1999 by
SEVERN HOUSE PUBLISHERS LTD of
9–15 High Street, Sutton, Surrey SM1 1DF.
This first hardcover edition published in the U.S.A. 1999 by
SEVERN HOUSE PUBLISHERS INC of
595 Madison Avenue, New York, N.Y. 10022,
by arrangement with HarperCollins*Publishers,* Inc.

British Library Cataloguing in Publication Data

Savarin, Julian Jay
The Queensland File
1. Suspense fiction
I. Title
823.9'14 [F]

ISBN 0-7278-5445-3

Printed and bound in Great Britain by
MPG Books Ltd, Bodmin, Cornwall.

First Moves

The rifle was something very special. As yet, none other like it existed. In a world without competition it was king, emperor, fearsome god. Its operator, well chosen, was also, it seemed, without peer. The best, equally fearsome. The two went together like well-matched twins: rifle and sniper, made for each other.

The sniper had planned well. It was going to be a kill that would be spectacular in its efficiency, with a subsequent escape from the area that would be so low key, it would be as if the killer had been invisible.

Late April, the north midlands, England.

The man sauntered along the terrace of Nottingham Castle. There was no one else about. The early sight-seers had remained within the building, for though it was a bright, clear day, it was also cold. A brief shower of morning rain had left the terrace gleaming and the man's reflection moved erratically in his wake as he walked. He passed a middle-aged couple, coated against the wind, using their large golfing umbrella as a shield as they cowered in an outside corner of the building. They were having a quiet argument. It was clear the woman did not want to be there.

The man smiled thinly as he walked on. He was tall, with heavy features and thinning black hair that frustrated the wind. His woolen suit, though reasonably smart, was not stylish and did not look expensive. It seemed merely functional, and fitted him indifferently. He didn't seem to care about the cold or the wind. But there was a strange dignity about him that contradicted his appearance, and his eyes, glowing darkly beneath thick, graying eyebrows, sparkled with an intelligence that was unexpected.

His walk took him to the southern edge of the terrace, where he stopped to look briefly down past a sheer drop, upon the sparse traffic of Castle Boulevard. A stranger to the city, he'd only identified the street because of the instructions he'd been given for getting to the rendezvous. Directly behind him and in front of the closed windows of the castle cafeteria was a tall, sturdy flagpole. On this particular cold day the cafeteria was doing good business. No flag had been hoisted; but the wind at times gusted so strongly, the top of the pole swayed quite perceptibly.

The man looked up at the distant copse that was Sparkhill Wood. The morning rain appeared to have given it an extra sheen so that it seemed to gleam in the bright sun. He turned away and walked to the flagpole. Turning once more to face in the direction of the wood, he leaned against the pole and lit a cigarette within cupped hands. He drew almost hungrily upon the cigarette; then he relaxed, and began to wait.

▪ ▪ ▪

The battered Land Rover, older than many of the drivers of the cars that passed it, made its way at a steady speed along the A52. Some drivers glanced up as they passed, smiling indulgently at the farmer at the wheel, who looked as battered by life as his vehicle. The Land Rover came to a roundabout, negotiated it with care, and carried on along the same route. A short distance later, it turned left off the road and onto a rough track that climbed gently. It kept going, taking the lumpy terrain in its stride until it could go no farther, balked by a slab of concrete that had been placed there for that very purpose.

The farmer didn't seem to mind and climbed out, taking a heavy-looking canvas sack from the back. He locked the Land Rover, then walked past the concrete block, the bag slung over his shoulder. The track had now become a footpath bordered by thick, wild hedges. The farmer walked along it until he came to an entrance to an open field on his right, beyond which was a thick wood. To the left was a cemetery. A few cars were there, their occupants scattered about, tending to various graves. The farmer took no notice and started walking across the field, making for the wood.

Coming towards him was a couple trailing two enormous Dobermans. The dogs came bounding up, looking mean. The farmer stopped and waited calmly. The dogs hesitated in their stride, slinking sheepishly to stop uncertainly before him. He stared at them. They looked back at their owners as if waiting for instructions. The farmer did not budge.

"Caesar!" the woman called. "Brutus! Back here!"

The dogs looked at the farmer, whimpered, then hurried back.

The farmer continued walking. When he came up to the couple, the woman looked at him apologetically.

"I'm sorry," she said. "I hope they didn't frighten you. They're just playful puppies, really."

The farmer walked on without speaking.

The woman paused to look back. "Well! Some people are quite rude. It's not as if the dogs tried to attack him."

Her husband said nothing.

The dogs had themselves stopped to look at the departing farmer.

"Brutus! Caesar!" the woman called. "Come *on!*"

The dogs whimpered once more before obeying.

The farmer made himself comfortable within the wood. He was well hidden, and even an inquisitive dog would find it hard to betray him—the surrounding area had been sprayed with a repellent that would cause both dogs and cats to give it a very wide berth.

After selecting his position, the farmer had swiftly taken the sections of the rifle out of the bag, snapped it together with practiced ease, and mounted the scope. Both rifle and scope were remarkable pieces of engineering. As he now sighted through the scope, the flagpole at Nottingham Castle sprang into sharp relief just over four and a half kilometers away.

And leaning against the pole was the target.

The rifle, resting now on its low tripod, had a very long barrel whose bore seemed larger than expected, even for a sniper's weapon. The stock was a spaceframe of molded plastic, making it considerably lighter than that of a standard gun, yet much stronger. The scope, purposely designed in a dull finish so as to eliminate all possible reflections, had a power of magnification that was similar to a telephoto lens of 2000 mm. But whereas such a lens would be cumbersome and weigh at least twelve kilograms, the scope was less than a quarter of the weight, and less than half the size.

More, the scope had a brain, a minute computer that performed remarkable feats. In addition to image-intensifying qualities that enabled it to see in pitch darkness, it could also match the image of its selected target, so that no mistakes could be made. If the match were not one hundred percent, the computer would shut down and the rifle would not fire.

The third component of this killing machine was a card no bigger than the program cards that slotted into the backs of certain autofocus cameras.

The fourth component, the farmer, now took the card from a selection in the hollow compartment of the rifle butt and slid it horizontally into the waiting side slot at the rear of the scope. Next, the farmer took a strange-looking short magazine from the bag and clicked it softly into the belly of the rifle. The magazine seemed bigger than was normal for such a weapon. It held no more than four rounds. The farmer expected to use just one.

Finally, he took what resembled a small stethoscope, put the phones to his ears, and plugged the single end into the scope. He then settled into a firing position and began to acquire the target.

Within the scope, something quite startling was happening. Green numerals measuring off distance and bearing began to whirl until they steadied, blinked rapidly, then pulsed once and became static. They read: *dist. 4.587 kms, brng 338.*

The image of the man smoking against the flagpole then flashed and another blur followed as the computer compared images. Then two images appeared and began to merge, with a count of the percentage of the possible match appearing, moving from 10 percent upwards until there was no anomaly. The images solidified as one.

Match 100%, the scope displayed. *Firing integrity achieved.*

All this had been done within fleeting seconds, accompanied by a soft bleeping on the headphones, terminating in a single tone each time the parameters had been satisfied. Within the scope, concentric rings were displayed before merging into one glowing ring around the target. The single tone continued to sound, signifying target lock.

The unsuspecting man stared out at Sparkhill, enjoying his smoke as he waited at his rendezvous.

The farmer stared at the face looking unseeingly at him, and fired.

There was hardly any sound. There was a sharp whoosh, at such a high frequency it was almost beyond the aural range of humans. The Dobermans, now in their owners' car after a good fifteen minutes of play since having met the farmer, pricked up their ears suddenly and whimpered. The woman stared at them uncomprehendingly. Her husband, at the wheel, sighed as he started the car. It was clear whose dogs they really were.

The bullet was unerringly on its way; but it was no ordinary bullet. Longer than the .303 rifle round from the old bolt-action Lee Enfield, it was really a miniature cruise missile traveling at well beyond the speed of sound. It possessed its own guidance system, programmed by the scope. It was a bullet that truly had its target's name—or more precisely, face—marked upon it.

In the wood, the farmer was already swiftly dismantling the weapon. He knew he had not missed.

The man at the flagpole drew in another satisfying lungful of nicotine. It was his last. Something indescribably hot entered his chest, with such force it pinned him against the pole and forced the cigarette explosively out of his wide-open mouth. It went sailing in a graceful arc across the terrace.

The man's eyes popped and he grimaced, already dying as a tiny detonation took place within him. The force of the explosion, minute though it had been, wrecked his insides. Blood leaked out of every orifice as he slid to the wet, glistening stone floor of the terrace. Someone in the cafeteria had looked out just at that moment and screamed, pointing at what she saw. People rushed to the windows to look. Mothers dragged their eager children away. Out on the terrace, a second man who had been coming to the rendezvous had arrived just as the man at the flagpole was hit. He turned swiftly and went back the way he had come. No one took any notice.

The farmer had disappeared. Walking away from the field, in a direction different from the one he had come, he was now dressed as a backpacker. There was no evidence left within the bushes to show that anyone had been there. The backpacker's route eventually took him back to the roundabout from an easterly direction. Near the roundabout was a parking lot belonging to a small hotel. The lot was not full, but among the cars was a cream-colored Citroën 2CV. The backpacker went up to the small car and opened it, slinging his pack inside. He then climbed in and drove the three miles to Nottingham.

In the city, he found an underground garage. The backpacker disappeared.

The businessman in the trendy hat and fashionably loose expensive suit hailed a taxi. He carried a large, equally expensive briefcase. He was taken to the railway station, where he showed his first-class ticket and climbed aboard the train for London. He had been picked up a long way from the underground garage.

▪ ▪ ▪

The police were trying to make sense of the mystery killing on the terrace at Nottingham Castle. To begin with, there was nothing upon the victim that could identify him. There were not even labels, either on his clothes or his shoes.

When the train was half an hour out of Nottingham, a sphere the size of a golf ball within the tank of the Land Rover, still parked by the concrete block, exploded with little force but astonishing heat. Within minutes, the vehicle had been consumed, leaving the barest of charred remains. Thirty minutes later, the Citroën suffered the same fate. The train got to London, and the businessman disappeared.

I

Gallagher was dressed in a designer suit, designer shirt and tie, and shoes by Russell and Bromley.

"Doesn't he look pretty," someone remarked, almost in his left ear.

Gallagher turned toward his friend. "If you want me to be a godparent to your brat," he said good-naturedly, "be nice."

They were outside a small church in a beautiful Kentish hamlet. The early May Saturday was pleasantly warm and dry. The brat in question, fast asleep in his mother's arms, was due for a rude awakening.

"Anyone would think I didn't own a suit," Gallagher added.

"As one who has known you through school," the proud father began, "university, the Service, and the Department, I'm well aware of your dress sense, and your somewhat extensive wardrobe. Fit to be in one of the glossies, we used to say. But ever since you resigned and took up the questionable pastime of photography, waving a tie at you seems to guarantee you'll head in the opposite direction at a high rate of knots."

"Perhaps it's a reaction against all those years of trying to strangle myself."

"Oh, deep. Very deep, Gordon."

The proud father was Alun Boyd-Callum, school chum, university chum, Service chum, Department chum. The school was the only institution they'd actually shared, but the friendship had endured over the years, despite the different places of study and service.

Boyd-Callum, a Royal Marine commando in his thirties with the rank of lieutenant colonel, was still active, though with a totally different department. At six foot three, he was nearly a full two inches taller than Gallagher, and with his close-cropped dark hair, he looked a bit like a rugby player who was going a little soft at the edges. Unwise people had made the mistake of believing that, to their eventual cost.

Boyd-Callum's wife, Eleanor, a raven-haired beauty who was herself at nearly six feet an imposing presence, joined them with the sleeping baby. In her mid-twenties, her features glowed with the pride of new motherhood. Having married the man she had loved since her teens and having now presented him with a firstborn, life, she felt, had been good to her.

"Alun's right," she said, "you do look pretty."

"Not you as well," Gallagher said.

"Such a shame about Rhiannon," Eleanor continued, ignoring the warning glance from her spouse. "We really wanted her to be godmum."

"Well she won't be," Gallagher said. He didn't want to talk about Rhiannon. After over a year of what he'd mistakenly believed to have been a relationship that seemed to promise a great deal, she had decided to leave. For the second time.

He did not need the reminder.

But Eleanor was not finished. "You're in luck," she said, looking round as a powerful car squealed to a halt on the road that bordered the churchyard. "We managed to grab my globe-trotting sister in between assignments for her glossy mag. You remember my older sis, don't you?"

Miranda Lacey was a year older and as tall as her sibling, with auburn hair and dark blue eyes. She was as stunning as her younger sister, but with the added power of a more overt sensuality. She was also tough, and it was said that men were generally terrified of her. Gallagher hadn't seen her for at least ten years. She'd been almost like a bean pole then.

The woman who climbed out of the metallic blue TVR Chimaera was no bean pole, and the gossamer-thin dress she wore proved that beyond doubt. All the guests, waiting for the christening to begin, had turned to look. It was quite an entrance.

She hurried up to where Gallagher and the proud parents were waiting.

"Thought you weren't going to make it," Eleanor remarked by way of a greeting.

Miranda smiled brightly. "I'm here. Though for a while, *I* thought I'd still be in Prague. Plane was delayed." The eyes surveyed Gallagher as she quickly kissed Eleanor and Boyd-Callum on each cheek.

"You do remember Gordon, don't you?" Eleanor went on.

"Yes indeed." The voice was warm and slightly challenging. "You do look pretty, Gordon. As I remember, you always were." She kissed him, but closer to the edges of the mouth.

Gallagher shut his eyes briefly. "Nice to see you too, Miranda."

"Am I missing something?" She glanced at each in turn.

Boyd-Callum was trying not to grin. "We've been

having a little joke at Gordon's expense while we were waiting for you. We'd better go in before we embarrass him further."

Everyone trooped in. Soon, the baby began to yell.

Well hidden in thick, green shrubbery atop a low hill half a mile away, the killer had a clear view of the pretty Romano-Saxon church. The killer had watched the blue car as it had raced into view while still some distance from the church. It had come to its screeching halt, and the driver had hurried out to join the three people standing slightly apart from the rest. Shortly, they had all gone inside.

The same rifle would be used, but this time the scope would be needed only for sighting. The killer had watched everything through it. It was to be a shot unaided by special bullets or minute computer brain. It would also be an easy shot.

The killer had again chosen his position well. Directly ahead, the cleared fields gave a perfect zone of fire all the way down to the front of the little church. Beyond it, the peaceful hills of Kent rolled as far as the eye could see.

The killer waited.

They came out of the church smiling and talking animatedly as they were fussed over by the photographer Boyd-Callum had hired for the occasion. He wouldn't have dreamed of asking Gallagher. Gallagher was family. Gallagher was himself quite pleased not to have been asked, and surrendered willingly to the bossiness of the man who would be taking the pictures.

The baby had long since stopped yelling and was gurgling happily.

A warm body was gently maneuvered close to

Gallagher. "Hullo, Godfather." Miranda's eyes seemed to be daring him.

"Behave, Miranda," Boyd-Callum said. "Can't you see he's still in shock?"

"I think he'd make a lovely daddy."

Gallagher was saved by the photographer shouting imperiously, "All right, ladies and gentlemen! Smile, please!"

On the hill, the killer moved the scope slowly along, picking out each guest. The scope paused on Boyd-Callum, then Eleanor, then the baby, as if unsure of which target it wanted. It moved to Gallagher, paused again before moving to Miranda. It stayed there for long moments, watching as she smiled and talked.

The scope moved back to Gallagher, passed him, retracing its steps. Then suddenly, it swung back to Miranda and froze there.

A finger tightened on the trigger.

"Do remain still, Miranda!" Boyd-Callum said through clenched teeth. "We want this photo taken before my smile stays permanently fixed on my face."

"But there's something crawling on my ankle!" she hissed back at him.

Gallagher, watching the photographer's exasperated stare, was trying hard not to burst out laughing. Next to him, Miranda gave up the struggle.

"Sorry," she said and began to bend towards the offending ankle. At that very moment she gave a piercing scream and was flung backwards to slam against the stone steps of the church.

Gallagher took one look at the blood welling from her left shoulder and yelled, "*Down, everybody!*" Then he lunged towards Eleanor and the baby as people screamed and panicked.

Boyd-Callum, taking in the situation as swiftly as Gallagher, also grabbed at his wife and child. Together, they had a startled Eleanor and the baby down on the ground, their bodies forming a shield.

"We're okay," Boyd-Callum said urgently. "See to Miranda."

"Right."

Gallagher crawled rapidly back to Miranda, who was shivering into shock. He inspected the wound. It looked more serious than it actually was. The bullet had gone right through, but damage appeared slight.

"You're very lucky," he told her. "The shoulder's going to be fine."

Her face was screwed up against the pain. "So you say. It bloody hurts!"

"Of course it hurts. What do you expect?" He began tending the wound, ripping the sleeve off her dress.

"Christ," she said, "do you know how much that cost?"

"Not much with a bullet hole in it. I need a bandage."

"Are you always so kind?"

"At least you can't be in such bad shape if you can muster the sarcasm."

"I could have died," she said with sudden understanding.

"Thank whatever bug was crawling on your ankle. You must have reached down at the exact moment whoever it was fired. That was meant for the spot where your heart is."

She went even paler.

"Gordon!" Boyd-Callum called from where he was still holding his family down. "How is she?"

"Very, very lucky."

People were all over the place, cowering behind any cover they could find, including the gravestones at one side of the church. The vicar, who had been next to Eleanor, was trying to squeeze himself into the ground and looking a veritable beacon in his white surplice.

"We should get out of here," Boyd-Callum said, glancing round at the surrounding woods, trying to identify where the shot had come from.

But Gallagher, having tended to Miranda, was looking for something else, eyes searching around the steps of the church. He visualized the likely trajectory after the bullet had left her shoulder. Soon, he found its resting place. It had plowed itself in the solid stone of the building near the door, a mere foot off the marbled floor of the entrance. He began to move towards it.

"*What do you think you're doing?*" Boyd-Callum asked, horrified. "That lunatic could still be out there!"

"Perhaps. But I doubt it. He could have shot again if he'd wanted to. He's not some nut with a passion for guns and popping off at people, and Miranda's in good cover for the moment. He was after a target."

"*Me?*" Miranda said, managing to sound shocked and weak at the same time. "A *target?*"

"You must have upset someone during your travels in eastern Europe."

"Don't be ridiculous."

"An irate lover then."

"That doesn't even require comment."

"If you two could humor us and force yourselves to stop arguing," Boyd-Callum began with heavy patience, "perhaps we can do something about getting out of here. I have a baby who seems to think it's all a game. Any moment now he's going to think different and let us all know about it."

Gallagher had reached the bullet, but it was so well embedded, he couldn't pry it loose without digging.

He stared at it. "Powerful rifle," he murmured to himself. "But silenced, and still able to do this. No lunatic, but a pro. Anyone got a penknife?" he called. "I've got to dig this bullet out."

The silence that greeted his request was eloquent.

Then a voice, muffled by grass, said, "Isn't that tampering with the evidence? Shouldn't you leave that for the police?"

Gallagher peered round, but could not identify the owner.

"Fine," he said, giving up. He wasn't in the mood for an argument. "All right. I think we can all get up now . . . except for Miranda, of course."

Nobody moved.

Gallagher stood up, wishing he didn't have to. "It really is all right. Whoever it is, has gone." He didn't believe that, but he was equally certain this was no random shooting. The person up there was not going to waste bullets if he couldn't see the target.

Feeling horribly exposed, Gallagher remained standing at the church door.

Up on the hill, the killer was indeed still there, and furious, knowing the shot had missed. It was one of the risks of the long-range shot without the computer. The cruise bullet would have found any target making such a basic maneuver as ducking or, as had apparently happened, unexpectedly moving to brush at something.

The killer focused the sight on Gallagher, who seemed to be looking directly into it. But he did not fire.

"You know something," the killer murmured, "but you're not sure what."

The scope made darting searches for its original target, and could not find her. The killer began to dismantle the weapon with practiced speed. Even in this sleepy place, someone would have rung for the police.

It would not do to be seen on the road while the local force of one was on his way to the incident. He would inevitably have contacted his superiors, and before long the place would be knee deep in police cars. Perhaps even a helicopter, or two. A shooting always got them excited.

It was time to leave. There would be other opportunities.

Boyd-Callum, still down, looked up at Gallagher. "Well, you're still alive. Do as he says, everybody," he called out to his guests. To Eleanor, he continued, "Come on, darling. Up you get. Whoever's out there is not using an automatic weapon, or he'd have sprayed the place by now. That means a shot at a time. Even if he's still intending to shoot, he can't possibly get more than one if we all hurry to the cars."

Her eyes were trying hard not to show fear as she looked at the baby. "What if it's Jamie?"

He had no answer to that. "It will be all right." He stood up, gently pulling her with him and shielding them as best he could. "Now let's go. Gordon will see to Miranda."

The others had stayed down even after Boyd-Callum's urging, but now, seeing him making his way to where the cars were parked, they all got up in a sudden rush like startled pheasants and headed for the cars in a controlled stampede. The vicar hurried past Gallagher and back into the church. The photographer was legging it at high speed for his own car.

Gallagher remained where he was. "Don't move," he said to Miranda. His eyes were still on a far hill.

"You've seen something?"

"No."

"Then why . . ."

"Just working out possibilities."

She gave a sudden gasp. "Work them out soon,

please. This shoulder is killing me. I think it's bleeding more heavily. It feels as if it is."

"Soon I'll get you to your local doc. Let the others sort themselves out first and get out of the way. We're going to have to move quickly. It wouldn't do to have someone blocking the way with a car that won't start."

The sounds of revving engines, manic starter motors, and crunched gears rent the once-peaceful air as people roared away in a chorus of squealing tires. The wonder was that none of them hit each other.

Gallagher smiled as in complete contrast Boyd-Callum's Range Rover moved sedately on with a parting wave from its driver. He nodded briefly in acknowledgment. Alun had never known how to panic. Gallagher thought the high-riding vehicle, with its acres of glass, looked frighteningly vulnerable and that Eleanor's car, a much lower Volvo estate, might have afforded more protection, but there was nothing he could do about it. No one had expected a shooting party.

"Right," he said, looking down at Miranda. "They've all managed to get away without running each other down. Our turn."

"What about my car? I've only just got it."

"She worries about her car. Well, you're in luck: I got a lift here. My car's back at Alun and Eleanor's. I'll drive you."

She seemed hesitant.

"Listen," he began, "I appreciate how you feel about your car. I don't let just anybody drive mine either, but this is not the time and place to get touchy about who . . ."

"All right. Keys in my bag. But do be careful."

"Yes, ma'am," Gallagher said dryly.

"It's not funny."

"No. Neither is that shoulder, nor that shooter up on one of those hills."

"How do you know he's up there?"

"I don't. But it's where I would be in his place."

"I forgot. You and Alun used to do that secret stuff together."

"We never worked together."

"Whatever. Well? Do we move?"

"We move, if you can walk."

"I can walk."

He got down quickly off the steps to help her. She gasped as she rose to her feet and they hurried for the TVR. Gallagher kept his body between her and the suspect hill as they walked. Her own body was pleasantly warm against his and the scent of her was powerful and heady; but there was no smell of fear.

She turned to briefly look at him, her mouth coming close to his. "Aren't you brave, protecting me with your body like that."

"I don't like getting shot any more than you do, so let's just make it to the car in one piece, if we can."

She looked away, a tiny smile showing fleetingly through the pain.

They got to the car without incident. Gallagher helped her in, then got behind the wheel and eased the Chimaera out of the hamlet, wondering if the rifle still had a bead on them.

No bullets came their way.

The killer was already well away after having made sure nothing had been left to betray a recent presence. This time, no car was used for the escape. As a backpacker, the killer walked away from the area. It was a good six miles before he saw any other person. A group of four ramblers passed by.

"Nice morning for it," one of the ramblers greeted.

The others smiled pleasantly.

"It certainly is," the killer said, and walked on.

▪ ▪ ▪

The Boyd-Callum home was a large, Georgian house that stood proudly on wide grounds, at the edge of a village about twelve miles from the church. A stream meandered along the bottom of the well-kept garden. The guests were dispersed about the place, some sitting on the grass, most with large drinks. A few were talking with a slight edge of hysteria in their voices. They would remember the day for the rest of their lives.

Miranda had been attended to by the local GP, and the police had been to take statements. The senior policeman for the district had been invited to the reception, and though he had come to the house in civilian clothes, he had not stayed long and had rushed off to supervise his officers. He was unmarried, and lived alone. He knew Alun Boyd-Callum well, and as the Laceys were a local family, knew the women from their childhood.

The policeman was also well aware that the man he called Colonel worked for a government agency, though he didn't know its identity. As a result, he'd been quite happy to pass the responsibility for the inquiry to higher authority. But he'd insisted on retaining some vestige of local control, and it had suited those above him to give him some autonomy.

Inside the house after the police had gone, Gallagher said to Boyd-Callum, "I'd like to go back to the church and get at that bullet, as well as checking out the hill."

"The bobbies might take a dim view of your prying out the evidence."

"I was hoping you could handle that side of things."

"Bit keen, aren't you? Ever since your resignation, I've had the impression that what you wanted most was nothing to do with the old sort of life. I'm naturally most disturbed that Miranda was shot, and that my family and guests were put in considerable danger by whoever was back there, but . . ."

"Something's itching at me, Alun, and I don't know what. My antennae tend to quiver when things happen without apparent reason. There's *always* a reason. What was Miranda really up to in Prague?"

"Don't look at me like that, old son. Foreign activities are not my brief, as well you know; and I certainly wouldn't use my own sister-in-law, even if they were. So not guilty. You know what she's like. Probably trod on a few toes while researching some article for her mag."

Gallagher shook his head slowly. "It's got to be—"

The ringing of the phone interrupted him.

Eleanor yelled from somewhere, "Get that, will you, darling?"

Boyd-Callum picked up one of the extensions that was close by, and announced the number. He listened, then said, "Of course." Then he hung up.

"You won't have to vandalize our little church, after all," he went on to Gallagher. "It's already been done. That was the police. They've dug out the bullet and are mystified. They wondered whether I could help them identify it, so they're bringing it over. We'll see them in my study."

The senior policeman, Henry Parring, brought the bullet himself. In the study, he handed the spent round to Boyd-Callum, who stared at it.

"Beats me," he said, and passed it to Gallagher.

Parring stared uncertainly.

"It's all right, Henry," Boyd-Callum said to him. "Gordon's an old friend. More, he was also a colleague. He knows his stuff."

"I see," Parring said, but clearly didn't.

Gallagher inspected the squashed lump. Much of it was sufficiently intact to give an idea of its former length and calibre. It had traveled with such force that its tip had acted like a punch that had virtually attempted to perforate the stonework of the church. The tip had remained practically unaltered. It was the rear end that had squashed in on itself with the force of the deceleration.

"Longer than the old .303," Gallagher said, "which is a real departure from the current trend of using compact, metric ammo. This thing doesn't tumble, either. It's like a minirocket, without the propellant. This is new stuff. Nothing else like it around." He looked up at Boyd-Callum. "Unless your lot are experimenting."

"We're hardly likely to shoot members of my own family."

Gallagher looked amused. "No. I suppose not." He handed the bullet back to Parring. "Sorry. Can't help."

Parring looked disappointed. "Very well, gentlemen. Perhaps London can tell my people more . . . always assuming they want to. They think we're yokels down here."

Boyd-Callum nodded sympathetically. "Know what you mean. Sorry not to have been of more use, Henry."

"Not your fault, Colonel. I do hope Miss Lacey will be all right."

"We'll look after her."

"Yes. Well, I'd better get back to my men." Parring gave a brief smile. "No rest for the wicked. Bit of an unusual christening for young Jamie."

"It was indeed."

They saw Parring to the door. They all shook hands and the policeman left.

"Good man," Boyd-Callum said to Gallagher as the policeman entered his car and was driven away. "Used to be a constable on the beat when the girls were kids. Now he commands his own force. All right, Gordon," he went on. "Give. I know you recognized that round."

Gallagher did not waste time denying it. "I didn't recognize it specifically, but I do recognize a similarity. Years ago someone I met briefly in the business—in the Middle East, of all places—told me of a special type of ammunition that was at the experimental stage. Our reasons for meeting had nothing to do with this new bullet, but he drew me a sketch. Unfortunately, he never made it to our next meeting, so I never found out more. His body was found on some rocks. 'Robbery' was the official cause of death given. Yet another tourist hit. No one asked too deeply about the total lack of identification, even on his clothing."

"So what are you saying?"

"The experimentation is clearly over, and that thing is being issued to special killers."

"By whom?"

"Perhaps we should talk to Miranda."

"Perhaps we should talk to me."

Gallagher stared at him.

"Back to my study," Boyd-Callum said. In the study, with the door shut, he continued, "I'm still not certain there is a connection, but your little story about the sketch and that bullet has crystallized something for me.

"A few days ago, a man was shot on the terrace of Nottingham Castle. Like your character in the Middle East, he had no identification whatsoever upon him. But the real prize in this particular incident is the way in which he was shot. From long range—no one has so far worked out how or where—by a bullet that exploded *inside* his chest."

"Jesus!"

"Quite. By the number of fragments that were found, even allowing for the possibility that a considerable number were not, it still added up to a monster of a slug. But there's more: This one was propelled, and judging by what the lab boffins have suggested, it also possessed a minature seeker."

Gallagher stared at him. "You've got to be joking."

"I didn't believe it either. Until I saw what showed up under the microscope. The damned thing had its own electronic brain, in a titanium jacket. Judging by the dark color of the tip of the one that was fired today, it's also in a titanium jacket. So we've got two kinds in use by the same people, if the incidents are connected. One is self-propelled and explosive, the other fires normally and is inert. Different ammunition for different jobs. Armor-piercing, too, of course, which is why this one did not attempt to turn itself into a coin on making contact with centuries-old English stonework. What the lab scientists—two men and a quite formidable lady—couldn't say was how the seeker locks on to target."

"My God," Gallagher said quietly as he considered his friend's revelations. "So that poor sod who was taken out was on to something when he made that sketch all those years ago."

"Certainly looks like it. Your unfortunate artist definitely knew something. Might well have been the true reason for his sudden demise." Boyd-Callum paused, looking sheepish. "Er . . . There's more."

The tone of his voice put Gallagher on the alert. "Am I going to like what's coming next?"

"That depends."

Gallagher waited.

"I'm afraid the investigation into the Nottingham killing, because of the possible foreign connotations . . ."

"I know I'm not going to like this. . . ."

" . . . has been taken over by your old department. Fowler . . ."

"I bloody *knew* I wasn't going to like it!"

"Fowler would like to see you."

Gallagher fixed his old friend with a baleful stare. "Alun, if you tell me that you asked me to be godfather at the behest of Fowler—"

"Good Lord, no!" Boyd-Callum was shocked by the

suggestion. "He knew the christening was coming up, and that we'd always wanted you to be godfather."

"And never one to miss an opportunity to use people," Gallagher said bitterly, "he made the suggestion."

"Er, yes."

"That man does not know the meaning of shame. Well, he can stuff it."

"You were keen enough to check out that bullet a while ago. Why not hear what he has to say?"

"Because Fowler always gets me into situations that can get me killed, and people around me usually wind up dead."

"He wasn't at the church," Boyd-Callum said reasonably. "Miranda could have died, and so could have you. So could have any of us. Fowler can't be held responsible."

"I wouldn't put it past him," Gallagher said grimly.

"You're being hard on him."

"I could never be too hard on Fowler."

2

"Now I do need to have that talk with Miranda," Gallagher said. As they came out of the study, the babble of voices hit them like a great wave. "She may know something, even if she's currently unaware of it. And after that, I'm off to the hill."

"What do you expect to find?"

"If he's good, not a lot. If he's very good, which I'm certain he must be, he'll have sanitized the area. But even the best of pros can sometimes make a mistake."

There's always one thing that escapes the first check, sir, and it can make all the difference between a successful mission, and disaster. Make sure you double-check to find whatever might have escaped your notice; but hope your opponent doesn't do the same. It does happen sometimes, and that could be to your advantage.

O'Keefe.

But O'Keefe was long dead.

"Want me to come up there with you?" Boyd-Callum was saying.

Gallagher shook his head. "Your place is here with your family and guests."

"As possibly the county's newest godfather, yours too."

"I won't be long. Make do with the godmother for a while."

"And here she is," Boyd-Callum said, "holding court."

They'd reached the wide terrace, where Miranda, arm in a sling, was reclining languidly on a lounger that had been brought out specially for her. She was surrounded by most of the male guests, some of whose respective partners were not looking pleased as from various vantage points in the garden and on the terrace they darted glances in her direction from time to time. She didn't seem to mind.

"Break into that at your peril," Boyd-Callum cautioned, an amused expression upon his features. "I'm off to see to my wife and son."

Gallagher went up to the group. They fell silent, and waited expectantly. Miranda looked up at him.

"We've got to talk," he said. He looked at each of the men in turn. "Privately."

They surveyed him with a mix of expressions that ranged from tolerant resignation to downright annoyance. One man stared at him haughtily.

He stared right back.

After some moments of silence, Miranda said, "He's not going to back down, so I'm afraid I'll have to see you all later."

There was a further stubborn silence before they reluctantly moved away.

"Brave, and tough," Miranda said to him, her eyes challenging him once more. "Want me all to yourself, do you?"

"Don't make the mistake of treating me like one of them," he said. There was an edge to his voice that made her eyes widen briefly in surprise. "I want to talk to you about Prague."

She sighed. "And here I was thinking you were interested in my company, or at least in my well-being."

He did not rise to the bait. "I can see you're all right."

"I'm not bloody all right," she told him in an aggrieved tone. "A bloody great bullet went through me."

"Cleanly through you," he corrected. "As I've said before, you were very lucky, and you're milking the sympathy for all you're worth."

Unexpectedly, she smiled broadly at him. "You're seeing cleanly through me as well. None of the others would have dared say that. Afraid they'd hurt my feelings. You win some brownie points. So what do you want to know about Prague? But I warn you, there was really nothing special about the trip. Here. Sit next to me." She moved her legs to make room. "This will kill them," she added, glancing at the men who had been crowding round. "They probably think we'll end up in bed."

He glanced idly at the legs, which were exceedingly beautiful. "What? With your wounded wing? I wouldn't do that."

"Dunno. Might be fun." She sounded as if she meant it. "I suppose I'll have to make do with boring old Prague."

"Prague is never boring," he said, remembering a city that just a very few years before was one of the most dangerous places the Department could send you. Gallagher wasn't taken in by Miranda's bold flirtation. He should probably run a mile, he thought, if he took her seriously. "Tell me about your trip."

"I went over to do an article on exiled royals who

hoped to reclaim whatever it was they had left behind. I know people sneer at the magazine for its gossip on who's spending what mini-fortune in which fashion house, or who's having what affair, and so on; but I didn't join to do that kind of work. My articles are meant to stand out. I go after other meat. I wanted to find out whether there were royals who had remained and embraced the regime, either because they genuinely wanted to, or because they could remain fat cats, or possibly because they had been blackmailed into doing so and it was a way of surviving."

"I can see all sorts of reasons why some people would be very reluctant to talk to you about that," Gallagher commented. "There may have been a 'velvet' revolution, but all those heavies didn't retire overnight. Besides, it's not looking so velvety these days. There must be quite a few Czechs and Slovaks who are having sleepless nights as they take in what's happened to Bosnia. And if they're not, they should be. The nightmare could be rolling down their street any day."

Miranda paused for a moment, and frowned. "Once or twice, I did think I was being watched, but I put that down to my own Western paranoia about being in what was not so long ago an Iron Curtain country. But I'm sure everyone from the West who goes out there for the first time, even today, must have a slight case of the chills. After all, think of all the Cold War movies we've seen. All those po-faced border guards with itchy trigger fingers, just waiting for you to run so they can have the excuse to let rip with a stream of bullets.

"So what happens? Nothing sinister in Prague, but I go to my nephew's christening right here in dear old England, and what happens? I get shot in a churchyard in peaceful Kent.

"And that's it, I'm afraid. No men in dark overcoats sat next to my table in some mysterious restaurant, listening to everything I said to my contacts. No microphones in the ashtrays, no packages passed under tables, and nothing slipped into my suitcases while I was away from my hotel."

Despite what she said, Gallagher was convinced she had missed something that might give a clue to what had just occurred, and why. It could have been something totally unconnected with what she might have been doing at any given time. Perhaps she had witnessed an incident, without realizing it. Stuff like that happened much more frequently than the average citizen would believe. Gallagher had himself succeeded in a mission, one he'd practically decided to abandon, by just such an occurrence: a chance sighting of an agent who'd supposedly been seen in a country thousands of miles away. There had even been documentation to prove he was where he wasn't.

Gallagher decided he'd leave it for the moment. Whatever the doctor had given her to kill the pain would soon be wearing off. That shoulder was not going to be fun. She'd be in no mood then to answer his questions.

"She must have hurt you very badly," Miranda remarked suddenly.

He'd been glancing about the garden as he marshaled his thoughts. His head snapped round, and he realized she had been studying him keenly.

"What? What are you talking about?"

The blue eyes held his gaze. For the moment, the pain of the shoulder was not in them.

"Of course, you're very good at hiding it," she went on conversationally. "Must be the training, or perhaps you're instinctively like that. But there are times when you drop the curtain a bit, like in church during the christening. You were relaxed, and something peeped out. Don't be surprised. I am a journalist, after all. I look for the things that people don't normally want you to see."

Gallagher said nothing.

"Whoever she is," Miranda went on, "she's a fool. Aah, shit!" she added with a sharp gasp. "I think the painkiller's wearing off, and I can't take any more for at least another two hours. Damn. This really hurts."

"Would you like to go in?"

She shook her head vigorously. "No. I can handle it."

"You don't have to prove how tough you are, you know."

"Don't patronize me."

Gallagher got to his feet. "I'm not patronizing you. There's nothing virtuous in pretending you don't feel pain."

She hated giving in, but in the end she said, "Perhaps I should go in for a bit. I'll go up to my room. Help me up?" She extended her good hand.

He took it, and she pulled herself upwards. "Thanks."

They walked into the house and when they got to the stairs, she paused. "I'll be fine. I meant what I said. She is a fool."

"Perhaps she's the smart one."

Again, Miranda shook her head. "You don't really believe that." She turned and made her way up to her room.

He waited until he heard her door close.

"Is she all right?" Boyd-Callum said from behind him. "I saw you two come in."

Gallagher turned to face him. "The painkiller's worn off. She's decided to sweat out the next couple of hours in her room. I'm off to the hill now. See if anything's been left behind." He paused. "By the way, it was a good idea not to cancel the reception because of what happened. Besides, by the look of them, your guests needed stiff drinks."

Boyd-Callum grinned. "Even if I'd wanted to, Eleanor would not have gone along. And as for both sets of grandparents . . . They've been showing off ever since he was born. But I did suggest it to her on the way back. Not a chance. Wasn't going to be put off by a psycho with a rifle. Her words. Great woman," he added proudly. "Someone I can depend on when the chips are down. I'm a very lucky man." Then a look of embarrassment came to his face. "Oh God, I'm sorry, Gordon. Not thinking."

"Don't look so miserable, Alun, for God's sake," Gallagher told him lightly. "All that is history. See you later."

As he left, he could sense Boyd-Callum staring worriedly at him.

Gallagher's pride and joy was waiting in the spacious drive. The gleaming black machine made the other cars seem positively mundane by comparison. The turbocharged Audi Quattro, its twenty-valve engine developing more power than was standard, its advanced four-wheel-drive system giving it leechlike roadholding abilities, was to Gallagher the epitome of all he desired in a car. It was fast and powerful, it was a superb long-distance cruiser, and it was safe in all weather conditions. It was thus a source of constant disbelief to him that the manufacturers had chosen to discontinue the model. He thought the decision a fine example of corporate madness.

The car was just a little under three years old. He would not dream of replacing it with anything else, and intended to cherish it for as long as it lasted. He had added a few of his own modifications. There were no handles on the doors. Instead, there were plates that would open the door at a slight pressure. There were sensors on it that would warn not only of attempted theft, but of efforts to attach tracers. He'd had good reason previously to take this precaution, even against those supposedly on his side. Like Fowler.

But the remote he carried on him had been silent. No one had interfered with the vehicle. Whatever was going on in Fowler's devious mind, at least the car had been left alone, for the time being.

He removed his jacket and loosened his tie as he approached it. Taking out the remote, he squeezed one of its buttons. The Quattro's indicator lights flashed briefly and the driver's door sprang open a few inches. He flung his jacket into the back and climbed in. The leather upholstery still smelled as fresh as it had on the first day of his ownership.

He liked the sense of oneness he felt every time he climbed in, the way he'd felt when he flew Phantoms. Climbing into the cockpit at the start of a mission, no matter how many times he'd done so, had always seemed to lift him to several higher levels within himself. When he flew, it was as if the aircraft had become part of him. The same thing had occurred with the quattro. Sometimes, he talked to it and called it Lauren.

There were very special reasons for that.

"Ah. Mr. Gallagher," a muffled voice said.

Gallagher snapped on his seat belt and looked across at the face that was peering in from the passenger's side. Henry Parring.

Gallagher turned the ignition key far enough to give power and pressed the switch to lower the window. "Mr. Parring. I expected you to be long gone."

"You don't seem particularly surprised to see me, however."

"Alun said you were a good copper. I'm never surprised by what a good copper does. I expect the unexpected."

"A wise precaution."

"And no doubt, you've got some men about the place to keep an eye on Miss Lacey, just in case."

"Right again, Mr. Gallagher. Going somewhere?"

"Only for a drive. Not for long."

Parring appeared to think about that. "The Colonel mentioned you were once colleagues. Can I assume this means you are no longer . . . ah . . . active?"

"I try my best not to be."

"I see. It occurs to me that both your good self and the Colonel had some ideas about that cannon shell of a bullet which you were not prepared to divulge."

"We had a few wild guesses, Mr. Parring. We could not have helped you. We had nothing of substance to contribute."

"I see," Parring repeated. "I could say I should be the judge of that, but we'll let it pass. I suppose if during your drive you happened to come across anything of interest, as a *private* citizen, you would naturally hand this over to the police to assist us in our inquiries."

"Of course."

"Of course," Parring echoed, not entirely convinced. He stood back, and appeared to be admiring the Quattro. "A very nice car indeed. Enjoy your drive, Mr. Gallagher."

"Thank you, Mr. Parring."

Gallagher raised the window and started the car. The five-cylinder engine gave its muted, but mean, lop-sided beat, and he moved off unhurriedly. Like a great beast of prey, a deep rumble coming from the large double exhaust pipes, the Quattro eased itself down the drive, seemingly eager to be unleashed.

Parring watched it leave, remaining where he was until it had gone out of sight. He carried a radio, but made no attempt to order one of his men to follow, knowing the man would be spotted. He stood there and listened until the powerful rumble eventually faded away.

Gallagher drove along the narrow country lane at a steady pace. He was in no particular hurry. If the police had already been to the hill, which he doubted, they would have found nothing. At least, not the things they would be looking for. As if to confirm his thoughts on the matter, a speck in the sky gained his attention. Helicopter. But looking in the wrong place.

Not his problem.

Other thoughts also occupied his mind as the Quattro's muted thunder beat against the tall hedges on either side of the lane. The comments of both Miranda and Boyd-Callum had brought unwelcome memories of certain aspects of his personal life into focus, where he least wanted them.

As he was constantly reminding himself, it seemed that every time he valued someone, he tended to lose that person. He was either betrayed or the person was taken from him. It was as if he were not meant to get too close to anyone; as if his road were destined to be solitary.

First had been Celia. He'd married her while still in the air force. But she'd hated being a Service wife, and hated it even more when he'd gone to work for the Department. Her antipathy had helped him make a decision he'd arrived at quite independently, and he'd resigned from the Department after becoming disillusioned. The death of O'Keefe on a mission had been the real deciding factor. O'Keefe was the man who'd trained him. Despite being assured to the contrary, he continued to think it had been his fault. As leader, the mission had been his responsibility; there could be no getting away from that.

But starting a new life had not been easy. He went into photography and after a slow beginning, things had picked up nicely. Then disaster had struck. Coming home early one day, he'd heard sounds he had never, in his worst of nightmares, expected to hear: Celia gasping and squealing into climax without him.

He had bounded up the stairs to be greeted by a

tableau that was now burned into his mind. In his bed had been an unknown man and woman with Celia. Celia had been astride the man, at full gallop. The shocked look on her face when she'd realized he was standing there was another vivid and unwelcome memory.

He had rushed out of the house, past a wedding photograph, he in full uniform, his wings seeming to gleam on his left breast as they walked through an arch of swords. He had paused just long enough to take a minimum requirement of clothes and his passport. Somehow he'd made it to Heathrow and grabbed the first available flight out of the country.

Then the flight had been hijacked, by a new type of terrorist. There had been no political reasons. It had been purely for cash, a job for a major international company. One of the passengers had been earmarked for assassination, and to make it look like a normal hijack, all the selected passengers were to be killed. Unfortunately, and mistakenly, Gallagher had been included. They had wound up in the Australian Outback, with the group of terrorists intending to turn them loose and then hunt them down.

But Gallagher had found a reason to live in Lauren Tanner, one of the trapped passengers. She was traveling with her grandfather, the intended victim of the assassination plot. Gallagher had led an escape attempt. Four of them survived, including Lauren's grandfather. Villiger, an Afrikaner agent on the flight, had worked with Gallagher in their flight for survival, and had shot the leader of the hijackers dead.

But a member of the group had survived and revenge had been taken. On a skiing holiday Gallagher and Lauren were taking in France, she had been killed by a sniper. The second bullet, meant for him, had missed; Lauren's dying body, in cannoning against him, had pushed him out of the line of fire.

Gallagher found his hands gripping the steering

wheel tightly as he remembered. He had wrought a terrible revenge upon the assassins, but in so doing, had found himself involved in something far more sinister. In addition, a good friend had betrayed him during the course of it.

And so it went. The people he had lost—Celia, Lauren, Diderot (who had betrayed him), Dalgleish (who had been captured and turned into a killer of those of his own side in desperation), Lucinda, O'Keefe—people close to him, betrayers or victims. There were still others. Now Rhiannon had been added to that list.

He relaxed his grip on the wheel, allowing himself to once more drive the car with sensitivity. He was now close to the hill he was certain the sniper had picked, and began looking for a suitable place to park. Frequent glances in his mirrors showed nothing to cause alarm. The helicopter had disappeared.

Gallagher eventually found a spot close to a farm gate. He was able to park the Quattro out of view, without blocking the entrance. He climbed out and began walking along the crest of the hill, every so often pausing to take a sighting on the church. Fifteen minutes later, he was certain he'd found the exact spot. There was an unimpeded view all the way to the churchyard. It was a clear fire zone.

He began to search the area minutely, not really expecting to find anything, but living in hope. Twenty minutes later, he was ready to admit defeat. The killer was what he feared: very, very good. It was as if no one had been there for a long time.

He almost missed it.

He was turning to head back to the car when the tiniest flash of white showed briefly in the tall grass. For a few anxious moments, he couldn't locate it. Then he saw it again and parted the screen of its natural hiding place. It was a partially smoked cigarette.

He stared at it before gingerly picking it up. There

was something not quite right about the way it looked. It was too clean, and looked as if the smoker had broken it and put a light to one end, without actually having bothered to draw on it. There was also a smudge of red on the filter.

Very carefully, Gallagher sniffed at it. Lipstick.

But it was not the imprint of a lip. It looked as if the red had been marked upon it. Had it been deliberately left to be found, but placed in such a way that only a searcher looking for something out of the ordinary would have discovered it?

"A strange calling card," he said to himself.

He could be wrong. It could easily have been discarded by some thoughtless walker who had no worries about accidental fires in the countryside, and had nothing whatsoever to do with any killer. But the lipstick washed out that idea. A cleanly broken cigarette stub with lipstick purposely marked upon it had been left lying around. It had to be deliberate.

So who was the message, or warning, for?

His antennae were almost singing. "Me?" he asked aloud.

Boyd-Callum was making his way up the stairs to check on Miranda when he noticed that the door to his study was slightly ajar. He clearly remembered shutting it when Gallagher had left.

He went back down the stairs to investigate. Miranda was there, one-handedly leafing through a large book that was spread open upon his desk. She looked up as he entered.

"Miranda!" he began. "Aren't you supposed to be resting?"

She flashed him a quick smile that tried to hide the pain of the shoulder. "It was a battle between lying up there uncomfortably and hating it, or doing something to keep my mind off this wretched ache. Do you mind my being in your study? I promise not to look at any secrets."

"Be my guest. I keep nothing remotely confidential here. I see you've found Gordon's book of photographs."

"Yes. The down-and-outs. Very impressive. I've got one, you know, but not personally signed like yours."

"I'm certain if you ask him nicely," Boyd-Callum said with a straight face, "he'll oblige. I've also got the second book. The one on the homeless."

She closed the book. "I don't have that one." She moved to a tall window that looked out on the drive. "I find him fascinating."

"Any man who does not immediately throw himself at your feet fascinates you, Miranda."

She did not look round. "It isn't that. I won't deny I do find him . . ." She didn't continue to voice that particular thought, but the meaning was clear enough. "It's something else. I saw a little of it back at the church after I'd been shot. There are so many different facets to him. He was looking at that hill as if he could see the person hiding up there. He does not appear to have great faith in people, yet he threw himself over Eleanor and the baby to protect them." She gave a short laugh. "I ought to feel miffed. After all, I was the one who got shot."

"Ah, but you see, the way Gordon reasoned, you were already down. He sought to protect the most vulnerable. We almost head-butted each other senseless as we both leapt for Eleanor. Yet, he's one of the most cautious people I know. Never goes in unless he knows he can get out."

"But he was quite prepared to risk his life for Eleanor, and for me too. Do you know that when he walked me to the car, he placed himself between the hill and me?" She paused, thinking about what had happened. "He reminds me of a lone hunter of myth and legend: instinctive, dangerous, searching for something . . . perhaps someone. If you were to ask what animal he most reminds me of, I'd say the wolf. The noble kind, not the idiotic sort you've got in your garden."

"Remarkable." Boyd-Callum spoke almost in hushed tones.

She turned. "What?" Her free hand made to touch the wounded shoulder, then thought the better of it.

"Er . . . nothing. Muttering to myself."

"What do you think he hopes to find on that hill?"

"God knows. Gordon goes his own way. Always has."

"Tell me about him."

Boyd-Callum hesitated.

"It's okay, Alun. In this house, my journalist's hat comes off. This is not an interview, and you don't have to tell me anything secret about him. This is personal interest only. Tell me about the man I last saw when I was a skinny teenager."

Moscow, the same day.

Colonel General Vladmir Mikhailovich Skoryatin, GRU, was a dissident before *glasnost, perestroika,* Gorbachev, and Yeltsin. Those very few in the West with whom he'd had contact knew him by a series of names, one of which was Borodin. He had survived the dangerous pre-Gorbachev times because he was an exceedingly clever individual. Now that the Soviet Union was technically no more, even Russia was unstable. His personal feeling was that despite the tentative steps towards a version of democracy, these were even more dangerous times, made so because the enemies were more numerous and faceless. Even greater care was needed in order to survive. Despite his liberal leanings, he was not a Yeltsin fan and was, in fact, diametrically opposed to all the new president stood for.

In his office, which he was constantly surprised to find had not yet been taken from him, Skoryatin was studying a thin file. The information in that file should never have left the country to which it rightfully belonged. Yet here it was in his hands.

The subject of the file was Gallagher.

Skoryatin, known as Borodin, began to read:

STAFF MOST CONFIDENTIAL

PSYSEC/1/6/39C/GGG

PROFILE ON GALLAGHER

NAME	GALLAGHER, GORDON GARETH
CODE NAME	GREYWOLF
HEIGHT	6FT 1IN (1.85M)
WEIGHT	13 STONE (182 LB)
EYES	HAZEL

REMARKS:

Gallagher is approaching his mid-thirties. Gained his degree at Cambridge, entered the Royal Air Force through University Air Squadron. Highly skilled fighter pilot; last posting before joining the Department was on Phantoms. His rank, Squadron Leader, was gained at the age of 27. A high flier indeed. In training for specialist duties, showed great aptitude for clandestine combat. Is deadly accurate with a variety of weapons, particularly 9mm automatic pistols and assault rifles. His favored weapon is the SIG Sauer P226 pistol. Strangely, shows antipathy for use of these, turning to them only as a last resort. His records show, however, that when called upon to do so, is devastating in their use.

Has completed several successful missions for the Department. Thus, the Department cannot afford to dispense with his services. All coercion to be used to keep him in harness, despite his resignation.

A combination of personal and professional troubles led to the resignation. His marriage failed. Wife unfaithful, *discovered by Gallagher in the act.* The psychological effects can only be guessed at.

His professional troubles began when O'Keefe was killed on a mission. Gallagher continues to maintain he was responsible. However, careful checking of his report and of others, show quite conclusively that his weapon jammed at the crucial moment, resulting in his inability to give O'Keefe covering fire when it was most needed. A more convincing reason for Gallagher's resignation is his disenchantment with the Department's activities. As previously indicated, he is far too valuable to lose. His faculties are in excellent order.

His father was an Oxford don, of Irish ancestry. His mother Jamaican, though of part-Scottish extraction (née Gordon). Despite this ancestral mix, Gallagher appears to have had a very stable upbringing, a tribute to both parents, considering the social pressures they may have experienced during that time. Both parents are now dead, father murdered by antagonists during one of Gallagher's missions. He blames himself for this, and the Department is a sharp focus for his anger.

He has no problems forming relationships with women. However, given his activities for the Department, these young women tend to come into considerable danger. There have, unfortunately, been casualties, including Gallagher's fiancée.

Currently, he makes a very comfortable living as a professional photographer, having apparently found a marketing niche for his own individual style. He owns his home, an attractive maisonette in Holland Park. In addition to money spent on the acquisition of professional materials which are of the very best, his single real extravagance appears to be his Audi Quattro, upon which he tends to lavish a great deal of money. It is substantially modified, with all manner of electronic wizardry, and is extremely fast and powerful. A point to note: It is believed that the grandfather of the dead bride-to-be gave Gallagher a considerable sum of money, meant to have been a wedding gift. Despite his refusal to take it, this large sum continues to gather substantial interest in the bank account opened in his name by the old man. Gallagher has never made use of it. This sum is fast approaching seven figures. Financial coercion will therefore not succeed. Another point to note: Gallagher travels extensively because of his work. This can be of great value to the Department.

There are unconfirmed reports that he sometimes talks to the car, addressing it as LAUREN, the dead fiancée's name. She was killed on the slopes of Courchevel. He exacted a terrible revenge, but he blames the Department for her death. The killing conveniently coincided with a mission we wanted him to undertake and his quest for revenge served the Department's interests. However, he continues to harbor a simmering resentment. The Quattro is black, a symbol of the grief he originally suffered. His current companion is RHIANNON JAMESON, who appears to have had a beneficial effect upon him. There are suggestions that all may not be right with them. I would venture to suggest we wait and see how this develops.

Conclusions are these: Despite the above trials, Gallagher remains what he has always been. He is a suberbly controlled individual who performs excellently under stress. His constant doubting of his own abilities leads him to perform efficiently, rather than the opposite. This is a healthy trait. We do not need gung ho merchants. He manages to draw extra resources from within himself, where others would have long since given up in defeat. As a result, it is to be reiterated that the Department cannot afford the loss of his services. The reasons for his initial selection for Department work are as relevant today as they were then; perhaps even more so, given his considerable experience and the current state of the international situation.

My conclusions are based upon detailed study of his mission reports, testimony from various sources, and unobtrusive observation of the subject. A measure of his capabilities can be gleaned from the fact that out of ten observation attempts made, he discovered eight and gave extreme difficulty with the other two, merely by taking it for granted he was being observed.

It is therefore highly recommended that efforts to keep Gallagher on strength be continued. Failing voluntary service, coercive methods should be employed. GREYWOLF is to be kept active.

R.D. Malton-Coombs
Senior Medical Executive Officer
Psychological Section, Int.1

cc: Sir John Winterbourne	Head of Department
Mr. Adrian Fowler	Deputy Head of Department

ENDS

Borodin shut the file slowly, thoughtfully. "Very impressive, but the thing is, my friend," he said, addressing the file softly, "there is an assassin on your trail. I do not know who, but I must find out and warn you."

The file he had read, all of whose copies should have been safely locked in Department safes, had been stolen from the offices of the KGB. The West insisted in calling the famous and notorious security organization the "former" KGB. To Borodin, KGB was KGB. He extracted the profiled report.

Then he put the entire file, its remaining contents

and cover, into the electronic shredder at the side of his desk.

The M20 motorway, Kent.

The killer, no longer a backpacker, turned the stylish car with French license plates off the motorway to rendezvous with another car waiting at the side of a quiet road two miles ahead. In the waiting car, which carried British plates, were two men, and they watched as the French car pulled up behind them.

The killer got out and approached, then leaned forward, eyes unfathomable behind dark glasses.

The man in the passenger seat was surly. "Where the hell have you been? We've been waiting for a good half hour."

The dark glasses surveyed the men in the car for long moments. Nothing was said. As the surly man once more began to speak, his companion behind the steering wheel placed a restraining hand upon his arm.

"This will be the first and only time you question my movements," the killer at last said coldly. "Your instructions are to cooperate fully with me. Do not attempt to exceed your authority, and do not get in my way. You would not survive it." A hand was thrust forward. "Give me the next assignment."

The surly man brought out a thick envelope and handed it over with bad grace. "All the information you need is in there. The money is already in the specified account. This one's to be in France."

"I never would have guessed."

The killer turned and walked back to the second car.

The surly man, cranking his head around to look, said, "I don't have to take orders from—"

"Don't even think it," the driver interrupted quickly. "Didn't you see those eyes?"

"What eyes? Those fucking dark glasses . . ."

"Exactly. Do you like cowboy movies?"

"What are you talking about?" The surly man watched as the other car accelerated past on its way to eventually rejoin the motorway for the channel port of Dover, where it would take the ferry to France. "What have cowboy movies to do with this?"

"There's a recurring theme in them," the driver said. He was also staring in the direction of the receding car. "You know . . . the one where the loudmouth with fancy guns slung low turns to look at a quiet man, usually sitting alone. 'He ain't so tough,' the loudmouth says loudly. Next thing, he's down on the floor of the sedan, quite dead, pretty guns barely out of their holsters. You're right. You don't have to take orders. If you're feeling suicidal, you can always make the point; then you won't have to take orders, ever again."

The surly man turned a vicious look upon his companion. "Shut up!"

But the driver was unperturbed. He was still looking out at the motorway, though the car had disappeared.

He shivered involuntarily. "You can try if you wish. Me, I just want to complete the job and say good-bye to that assassin. Gives me the chills."

He started the car, turning it around to head back to London.

The cautiously pragmatic driver had a broad Scottish accent. His surly companion's was indeterminate. Neither man was British.

3

Miranda was still in the study, Boyd-Callum having left to see to his guests. She was standing at the window and looking out at the drive when the Quattro's snout poked itself between two cars as Gallagher parked it. He did not appear to have seen her.

She felt she now understood a little more about him. Though Boyd-Callum had divulged nothing about his work for the Department, enough had been said about the man Boyd-Callum knew to give her what she felt was a reasonable insight into Gallagher's character, attitudes, and feelings. Boyd-Callum had warned her not to come to hasty conclusions. Gallagher was not easily pigeonholed. But she understood; she understood the lone wolf in him.

She had also been cautioned about becoming emotionally involved. That advice, she decided, she could take or leave as she saw fit.

She left the study to go out to meet him. They met

on the low steps of the house just as he was about to enter.

"Shouldn't you be taking it easy upstairs?" he greeted.

"It was worse lying up there. Anyway, I'll soon be able to take another painkiller; the two hours are almost up. Did you find anything?"

"No," he replied easily. "Whoever it was was too good."

The dark blue eyes held his steadily.

"What?" he said, innocence itself.

"Nothing at all?"

"What's this? The probing journalist?"

"Experience has taught me that it's what people don't say that's most interesting."

He gave her a quick grin. "You've never interviewed me before or you'd know—"

"I've got your book on the down-and-outs. I was looking at the one you gave to Alun."

"Very neat," Gallagher said. "Change of tack. I still found nothing."

Her eyes searched his face for some moments, and then she said, "Okay." She began to turn away.

"Ah, Mr. Gallagher," a familiar voice called.

"Shit," Gallagher said to himself.

Miranda heard and paused to look on interestedly. "Let's see you work your way out of this one," she remarked in conspiratorial tones.

He turned to face his nemesis, in the shape of Henry Parring. "Mr. Parring," he greeted with a brightness he did not feel.

"Enjoyed your drive?"

"Yes. I did, thank you. Lovely day for it."

"Indeed. I was up in the chopper for a while," Parring went on. "If you remember, we flew over you."

Gallagher remembered. He had been on the way back from the hill when the helicopter had passed over again, heading in the same direction.

"I do remember," he admitted. "Any luck with your search?"

"Well now. I was about to ask you the same thing."

"Me?"

"Well, yes. You see, the pilot—I was not up with him then—seems to think you stopped near a hill overlooking the church."

Bloody hell, Gallagher thought. They must have been using binoculars while still some distance away. No point denying it.

"I did stop, but really to admire the view."

"Come, come, Mr. Gallagher. You can do better than that, surely. With your background, I would think the last thing on your mind at the moment would have been the picture-postcard beauty of the countryside."

"I am a photographer," Gallagher reminded him. "I'm always interested in landscape."

"I thought cityscapes were more your line."

"Ever the good copper," Gallagher said. "So you checked out Alun's book of my photos."

"I've got one of my own. I thought it very good work."

Gallagher was genuinely surprised. "That's one unexpected thing I didn't expect. Thank you for the compliment, and for buying the book."

"Ah, I have to confess it was a gift. From a socially concerned person who felt the police should study it and perhaps be a little less, ah . . . rigorous with vagrants. I admit to being less than enthusiastic when first receiving it."

"And now you're converted."

"I wouldn't put it quite like that, but I am impressed, yes. And so, Mr. Gallagher, find anything?"

It was a neat maneuver, but Gallagher had been waiting for it. "No," he replied smoothly. "I'm afraid not."

"Oh, well. There was just a slight chance. Good to see you up and about, Miss Lacey. Thank you, Mr. Gallagher."

"Mr. Parring," Gallagher said, watching him leave.

After Parring had moved out of earshot, Miranda said, "You knew he was going to pull that one, didn't you?"

"Of course. All that stuff about the pictures."

"But he sounded genuinely impressed."

"He was. That's why it was such a good move."

She smiled at him. "I think I'm going to like you."

"Should that worry me?"

"Who knows?"

London, three days later.

Fowler studied the reports on his desk. They concerned the shooting of the still-unknown man in Nottingham, the failed attack on Miranda Lacey, and a new report that had come in from France. A politician with overtly rightish tendencies had been shot dead, with the same kind of bullet that had killed the man at Nottingham Castle.

"So where's the connection?" he asked aloud.

"There is one," his companion replied. "You've just got to find it."

"Thank you for that vote of confidence, George," Fowler said dryly.

George Haslam. Tall and big and remarkably fit, a bluff man approaching his seventies. Officially retired, he somehow always managed to become involved in Department business. He constantly bemoaned the fact, claiming he would much rather tend to his garden and enjoy his much-needed retirement. Others knew the real reason was that he simply could not keep away and was quite happy when from time to time Fowler dragooned him into service. His thinning hair was so short, it was difficult to tell whether he actually possessed any or was actually bald. His eyes were those of one still young, yet they looked out upon the world with the wisdom of many years spent in the observation of human frailty. George Haslam had grown detached from the stupidities of his fellowmen. Nothing they got up to could surprise or shock him.

Fowler was secretly very pleased with this continuing access to Haslam, whose experience was invaluable. Barely twenty years old during the Second World War, Haslam had seen service with the maquis, the French guerrilla movement. Legend had it that in his day, he was as good as Gallagher. Fowler frequently drew on Haslam's expertise when dealing with Gallagher.

"The question, George," Fowler now continued, "is who and what's behind it. Where does Miranda Lacey come into the equation? Could she have indeed become involved in something out of her depth in Prague?"

"Could she have discovered a group, or seen someone involved with the killings, you mean."

"Exactly. And was she then pursued here because of it?"

"Perhaps Gallagher has some idea. He was on the spot."

"Which is why I've asked him to pay us a visit."

"And that's really going to please him."

Fowler was not as tall as Haslam, but his slim, aesthetic build made him seem equal in height when the two of them were seen walking together. His neatly cut hair, with graying wings, was longer than would have been expected. He wore glasses that seemed to sparkle with their clarity, giving the impression that his eyes were larger than they really were. Many believed that Fowler did not need those glasses at all and that they were an effective psychological tool that he used ruthlessly when the occasion demanded it. A full-power stare from Fowler, those unfortunate enough to have experienced it had sworn, was like being caught in the beams of a laser. Everyone agreed this was an outrageous exaggeration; but only just.

Fowler now turned one of his milder looks upon

Haslam, who was impervious to even the strongest. "Your wit does you credit."

"Oh, good," Haslam said.

The sleepy London square, overlooked by the anonymous offices of the Department, was reasonably quiet, save for the occasional car desperately cruising the one-way system looking for a free parking space. The broad roadway neatly surrounded a small, perfectly manicured park within which were benches placed there for public use. The park was itself protected by tall iron railings, and a keeper who descended like the wrath of God upon anyone foolhardy enough to drop the smallest piece of litter. The surrounding road was patterned by marked-out parking spaces, access to which was gained by buying a timed ticket from strategically placed machines. Like a prowling shark, a privately run wheel-clamp vehicle patrolled the square, looking for hapless prey.

Gallagher, in common with many car owners, despised the wheel-clamp units with a vengeance. As far as he was concerned, they added to rather than reduced traffic congestion. A clamped car was an even more annoying obstruction, until it was either towed or lifted away.

Cruising round looking for a space, Gallagher frowned. On his third circuit of the square, there was still nowhere to park legally. He decided that if Fowler had dragged him here, the Department could bloody well sort out the clampers.

He parked the Quattro where it caused no obstruction, got out, and walked off. Within seconds, it seemed, the wheel clampers arrived. Gallagher turned to watch. They must have been lying in wait. The driver had actually got the yellow menace out, when the policeman given the unwelcome job of escort stopped him. The disappointed man put the clamp back in the vehicle. Fowler must have detailed someone from the Department—who had obviously radioed the policeman—to watch out for him.

Gallagher smiled broadly as they drove frustratedly past, then made his way to the offices.

"Nice to see you, Gordon." Delphine Arundel, widow of a colonel who'd been killed years before in Northern Ireland.

"Not so sure it's nice to be here, Delphine," he said, "but of course, with the usual exception."

She smiled at him. "You know all the right words."

"And as usual, sincerely meant."

She gave him an anxious look. "How are you keeping?"

"I'm okay." He knew she was thinking of Rhiannon's departure.

"Are you sure?"

He nodded. "Yes. And I'm eating well, and I'm not moping. Shall I go on? I'm really okay."

She didn't seem entirely convinced. "Mr. Fowler's waiting. George Haslam's with him." Her eyes studied him, as if searching out a clue that would confirm her anxieties. "Shall I bring you a coffee and shortbread? Or tea and shortbread?"

"Let's be daring. Coffee. Now I'd better go and see what kind of misery Fowler's got in store for me."

"Don't make jokes about it, Gordon. He ought to leave you be. You've done enough for this department."

"Just keep telling him that. He might listen one day."

Gallagher walked along the familiar corridor to Fowler's Spartan office.

"Glad you could make it, Gordon!" Fowler greeted him with the sort of expansiveness that would cause worry to anyone who knew Fowler well.

Gallagher gave him a jaundiced look. "And I really

had a choice, of course." He offered his hand to Haslam. "George. Still dragging you in, is he?" They shook hands. Gallagher actually liked Haslam, whom he considered to be reasonably honest; but even with Haslam, it was wise to be circumspect.

"You know how it is," Haslam said.

Fowler's eyes gleamed at Gallagher. "You didn't even wait for us to send someone to get you this time, Gordon. You must want something."

"Makes a change," Gallagher said. "And thanks for getting rid of the clampers. Brightened the day."

"Always happy to help our people."

"I'm not your people." Gallagher took a transparent plastic bag about the size of a matchbox out of a pocket. There was something in it. He placed it on Fowler's desk, and waited.

Fowler stared at it, but did not pick it up. He then looked at Gallagher. "A partially smoked cigarette. Share the mystery."

"Found on a hill overlooking the church."

"Ah!" Fowler said, and picked up the bag, opening it carefully. "It's got a smudge of red. Blood?" He put it down.

"Lipstick."

"A killer who wears lipstick. A woman?"

Gallagher shook his head. "I thought about that. The smudge was not made by anyone's lips. This cigarette was not even smoked, but was deliberately broken and then lit before being put out. Then the lipstick mark was made."

"Are you certain of this?"

"No professional assassin would leave such a clue, unless he meant to. And I can't see someone like that being stupid enough to give his position away by smoking. Take a good look at it. It's as if it just came out of the pack."

"And the purpose?"

"I'm trying to work that one out," Gallagher said.

"He wants us to think it's a woman," Haslam suggested.

Again, Gallagher shook his head. "Too crude. There's another meaning. I really had to look for that cigarette; as if the killer expected it. I think it's a challenge."

Fowler gave a tight smile. "A duel? And who is being challenged?"

Gallagher took his time before replying. "It's either the security services in general, the local police on whose patch he's made the kill . . ."

"Or?" Haslam was looking directly at him.

"Or me," Gallagher said quietly.

Now Fowler was also staring at him. "That would indicate prior knowledge of your movements, or even of you personally."

Gallagher nodded slowly, but said nothing.

"But how?" Fowler demanded. "And why the challenge?"

"That's what I'm hoping the Department could try to find out. Do a little probing," Gallagher went on. "I want to know who the hell's got tabs on me."

"Probing." Fowler repeated the word as if he didn't particularly like its taste. "If it is you, how do you explain Miss Lacey? And the man in Nottingham?"

"I can't. That's the problem. But my antennae are practically off the scale."

"There's been another killing," Haslam said.

Gallagher looked at him. Fowler glanced at Haslam, a brief flash of annoyance flitting across his face. He'd obviously wanted to choose his own time to tell Gallagher.

Gallagher turned to Fowler. "What other killing?"

"France this time. A politician to the right of Genghis Khan. Yesterday. It's not been on the news. We're cooperating with the French to keep it low key until we can make sense of it all."

"You won't be able to sit on that for long."

"We don't intend to. What price your theory now?"

"All I know is that my instincts are screaming warnings. I have no idea what these killings mean, and as for the failed hit on Miranda Lacey, it was pure fluke. Something was crawling on her ankle and she took a swipe at it just as the killer fired. But she was still hit. By any standards, it was pretty good shooting."

"But there were no other shots."

"No. I think he was up there for a while, watching us all through his scope. I'd got Miranda Lacey into some cover, so he was unable to get another shot at her."

"He might have gone for you instead."

"He could have done that with the first shot, if he'd really wanted to."

"Yet you still think it's a challenge." Fowler was poking at the tiny bag, but did not remove the cigarette.

"I do. And you can do something for me for a change. It might even be helpful to you."

"We'll certainly do all we can, Gordon."

Too bloody easy.

"What's the price?" Gallagher asked.

Haslam, arms folded, looked on with benign interest.

"Why do you think there's going to be a price?" Fowler asked.

"There's always a price with you."

Fowler chose to ignore the seeming aspersion. He again poked at the bag. "I'm assuming no one else has seen this? Not the local bobbies, nor your commando friend?"

"You two are the first."

"Departmental loyalty. I like that."

"You keep forgetting," Gallagher said. "I'm no longer with the Department. I'll say that slowly if it will help."

Fowler's eyes were neutral. "I've got some good news for you."

"That should be a laugh."

"Winterbourne's gone."

It certainly got Gallagher's attention. "At last. Someone woke up long enough to get rid of the dead admiral."

"He finally succeeded in getting what he wanted.

He's been made an ambassador." Fowler, who had barely been able to stomach his former head of department, appeared to be smiling. "But not Washington, I'm afraid. One of those little republics springing up like boils over in the East."

Gallagher wondered whether Fowler had somehow managed to engineer it. Winterbourne, who looked like a petulant cherub even on good days, had been, as far as Gallagher was concerned, the worst kind of incompetent: dangerous to those in the field.

"So you're now department head?"

But Fowler was in the wrong office. Head of department resided in a room that looked like the inner sanctum of a very exclusive club.

"Alas, no," Fowler replied. He did not seem particularly disturbed by that fact. "New man. Major General Sir James Crombie."

Fowler's voice gave no indication of how he felt about Crombie, or of having yet another man brought into the top job. It was, Gallagher decided, because Fowler was in reality in charge. Fowler, vastly intellectually superior to Winterbourne, had successfully played the tunes his erstwhile chief had wanted to hear, while doing something else entirely. Everyone except Winterbourne had worked that one out. It would be interesting to see how Crombie fared.

"Would you like to meet him?" Fowler was saying. "He's very interested in you."

"I can wait," Gallagher said. He was in no hurry to meet the major general. Fowler was being too accommodating.

Haslam permitted himself a tiny smile as Delphine Arundel brought in Gallagher's coffee and shortbread, along with a plain folder, which she handed to Fowler.

Gallagher thanked her and Fowler took the folder with a slight nod. He opened it and began to read the two sheets of paper in it as she went out.

"Interesting," he said when he'd finished, then

looked up at Gallagher. "A report on the clothing worn by the victim in Nottingham. It's taken a few days, but that's understandable, considering where our unidentified man got his suit. He'd bought it in Hungary. Doesn't mean he was Hungarian, of course. So many people crossing borders these days, he could have come from anywhere out there. Still, nothing to give us the connection between the two victims, and the lucky one—Miss Lacey—who escaped. The Hungarian suit brings Miss Lacey's Prague trip into closer focus. You know where she lives, don't you?"

Fowler knew very well that Gallagher knew.

Gallagher nodded. "Yes."

"And I suppose she's hoping you'll stay close—watching her back, so to speak—even though we've already got some people keeping an eye out?"

"Who's keeping the eye out?"

"Your old pal Prinknash and another seconded copper from the armed team."

Gallagher shut his eyes briefly in resignation. "*Prinknash?*"

Prinknash was no pal. The very first time Gallagher had met him had set the tone. Prinknash had been sent by Fowler to request Gallagher's attendance. Not understanding his relationship with the Department, Prinknash had played the heavy policeman. Gallagher had struck out, seriously hurting the man's arm. It had been a strike on the most painful part of an elbow, and Prinknash had never forgotten it.

"Don't be too hard on him," Haslam said mildly. "He's a good copper. He's been shot while working for us, as you know. Yet he's still willing to stay in secondment. He can't be all bad. He just needs careful handling."

"You've worked with him, George. You can stand him."

"I didn't say I could stand him. That's a different thing altogether."

▪ ▪ ▪

The killer drove slowly past the small, white, stucco-fronted town house on a corner in Little Venice, one of the more sought-after areas of town, and noted the discreetly parked car. One man was in it. Obviously, his partner was somewhere around.

The killer knew that to make a second pass would arouse suspicion. It had to be now. After a swift check to ensure there would be no nasty surprises, the killer parked and walked unconcernedly back towards the unmarked security car.

"Excuse me."

Prinknash's partner looked up expectantly, completely relaxed. He only began to react when he saw the silenced pistol. He was already much too late.

The gun coughed twice. The policeman reared in his seat, grimacing with the shock and pain before relaxing forever. His head slumped casually onto his chest. He looked as if he had decided to doze.

The killer walked unhurriedly back to the car with British plates that had been hired under a false name, got in, and drove slowly off.

Prinknash was nowhere to be seen.

Twenty minutes later, the killer pulled up behind a parked car at the Knightbridge end of Hyde Park, and climbed out. The same two men from the meeting in Kent were waiting.

The surly one glanced at his watch. "Our assassin's on time. Makes a change, I suppose. Dark glasses, as usual."

"Just don't start anything," his companion said anxiously.

"Why should we have to make allowances for—"

"The next assignment." The killer was at the car window.

The surly one shut up and handed over the expected envelope. His silence didn't last for long.

"Germany this time," he said.

"I know." The killer turned away.

"If you know so much . . ."

The killer paused.

Almost in panic, the driver got out of the car and said hurriedly. "Ignore him. Let's just get out of here before someone takes an interest."

The killer surveyed them both, the dark glasses menacing. Then the tense moment was over. The killer walked back to the hired car.

The driver once more took his seat. "Look. You may be suicidal, but I'm not. If you want to pull stunts like that, you make the next meet alone."

"You don't have to fight my battles for me," the other said furiously. "I'm highly skilled, and dangerous. People run away from me . . ."

"I know. I've seen it happen. But just remember the fancy gunman in the cowboy movies. This one is not going to run away, and if you don't realize that soon, you won't live to regret it."

The hired car swept by. They stared after it.

"Why the devil did we have to meet in England, anyway?" the surly one complained. "This job's in Germany. We've got people over there who could have met our high-and-mighty mercenary."

"That was not the arrangement."

"Screw the arrangement."

The driver looked at his companion, and shook his head slowly with exasperation. You could warn a man about sticking his head between a lion's jaws only so often.

"It's not my neck," the driver said, more to himself.

The car's engine had been running. He now put it into gear and drove sedately round the park, before turning unhurriedly into Bayswater Road.

4

Gallagher drove the Quattro fast along the Edgware Road. Haslam, in the passenger seat, stared grimly out at the world. They came to a set of traffic lights which were on green and Gallagher turned left, barely slowing down. The car powered into the turn, not budging an inch from its line. He slowed down as they approached the road where Miranda lived.

A big, tough-looking policeman in the dark blue flak-jacketed rig of the armed response team stood in the middle of the road facing them. A mean Heckler & Koch submachine gun was held across his chest. He raised an imperious hand.

Gallagher stopped. Beyond the policeman, he could see others, plus two unmarked vehicles blocking the road. Past them, a third vehicle was parked behind Prinknash's car. There was no sign of Prinknash.

Prinknash's strained message had been received by the Department's communications duty officer, who had contacted Fowler immediately.

Haslam had simply said to Gallagher, "Come on. Let's go."

Gallagher had not hesitated.

The policeman, eyes firmly on the Quattro, cocked his head slightly, listening to his communicator. Then one of his hands moved briefly to beckon the car through. The message had obviously told him to do so. As they drove past, the policeman stared at Gallagher, as if wondering what he was doing there.

Gallagher parked nose-on to Prinknash's car, which was now empty, the dead man's body having already been removed. Followed by Haslam, he walked towards Miranda Lacey's home. The watchful policemen regarded them with a brief, restrained curiosity, eyes constantly checking out the surrounding area.

Not much use now, Gallagher thought. All that hardware was already too late.

They entered the house and found a miserable-looking Prinknash and a very scared Miranda, waiting in the large reception room. She came off the sofa on which she had been sitting, almost as if she had been catapulted off it, as Gallagher entered the room. She hurried towards him, and then, apparently suddenly remembering she was supposed to be a strong journalist and not a wilting female, stopped just short of throwing her good arm about him. But her eyes, a haunted darkness in them, told him she was very pleased he had come.

"You okay?" he said to her.

She bit at her lip and nodded. "Yes."

"Mr. Gallagher," Prinknash began. "Mr. Haslam . . . I'm sorry. I was in the house with Miss Lacey. Bob was outside doing his stint in the car. I never heard a thing. Silencer."

Normally, Prinknash was like an aggressive bantam looking for a fight. His favorite stance was feet spread, cropped head jerking belligerently; and though the rest of his body would be perfectly still, there was always the strong impression that he was hopping from foot to foot. He was now looking so miserable because of what had happened, Gallagher actually felt sorry for him.

"It wasn't your fault," Haslam told him. "We were all caught out. This is being played by rules we do not as yet understand."

"But why shoot Bob like that? He's got a wife and two little kids! What am I going to say to them?"

"We can take care of it."

"But he was my mate. I asked for him to come on this with me. It was because of me that he volunteered."

"Simmer down, Prinknash. Look, you go outside and have a break. We'll carry on from here."

Prinknash looked at Gallagher. "Mr. Gallagher . . ."

"Not your fault," Gallagher said. "Do as Mr. Haslam says. Gallagher turned to Haslam as Prinknash went out, looking very unhappy, and shook his head. "He's never been so polite to me before."

"The shock of losing a friend. It's true, you know," Haslam went on. "That copper, Bob Denton, was a good friend of his. One of the few who were prepared to be real friends with him. Besides, you were kinder to him than you've ever been."

"I know what it's like to lose a friend and feel it's your fault."

Understanding, Haslam made no comment and turned to Miranda. "Well, Miss Lacey. It looks as if our mystery killer was not satisfied with the job he did at the church."

She turned bewildered eyes upon him. "But why kill that policeman and make no attempt to come to the house?"

"He had no intention of coming to the house," Gallagher answered. "What he's saying quite plainly is that if he'd wanted to get at you, he could have done it. This was a deliberate kill, to increase the psychological pressure, and to tell us he's in control of events."

She hugged herself with the good arm, briefly touching the wounded shoulder, and shivered. "How cold-blooded. But what could I have done to bring this . . . this person after me?"

"You are quite certain," Haslam said, "that there was nothing whatsoever in Prague . . ."

"Look. I don't mean to be rude, but I've said this over and over again. There is nothing, *nothing* that I can remember. I met a few people, yes. But I've done nothing I can think of that gives even the most remote of reasons for a killer to set off after me. Believe me, I've gone over all my movements out there so many times, I've lost count. It's all so crazy!"

She turned and walked towards the large French windows that normally looked out upon the Paddington Basin, the mooring and turning area for canal barges and other craft formed by the Regent's Canal. But now, the curtains were drawn, shutting out the frightening world beyond.

"I chose this house," she began quietly, "because it's so pretty, and because it's in a part of London that I like. Cost me an arm and a leg." She smiled wistfully to herself at the unintended joke. "Normally, it's peaceful enough. I've got a lovely view of the basin and canal, and there are nice little restaurants nearby where I take friends and colleagues. On sunny days I can open the French windows and just enjoy the view, or entertain a few friends. If someone had said a policeman looking after me would be killed right outside my door . . ." She stopped and turned to look at Gallagher. "Gordon, what am I going to do?" The frightened eyes were pleading.

"You pack. We're taking you out of here. You're going to disappear for a while."

"But the magazine . . . I promised an article—"

"You're not going to be of much use to them if you're dead," he cut in with more brutality than he'd intended;

but he had to galvanize her. "So you might as well take some extended leave until we sort this out. Give them a call. Make any excuse. Say you're working on something and will be in touch. Did you give them the explanation Alun and I suggested for that arm of yours?"

"Yes. I said I'd fallen off a horse. They know I'm a good rider, but I told them I'd chosen a brute of a mount on a bet. They'd expect that of me."

"Then you've got the perfect excuse. Say the arm's acting up. You're going off for some peace and quiet, and you'll work better if you're away from phones and faxes for a while. That ought to do it."

She went to the phone and did just that. The person at the other end accepted the explanation.

"I'll be in touch," Miranda finished, and hung up.

"And now, you pack," Gallagher said.

"How long for?"

"As long as it takes."

"Is there a washing machine at this place?"

Bloody hell, Gallagher thought. Is there a washing machine. She would think about that. Jesus.

"Yes," he replied.

"Then I'll take only a few things and my laptop computer. I'm accustomed to traveling light." She hurried out and up the stairs to her bedroom. "What about my car?" she called down.

"As you can't drive with that arm and the car's still down in Kent," Gallagher answered, "it hardly matters."

"But what about when my arm's okay? How do I get back?"

"I'll be taking you, and I'll be bringing you back."

"Oh, good."

Gallagher looked at Haslam. "Don't say it."

There was on Haslam's face what looked very suspiciously like a smirk. "Not a word," he promised.

Gallagher gave him a doubting stare, then called up at Miranda. "Need any help?"

"If someone could take the laptop. It's a bit difficult with the one arm. I'm taking all my disks and notes."

"Would someone like to go up?" Haslam said in a low voice that definitely had a smirk in it. "Better than shouting the house down."

"*You* go."

"Coward." Haslam made no move.

"Ready!" came from upstairs.

"That was fast," Haslam commented. He still made no move to go. "I don't think she wants the older man. I'll be outside." Without waiting for Gallagher's reaction, he made his way out.

Gallagher went up the stairs.

Haslam was back in the house, waiting for them downstairs. He was carrying a fat briefcase.

Gallagher turned to Miranda. "Can we get out round the back?"

"Yes. There's a high door at the end of the garden; but I always keep it locked and bolted. I never leave the house that way."

"Today will have to be the exception." He turned to Haslam.

Haslam knew immediately. "One of the coppers can do the locking and bolting after we've gone, then give you the keys."

Miranda looked at each in turn. "But I thought Gordon—"

"He is," Haslam cut in, "but after we've left the area. Best if he's not seen leaving with you. No one may be taking the sort of interest we wouldn't like; but you never know. That's why Gordon shouldn't even lock the door himself."

"I've also got to stop off at my place first," Gallagher told her. "We'll meet up after that. Well, off you go. Through the garden. I'll send in one of the coppers."

Haslam handed him the briefcase. "A present for you. Check it out at your house. I'll take Miss Lacey's things," he went on with a straight face, before adding to Miranda, "All right, Miss Lacey. Prinknash is waiting."

"The sergeant?" She looked worried. "He's not using the same car that . . ."

"No, no, Miss Lacey," Haslam said patiently. "Not the same one. The forensic people have already claimed it."

Gallagher watched them leave before going out through the front door to talk to the nearest policeman. It was the same one who had stood in front of the Quattro, barring its way. "Please come with me."

The policeman stared at him without moving. Gallagher glanced quickly at the team leader, who was close by.

"Go with him, Wilson," the senior man ordered.

Wilson did not look particularly ecstatic as he did as he was told.

In the house, Gallagher said, "There's a big door at the end of the garden. Could you lock and bolt it, please, then bring me the keys? Miss Lacey's got them."

Wilson wasn't going to give up easily. "Shouldn't we be having those keys?"

"What's your problem, Wilson? You don't like taking orders from me?"

Wilson looked for an excuse. "You're an unknown civilian . . . sir."

"Life's hell, isn't it? I wouldn't keep Mr. Haslam waiting, if I were you. Shocking temper."

Wilson stomped off. Presently he returned, and handed the keys over with as much bad grace as he could muster without leaving himself open to a disciplinary charge. Not sure of Gallagher's status, he was hedging his bets.

"Why, thank you, Wilson," Gallagher said.

Wilson said nothing, and stumped out.

Gallagher waited just long enough to give the other car time to get away before going out to the Quattro.

He did so unhurriedly. If the killer or his helpers were still in the area, Gallagher wanted them to keep focused on him while Haslam got Miranda away. Haslam would have got her down behind the front seats with a rug over her. She would not resurface until the exchange of cars.

Gallagher put the briefcase behind his seat, then climbed into the black car. He started it and drove slowly away. Wilson tracked the car with eyes that were like hostile radar.

Have a nice day, Wilson.

Gallagher took a roundabout route through the city, going well out of his way before heading home back towards Holland Park, not very far from Miranda's house. He used the time to check for any followers, but detected none. There were no tracers on the car.

He made it without incident and got out, taking the briefcase with him. He had totally renewed the security system and there were no keyholes in the solid outer door, the only blemishes being the mail slot and a thin horizontal slot the size of a credit card at keyhole level. He slid a card into the narrow opening. There was a soft whirring and the card was ejected while the door eased slightly open.

Gallagher entered, shutting the door behind him. There was no need to deactivate the security system. The card had already done that.

There was a lot of mail in the secure box, and he got it out before walking the six feet to the opaque-paneled second door. This too was opened by the card. He hurried up the stairs and first checked out the mail. He left all bills and obvious mailshots, taking only letters he recognized as photo assignments. Then he opened the briefcase.

Haslam had left him an armory.

Nestling in embedded splendor were a big and gleaming SIG Sauer P226 automatic pistol with a supply of 15-round magazines *and* silencer, and a dismantled quick-assembly Beretta PM 12S submachine gun with its own supply of 32-round magazines. Haslam had also left a note with the SIG.

"*Your favorite,*" it said.

Gallagher shut the case. "Thank you, Haslam. But I hope I won't need this little lot."

He then checked his answering machine. The bugging light was not blinking. That meant neither Fowler nor one of his minions had attempted to tap his phone. Experience had taught him that Fowler was not averse to a little eavesdropping.

The machine delivered its usual crop of assignment messages and social invitations. His faint hope of a message from Rhiannon did not materialize. Then the last one made him very thankful that Fowler had not yet attempted a bugging.

"Meet me in Faro," the voice said. "The airport in three days, fifteen hundred hours local. Very important. To you."

It was a long time since he'd heard the speaker, but he recognized the voice instantly.

Borodin.

As he made his way towards the rendezvous with Haslam, Gallagher tried yet again to make sense of Borodin's message. Finding a reason for going to Faro on Portugal's Algarve coast was not difficult. One of his pending assignments was in that location. Telling Fowler it had become urgent would not sound too suspicious, even to Fowler's naturally suspicious mind. Borodin would not have personally come out, even in these days of supposed open access, unless something very urgent had come up. Clearly, he was trusting no one with whatever he had to say.

"But what?" Gallagher said aloud as he drove along

the M40 motorway towards Oxford. "And what could be so important to me?"

The rumble of the big tires upon the road surface was the only reply he got. It would not do to give Fowler an inkling of Borodin's presence in western Europe. You never knew with Fowler.

He made a periodic check of his mirrors. No tail.

"Anyway," Gallagher reasoned to himself, "this concerns *me.* It's personal. Nothing to do with the Department." The problem now was what to do with Miranda.

"Take her with you," Haslam suggested at the rendezvous.

"You've got to be joking!"

They were at a petrol station on the outskirts of Oxford, away from the motorway. Miranda was in the lavatory, her cases having already been put into the Quattro by Prinknash, who sat waiting for Haslam in the other car.

"No, I'm not," Haslam countered mildly. "This takes her well out of the way. Portugal's very nice at this time of year, I believe. The school holidays have not yet started, and the tourists have not yet descended in their hordes. Perfect for your working needs. And of course, the weather's also perfect for . . ."

"Spare me the tourist board advert, Haslam."

"Gone from George to Haslam, have we? Since when?"

"Since you started making daft suggestions. I'm going out to earn my crust. I can't—" Gallagher stopped.

Miranda had come out of the lavatory and was walking towards them, a big smile on her face when she saw Gallagher.

"Going to dump her to her fate, are you?" Haslam whispered.

"Shut up, Haslam," Gallagher said, keeping his own

voice low. "And don't claim the high moral ground with me. I know you too well."

"Look at it this way," Haslam said, unmoved. "She's a professional journalist. She's been in tight spots, so she's not likely to be totally helpless."

"Aren't you forgetting something? She can only use one arm."

"It's healing quickly. She'll be all right soon."

"Thank you, doctor."

There was no time for further discussion, because Miranda was now within earshot.

"You two are looking a little intense," she began. "Anything wrong?" Her eyes studied them in turn.

"No," Gallagher replied. "I was just telling . . . *George* here that a job of mine has become urgent. I've got to be in Portugal in three days."

Her face clouded in disappointment. "Oh." Then suddenly, it brightened. "That's perfect! I'll come with you. I'll pay my own way, of course."

Gallagher looked poisonously at Haslam, who was very successful at keeping a straight face.

"I won't be going back to town," Gallagher told her. "I've already got my passport and everything I'll need." That ought to put an end to her ideas. "You'll have to get your passport and—"

"Oh, I've already got that," she said as if she'd planned it all along. "The job, you know. Always ready to move at a moment's notice. Got it here." She patted the small shoulder bag at her hip, where it hung from its sling across her chest. "And don't worry about my clothes. As I've said, I travel light."

"That's settled then," Haslam said, still keeping a very straight face and ignoring the hard look Gallagher had fired his way. "We'll make the arrangements to ensure you get securely on the flight." He looked at Gallagher. "What time of day?"

Feeling neatly ambushed, Gallagher said, "Early

evening, the day before." His eyes continued to drill into Haslam, who didn't blink.

"Early evening it is," Haslam said. "We could always fly you out ourselves, of course. The Department—"

"No!" Gallagher interrupted. "Thank you. You've done enough already, *George.* Besides, you'd have to justify it in the budget."

"I'm certain a way could be found . . ."

"Forget it, Haslam. Right, Miranda. In you get. The longer we remain here making small talk, the likelier we are to be spotted."

Something in Gallagher's voice made her comply without further comment. He got in behind the wheel.

Haslam came round to lean on the car. "Did you like the briefcase?"

"I won't need it."

"Even so, I hope you brought with you."

"Yes."

"Good." Haslam straightened. "Leave the rest to us."

"Ha!" Gallagher said, then started the Quattro and drove off in a surge of power.

Haslam rapidly grew small in the mirror as they rejoined the A40, bypassing the university town.

"Something's upset you," Miranda began tentatively.

"That obvious, is it?" he snapped.

She looked away. An edgy silence descended.

Gallagher sighed. "I'm sorry. I didn't mean to be rude. But I don't like Haslam's mob making my decisions for me."

"And *I'm* sorry . . . sorry to be in the way. I know this is an interruption in your life that you'd rather be without . . ."

"You're not an inter . . . Look. It was wrong of me to take it out on you. But we do have the little problem of how to look after you if you come to Portugal with me. For starters, that suitcase Haslam gave me has got a small armory in it. I can't see the Portuguese letting me cart that into their country."

"Didn't Haslam say he'd handle things?"

Gallagher nodded.

"So he'll arrange for you to get the briefcase through."

"Probably."

"Well then."

"I don't like guns."

"But you've used them."

"Too bloody often. I try to keep them well away from me, not always successfully. I'm not in that line of business anymore."

"And now I've dragged you back."

"I didn't say that."

"You didn't have to." She looked away again.

Bloody great.

Soon, Gallagher was turning left off a roundabout on the A40 and onto a smaller road on the northwestern outskirts of Oxford. The road led to Wytham, and eventually they came to a narrow bridge that crossed the Isis next to a weir. They had to stop briefly to allow for an oncoming car, as there was not enough room for the two cars to pass each other. He wasn't about to have his car scratched for anybody.

The road curved sharply right from the bridge, but Gallagher did not continue along it. Instead, he turned left off it and onto a track that went along the riverbank. The roar of the weir could be heard above the muted rumble of the Quattro's exhaust.

He drove slowly over the uneven ground. A couple of cars had parked on the rough grass just off the track, nose-on to the river. Their passengers were nowhere to be seen. Probably off walking, Gallagher assumed, though he did give the cars close scrutiny as he drove by. The area was a favorite for walks.

Ahead was a lock. People always came to see it operating as small pleasure craft moved up and down the river.

They drove past the neatly kept lockkeeper's cottage, and a short distance later Gallagher turned off to the right and into some woods. Just under a quarter of a mile farther on they stopped on a graveled patch in a large clearing, in front of a stone cottage. Like the cottage by the lock, it looked well tended. There was even a small flower garden. It was obvious someone came regularly to look after the place. Two stories high, it was bigger than the lockkeeper's home. A garage, with a strong-looking up-and-over steel door, was set within the structure of the house.

Gallagher remained in the car for a few moments, studying the area. He placed a hand briefly on Miranda's.

"Wait," he cautioned.

She stared at him. "You don't think anyone . . ."

"Just being certain. Okay," he added after a while. "We're clear."

He'd been looking for signs that someone might have come off the gravel and walked up to the door. The low slab of stone at the entrance would have shown gravel smears from the shoes. According to Haslam, the people who looked after the cottage had been told not to attend for a few days.

"Are you always like this?" she asked.

"It's kept me alive," he replied, getting out. "All right. Let's get our things, but wait here while I check out the place."

He went up to the door and studied it carefully. There was no sign of tampering. He inserted the large key that Haslam had given him on the way to Miranda's house, and turned it carefully in the massive lock. It turned smoothly.

He pushed the thick door gently open, making as small a silhouette of himself as possible. The door itself was a sandwich of solid oak, with a light armored sheet of steel in the middle. It swung inwards soundlessly. Continuing his cautious approach, he entered swiftly to get himself out of silhouette. He checked the place thoroughly. The house was clean. No one who shouldn't have, had been there. It didn't mean Fowler's people hadn't planted bugs. He'd have to watch what he said to Miranda. Any conversations they had inside the cottage would have to be of the kind he wouldn't mind Fowler hearing.

He opened the curtains and light flooded into the house. The windows were securely glazed with smash-proof panels. The place was very comfortably furnished, even expensively so, and outside the entire surrounds gave a clear field of fire, with no cover for an intending intruder for fifty meters. Buried within the grounds were sensors that would alert the house. These would be activated only by the weight of a human being or something heavier. Even if an animal like a horse set off one of the alarms, it could easily mean it was being ridden or had been used as a decoy, and it would thus be treated seriously.

Gallagher checked the kitchen stocks. There was plenty of food, plus wine and other beverages. They certainly would not starve, even if they had to remain inside for a month or more. There were other weapons, too, and in a cupboard hidden behind sliding doors in the lounge was the sensor display.

He stood in the middle of the lounge and said loudly, "Testing . . . one, two, three . . ." He stopped, grinning. If Fowler had indeed put the bugging system on-line, he might as well know it was suspected. He'd also know that anything eavesdropped upon had been deliberately said for his benefit.

Gallagher went back out to the car and opened Miranda's door. "We're okay. Let's get the stuff in."

"You didn't use a gun," she said.

"Should I have?"

"I thought people in your line of business always checked houses with guns."

"Not me. When I pick up a gun, it's because I intend to use it. As I said earlier, I try very hard to make sure those instances are very few and far between. And it's not my line of business. Not anymore, thank God."

"That doesn't answer the question."

"No. But here endeth the first lesson. Let's go in, then I must put the car away. Keep it out of sight."

"Very, very nice," she said as she looked about her when he'd returned from garaging the Quattro. "Oak beams, walls solid enough to withstand a siege, furnishings and decoration that would not be out of place in my glossy rag. A refurbished old building. Who pays for all this?"

"In a general sense? Or in the particular?"

"Both."

"In a general sense, the nation. In the particular, the . . . er . . . Haslam's lot."

"Your old mob."

"Yes."

"Bet you've had some interesting people here. What an article—"

"You'll never write," Gallagher cut in firmly. "This place has saved many lives. It will save yours. Other people might need to be safe."

The tone of his voice made her say, "I'm . . . I'm sorry. Damn! I'm always saying that to you. I was only joking. I'm a journalist, but I do have my scruples, you know."

He made no comment about that. "Well, I've got the best guarantee of your silence that anyone can have."

"And that is?"

"Your life. Think about it."

She stared at him. "There's something really cold and dangerous about you," she said quietly. "Alun was right."

"Alun? What's he got to do with it?"

"It doesn't matter," she said. "Can you show me my room, please?"

Bloody great.

▪ ▪ ▪

Whitehall, London.

Fowler permitted himself a fleeting smile when he read the transcript that Delphine Arundel had brought in to him. Its contents had come through a secure line to those who'd been listening.

"Testing indeed, Gordon," he said to the sheet of paper. "Very droll." He looked up at Delphine. "Tell them to shut down the system in the house, and the garage; but leave the one outside on-line."

She nodded. "Yes, sir." She paused. "You seem almost pleased he found you out."

"Do I?"

"You won't catch him out, you know."

"I detect a note of pride. We're all proud of our Gordon," Fowler continued smoothly. "That's why we can't afford to lose him. Too good."

Delphine Arundel made no comment as she went out. Fowler was well aware of her feelings on that particular matter. After she'd gone, Fowler removed his glasses briefly to pinch at the bridge of his nose.

"The one outside was put in after your time, Gordon," he said mildly.

He picked up a purple file, opened it, and selected a particular section.

Profile on Gallagher,

it began.

5

The safe house, Oxfordshire.

Miranda came down the stairs to the lounge. Gallagher sat on a sofa, with the suitcase Haslam had given him wide open on a low table. He was putting the Beretta together.

"I thought you weren't going to use guns," she began.

"There's a difference between not wanting to use them, and having one that's ready to shoot if you need to. This thing's no use to man or beast sleeping in its case."

She took an armchair close to the sofa. "If you resent looking after me . . ."

"First, I don't resent looking after you, as you put it. And I'm not doing it just because my old firm wants it done. Second, I do need to go to Portugal on an important assignment and I am worried about keeping you alive out there, should the man who seems determined to hunt you down realize where you've gone. Third, this is personal. Someone fired a bloody great gun at my godson's christening . . ."

"*Our* godson. I have the extra stake in this too."

Gallagher paused. "Our godson. It's just not on. I want to know why this has happened. Haslam and the others are involved because it's their job to sort out these things. But I have a vested interest. Okay?"

"Are you telling me everything?" Her eyes were riveted upon him.

"As much as you need to know."

"Now I wonder why I *thought* that was the answer I was going to get."

The Beretta was assembled. Gallagher said nothing as he checked and double-checked it to ensure that it was working properly, while she looked on with a mixture of avid curiosity and anxiety. He snapped a loaded magazine into it. Both the P226 and the submachine gun were now ready for action. He hoped the need would not arise.

He looked at her. "Hungry? There's lots of food, wine, spirits . . . you name it. This place is always well stocked."

"I suppose there are others like it throughout the country."

"You're the journalist. What do you think?"

"I think there probably are."

And in other countries. But he didn't tell her that.

She stood up. "I'll check out the kitchen."

"I can do that. I'll cook. You've got one good hand. Remember?" He shut the case, then got to his feet, taking both the pistol and the Beretta with him as he went into the kitchen.

She followed him.

"I'm frightened, but not helpless," she protested. "How do you think I ate at my house? Who do you think cooked? Prinknash?"

"I know, I know. But I don't want you to think you're

expected to do the cooking. I'm actually not a bad cook, as it happens."

Her expression softened. "What a mass of contradictions you are. Nearly every man I've been out with would sit and wait for me to do my stuff in the kitchen. You order me around, but now you want to cook for me."

"There you are. No pigeonhole for me."

"New Man, are you?"

"Nope. Whatever 'New Man' is supposed to be, I'm not it. That's another pigeonhole. You've got a busted arm, and I can cook. So I cook. It's no big deal."

She smiled at him. "Here's a deal. We take turns."

"Fine. Who gets first shift?"

"You did offer."

"Miss Lacey, Miss Lacey. You drive a hard bargain."

Suddenly, she kissed him fleetingly, fully on the lips. "You're not so tough."

It was about four in the afternoon when they sat down to eat in the small dining room. Outside, a fine rain had begun to fall and the flowers and shrubs glistened as if polished. Gallagher had positioned their chairs so they did not sit with their backs to any of the windows, while still having a clear view of the space in front of the house.

He'd cooked roasted chicken with a cream and wine sauce, roasted potatoes, and a generous mixed salad. A bottle of pouilly-fumé accompanied it.

"Somewhere between lunch and dinner," he said. "Hope you don't mind."

"Mind? This is good!" Miranda raised her glass. "To my cook, guardian, and bossy sod."

He raised his own glass. "Enough of the 'bossy.'"

"This really is good cooking, Gordon," she said approvingly as she put down her glass. "I mean it." She went eagerly at the food. Using one hand was not a problem. "And that salad. What bottle did that dressing come from?"

"I made it."

She put down her fork. "You made it. I don't think I'm going to cook. I'll give up now."

"Oh, no you don't. A bargain's a bargain."

"You'll hate it," she warned.

"Let me be the judge. There are a couple of fresh lobsters in the fridge. Know how to cook them?"

"You're in luck. Lobsters happen to be my specialty." Miranda seemed to have forgotten her fears for the time being as the wine and the food began to mellow her. "Just you wait."

She picked up her fork, and halted in midair.

The phone had begun to ring.

Gallagher did not move. She stared at him, fear returning as she realized he was not going to answer it. She put the fork down slowly, as if afraid whoever was ringing would hear.

Gallagher stayed where he was. The phone rang ten times before ending in the middle of the last ring. It sounded as if it had been throttled.

Miranda let out her breath slowly, unaware that she had been holding it.

"Why didn't you pick it up?" she asked in a whisper.

"There's no need to whisper," he said. "I didn't pick it up because no one is supposed to ring."

"Perhaps it's something very urgent."

Gallagher shook his head and brought something out of a trouser pocket. It was about the size of the remote for his answering machine. He held it up for her to see.

"There's a very powerful dish aerial hidden at one end of the roof. If there had been an emergency, a pulse would have been transmitted to this little gizmo. The shriek will wake you from a deep sleep. This is the only signal we get. One shriek, and we prepare to batten down. This means we can hold off till reinforcements arrive. Two shrieks mean we'll have to stay longer before help arrives; but the house is solid and it would need a few rocket-propelled grenade rounds to do damage. Three shrieks and it's bad news. We leave in rapid order, and call from the first telephone that's a safe distance away. Those three shrieks mean there's no way they can get to us in time. So we get out before whoever or whatever it is gets here. That phone call was not on the agenda."

Gallagher wondered whether the house bugging system had already been switched off. Fowler should by now have had the transcript showing the fact that Gallagher was aware of its activation. If it was still on, the ringing of the phone would have been picked up, as well as their comments. Fowler's people would know of the unscheduled call and would take appropriate steps.

If the system were still on-line.

Gallagher decided he would have to assume it wasn't, and act accordingly.

"A wrong number?"

"Nobody is even supposed to get this by mistake. The system blocks out any call made in error. Whoever it was dialed correctly."

"My God! You mean someone on your side—"

"Not my bloody side."

"Then whoever! Someone with Haslam might be working for—"

"We don't know that. Perhaps the beeper system's been changed and it was Haslam—

"But you just said—"

"I know what I just said." Gallagher had left his chair and begun prowling, going flat against the edge of a window to peer out. He'd picked up the P226. "It could be something quite simple. On the other hand . . ."

"Would people really use grenades against this house," she began hesitantly, "in a place like this?"

"Why not? If they were determined enough, of course they would. People fire rockets in the middle of London, or leave bloody great bombs in the city. Someone shoots at you at a christening. Attacking this place with grenades would be nothing by comparison. It's all too easy to get that sort of weaponry these days. Eastern Europe's a bloody bazaar. Sad fact of life."

He stared out at the flower garden. "You may be thinking that perhaps Haslam was calling to make arrangements for the flight. Not a chance. He wouldn't do that by phone. That patch of open ground has an additional, but very important function. Helicopters land there. That's how we'll be leaving. By chopper."

Gallagher studied the woods beyond the clearing. Suddenly, the tranquil beauty of the Oxfordshire countryside had changed.

It had become menacing.

"On the other hand," he repeated, "that phone call could have been a fishing expedition to see if anyone *is* here. It's an old trick, but it sometimes still works. All sorts of people do it. As a journalist, have you never made a call just to see if a person from whom you've been finding it difficult to get an interview is actually around, when you've been told otherwise?"

She nodded. "I've caught out one or two people."

"There you are." He moved away from the window. "Let's see if they try again. I'll have words with Haslam. Find out who the hell's got access to this number."

The phone never rang again, and no intruder came into their haven that day.

At twilight, Gallagher went out to do a systematic check of the immediate environs of the house. Miranda was reluctant to remain by herself, but he convinced her it would be all right. As long as she did not open the door until his return, she would be safe within the house. He did not take the key with him.

There was still plenty of light to see by and as he

moved swiftly round the building, something beneath an eave caught his eye. He didn't pause, but kept moving. He saw several more of the objects. They had been very cleverly placed, and had he not gone out to do the detailed check he would have missed them. They looked like part of the house, and even in full daylight would not have been easily discovered.

The outside of the house had been wired for sound. The powerful microphones would pick up any conversation, or footfalls, within the clearing around the cottage. He kept on moving, so as not to let the listeners know their hidden mikes had been spotted. The system had not been installed during his time with the Department. Gallagher's luck had been in noticing one that had been shifted from its position. Perhaps a nesting bird had pecked at it once too often. On such small happenings . . .

Finding the others had been relatively easy after that.

Very clever, Fowler, Gallagher thought as he eventually returned to the front door. He knocked on it softly. He was now quite certain Fowler had ordered the internal bugging system turned off, expecting to catch unguarded words outside.

"It's Gordon." He spoke loudly, both for Miranda to hear clearly and for the benefit of Fowler's minions.

The door swung open and he entered, shutting and locking it behind him. She was looking at him expectantly.

"We're clean," he assured her. He made no mention of the microphones. "Now I'll just do another check inside to make quite sure we're secure for the night."

She followed him all over the house as he did so.

"I'm not sleeping in my room," she stated badly when he'd at last finished.

"There have been fugitive heads of state here," he told her calmly, "and they've been perfectly safe."

"I'm not sleeping in my room," she repeated. "I'll share yours."

He looked at her steadily. She was clearly not going to change her mind.

"All right. You have the bed. I'll take the floor."

"Why?"

"Why what?"

"Why sleep on the floor? Your bed's big enough for two."

"But . . ."

"I won't make any advances if you don't."

She'd left him no room for a reply. Instead, he concentrated on setting up the ground sensors.

She watched as he slid open the doors to the monitor and turned it on. A graphic display showed the house at its center, with the position of each sensor marked by a multipointed star. Around each star a circular dashed line expanded outwards to a prescribed limit, before repeating the sequence. The entire area was dotted.

"What's that?" she asked.

"The warning system. Buried in the grounds are small sensors, like antipersonnel mines. Instead of blowing you up when you step on them, these little geniuses sense the pressure, then pulse on the monitor so that you know exactly where the intruder is. The dashed circles become solid to display which sensor has been activated. That's how we'll know the precise location of the intruder.

"They're so sensitive, if you walk within four feet they'll register, and they're laid down in such a way that each sensor zone overlaps by about three feet. See the way the circles cross into each other? The whole display area is blanketed. There's no blind spot unless one of the sensors goes down. If that happens, the star in question glows red. As you can see, everything's online. I'm about to rig the monitor so that it activates the shrieker. Believe me, it will wake us up if anyone tries to sneak, or drive, into the clearing."

"You think of everything."

"Not always," Gallagher said, remembering O'Keefe.

It's sometimes the simplest of things, sir, that can blow up a mission in your face. Check and check again.

O'Keefe.

Gallagher did another check inside the house. He was satisfied he'd left nothing to chance.

The men on eavesdropping duty had picked up Gallagher's footsteps while he was outside the house.

"Think he's spotted them?" one asked.

"No. There was no pause. He didn't stop to check. We're okay."

"Wonder what they'll get up to in there tonight."

"How far *he'll* get up to, you mean."

They laughed.

"Pity we can't hear," the one who had first spoken said wistfully. "We could always—"

"We were told to leave the house system deactivated, and that's exactly what we do. Other people can do unauthorized bugging if they want. *I* don't want Fowler descending on me like a ton of bricks. If you want to risk your career for a bit of titillation, wait until I'm not sharing a duty with you."

"Pity. It might have been juicy."

"A word of advice from someone who's been a little longer with this department than you have: Disobeying Fowler is terminal for budding careers, in a very serious way. You go to zero, deep in the brown, and stay there. Gallagher is the only person I know who got away with it; but considering some of the shit Fowler gets him into, even now that he's out of the business, he's very welcome to his leeway."

"Good, is he?"

"Let's put it this way: If you'd been in some of the situations he's had to handle in his time, a snowflake in hell would grow old when compared to your chances."

"That good."

"Better. The best the Department's ever had."

She came into his room wearing a huge blue T-shirt that bore the logo of a new restaurant that had recently opened in London's West End cinemaland. It reached just past her knees.

He stared at it as she hesitated by the door. "Eating in bed, are we?"

She gave him a weak, nervous smile. "Not mine," she began apologetically, glancing down at the logo. "A friend dumped it on me when she came to stay at my place. I just grabbed the nearest thing when you said I had to leave immediately. I never expected you to see me in it."

"You look fine," he said.

That seemed to make her less hesitant. "Which side do you sleep on?"

"The left, if you're standing at the foot of the bed."

"That's handy. I prefer the right."

"No chance of making a mistake and ending up on the same side."

"No."

Gallagher was already in the bed, sitting up. "I normally sleep nude," he said, "but in your honor I've put on fresh underpants and this T-shirt." He indicated a black, short-sleeved garment that fitted him closely.

He'd chosen black for a purpose. If the sensors went mad, he intended to go hunting. All he'd have to put on would be his jeans and snap-on soft black boots, which were ready by the side of the bed. Close to hand next to them was the P226, fitted with the special silencer that Haslam had thoughtfully included in the armory. Haslam had also put in a shoulder harness made of black leather, unpolished to eliminate reflections.

If he had to go out there tonight, Gallagher decided, there'd be little point in wearing it. The pistol was thus lying free of its holster.

The heavy curtains in the room had been drawn closed, and not even the faintest translucence would be visible from outside.

She pushed the door firmly shut with her behind, then came round to her side of the bed. She climbed in beneath the duvet, sliding down and pulling at it with the good hand until it came up to her chin.

He looked at her with some amusement. "Comfy?"

She nodded. "I have shared a bed with a man before, you know," she began defensively, "without anything happening. A researcher came with me to some outlandish place where there was just the one room free, with one bed. We were too fed up to try and find another wretched hotel with more beds."

"So what's happened to the nothing-can-faze-me journalist?" Gallagher asked, thinking of her sudden onrush of modesty.

"Someone's trying to kill her and she's very scared. That's what."

"As long as I'm here, they won't get at you. Now let's see about some sleep." He turned away to switch off the bedside lamp, and so missed the softening of her features as she looked at him.

He eased himself closer to the edge of the bed and turned on his side, away from her. From that position, he could get at the gun quickly. He still hoped he wouldn't have to use it.

The darkness enveloped them, and the house seemed to be holding its breath, waiting. Gallagher lay still, allowing his senses to amplify themselves, catching every nuance in the night. Presently, he could feel the rhythm of the house. The sounds it made; the infinitesimal movement of the oak beams as the wood creaked softly; the dying sighs of the heating system that he'd put on briefly to kill the slight chill of the evening; the soft, barely identifiable hum of the electronics that ran the security system; and many more sounds that came alive upon the night. He sensed them all, waiting for any that did not belong.

Greywolf was active.

Half an hour later, her voice came softly. "You awake?"

He toyed with the idea of not replying before saying, "Yes."

"Thought you were ready to sleep."

"I can sleep lightly and still feel refreshed."

"You're on guard, aren't you."

"Go to sleep, Miranda. I'm okay."

She fell silent, but a few minutes later, she was at it again. "I'm sorry about your father."

"What?"

"Alun told me . . ."

"Alun talks too much. Remind me to speak to him. He's becoming a bloody public-address system."

"Did you go to Cambridge because your father was a don at Oxford?"

"You know how it is with generations. They never do the same things. Or at least they try not to. Now go to sleep. Please."

She fell silent. After a short while she began to move, shuffling closer until the front of her body was against his back. The warmth and softness of her permeated through the thin clothes he wore.

"Do you mind?" she murmured against his back.

"No," he said.

He realized there was no overt sexuality in what she'd done. What she wanted most was comfort.

He reached behind him with a hand to briefly touch

her reassuringly. Her movements had caused the T-shirt to ride high, and his hand touched the bare, warm curve of hip and upper thigh. She didn't shift away. There was nothing under the T-shirt.

Gallagher moved his hand away quickly.

"Thanks," she said softly.

He turned his head briefly. "Sorry, I didn't mean . . ."

"Oh, that. I don't mind. I said thanks for the pat." She sounded drowsy. One of her legs moved and placed itself over his, and very soon her breathing relaxed into a subdued rhythm.

Gallagher felt the heat of her leg and thigh burning through him. At last, she had fallen asleep.

It was three o'clock in the morning when the alarm shrieked them awake. It was a good time to come, one he himself would have chosen, Gallagher thought as he swiftly squeezed the mute button. At this time of year, dawn came around 4 A.M., creating too much light.

He was out of the bed almost before the shrieking had stopped and getting into his jeans, fully on the alert. The boots were on next, then he picked up the P226. Now that the alarm had stopped, Miranda was groggily trying to get back to sleep.

"Up, Miranda!" he commanded. "I'm moving you somewhere safe until I check this out. Come on! Move it!"

His mind raced, evaluating tactics and trying to work out how whoever was out there had managed to make it to the cottage in the first place. He knew the Quattro had not been tagged. At no time had anyone been near it to attempt placing a tracer. The car's sensors would have gone ape. He had also double-checked when he'd put it away, just to be sure. It was definitely clean.

Eyes accustomed to the dark, he reached for a switch near the bed and clicked it on. A dim red light flooded the bedroom, enabling Miranda to see where she was going, without sacrificing his night vision with normal lighting.

He turned back to the bed and grabbed her by the good arm. "Come on, kid. Up with you. We've got visitors."

That brought her fully awake. She shoved the duvet away in her hurry to get out. The T-shirt had ridden up to her waist, baring her entire lower body; but the glorious legs and thighs were the last thing on his mind as she left the bed. She seemed to hit the floor running.

"I'm taking you to a secure room under the house," he told her quickly. "Stay there until I return. Don't open up unless it's me, or Haslam."

She halted abruptly and turned upon him a face made ghostly by the redness of the lighting. She noticed the gun and looked very scared indeed.

"Haslam! What do you mean? You've got to come back!"

"I intend to, but this is a precaution—just in case. No more time to waste; we can talk on the way there."

"My knickers! I've got to get them. I'm not going in some hole in the ground with no knickers." She was adamant.

"Hurry!" He tried not to smile. Her knickers.

As she went to her room, he reflected that all things considered, she had moved reasonably quickly. Less than a minute had passed, he judged.

Soon, she was back. She hadn't just gone for the knickers. She'd brought her small suitcase and the laptop.

"Jesus," he said. "Give me one of those and let's go."

"If I'm going to be down there for a while," she began defiantly as they hurried downstairs, "I might as well have something to do."

"It's not just a hole in the ground," he told her. "It's as big as an entire floor and is fully stocked with everything you're likely to need, including books and videos. There's a kitchen, a lounge, bathroom, and bedroom. There's a filtration unit so your air will be pure."

"A nuclear shelter?"

"It would have doubled as that, if the need required it," he said, "but it's mainly a secure hide."

"You never told me."

"You only get told the things you need to know. I was hoping we'd not have to use it."

"Are there many places like that around?"

"Who knows?" He had no intention of saying more.

She did not probe further.

He led her to a small study. Every time he'd clicked a switch on as they'd hurried through the house, red lighting had come on. Before going up to bed, he had programmed the lighting system to give the illumination in case of an alert.

In the study, he rolled back a portion of a large rug. No identifiable outline could be seen in the small dark squares of the wood-laid floor. He went to a bookshelf, pulled out a book, and pressed at something in the recess. A section of the floor, accurately matching a larger square created by the smaller ones, rose soundlessly. Red lighting came on beneath to show carpeted stairs leading downwards.

"Okay," Gallagher said to her. "Down you go. When the trapdoor's shut, normal lighting will come on. You'll then be able to find your way around. I'll pass you the laptop when you put your case down. When you're all secure go to bed, and get some sleep."

She stopped midway down to turn to look up at him, a forlorn expression upon her face. "How can I, when—"

"Tell me later. Come on, love. Let's do it." He wanted her safely away so he could get on with the serious business of hunting out whoever was out there.

She went down, dropped the case, then came partially back up for the laptop, which he handed to her. When she'd again reached the bottom, she turned to look up at him once more.

"You'll be very safe down there," he said. "If for any

reason I'm not back, you won't have to wait long before Haslam arrives. Hours at most. There's an intercom, and a telephone. Don't touch the phone for any reason, even if it rings. And use the intercom only if you hear my voice, or Haslam's. There's a red push button over to your right . . ." He paused as she turned her head briefly to locate it. "It will raise the trapdoor. The weight of the rug will make little difference. However, I suggest you do not use it. Wait for me, or Haslam."

"You must come back!"

"Don't worry. You'll be fine."

"I wasn't thinking of me," she said. "Be careful."

As he shut the trapdoor on the pleading face, he wondered whether he'd be seeing her again. He was quite right when he'd told her she would be safe. The shelter was in an armored steel envelope, and only a direct hit from a nuclear weapon would harm her—provided no one found the trapdoor. He quickly rolled the rug back into place and slid the book back where it belonged. Then he turned off the lights as he left the study to go to the lounge.

A check of the security display showed two of the stars with solid pulsing rings, one on either side of the house. They were trying for a bracket, in case anyone was about.

They would not have heard any alarm, and would not have realized they were betraying their presence so completely.

Gallagher had already worked out his tactics. First to go would be the one at the back.

Beneath the monitor was a control panel filled with push buttons. He pressed one and the display was replaced by a greenish, light-enhanced view of the area at the back of the house, relayed by the night vision system. The cameras had automatically tracked to the activated sensor, zooming in on the spot. The figure of a man, gun in hand and in what looked like unpatterned combat gear, was shown cautiously looking about as he inched towards the house. Gallagher pressed another button and the cameras switched to infrared. A photonegative view of the same scene appeared, artificially tinged with red. The man's heat source was a beacon.

Gallagher now turned his attention to the intruder's companion at the front of the house. This one, dressed similarly, was lying on his stomach. He was speaking into a communicator.

Gallagher reverted to the first view. The standing man had stopped and was obviously talking to his colleague.

It was time to move.

Gallagher switched the monitor back to the graphic display, then slid the doors shut. There was an exit in the kitchen, sealed by a heavy sliding door. For the time being, it was out of the line of sight of both intruders. Once out, Gallagher knew, he would be unable reenter that way and would have to use the front entrance. He hoped he'd still be alive to do so.

He checked that he had the key as he made his way to the kitchen and decided he would hide it outside, in case he became incapacitated. That way at least whoever was out there would not be able to gain entry, and Miranda would be safe until Haslam came to the rescue.

In the kitchen, he pressed the switch to open the door. When it had slid noiselessly open far enough for him to slip through, he pressed the switch again. The door halted, and began to close. He just made it before it locked silently home.

Inside the house, any red lighting still on went out within seconds. No one outside would have seen any evidence of the lights being turned on and off.

6

Gallagher remained perfectly still, crouching low by the door for long seconds, allowing his eyes to adjust to the new conditions. When he was satisfied, he got out the key. A mere two feet to his right, a bushy shrub grew, and he quickly buried the key at its base. No one would find it without knowing precisely where to look.

He relaxed, holding the P226 ready, stilling himself once more. Nothing came within range of his vision.

He thought of Miranda waiting apprehensively in the hide beneath his feet, and that brought unwelcome thoughts of Rhiannon, which in turn dragged others, even more unwelcome, in its wake.

Gallagher caught himself. Wake up! If those two out there catch you dreaming, you're dead meat.

But he didn't move.

Stillness, sir. Stillness is all. Wait. Wait!

O'Keefe.

Gallagher waited, letting the night and its sounds seep into him. In the distance, he could see pinpricks of light through the trees beyond the clearing. The faint sounds of the river, the groan of moored boats, reached for him. The muted thunder of heavy lorries, carrying goods of the day and hurrying to make their deliveries before the start of business, could be heard on the A34 just half a kilometer away. But they did not overwhelm the closer sounds of the night: the scurrying of woodland creatures; the sudden hoot of a marauding owl; the sharp squeal of death as it struck.

The cautious footfall of an intruder.

The man was working his way towards Gallagher's position, possibly looking for a way in. He would already have studied the back of the house and discovered it was no go.

Gallagher did not move.

The footsteps approached. Wisely, the man did not hurry. A step, pause to listen, another step . . .

But Gallagher's ears were attuned to the nuances of the night. The man ruined his chances by moving. Every step taken meant his own ears had to readjust. To Gallagher, the unknown man might as well have been carrying amplifiers on his feet.

A shape cautiously moved into view. Still too far to take out without use of the gun.

Gallagher waited.

But something had warned the man. Maybe his instincts, heightened by the night, had told him he was close to danger.

Gallagher had not moved, but he knew that like a creature of the wild, the man had sensed that something inimical was close. Gallagher also knew that the man would be confused. What could possibly be waiting out there at three o'clock in the morning? The man had to feel certain that the approach of he and his colleague had been undiscovered. Resistance at this stage had not been expected. He remained where he was, irresolute.

Like a predator that knew it had all the time in the world, Gallagher waited.

The man began to move again. This time, there was an added edge of caution. He stopped again, and seemed to be staring directly where Gallagher was.

Gallagher was positive the man had not yet seen him, but the alarm bells must have been going mad. The man was a pro. He *knew,* even if he could not as yet see, that danger lurked. He went for his communicator and pointed his gun at the same time. The nature of his stance was a clear telegraphing of intent. The bastard was going to shoot. There was only one thing more dangerous than a nonpro in a panic: that was a pro in a panic. The nonpro wouldn't shoot straight. The pro would.

Shit, Gallagher thought.

The man was still too far away to risk a lunge. It would have to be the gun, before the other had time either to shoot or to warn his colleague.

Even as he was thinking it, Gallagher had brought the SIG to bear. The P226 coughed twice. The man gave a strange, almost resigned sigh as he crumpled. He never managed to make the call. His gun had remained silent.

Gallagher did not move. There was no need to check. He had not shot to disable.

The men who were listening in were the same two who had argued about whether to eavesdrop on the goings-on within the house.

"Something's happening out there," the senior one said. He placed his hands to the headphones, as if to hear more clearly.

His companion, who was sipping at a plastic cup of coffee, paused to look at him.

"Pick up your phones and tell me," the senior man continued.

The other put the coffee down and took his place at the second machine. "Nothing."

"I did hear something."

"If you did, it will have been recorded. So why worry?"

The senior man stared briefly at his companion, shook his head despairingly, but said nothing.

Gallagher decided it was time for the second man. Any moment now, he'd be checking to see whether his partner was still operational.

At last, Gallagher began to move.

The second man was still on his stomach, inching his way towards the house. Though the night cloaked him, he felt horribly exposed in the clearing. He paused and spoke softly into his communicator. There was no reply.

He stopped moving and spoke again, this time with urgency. Still no reply. He tried a third time. The result was the same.

The mission was blown, he decided. His partner was down. It was not worth compromising it further.

The man got to his feet and took off for the relative safety of the woods. At least one thing was certain: The house was occupied.

Gallagher arrived at the position he had set himself in time to hear softly running feet. He remained absolutely still, listening. He heard the man reach the woods.

He continued to wait.

Presently, he heard the distant sound of a car moving in a hurry. He remained where he was until the sound faded.

He allowed himself to relax. That would be it for the night. Only then did he return to check on the man he had shot. The unknown man was quite dead.

Gallagher retrieved the key, then looked up at the house.

"Tell Fowler someone's screwed up," he said loudly enough to be picked up by the listeners. "There's a dead man that will need attending to, and I want Haslam out here sharpish. We're going to have to move. That means immediately. Do it!"

"Shit!" the junior man exclaimed. "He knew all along!"

"What did I tell you?" The senior man allowed himself the brief luxury of smugness. "He's good, mate. Very good. Better get Mr. Fowler on the direct line," he continued firmly. "Some heads will go on the block for this cock-up. Let's make sure ours are not among them."

Miranda sat in the kitchen of the shelter wondering about what might be taking place above her head. She could hear nothing, and this made her imagination run riot. She envisaged all kinds of scenarios, all bad. Would Gallagher survive? And if he didn't, who would get to her first? Haslam's people? Or those who wanted her dead?

Though the kitchen was indeed well stocked, as Gallagher had said, she had touched nothing. Every so often, she would look up at the ceiling, as if expecting to be able to see what was going on outside.

She was literally startled off her chair when Gallagher's voice came at her from the intercom. She beamed with relief and pleasure.

"All over!" his voice announced. "Time to leave your underground hotel."

The trapdoor was already being raised, and soon he was on his way down the stairs to meet her. She rushed forward and, embracing him with her good arm, held on tightly.

"Hey," he said gently. "I'm enjoying this, but I wasn't gone that long."

"It seemed like ages," she said against his neck. "I imagined all sorts of horrible things going on out there, and that you . . ." She stopped, not wanting to take the thought to its logical conclusion. At last, she released him and glanced down. He had brought the gun with him. "What happened?"

"There were two of them," he began. "It was just a reconnaissance. They took off as soon as they knew someone was out in the dark with them." No point telling her about the body. By the time they were ready to leave, Haslam's people would have cleared it away. "Now let's get you out of here."

With the shelter closed down once more and the trapdoor secured, they returned to Gallagher's bedroom.

"I'm not going back to my room," she said in a voice that told him it would be quite pointless to argue. "It's the only way I'll be able to sleep."

"Not much time for that. I expect Haslam within the hour, or ninety minutes at most. We're catching the earliest flight out of Heathrow that he manages to book us on; it's not such a good idea remaining here now. You'll be able to snatch a couple of hours once we're airborne."

There was an upright chair placed against the wall near his side of the bed. He put the gun down where he'd placed it before the alarm had gone off, then sat on the chair to remove his boots and socks. Next came his jeans.

"I've got my gear ready," he continued as he turned to fold them once across the back of the chair, "so if you prepare yours, we'll be out of here as soon as Haslam arrives." He turned again to face her, straightened in the chair, and brought his hands to his face. He rubbed vigorously at it.

"My own stuff is practically ready. You're tired," she observed. "You have a quick snooze, and I'll sit up to keep watch. I don't think I'll be able sleep now, even in here. I can always yell if anything happens. That'll get you up."

"We've got the alarm system. It didn't fail us, so we're quite safe without your yell." Gallagher rubbed his face once more. "I'm fine."

She moved slowly to stand before him. "If you're not tired . . ." She let her words hang.

The way she said it made him look up at her. The room was still on alert lighting, and its pale crimson glow gave her an ethereal presence. She was looking down at him, legs slightly apart. Even as he stared she began, with deliberate slowness, to remove her briefs from beneath the voluminous T-shirt. She stepped out of them, thighs flashing a tantalizing pink in the redness of the light.

"It occurred to me," she said, "while I was locked up in that luxurious hole down there like some medieval virgin hidden from marauding raiders, that if it all went dreadfully wrong and we were both killed, we'd have wasted valuable time."

She came forward, hitching up the T-shirt and spreading her legs to straddle him. She reached forward with her good hand to take hold of the waistband of his underpants. The heat and smell of her were beginning to arouse him.

"You're going to have to help me," she said into his stunned silence. Her voice had gone lower, and she was beginning to sound uncertain.

"You don't have to do this," he said.

"I want to. I'm not doing this in gratitude, and I'm not asking you to fall in love with me or anything . . ."

"Miranda . . ."

"Shhh." She kissed him on the mouth with a brief but sensual pressure. "And no excuses about my shoulder. This way won't hurt it. Help me, Gordon, before I begin to feel a fool." It was a plea, but it didn't prevent her from raising herself slightly to give a gentle tug at the pants.

The feel of her thigh muscles as she balanced herself increased his arousal, despite his misgivings.

"Gordon?" she began with a tremulous softness, the uncertainty in her voice growing. "Are you going to let me stay like this?" The busy hand began to hesitate.

"No," he said, and gently reached forward to ease her off him.

She did not move. "Do you find me so unattractive?"

"God, no! It's all I can do to keep myself from—"

"All right then." She lowered herself once more and began to kiss him. This time she kept at it, pressing hard against him.

"Miranda!" Gallagher said. "Haslam . . ." The pressure of her lips turned the rest of what he intended to say into an incomprehensible jumble.

"Sod Haslam!" she said fiercely.

She raised herself again, because he was now pulling at the underpants himself. She continued to kiss him, giving a brief wiggle to better position herself for a smooth entry. Moving her hand to his shoulder and using that for leverage, she descended for a third time, impaling herself upon him with a plunge that brought a shuddering gasp out of her.

"*Aah!*" she cried in a thin, high voice. Slowly at first, then with increasing rhythm, she began moving vigorously against him.

Gallagher had placed both arms about her, but did not squeeze too tightly for fear of hurting the wounded shoulder. In her abandon, however, she seemed to have forgotten all about it.

She began to make whimpering noises that grew

rapidly in intensity. Then she snatched her head away, throwing it back as she reared and arched against him, her feet pounding at the floor.

"Oh my God!" The squealed whisper was forced out of her as she tightened and pulsed about him. "I'm . . . I'm going to scream! Oh God . . . *I'm going to scream!*"

And so she did.

The man who had run away drove fast along the empty country road. He had removed his combat jacket, which was now in the trunk of the car, to reveal a plain blue open-necked shirt, and had pulled the trouser bottoms out of his boots. His face was expressionless as he negotiated a bend at high speed. The car briefly twitched off its line, using up a lot of road, but held. The first streaks of daylight were beginning to appear high in the sky, but on the ground it was still dark and headlights were required.

He had now crossed into Buckinghamshire, and the road was totally devoid of traffic. Soon, he was turning off onto an even narrower road. He drove for another three miles until the rear reflectors of another car appeared in his headlights. It was parked slightly off the road. Beyond it was a shallow ditch. He drew up behind the car and stopped.

He wound his window down.

"Turn off those bloody lights!" a voice ordered curtly out of the darkness.

The suddenness of it startled him but he did as he was told, feeling momentarily blind and strangely vulnerable.

"Where's your partner?" a new voice demanded.

"He's . . . he's down." The man began to get out. He'd feel less exposed.

"Stay where you are!" the second voice commanded. "What do you mean he's down?"

"They were waiting for us."

"'They'? You mean *he* was waiting for you." The second voice was now doing all the interrogating. "I might have known you two would bungle this. He's too good for idiots like you." There was almost respect in the voice. "You're sent on a reconnaissance, and you return one down. And the woman? Is she there?"

"She must be if he's—"

"Fool! How can you be certain if you haven't seen her? One of you was meant to distract him while the other gained entry to see if the woman was indeed there. Nothing else was to be done—"

"At least we know the place is occupied."

There was an absolute silence over the interruption, and menace oozed out of the darkness.

"You won't interrupt me again," the voice said coldly. "Are you really so stupid that you seriously believe they'll remain there after all this?"

Two shots barked suddenly into the night. The unexpectedness of it took the man in the car completely by surprise. He was hit at close range, in the chest.

"Why?" The strangely mournful question wheezed out of him just before he died.

"Why?" The voice, closer now, carried a restrained savagery. "Because you failed."

"What do we do with it?" the first voice asked.

"This." Something was dropped into the dead man's car. "Now push it into the ditch." It was a command.

The car was pushed off the road, then they got into their vehicle and drove off. Some minutes later, the car in the ditch erupted into flame.

By that time, the other car was a long way from the scene.

Miranda's head rested in the crook of Gallagher's neck, her face damp from her recent exertions. She breathed softly, her body propped in relaxed contentment.

"Not the best of times," she began in languid tones, "to ask if you're free of nasty infections."

"Bit too late for that. Lucky for you, I am."

"And lucky for *you,*" she retorted, nuzzling his ear, "*I* am." She giggled.

They had remained on the chair, and the giggling sent a tremor through her body. She felt him twitch within her in response. Rearing slightly, she moved languorously as she shifted into a better position. The twitching turned into something more potent.

"Oh yes," she murmured. "More, please."

She raised her head to look at him. In the subdued reddish glow of the lighting, her eyes were dark hiding places full of secrets. She began to make slow, sinuous movements, kissing him as she did so.

Gallagher, now in the grip of a powerful new arousal, squeezed her tightly to him, his earlier concern for her shoulder driven from his mind by her slow gyrations. Then the gyrations increased, and soon her wails were mingling with his own sounds. At last, bodies trembling, they fell silent.

Then they heard the helicopter.

"Shit!" Gallagher exclaimed. "Trust Haslam to get here quicker than expected. Bloody typical." He began to move.

But Miranda was holding on tightly to him. "Oh, no no no! Not yet. Let's just stay like this a little longer."

"Miranda, they're going to be here any minute!"

"Oh." Her voice was a long, drawn-out sigh of disappointment, like that of someone denied her favorite sweet. She rose slowly, with great reluctance, a shudder going through her as she did so. There was the faint noise of suction as their bodies separated, and an involountary little gasp was forced out of her. "Oh," she whispered, feeling cheated, before adding with some vehemence, "Sodding Haslam! Why couldn't he be late for a change?"

But she moved quickly after that, rushing to her bathroom. Gallagher moved swiftly, too, to tidy himself and to get everything sorted before the aircraft landed.

By the time the helicopter had set down they were waiting downstairs, fully dressed and ready to travel. Outside, the day had claimed its place from the night.

Gallagher opened the door to see Haslam standing there. Beyond was the waiting helicopter, its blades turning slowly.

Haslam entered and looked pointedly at each in turn. "I can see you got plenty of sleep. Anything I should know?" His eyes said he already knew.

Gallagher just stared neutrally back at him.

"We got you an early flight," Haslam said. "Eleven hundred hours."

Gallagher favored him with a disbelieving look. "You call that early?"

"Best we could do under the circumstances. You are a day early."

"I didn't choose to be."

The helicopter was beating its way towards Heathrow. As it had lifted off from the clearing, Gallagher had noticed a second one swooping in to land. The cleanup team.

Miranda was sitting up front next to the pilot while Gallagher and Haslam, wearing headsets, talked privately on a secure channel. Miranda was also wearing a headset, but that was to allow her to listen in on the pilot's conversations with the various air traffic control areas.

"I take it she knows nothing of the man you shot?" Haslam now asked Gallagher.

"Thought it best not to tell her more than is absolutely necessary."

Haslam nodded his approval. "Just as well. There's more news on what I believe may be the work of our friend with the rifle. A West German industrialist, allegedly with links to the Stasi in what was East Germany, was found shot dead in the toilets of an autobahn restaurant. His driver was quite unaware and only discovered what had happened when he became worried that they would be late for a meeting and went in to check on him. It took him a while to do this because, understandably, he didn't want to disturb the big cheese while said cheese was on the throne, so to speak." Haslam sometimes had a way with words.

Gallagher waited, knowing there was more.

"On the way to pick you up," Haslam continued, "we made a slight detour. A couple of county bobbies on patrol were coming to the end of their shift when they saw a bloody great fire about a mile away. First thought was that a group of New Age hippies had set fire to a field around one of their illegal encampments on some poor farmer's land. With summer approaching, their tribes are gathering for their usual visits to their festivals and, of course, Stonehenge. Although they're now forbidden to go near it, they were still on their travels to the site, and some had obviously decided to camp along the way.

"At least, that's what the bobbies thought, but the bobbies were wrong. What they found was a burning car in a ditch, with a man in it. Although we'll have to wait for the forensic report, I think that was your second man."

Gallagher stared at him. "The killer took him out?"

Haslam nodded. "Seems most likely. The man and his partner had bungled. One down, the quarry now alerted and, as a result, obviously evacuated from the area as quickly as possible. To someone like our friend, that would be a major failure. I don't think he'd take kindly to that. He's the sort who cuts out the dead wood ruthlessly."

"That still leaves the question of time available to do all that. To take out both the copper in London *and* that businessman in Germany yesterday, then get back to be able to attend to his helper in the early hours of the morning, would need very good organization."

"Oh, I don't know. We've moved you into places quickly before, unless you've magically forgotten."

"I haven't forgotten," Gallagher replied grimly.

"He's clearly got the organization. Whoever is running him has plenty of resources."

A silence fell between them as Gallagher turned to look out of the helicopter and down at the still-sleeping landscape. The number of moving lights on the roads showed that many commuters were trying to beat the inevitable jams to come.

"I admire your restraint," Haslam now said.

Gallagher turned his head briefly to glance back at him before once more studying the world outside the aircraft.

"Oh, I don't mean Miss Lacey, our intrepid journalist," Haslam's voice continued cheerfully. "One look at the dewy-eyed expression planted on her face would have been enough to damn you without further evidence. I'm talking about the fact that you haven't yet asked me how those men came to be checking out an area that only a very few within the Department are supposed to know . . . and that phone call."

"I'm waiting for the excuse," Gallagher said without turning round.

"No excuse," Haslam said. "I haven't the foggiest idea how any of it came about."

"Oh, great. I feel better now."

There was no further discussion before the helicopter landed within the perimeter at Heathrow. But the car that picked them up did not head for the terminal buildings. Instead, it made its way out of the airport.

Haslam was sitting next to the driver. From the back, where he sat with Miranda, Gallagher reached forward to tap him on the shoulder.

"What's this, Haslam?" he demanded sharply.

Haslam turned round. "Change of plan," he announced calmly. "I'm just as anxious as you are, so it was decided to play safe. Tell you more later. Sit back and enjoy the drive."

Haslam was again facing front. Gallagher looked at Miranda, who gave him a worried look.

"Can you trust him?" she whispered.

Gallagher nodded, but as he stared at Haslam's back, he hoped he could. Then he noted the route the car was taking. It had joined the M25 orbital motorway and was heading southwards at high speed. The motorway curved eastwards and when thirty or so miles and twenty minutes later they joined the M23 heading south, Gallagher had his suspicions confirmed. They were on their way to Gatwick.

London's second international airport was busy enough throughout the year, but even more so during the run-up to and the summer itself. Because of the many holiday charter flights that took off from there, Haslam was obviously hoping to make them inconspicuous among the crowding holidaymakers.

But Haslam had other plans as well.

The car did not head for the terminals. Instead, it made for the private aircraft park, where it came to a halt.

"And here we are," Haslam said, getting out.

Gallagher and Miranda climbed out. Gallagher's eyes settled on a gleaming white Cessna Citation VII, and he felt a sudden tightening in his stomach. It carried an American registration and looked brand new. The flight deck was occupied.

The aircraft sent a wave of conflicting emotions through him. It brought back memories, some of which he'd rather have done without. Memories of being hunted in the Australian Outback; of flying a craft very similar, with the headless corpse of its original pilot in the left-hand seat; and, inevitably, of Lauren dying on the slopes of Courchevel.

But this was a very different Citation, though its genesis was unmistakable. Based upon the beautiful gull-like shape of its predecessor, the Citation III, the graceful swept wings, seemingly fragile and too slender, were in reality immensely strong and efficient. It was a high-performance, high-flying business jet. As he remembered it, the earlier version had a ceiling of 51,000 feet. This one would no doubt be equal to it.

Haslam noted his gaze. "Yes," he confirmed. "That's your flight."

"The taxpayer's paying for this?"

"No. Let's just say someone who owes us a favor was very pleased to place his private jet at our disposal."

"I'll bet," Gallagher commented dryly. He wondered what leverage Fowler had used.

"It's really a two-pilot airplane, but we're using the one plus the . . . er, flight attendant, who's quite useful on the flight deck. Security in small numbers. Our own pilot, of course."

"Naturally."

Miranda was staring at the Citation. "If it weren't for the reason we're here, I could get to like this."

Haslam gave her a brief smile. "Make the most of it. Might as well. Now let's get your things aboard."

The pilot came to the door of the aircraft. He seemed vaguely familiar to Gallagher. As they approached with their luggage, Gallagher recognized him.

"We meet again, sir," the pilot greeted. "Hammond."

"Yes. I remember." They shook hands. Hammond had been flying military helicopters then.

"So you're still at it."

Hammond grinned. "For my sins. Took a fixed-wing course. Bit older, but still going strong." Hammond looked at Miranda. "We'll give you as smooth a flight as possible, miss." He stepped out to help with the bags, the heaviest of which were then stowed in the aircraft's luggage compartment.

"We?" Gallagher repeated as they climbed in. Then he saw a young woman he didn't recognize. Haslam's "flight attendant."

"Welcome aboard." She greeted them with a genuinely friendly smile. "I'll be looking after you on the flight. I'm Sian."

"Thank you, Sian," Gallagher said, as he watched Hammond lead her onto the flight deck.

Miranda looked about her as they took seats that looked like armchairs. Highly polished retractable tables with cushioned surrounds were slotted neatly into the sides of the cabin. The seating, configured for six passengers and one attendant, faced towards the flight deck in three pairs, with the equally luxurious seat for the attendant positioned near the galley at the rear.

"So," Miranda began, "even multimillionaires at your beck and call. Smell that leather!" She stroked the rich upholstery.

"Not *my* beck and call," Gallagher retorted.

Haslam had come abroad and had perched on a seat behind them. He held the briefcase out to Gallagher.

"I don't need it," Gallagher said.

"You needed it back at the house."

"That's because someone knew where we'd gone. This time, only I know where we'll be going."

"You might still need it."

"And how am I supposed to get that through Portuguese customs?"

"You won't be stopped. Take it. If not for your sake, for hers."

Gallagher reluctantly took the case.

"And I can get the Portuguese to give you back up—"

"Thanks, but no thanks," Gallagher interrupted. "I don't want to broadcast our presence to all and sundry. The less people involved, the better I'll like it. Do they know what's in the briefcase?"

"No. Only that they shouldn't stop you."

"Fabulous. And what happens if I meet a customs man who's just come on duty and doesn't know the drill, or who's a new man and keen, or who's just simply in a bad temper because his wife gave him a bad time this morning and so he wants to vent his frustrations on someone? I'd look great with a load of guns on me."

"It won't happen."

"Trust you?"

"Yes."

"You've got to be joking."

Haslam glanced at Miranda. "He's always like this."

"My car," Gallagher said. "Tell your people not to put their paws all over it. I'll collect it when I get back."

"They've already been warned. I know how you feel about that car of yours. Incidentally," Haslam continued, "Sian's fully qualified with weapons, should you need help on arrival. In fact, she's bloody good. If you won't have a backup in Portugal," Haslam carried on before Gallagher could object, "and you won't let us know where you're going, at least keep in contact."

"How? By wide-open international phone?"

"Don't be difficult, Gordon. Call the consulate. Use your code word."

"What code word?"

Haslam was reluctant to say, clearly not wanting to divulge it in Miranda's presence. "You know the one."

"I don't have that anymore."

"Oh, yes you do," Haslam insisted, getting up. "Have a good flight." He made for the door, paused to give each a parting look, and then, with a brief smile, climbed out.

Sian came back from the flight deck to secure the door before returning to take the seat next to Hammond.

Then the Citation VII's twin engines began to spool up.

7

The Citation was cruising smoothly at 45,000 feet, its engines barely audible from within the opulent cocoon of the cabin. Sian came up to them and, standing in the recessed channel of the aisle, began to extend their tables.

"How about some breakfast?" she asked when she'd finished. "We've got hot rolls, croissants, hot coffee or tea, marmalade and other preserves, and even fresh bacon that's keeping nice and hot."

"Spoiled for choice," Gallagher said. "I could eat a large breakfast. I'll have everything, with coffee."

She gave him a huge smile. "Everything, with coffee." She turned to Miranda. "And you, miss?"

"I'll have what he's having, with tea."

"With tea it is." Sian gave Gallagher another friendly smile before going to the comprehensively equipped galley.

Miranda shifted briefly to look back along the aisle to watch her departure before turning to Gallagher.

"I could eat a large breakfast. I'll have everything, with coffee," she mimicked in a whisper. "Pretty thing, isn't she? Another redhead. Freckles too. How sweet. Wonder what she'd think if she knew why you need your large breakfast. Nice legs, if a trifle heavy. I know I'm no fragile flower, but . . ."

"Meow!" Gallagher said.

"Well," she said, managing to apply admonishment as well as projecting a sense of injury with that single word. "The way she smiled at you. Sickening. She just about managed to hold on to it when it was my turn."

"Miranda, Miranda. Jealousy from a hard-nosed journo?"

"Jealous? Ha!"

He gave her an amused look. "She's one of Haslam's people," he told her. "And when we land, I'll be concentrating on losing her as quickly as possible."

Miranda was surprised. "So he really was serious about her? That girl?"

"Haslam is always serious about such things. I'd be even more worried than I am if he weren't. And what do you mean by 'that girl'? Think she's a bimbo? How do you like it when male journalists see you like that?"

"Touché," Miranda conceded, if a little reluctantly.

"She wouldn't be here," Gallagher continued, "if Haslam's boss didn't think very highly of her. I'm going to have to sort her out when she least expects it."

"You're that certain she'll try to follow us?" Miranda kept her voice low, glancing quickly over her shoulder. "Shouldn't she be going back with the plane?"

"I learned a long time ago," he said, "never to take anything for granted. I'm assuming she's under orders to follow. If I'm wrong, fine. But if I am right, I'll be expecting it and won't be caught by surprise."

She was staring at him. "Are you always like this, as Haslam said? Suspecting everyone all the time?"

"In your job, don't you sometimes doubt people's motives by the replies they give during an interview?

Or more interestingly, by what they *don't* say to you?"

"Yes, but it's not the same thing . . ."

"Different, but similar."

"You call that an answer?"

"It will have to do."

The sleepy square, London.

Haslam entered Fowler's office and sat down.

Fowler looked up from his desk. "Safely on their way?"

Haslam nodded. "Up in the blue yonder."

"And Sian?"

"I told her to keep an eye. See where they go. But he's probably expecting it anyway. He'll lose her the first chance he gets. So I suggested she give it up if it seems he knows she's on the trail."

"That will be from the moment they land," Fowler commented dryly. "Sian's good, but Gordon's way ahead. Oh, well. Worth a try."

Haslam was not fooled. Fowler had accepted the inevitable too easily. He wondered what his former colleague was really up to. When it came to deviousness, Haslam always thought Fowler could have given Machiavelli a lesson or two.

"Got the report on that burned car," Fowler now said. "The driver was shot twice, killing shots in the chest. You were correct, George: It's our rifleman. It must be. The same thermal device was used. Like the others, it's of American manufacture; but I believe that to be a deliberate smoke screen. With the right connections, one does not have to be American to buy these."

"Any more than one has to be British to buy some of our stuff," Haslam pointed out mildly.

The glasses stared at him. "Quite. Took out his own helper," Fowler went on. "Cold-blooded bastard, isn't he?"

If Haslam thought that was rich coming from Fowler, he chose not to say so.

"Let's hope that this time, he won't discover where Miranda Lacey has gone," he remarked instead.

"We can but hope indeed. But we still don't know *why* Miranda Lacey. It's not even as if she's interviewed any of the assassinated victims. What the devil could she have seen? What's the connection? That's the question exercising my brain at the moment." Fowler studied Haslam closely. "You look worn out, George. Go home and continue with your interrupted sleep. Lounge in your garden. I'll keep you posted."

Haslam got wearily to his feet. "Perhaps you're right. I'm too old for this."

Fowler gave one of his tight smiles. "So you keep saying."

Lisbon Airport, Portugal.

Borodin, traveling as a French citizen named Delacroix, signed for the rental car with a flourish. All his documents were in perfect order, including the credit card he'd used to hire the dark blue Citroën Xantia.

He smiled at the young Portuguese woman as she handed him the keys. He'd told her a story about meeting his family who were already on their holiday in the south, and who were waiting for him. But first, he had business in Lisbon.

"*Merci,*" he now said to her as he took the keys, his French pronunciation properly accented.

"*Vous en pris,*" the multilingual young woman replied.

She wished him a safe journey south to the Algarve when he'd finished his business in Lisbon.

▪ ▪ ▪

The Citation cruised its way towards Faro Airport on the Algarve. Having consumed a truly substantial breakfast, Gallagher dozed contentedly. From her seat, a wide-awake Miranda glaced at him from time to time. Movement on the periphery of her vision made her look round.

Sian was approaching from the flight deck, where she'd spent most of the flight when not attending to her charges.

She stopped between the seats and smiled almost fondly, Miranda thought, at the sleeping Gallagher.

"Needs his sleep, does he?" she asked Miranda.

Miranda found herself looking into very green eyes that certainly did not belong to a bimbo, and restrained the witty but barbed comment she was tempted to make.

"He's been up most of the night," was what she said.

"Best leave him to his rest then."

"Yes."

"Is your arm okay? I've got some painkillers if you need them."

"I'm fine. Thank you."

"Just sing out if you do need anything."

"I will."

The green eyes seemed amused by a private joke. Then Sian returned to the flight deck.

Gallagher popped open an eye. "You two are squaring off like a pair of cats. And you sounded as if you were trying hard not to speak through gritted teeth. I hope you're not going to give me trouble." Both eyes were now studying her.

Miranda stared at him furiously. "You're awake?" she accused in a sharp whisper. "You eavesdropped!"

"I could hardly fail to hear. For a moment, I thought you were going to give her your version of why I needed my sleep."

She gave him another furious look.

"Don't look so put out," he said to her.

"I'm glad you think it's funny."

"She was doing her job. Checking up on me." Gallagher closed his eyes once more. "Wake me when we land."

The Citation curved gracefully in on the seaward approach pattern, which scrupulously avoided overflying the exclusive zones of residential and holiday villas. Hammond made a perfect landing and the sleek jet taxied swiftly off the runway to where two cars waited, well away from other airport traffic. One of the cars was a steel gray Jaguar sedan.

Four men stood expectantly by the cars. Three were in civilian clothes, while the fourth was in the jeans-blue uniform of the airport police. In keeping with normal practice, he was armed. He also wore dark glasses.

The Citation came to a gentle halt and the engines began to spool down. Gallagher waited until Sian had returned to the cabin to release the door before indicating to Miranda that she should leave her seat. Carrying the briefcase with the guns, he first went up to the flight deck.

"A very smooth flight and a greaser of a landing," he said to Hammond, who had turned in his seat expectantly. "Thank you."

Hammond grinned. "We aim to please."

"Heading back, are you?"

"We'll be waiting for instructions, but that's the general idea. Yes."

Gallagher held out his hand. "Have a good return trip."

Hammond shook the hand. "I intend to."

Gallagher went back along the aisle to follow Miranda out. Sian waited by the exit. Her expression carried its usual friendly openness.

"A good flight," he told her. "Thank you."

"A pleasure," she said.

Still certain she'd been primed by Haslam, he moved past her to step into the bright warmth of Portugal.

"God," Miranda whispered fiercely as he caught up with her and they walked towards the reception committee. "I *hate* that smile she's got pasted on her face. So bloody smug."

"You're imagining it."

Two of the suits, in different shades of cream, were approaching.

"Imagining . . ." she began indignantly.

The arrival of the men ended whatever she had to say. Like the two who remained by the cars, both appeared to be Portuguese. One had a full but neatly groomed mustache.

The taller one held out a welcoming hand to them. "Miss Lacey, Mr. Gallagher . . . I'm Roberto Haxton, from the consul general's office, and this is Captain Mario Pinheiro of the district police. Our instructions are to give you any assistance you may need."

They all shook hands. Haxton was the one with the mustache.

Any assistance. Nice try, Fowler, Gallagher thought. He had no intention of allowing the Department to keep tabs on him. Pinheiro loked interestedly at Miranda's sling, but made no comment.

"Thank you, Mr. Haxton . . ." Gallagher began.

"Roberto, please. Or Robert. If you prefer. Some of the people we deal with—tourists and such like—tend to prefer the anglicized version. My mother's Portuguese, father English."

"Roberto will do," Gallagher said.

Haxton looked pleased. "And so, what are your instructions?"

Gallagher glanced quickly back at the aircraft. Both Hammond and Sian were outside. Hammond was unloading the luggage. The civilian next to the uniformed policeman hurried over to help.

"Excuse me for a moment, gentlemen," Gallagher said to Haxton and Pinheiro. "Something I've got to do. Won't be long," he added to Miranda.

He went back to the aircraft, leaving them to stare puzzledly after him.

Both Sian and Hammond paused to watch his approach. He went up to Sian. The green eyes regarded him expectantly, but gave nothing away.

"I'll come straight to the point," he began pleasantly. "I know Haslam's given you a bloodhound job. Forget it. I'll lose you."

She beamed at him. "Definitely straight to the point."

"I'm glad you didn't try to deny it."

"To what purpose? Mr. Haslam did warn me you'd be no pushover. Besides, I already knew you wouldn't be. I know of you by reputation."

"Then you're one up on me. I know nothing about you at all."

"I joined after your time with the Department."

"Obviously. So what are we going to do about this situation?"

The green eyes seemed speculative. "I might as well return with the aircraft."

"Good idea." He turned to go.

"It might have been interesting fun," she said.

He paused. "'Interesting fun.' That's one way of putting it. What might?"

"Working with you."

"Who knows," he said and went back to where Miranda and the others waited.

He could feel the eyes of both women upon him. One at the front, the other at the back. Laser beams would have been puny by comparison. Great.

"Problems?" Haxton queried.

"Sorted," Gallagher replied. He studiously avoided

Miranda's probing stare. "You asked for instructions, Roberto. Well, if you can get us out of here and to the car park, I'd be very grateful."

"The car park?" Haxton looked as if he thought Gallagher had suddenly gone mad. "But we've got a car for you, and a driver . . ."

"And greatly appreciated. But there's a company I usually hire a car from when I'm here . . ."

"But Mr. Gallagher," Pinheiro began carefully, "we're to give you protection . . ."

"Again, I really do appreciate it, Captain. But the best service you can grant me right now is to get us over to the other side. I do promise, however, should we be in the need of urgent help I'll get in touch with you both, through the consulate."

Looking distinctly unhappy, Haxton reached into his inner jacket pocket for a business card. "If you're really determined, at least take this. It's got my direct office number, and my home number."

"This is no reflection on you, Roberto," Gallagher said, taking the card. "I did warn Haslam."

"And he cautioned us you might refuse," Haxton said ruefully. "He said you preferred working on your own."

Pinheiro was himself offering a card. "Also direct number," he began, "and home number. Portugal is Britain's oldest ally, but you will try, won't you, Mr. Gallagher, not to start any wars on your own?"

"I always avoid doing that as a matter of principle."

Pinheiro did not look as if he believed it. "We shall escort you to the other side." He again offered his hand, in parting. "Miss Lacey. Mr. Gallagher." He went back to the smaller car and climbed in. He had barely glanced at the briefcase.

A sure sign, Gallagher thought, that Pinheiro suspected its importance, even if he were uncertain of what might be in it. Under normal circumstances, his policeman's instincts would have led him to demand its inspection.

The uniformed policeman got in behind the wheel. The civilian driver that Haxton had mentioned was behind the wheel of the Jaguar.

"Your car awaits," Haxton said, indicating with an outstretched arm, "if only for brief use."

They got in, Miranda and Gallagher ushered into the back of the air-conditioned splendor of the Jaguar by Haxton, who then took his place next to the driver. The police car set off at speed. The Jaguar took off after it as if scenting prey.

It wasn't exactly a low-profile arrival, Gallagher thought dryly. At least they hadn't used sirens.

As they flashed past the Citation, he saw that both Hammond and Sian were tracking their departure with interested eyes. Sian raised a hand in a brief wave. They seemed in no particular hurry to get back aboard the aircraft.

In the speeding car, Haxton had twisted in his seat to say, "Good man, Mario Pinheiro. Sensitive sort of chap. Usually he has to deal with the sort of tourist lout we mercifully don't have plenty of. Not like Spain, anyway. Not in this area, of course, but further afield. Places like Albuféira and Vilamoura. Not really his districts, but he has a wide brief."

Which told Gallagher quite clearly that Pinheiro was no ordinary "district" cop. Given the private boats that came to the warm Portuguese coast, Pinheiro was probably seconded from an anti-drug-smuggling unit, his "wide brief" the entire Algarve.

"I love the Algarve," Haxton was saying. "The authorities got wise very quickly when they saw what unchecked high-rise buildings had done to Spain. Now, all building is strictly regulated. You'll see that most houses are limited to two stories, with plenty of space and vegetation in between. You'll find some very pleasant ones in the area."

Now even Haxton was at it. Gallagher did not fall for that little fishing expedition.

"I love the Algarve too," he said. "I know it quite well."

"Ah." Haxton smiled sheepishly. "Was I that obvious?"

"He's just naturally suspicious," Miranda put in pointedly. She was clearly saving her comments about Sian for later.

Gallagher presented her with a benign look, which only served to infuriate her. She looked away. Haxton looked from one to the other, unsure of what expression to wear. A whole range flitted across his features. In the end, he gave up and turned to stare at the speeding airport landscape.

The cars came to a sudden bumper-to-bumper halt at the front of the low terminal building. The large car park, sectioned off into lettered areas, was quite full. But it was not static. Cars were constantly coming and going as arriving and departing holidaymakers picked up or left their hired vehicles. People with pieces of paper in their hands wandered among the cars, searching for the ones that had been prebooked with their flights. Some were looking worried, trying to identify which of the multitude of cars, virtual clones even down to color, had been allocated to them.

Gallagher climbed out, keeping hold of the briefcase, while Haxton left his seat to open the other door for Miranda.

"So I can't change your mind," Haxton said to Gallagher.

"No. But I've got your cards. Any problems, and I'll be on the phone."

The driver unloaded their luggage as Pinheiro left his police car to join them. He glanced round the car park.

"Your car is here?" he said to Gallagher, dark eyes asking far more.

"I think so," came the vague reply. "I'll have to check."

Pinheiro nodded, as if convincing himself of something. "I must leave you then, Mr. Gallagher. Miss

Lacey. You have my number if you need me. I wish you both a very pleasant stay."

"Thank you," they said together.

Pinheiro nodded once more and returned to his car, which set off as if at a grand prix.

Gallagher watched it leave the parking area to head for the road into Faro. He didn't believe it for one moment. Pinheiro had almost certainly left another unmarked car behind. Gallagher had ideas on how to flush it out.

He turned to Haxton as their luggage was assembled in a neat little pile by the driver.

He held out his hand. "Thanks again, Roberto. I'll handle it from here."

They shook hands, Haxton still reluctant to leave.

For Gallagher's part, he wanted both Haxton and Pinheiro out of the way, not simply because he preferred to work on his own, but also because it was the surest way of keeping them alive should the killer manage to pick up the trail to Portugal. If Haxton and Pinheiro got in the killer's way, like the unfortunate policeman who had been with Prinknash, they would be surgically removed from the scene. The killer would feel no more compassion for them than he would for a fly he was about to swat.

Thinking of this, he said to Haxton, "As I told the captain, I've got your number. If I do need you, I promise to call."

Haxton accepted the inevitable. "All right. We'll leave it at that for the moment. Miss Lacey."

Haxton climbed back into the Jaguar, which took off in a squeal of tires that caused people to turn to look.

Staring after it, Miranda said, "Same old Portugal."

"Been down here before?"

"No. I've been to the Douro region in the north. The driving's the same. And now, sir, what's the next move? And don't think I didn't see your tête-à-tête with Miss Green Eyes."

"I wondered when that would surface. Your 'Miss Green Eyes' is right now thinking of ways to track us. I was telling her not to bother."

"Is that why she waved?"

Gallagher looked at her.

"What?" she began defensively. "Are you the sort of man who believes a career woman doesn't have feelings?"

"I wouldn't dream of thinking that. Now let's start losing a few nosy people. First, the good captain's snoop."

"But he just left . . ."

"Ah, the innocence. He's got someone lurking around; perhaps even two of them. Wait here while I get a trolley."

Gallagher walked across the wide pavement to where a line of luggage trolleys were packed into each other. People were adding to and taking from the pack. He pulled one out, glancing with apparent disinterest about him as he did so. A man lounging casually against one of the car park booths was staring in his direction, then suddenly became very interested in conversation with the female attendant in the booth.

Gallagher gave no indication that he'd noticed.

On his return to where Miranda waited, he put the luggage onto the trolley and began moving towards the entrance to the terminal.

"What are you doing?" Miranda asked as she followed. "We're not flying back, are we?" She sounded terrified by the idea. "I thought we were going to hire a car."

"We are going to pick up a car," he assured her, "but not just yet. Let's go and have a coffee."

Without waiting for her to comment, he went through the automatic doors and into the building.

The concourse, with its gleaming floor and low, yellow-painted convex girders across the awninglike ceiling, was a familiar sight to Gallagher. To his left were four glass-enclosed balconies, seemingly suspended like flying buttresses above the floor. A wide staircase led up to them.

"We'll have our coffees up there," he said to a bemused Miranda, who was now at his side. "In one of those balconies. Perfect for observation."

"What are we observing?"

"We'll wait and see what develops."

Half an hour later, their coffees grown cold in plastic cups, Gallagher stared down at the now-empty concourse. Like migrating birds, the bustling passengers had suddenly vanished. The airline, car hire, and information desks within his field of vision were in full, uninterrupted view.

Miranda was no longer able to contain her curiosity. "What are you waiting for?"

Gallagher restrained the sigh he felt coming. He could have sat there all day if necessary; but with Miranda in tow . . .

Movement.

"That's what we're waiting for," he replied, indicating briefly with his head.

The man who had been in earnest conversation with the car park attendant had entered, and was looking up and down the concourse.

"That man? But—"

"Don't . . . stare at him. Pretend you're deeply interested in what I have to say."

"I am. I what to know what you're up to."

He reached for her hand and began to gently stroke it.

She gave him an uncertain smile. "I rather like that, but shouldn't we wait till we get to where we're—" Then she understood. "Now I see." She began to pull her hand away.

"Leave it! And calm that volatile temperament of yours."

Gallagher kept the man in view, watching the panicky jerking of the head as he searched this way and that, clearly not relishing the bawling-out he would receive from his boss for the failure. Finally, the man looked up and saw them, apparently engrossed with each other. The man relaxed and stayed where he was, leaning against one of the self-drive hire car company desks.

Now that he had positively identified the man as one of Pinheiro's tags, Gallagher released Miranda's hand and stood up.

"Time to go," he said.

"And here I was, thinking you were really enjoying stroking my hand."

"Miranda . . ."

"All right, all right. To hear is to obey."

They went back down the stairs and out of the building, as if totally unaware of the man's presence. Gallagher paused briefly, looking around until he saw what he wanted.

"We're in luck," he said, looking to his left. "Antonio's here."

"And who's Antonio?"

"The driver dozing in that green and black Mercedes 190 taxi over there."

The Mercedes was a short distance from the setting-down point, parked tightly into the curb.

"How did he know you'd be here?"

"He didn't. He's probably waiting for a flight to take people to one of the hotels. I'm about to commandeer him. Come on!"

"He'll dump a fare?" she said disbelievingly as they hurried.

"No. He'll get one of his mates to stand in."

Gallagher knew that Pinheiro's man would wait for a decent interval before following, still believing he hadn't yet been spotted. As far as the man was concerned, Gallagher was about to pick up a hired car, and he would judge, wrongly, that there was time to follow.

Gallagher rapped sharply on the car window. The

driver woke up with a start, grinning hugely when he recognized Gallagher.

"*Senhor* Gordon! But I did not know. You did not—"

"No time to explain, Antonio. Can you get us out of here immediately?"

"But of course."

Antonio was out of the taxi and grabbing at the bags while Gallagher and Miranda bundled themselves into the back. The luggage was stowed in the trunk and Antonio was back behind the wheel, rocketing off before Pinheiro's man had decided to come out to check. They were already on the filter road out of the small airport when Gallagher, looking back, saw the man come hurrying out to look desperately about him. With a bit of luck the second man—if there indeed was one—not having expected them to get into a taxi, had omitted to take its number.

"Good work, Antonio," Gallagher now said as the Mercedes entered its own private grand prix. "What about your passengers for the hotel? Can you make arrangements?"

Antonio picked up his microphone and spoke rapid Portuguese into it. "Taken care of, *Senhor* Gordon," he said calmly as he replaced the mike. "Now I will take you to your car."

Miranda was staring at Gallagher. "You control the taxis?"

"Of course not. Antonio and I are old friends."

Glancing up at them in his rearview mirror, Antonio smiled benignly.

"Friends," he confirmed. "*Sim,*" he emphasized, adding the "yes" in Portuguese for good measure.

Friends.

It had happened in a strange way. Gallagher and Friedrich von Talheim—a former colleague who had himself become a close friend—had once decided to fly from Munich to the Crusader island of Rhodes for a long weekend, just for the hell of it. Von Talheim had recently been invalided out of the then West German intelligence services, due to wounds received while on a mission to Czechoslovakia with Gallagher. They had deviated slightly from the mission requirements by smuggling out a young Czech woman, who had since become von Talheim's wife. But Gallagher and von Talheim had traveled to the Greek island unaccompanied.

They had been sitting in a waterfront bar, relaxing and pleased about not having to think about staying alive within some Iron Curtain border, when Antonio and his wife, clearly on holiday, had walked past. Not long after that a gang of six youths, the worse for drink, had followed in the couple's wake. The youths were at that point of drunken nastiness that preceded eventual stupor. They were English, and two of them were black.

Gallagher and von Talheim had sensed trouble. Gallagher had also felt that the black youths, to impress their white friends, might be the more vicious. They would have to be taken out first.

Both he and von Talheim had got up from their seats, almost as one. The injuries that had enforced early retirement upon the German had fully healed, and though no longer at the peak of his prowess, he was still a formidable opponent.

Within minutes, the youths were attacking the couple. The white ones, despite the presence of their black colleagues, were calling their victims wogs as they struck at them. Antonio, like many natives of the Iberian peninsula, had a fair dose of Moorish blood in his veins. Genes and the Algarve sun had blessed him with a complexion like burnt oak. To the morons kicking him, that made him a wog.

Gallagher and von Talheim had waded in, and within a very short time the six youths were experiencing a kind of pain they had never thought possible, on their way to various states of incapacitation. Then Gallagher and von Talheim had hurried Antonio and his wife out of the area before the local police put in an appearance. Friends had been gained for life.

In another café bar, while Antonio and his wife were recovering from the ordeal, Antonio told them he drove a taxi on the Algarve and that this was their very first time in Greece. Months later, on a shoot in Faro, Gallagher had left the terminal building to be greeted by an excited hail. Grinning up at him from behind the wheel of a battered taxi had been Antonio.

In the intervening years, the tourist trade had been very kind to Antonio, who now owned not just a single cab but a pristine fleet of six, a motorized fishing boat that landed fresh fish daily for an exclusive restaurant, and a substantial home in the hills of Loulé, just twenty kilometers north of the airport.

"You are remembering," Antonio now said.

Gallagher looked into the eyes in the mirror, and nodded.

"And *Senhor* Freddy? He is well?"

Again, Gallagher nodded. "He's fine, Antonio." He hadn't spoken to von Talheim for a while, but he would have known soon enough if things were not okay in Munich.

"What were you remembering?" Miranda asked, her journalistic nose twitching.

"Oh, just something that happened a long time ago," Gallagher replied lightly. He glanced out of the rear window to check for a tag; but no one seemed to be following.

"And that's it? No further explanation?"

"Nothing to explain."

"What a surprise."

Antonio was again favoring them with a benign look. "You are like man and wife," he observed.

"That's a joke," she said.

Gallagher felt a smile coming, but kept a straight face.

8

Antonio's home, on the outskirts of Loulé, was a surprise for Miranda. It was not the kind of house she'd expected would be owned by someone who plied the airport taxi trade.

The big villa, with its cobbled drive, plunge pool, large, well-kept garden full of exotic flowers, and triple garage, was a revelation. It gleamed whitely in the warm sunshine, its position giving it a magnificent view over the surrounding countryside.

"This is the home of a taxi driver?" she whispered to Gallagher as Antonio drove through a pristine Moorish arch with open double gates and pulled up before the house. "So what do the truck drivers have?"

"Antonio's no ordinary taxi driver. He owns his fleet and a fishing boat, and he and his wife also own some other property. They don't do too badly."

"You can say that again," she said, looking about her.

Antonio had climbed out and was opening the door for her. "Welcome to our humble home."

Miranda got out, peering at Antonio's face for evidence of irony. She decided he really meant it.

A very pretty, sturdily sensuous woman with gleaming dark hair had hurried with unexpected grace out of the house, beaming at Gallagher. She gave him an uninhibited hug while Miranda looked curiously on.

"*Senhor* Gordon! This is such a surprise!" Estella Aguiar kissed Gallagher at the corners of his mouth while Antonio grinned happily.

"My wife is very pleased. *Sim?*" Antonio remarked to Miranda.

"She certainly is," Miranda commented dryly.

"I was a little worried," Antonio went on, speaking the language carefully, "that she would be angry because she did not know. She likes to prepare when he comes to see us."

Antonio had either missed or had chosen to ignore the gentle barb lurking in Miranda's words.

As if on cue Estella, still holding on to Gallagher and looking at him, leaned back to say, "Antonio! You did not warn me. I have nothing prepared. I must feed this one." She inspected Gallagher as if looking for signs of emaciation.

Antonio glanced at Miranda. "She is a little angry," he said easily. "Estella, this is . . ."

But Miranda was already striding firmly towards Gallagher and Antonio's wife. She held out her good hand.

"Hullo. I'm Miranda."

Estella let go of Gallagher with seeming reluctance to take Miranda's hand, which she shook limply. Her eyes surveyed Miranda and studied the wounded shoulder with interest, but she made no comment.

"I am Estella," she said. To Gallagher, she added, "This one is jealous." She spoke English with more confidence than her husband and gave Miranda a sweetly welcoming smile. "Welcome to our house."

Taken off guard, Miranda could only say, "Thank you. It's very beautiful."

"Thank you," Estella said. "Come. We will go in. The men can carry the bags. You will stay with us tonight? Perhaps tomorrow night also?"

"Well . . . it depends . . ."

Estella made a dismissive motion with a hand. "Do not worry. *Senhor* Gordon will not refuse me. You will stay, and I shall make a truly wonderful dinner tonight. Come. You must have lunch. Just something quick." There was no chance allowed for refusal.

Watching them enter the house, Gallagher said to Antonio, "I think Estella can control her."

"My wife can control anyone when she wants to," Antonio said benignly. "She will of course expect you to stay with us tonight, or longer if you wish. My house is always yours." He gave a sigh of pleasure. "Even after all the years, she is still so beautiful. I am very lucky."

"Definitely," Gallagher said, thinking of his own disastrous romantic history. "So make the most of it."

"Even now, I still cannot believe she married a poor man like me," Antonio said.

Estella had come from a rich wine-growing family who had cut her off when she'd decided to marry the son of a coastal fisherman. Years of tribulations had not dimmed their love for each other. Now that tourism had given Antonio material success, the family had attempted a reconciliation. Strongly supported by his wife, Antonio had rejected the overtures.

"Don't wonder about it, Antonio. Just be thankful. We'll stay the night," Gallagher continued, "but I'm not so sure about longer. We really should leave tomorrow for the other place. Let's see how things develop. I don't want to bring trouble to your home."

"You never bring me trouble, *Senhor* Gordon," Antonio said, as if somehow feeling deprived.

"Which is exactly how I want it to remain. However, I'll need you to go back to the airport for me the day after tomorrow with a message for someone. Will that be all right?"

"But of course."

"Don't get into trouble, Antonio. Just deliver the message exactly as I ask you to, and keep out of the way."

"I will not have trouble, and I will keep out of the way."

Gallagher studied him for long moments. "Fine. Is the car okay?"

"*Sim.* Come and look."

They walked over to the garage and Antonio opened the roller door. A gleaming Ford Sierra 4 × 4, in gunmetal gray, lurked within. The car was over two years old, but Antonio looked after it so well, it might have come straight from a showroom. It was of a high specification with black leather upholstery, air-conditioning, strengthened suspension, and an expensive stereo CD system. The engine was a nonstandard, turbocharged V6 of 2.9 liters that was lovingly cared for by Antonio. Years of squeezing reliable service out of the battered engine of his father's original fishing boat had turned him into a mechanical wizard.

Gallagher had bought the car sometime before at a virtual bargain price from an expatriate islander Scotsman who'd been yearning once more for the mists of the Hebrides. All the equipment, with the exception of the turbocharger, had already been fitted. Gallagher had then bought the turbo, upon which Antonio had subsequently worked his mechanical magic. Gallagher had also installed other items.

It was no Quattro, but it suited him perfectly when he was in Portugal. The five-door sedan body had good load-carrying capacity, and frequently his search for photographic locations took him over less-than-ideal road surfaces.

The Ford was registered in Antonio's name, but such was his sense of correctness that he refused to drive it, the sole exception being on tests after servicing. Even then, he tended to drive it no longer than was absolutely necessary. It was Gallagher's special car, and that was that.

Gallagher gave the Ford a swift check, knowing there was no need for a detailed one.

"It is okay?" Antonio queried anxiously.

"It's perfect, as always."

Antonio looked pleased.

Estella stood by a window in the bedroom that she had selected for Gallagher and Miranda, and looked down at the garage entrance where Gallagher was talking to her husband. Miranda stood next to her, also looking at the two men.

"Do you love him?" Estella demanded suddenly.

Unsure of how to reply, Miranda began, "Well . . . I . . ."

"Then you are falling in love with him."

"Estella . . . I don't know . . ."

"He needs someone to look after him, although he does not seem to know it. Everybody does. Even you, the very successful woman."

"Deep down inside where he hides himself, I'm sure he realizes it. Well, maybe. But I'm not certain I'm the one he needs."

"Like so many men today," Estella said, "he is also confused about women, and we women must not pretend we are not also responsible for this . . . confusion. One person cannot have a quarrel. When I was a child, my family was in Moçambique. The African woman who worked for us had a son who was fourteen. He was old for his age. I used to like talking to him, although my parents would not allow it.

"One day, he said to me that the curse of the

oppressed, if they were not very careful, was to become the oppressors when they had won. That way, everyone loses. He said that was what a big African in the bush had said to them. The boy's name was Joao. He had joined the guerrillas, you see." Estella paused, remembering the past days of childhood in a far-off land. "I have never forgotten.

"There are times," she continued, "when I think that we women, because of the little we have already won, are perhaps risking behaving like oppressors if *we* are not careful. And of course, we all lose also. So how can you know what *he* wants?" Estella asked, indicating Gallagher with a nod. "Unless you allow yourself to find out. So . . ."—she drew the word out—" . . . perhaps it is a little dangerous with him. Ah, but he is such a *good* man!" The stressed word appeared to have many meanings. "Yes. A good man. You have known him for a long time?"

"Many years," Miranda answered, taken aback by the unexpected profundity of Estella's words and the barrage of questions. "My brother-in-law is a friend of his, but Gordon and I never saw each other much. Hardly at all, as a matter of fact. We were more like strangers. Then a few days ago at my nephew's christening, someone shot at me, and here we are."

Estella was still looking at Gallagher. "Ah. The shoulder. And he came to your rescue." She spoke very quietly, almost to herself.

Miranda stared at her. "Yes, but . . ."

"Do you know how my husband and I became his friends?" Estella had now turned to Miranda.

"No. He never gives anything away. Only what he feels you should know."

Estella nodded in understanding as she turned away to look out once more. She told Miranda about what had happened in Greece, staring out of the window as she spoke.

"So . . ." she added in conclusion, using her seemingly favorite word, " . . . we are here to enjoy this house and our businesses because of what he and his German friend did. We can never repay him."

Miranda had herself once again turned to study Gallagher. "I don't think he expects payment. If he thought you wanted to, you'd never see him again."

"That makes it harder, you understand. To do something in repayment is to lose him. In a way, his price is very high because he has none. Do I make sense? My English—"

"Is much better than that of some people I know." Miranda gave her a sheepish smile. "Although it's supposed to be their language. And you do make sense. I understand exactly what you mean. You love him a little yourself, don't you."

Estella was silent for long moments. "I do not understand what it is he does, and I do not wish to know. I have never asked why he and his German friend were in Greece. They were not like tourists, but I am very glad they were there. I watched the way they helped us. They were like . . ." She paused, searching for the correct expression. " . . . like wild creatures, but not savage. Very cold . . . very pre . . . precise . . . yes, that is the word I want. They were like hawks . . . no. Not like hawks, more like wolves.

"They worked without speaking. No shouting. No noise. It was frightening, but also exciting to watch. And all the time, those boys . . . *they* were the savage ones . . . they were jumping and shouting, making much noise. And then like that"—Estella snapped her fingers—"they were all on the ground, some very quiet . . . the others crying in pain. They were hurt very badly. For a small moment, I was sorry for them. Then I remembered they would have beaten us, perhaps even killed us, for our money, and I was not sorry anymore but very glad we were not hurt.

"He keeps much of himself secret," Estella went on, eyes still on Gallagher, "perhaps because he does not like being vulnerable. But in some ways, he is also innocent. He trusts very few people . . . like his friend in Greece; you could see they trusted each other completely. Those he trusts, he trusts completely. Those are the ones who can hurt him, because then he is vulnerable. Of course, no one can own him."

She had not answered Miranda's question.

Pinheiro visited Haxton's office that afternoon, looking at once furious and sheepish.

"It is as if he has vanished!" Pinheiro fumed. "My men can find no one who has seen him—at least, no one who will admit to having seen him."

"We were advised he would do that," Haxton reminded him. "He prefers to work his way, and usually alone. And after all, we are here to give him support . . . not chase him."

Pinheiro's eyes were fathomless. "I will keep you informed if I learn of anything," he said after a while. "I hope you will do the same for me."

Haxton nodded. "Of course."

Pinheiro gave a curt nod and went out.

A few moments later, Haxton had another visitor.

"The good captain does not look a happy man," Sian greeted. She sounded as if she thought it funny.

Haxton did not appear particularly surprised to see her. "He's lost Gallagher."

"We've all lost him."

"So will you now be flying back?"

"I think I'll wait a while longer. You never know what might turn up." She gave him a disarming smile.

"Do you know," Haxton began mournfully, "I like this job. Nothing much to worry about. The odd lager lout getting his head kicked in or vomiting all over himself and other people, then having to get him out of the police cells to dispatch him home, none the wiser and broke. Muggers coming in with the holiday crowds looking for likely victims. All the things that go to make a vice-consul's day. I have a feeling that I'll be happy to go back to the lager louts by the time this is all over."

"Cheer up, Roberto," Sian said brightly. "You're beginning to look like the good captain. It may never happen."

"You've got confirmation on that, have you?"

"Of course not. I didn't say it was going to be easy."

"Do you think he'll get in touch?"

"Gallagher?" She seemed to give that some thought. "You never know with Gallagher. Anything's possible."

"You're a great help," Haxton said gloomily.

She grinned at him. "Anytime."

Fowler's office, London.

Haslam slouched in a chair in the Spartan room and stared neutrally while Fowler read a transcript. He'd had as much sleep as he'd wanted, and despite his earlier protestations about being too old, had returned without being summoned.

Fowler came to the end and, still holding on to the sheet of paper, looked up at Haslam.

"He's gone to ground," Fowler said.

Haslam was not surprised. "We did expect it."

Fowler nodded slowly in agreement. "According to Sian, this police captain fellow—Pinheiro—is quite put out."

Haslam was unmoved. "He won't be the first local law whose nose Gallagher's managed to put out of joint. Nor the last," he added for good measure.

Fowler gave the briefest of smiles. "He's been doing it to us for years."

"And it suits us," Haslam amended dryly.

Fowler's eyes seemed to give their strange gleam behind the glasses as he put the transcript down and picked up another sheet of paper, which he passed to Haslam.

Haslam read it silently before passing it back to Fowler.

"Another killing," Haslam said. "Italy." He glanced at his watch. "Given the apparent organization, I suppose the killer had plenty of time—"

Fowler interrupted him. "This wasn't done today. Here." He passed Haslam another sheet. "The report from Tuscany, where the killing took place."

Haslam spoke softly as he read. "Industrialist . . . found on a back road . . . no car or chauffeur in the vicinity . . . *before* that hit in Nottingham . . . same kind of weapon, whatever it is . . . same modus operandi." He looked up at Fowler. "And I take it we are quite certain that Miranda Lacey never even met this particular industrialist?"

"Not from what we currently know about her. One or two of the international glossies did articles on him and his rather lurid . . . er . . . adventures. Usual fare for such journals. Successful businessman wines and dines aspiring young 'model' or 'starlet' and enjoys her favors in return. She then breaks with him or is chucked over and hey, presto, poor little Miss Misunderstood rakes in a mint selling the story to some rag and suddenly, she's a 'personality' as well. Wife stands by businessman, till the next time."

Fowler looked as if he wanted to spit. "Not the sort of yellow stuff Miss Lacey tends to deal in, I'd have thought."

Haslam was more charitable. "Nice work if you can get it."

Fowler looked at him suspiciously. "Are you talking about the starlet? The businessman? Or Miss Lacey?"

Haslam smiled.

■ ■ ■

"Oh, look!" Miranda exclaimed softly, pointing across the terrace where they lay relaxing.

"I'll take your word for it," Gallagher said.

"I'm being watched by an owl."

"I'm sure he's having fun."

"Could be a she."

"Whatever."

The house had been built among a robust colony of umbrella pines. They were mature trees, none less than twenty meters high. A particularly tall one, perhaps a good thirty meters, stood close to the end of the terrace where the parasol had been erected. On one of its lower branches, a small owl was indeed looking down at Miranda laying on the lounger.

"It's really lovely," she said, her tone of voice urging him to check for himself. She sounded as if she wanted to stroke it. "Seems tame enough."

Gallagher reluctantly opened his eyes, searched for and found the object of her excitement.

"Ah," he said. "The Little Owl. He likes watching the world go by in the daytime, unless of course something he fancies passes his way. This is his favorite tree. According to Estella and Antonio, he's been using it ever since they've been here. May not be the same one, of course. But don't let that cute face fool you. He's a ferocious little beast and is an implacable hunter."

"Like someone I know."

"You say all the nice things," Gallagher said, looking at the owl. "You're right, he is pretty. But deadly too in his own way. Like someone *I* used to know."

Gallagher paused, feeling a sudden chill along his spine. Funny, he thought. Wonder what made me think of that.

Miranda was staring at him. "Are you all right? You look as if you've seen a ghost."

"I'm fine. I haven't seen any ghost." He paused once more, then added quietly, "But I just thought of one."

Miranda watched, frowning slightly and trying to understand, as Gallagher eased himself off the lounger and walked slowly across the terrace towards the tree. The owl had zeroed upon him immediately, swiveling its head to track his every move, its eyes unblinking. Gallagher stopped by the waist-high perimeter wall. The owl, ignoring Miranda now, concentrated totally upon him. It was totally in command of itself and was not even remotely agitated by his presence.

"Well, owl," he began, staring up at the disdainful bird. "What do you know?"

The wide stare remained fastened upon him, and he had the bizarre impression that the owl actually wanted to speak.

Then, very slowly, one eye winked.

Hyde Park, London, later the same day.

The portly man in the smart three-piece walked over to one of the big windows in the hotel suite and looked down upon the motor race that was the Park Lane traffic. His walk was a strange one: quick little steps that flung his legs jerkily forward as if they were scared to be off the floor for too long. Amusement showed in the thin smile on his lips.

"I love London," he said. "It is so crazy. But it is a nice craziness compared to the murderous insanity of some cities we know. Eh?" He turned to face his companion, briefly waving a hand to indicate the luxurious furnishings. "You live well while you're in town. Penthouse." He was not speaking English.

"I've earned it." The reply, in the same language, was cold and devoid of emotion. "Or perhaps you think this is a strain on the budget?" There was no threat, but the warning was implicit in the voice.

The portly one made a placating gesture with the same hand. "I was merely passing comment. It is a very neat move using a place like this. It would be very difficult to suspect that someone helping us in the way you are would be staying openly in such an example of self-indulgent luxury. I meant no criticism."

"Whether you did or not is of no interest to me. Now tell me: Have you found out where they've gone?"

"Not yet, I regret to say. We watched the three main London airports . . . Heathrow, Gatwick, and Stansted. We even checked the small city airport in the dock area. Nothing."

"I would have been surprised if they had used scheduled flights." There was open contempt now, as if the idea of watching just the airlines at the main airports had been a grossly stupid waste of time. "It is obvious he continues to work for his former Intelligence unit, and that they have put facilities at his disposal; you should have prepared for that after the house near Oxford. But I believe he has other facilities."

"We . . . are continuing with the pursuit. By the way, I have been instructed to pass on to you that there is great satisfaction with the manner in which you have . . . er . . . terminated the selected targets . . ."

"I care little for their satisfaction. The entire list will be completed as arranged."

"Of course. We are well aware of your capabilities. I have also been instructed to allocate you two more helpers to replace those who—"

"No! Those two were useless. I'll choose my own this time, as I should have done in the first place."

"Is that wise? You will only draw attention to yourself if you start recruiting, and at such a delicate stage. Let us find you the replacements; but this time you will be allowed total freedom to choose from a group of candidates, instead of having to accept those you've been given."

There was so long a silence that the portly man became fidgety.

"Very well," was the eventual, grudging agreement. "But I want you to check with his known contacts, and find the unknown ones. *Someone* will know where he's gone. Even the most careful person leaves a trail. It's simply a matter of finding it, and recognizing it when you do. Nothing stays hidden forever when you know what to look for."

"We have no one in contact with his department—"

"Not his department." The words were said slowly and with weary emphasis. The "you fool" was more palpable for being unspoken. "I mean those even the Department knows little about."

"But that will be his own private network. Something he may have deliberately kept to himself. He could be anywhere." The portly man stopped, not wanting to risk giving further offense. "We have no idea of knowing who—"

"*I* have. Here are some names. Check on them. I expect him to have a closed network. These people may be part of it, or they may know those who are. If only one does, it will be enough. We can proceed from there."

The man took the loose filofax sheet gingerly, as if expecting it to give him a venomous bite. There were suggested countries accompanying the names. "But . . . but they themselves could be anywhere, not necessarily in those countries. And it could be dangerous sending our people unprepared against them."

Eyes that were devoid of life fixed him in a mesmerizing glare. "Check them! If your people can't look after themselves they deserve to get hurt. I want answers within forty-eight hours. Unless, of course, you would like me to report your reluctance, Siminiev."

The portly man blenched. He felt as if the cold voice and eyes were chilling the very blood in his veins. "No! I . . . I shall see to it."

"Wait!"

Siminiev waited, wariness showing in his eyes.

"Check the plane spotters."

"Plane spotters?" the portly Siminiev queried weakly.

There was a world-weary sigh. "Yes, Siminiev. Plane spotters. You must have heard of the breed. Like train spotters who haunt the railways to log every type of rolling stock, the plane spotters haunt airports, airfields, air bases . . . Are you following my thoughts?"

"Yes!" Siminiev was squeaky in his eagerness to please. "These spotters might have seen something."

"You see? Your brain does work when you want it to. Send your people back to the airports to find these spotters. Find out if they saw anything unusual. *Anything.* And, Siminiev: Try to get your people to work in a subtle manner."

"I'll . . . I'll see to it."

There was a cold silence. Siminiev left the room in haste, as if he could hardly wait to get out.

Five hours later, Siminiev knocked on the door of the penthouse suite. There was no reply. He was about to leave, when someone spoke behind him.

"You have news for me, I hope."

Siminiev jumped, face turning sickly. There was naked fear in his eyes as he whirled. He'd heard nothing to warn him of the approach.

"Yes. Yes! There was—"

"Not out here." The cold voice, soft and contemptuous, cut into whatever he'd been about to say. The key turned in the lock. "In!"

Siminiev dutifully complied. The door slammed shut and the killer strode to a window, back turned to Siminiev.

"Now tell me."

Siminiev cleared his throat. "We checked the three London airports and other small airfields within the area. We found one anomaly . . ." He paused, waiting for comment. There was none. "At Gatwick," he went on hurriedly, "several spotters noted one particular aircraft. It was unusual in that it was the first of its kind they had seen."

Again, Siminiev paused, expecting some kind of reaction. Again, there was none.

For a second time, he cleared his throat. "The aircraft," he continued, "was a new business jet . . . the Citation VII . . ."

"The Citation . . ."

The words were spoken so softly, Siminiev almost failed to hear them. Yet there was a resonance to them. Knowing he had at last brought some measure of satisfaction, he waited for the other to continue speaking.

The killer still did not turn from the window. "The Citation. Find out where it was going. Even the most secret of flight plans is not secure. Someone, somewhere, will know. I don't care how you do it, but *find out!*"

"And what about Gallagher's personal contacts? Do . . . do we still check them out?"

The killer turned, eyes gazing balefully at Siminiev, appearing to impale him where he stood.

"Did I say you should stop?"

"No. No . . ."

There was no further conversation.

9

Faro Airport, two days later, 1500 hours.

Antonio waited in the arrivals concourse, prominently displaying a handwritten sign. To anyone watching, he was just another taxi driver who, like the other drivers and hotel or tour representatives, was there to meet guests or tourists coming off a plane. His sign read, MR. THOMSEN.

Borodin, who had not come off an aircraft but had unobtrusively walked in some minutes earlier, immediately knew the message was from Gallagher. Thomsen was the name he had used when they'd last seen each other in Norway.

Borodin waited a few more minutes, checking to make certain no one was interested in him. When a throng of arriving passengers spilled into the concourse, he mingled with them, complete with travel bag, looking as if he too had just landed.

He went up to Antonio. "I am Thomsen."

Antonio looked at the big man in the lightweight suit, his build seeming strangely at odds with his elegance, and lowered the sign. A full head of cropped dark hair crowned the solid features, and piercingly shrewd eyes studied him from beneath thick black eyebrows. This was not a man that anyone, Antonio decided, with even the smallest amount of common sense would choose to cross.

"I have a message from *Senhor* Gallagher," Antonio said as they walked out towards the taxi.

Borodin instructed Antonio to take him a short distance from the airport car park to where he'd left the hired Citroën. He got out and climbed into the car, and with a brief wave to Antonio, set off for the rendezvous with Gallagher.

Not having expected Gallagher to come anywhere near the airport since he'd gone to ground, Pinheiro had not considered leaving a man on watch. As a result, Borodin's arrival and departure had occurred completely without his knowledge.

The Ilha da Faro is a thin strip of land, ten kilometers long and mostly sandbar, that forms part of the natural barrier separating the Faro estuary and its multiplicity of low-lying tidal islands and lagoons from the warm Atlantic.

The normal route on the exit road from the airport to the town of Faro was a right turn to the junction with the main trunk road. The airport road, however, also continued in the opposite direction for another three kilometers, where it virtually came to an end. This section curved past the western end of the runway to cross the estuary via a single-lane road bridge. Only one-way, alternate traffic flow was allowed in each direction. This system was controlled by lights at each end of the bridge, which ended the road more or less at the middle of the strip of land itself.

This part had been mildly developed with unpretentious holiday homes, a minimum of restaurants, bars, and shops, a sailing center, and a camp site. People lived on the Ilha permanently. The only road to speak of was a narrow, sand-swept street that went along the middle for four kilometers, with many short alleyways branching off it. Seaward, a beach created by the ceaseless ocean formed the natural barrier.

Gallagher had driven there in the Sierra 4 × 4 and had parked it out of sight, in an unpaved alley that almost fed itself into the waters of the estuary. He had waited and watched as the Citroën approached. He now walked towards the spot at which he had told Borodin to meet him.

He found the man who called himself Borodin waiting, and eating a fully peeled banana. The peel itself was nowhere to be seen.

"Wonderful fruit, the banana," Borodin began in greeting, his English flowing easily. "Full of nutrients and, if the latest rumors are to be believed, highly medicinal." He smiled hugely as he finished the last piece. "I believe some of your soccer hooligans throw these at black players to the accompaniment of monkey noises. The ignorance of it. If the monkeys are clever enough to know the value of this food, how smart does that make the hooligans? You'd have thought they would have worked that one out by now."

"Nice to see you too," Gallagher said dryly.

Borodin grinned and gave Gallagher an unrestrained hug. "Good to see you too, my friend. Especially alive, and still the expert survivor. Excellent." Borodin turned towards the vast calm of the ocean and stared at the distant horizon. A few coastal fishing boats, perhaps a mile offshore, rode at anchor like seabirds taking a rest. He breathed deeply. "Aah!" he continued, spreading his arms as if to gather the entire scene. "Pure sea air! A little different from the Baltic, eh?"

Borodin, Gallagher knew, had not made what must have been a hazardous journey merely to discuss the ethics of hooligans or to make comparisons with the polluted Baltic Sea. But he chose not to hurry the Russian. Borodin would give over the information when he was quite ready.

The short alley within which Gallagher had chosen to leave the car was practically at the end of the road, which had simply stopped, allowing the sand dunes to take over from there. On either side, single-story, weather-beaten houses seemed, even in the calm of the day, to be cowering against the winds that could come hurtling off the sea. Here, the exposed sections of the edge of the road and the dunelike beach seemed to merge.

The holiday season appeared slow to begin on this narrow peninsula, and the place was deserted; which was why Gallagher had chosen it in the first place. There seemed to be no one else about and even if some of the houses were occupied, their owners had apparently chosen to remain inside.

Gallagher was happy with that. If anyone had followed, there would be no crowds within which to hide. Borodin, he noted, despite an air of casual indifference, was quietly checking the surroundings every so often. There was plenty of cover among the houses, should there be need of it.

"Let us walk on this empty beach," Borodin said, then set off without waiting to see if Gallagher followed.

"Your people are making a mess of this Yugoslavia business," Borodin continued as they walked. "And you'll live to regret it. For a start, the Bosnians will never forgive you. There will be more casualties the longer you fool around because in the end, you may well have to go in—maybe within weeks, months, or even years. There's a bigger war brewing on your doorstep and you're allowing the flames to rise while you contemplate your navels."

"Not my people. I'm out."

"The *West* then. It's going to get a lot worse. Already, you are two years too late." Borodin shook his head briefly. "Missed opportunities. There are people back home who look at what's happening and who ask themselves whether they had really bankrupted the nation in an effort to keep up with what they now see as a bunch of disunited incompetents. Despite the fact that the West had been quite heavily infiltrated in some countries during what you laughingly termed the Cold War, we still did not expect to see such a display of naked self-interest fracturing your facade of unity. These are very, very angry people who believe our own politicians betrayed the motherland. Naturally, we have our own incompetents, but *this!* We truly expected more of the West.

"There are also those, even more hard-line, who believe we would have won the war, given what we now know. Never mind what happened in the Gulf. Yugoslavia has shown that cooperation was the exception, rather than the rule. These people want the old days back, and don't make the mistake of believing it's only the hard-liners. Sure, it was not good then; but things are much worse now. There is no dignity. It's a zoo out there."

Borodin paused, and looked about him. "Look at this sand. If it were not constantly cleared off that road and those houses, it would soon cover everything. Nature doing what she's always done. Life, we are often told, is a bitch. There's nothing wrong with life. It's the people who are the problem. There's no such thing as a fuel shortage, or a famine, or a financial crisis. It's like blaming the computer when a program goes down and an aircraft falls out of the sky, rather than looking for the idiot who set up the program in the first place.

"People by their own stupidity, greed, incompetence—choose your reason—make these things happen throughout the world. Someone is *always* responsible. This I came to realize very early in my career. The war in Bosnia did not spring into being perfectly formed. It had to be started. A single action by one person precipitated what has followed in its wake. It could have been a word, a simple statement, a moment of insanity dressed up as perceived destiny. There is always a point in time that is the genesis of any horror we bring to this planet. The icebergs were always doing what they'd done for centuries. It was the Titanic that got in the way." He stared at Gallagher. "Do you understand what I'm saying?" Sometimes, Borodin's speech hovered between English and American accents.

"Yes," Gallagher said. "I do understand."

"Is that why you got out?"

"Partly. There were other reasons."

"Are you *really* out?"

"Yes," Gallagher repeated firmly.

Borodin looked at Gallagher a while longer before nodding to himself as he continued walking, clumping his way across the softness of the beach.

"But I did not come here to talk about Bosnia, as I am sure you have realized. I commend you on your patience. What do you know of Queensland?"

"An Australian state, twice the size of Texas, so they say, five times the size of the UK, the Barrier Reef . . ."

"I don't mean the geography lesson."

At the mention of Australia, Gallagher had sensed the faint pinging of alarm bells, remembering what had occurred in the Outback. He had also been to Queensland before, but that had been during his career with the Service and not something he was prepared to share with Borodin.

"Then I don't know what you're talking about."

"Not the geography lesson," Borodin repeated. "I was talking about a code word."

The alarm bells were beginning to chime.

"I still don't know what you're on about."

Borodin kept on walking. "Are you quite sure?"

"Of course I'm bloody sure."

"Then it's all a mystery, because it concerns you."

Gallagher stopped dead in his tracks. "You've got to be joking." The alarm bells were pealing madly now.

Borodin too had stopped. He turned, hands in pockets, to face Gallagher. "I have not traveled thousands of miles, setting up a false trail for my opponents so that they believe me to be somewhere else while I am here, just to make jokes. I could have sent a postcard."

"To do that you would need an address to send it to. Or a phone number to leave messages on."

Borodin smiled thinly. "So you have been wondering about that."

"As I'm not listed, yes."

"The Queensland file will explain it all."

"And what is that, when it's not on holiday?"

"I've always admired that strange sense of humor of yours. That, my friend, is the code name of an assassin. The file is of an operation that has been running for some time."

Gallagher felt his blood congeal. "Are you telling me that I am on this . . . Queensland's hit list?"

"Oh, my friend," Borodin said in what sounded to Gallagher like an unnaturally mild voice, "it's much worse than that. You are *the* primary target." Borodin looked at Gallagher keenly, to see how he was taking the news. "I must say you're looking quite calm about it."

"Don't let my frozen stance fool you. There's a tundra growing on my spine." Gallagher paused, recalling all that had happened since the christening. "It's all beginning to make some crazy kind of sense," he went on, confirming something to himself. *He* was the real target! But why?

The alarm bells had by now gone berserk.

"What's making sense?" Borodin's eyes had narrowed briefly as he spoke.

"Give me the rest of the bad news, then I'll explain."

Gallagher felt as if his entire body had turned into an antenna, searching out the hidden and unknown enemy; an enemy so implacable, he was prepared to deliberately kill innocent bystanders as a means of pressurizing Gallagher. It was a cold-blooded deliberation that was as nasty as it was vicious.

Miranda Lacey had not been a target at all. She had simply been a convenient sacrifice. Luckily, she was still alive. But the policeman who had been guarding her in London had not been so fortunate. Even so, the killer had made mistakes. Unless they, too, had been deliberate.

All this for me? Gallagher now thought. He realized that from the very beginning his instincts, despite being unable to identify the nature of the threat, had been putting him on the alert. He had felt the warning when he'd found the sniper's position on the hill in Kent, and the deliberately "forgotten" cigarette stub. A bold challenge that even then he'd accepted, when he had picked it up. And on the terrace in Loulé, what he had felt was the presence of the unseen and unknown stalker, perhaps still somewhere in the UK.

As long as he towed Miranda along, she would be in constant danger: the perfect sacrificial goat, tethered and awaiting the killer's murderous pleasure. He'd have to see that she was returned to London immediately, and out of the firing line.

Gallagher's thoughts came to a screeching halt. *Antonio and Estella.* The killer, if he eventually made it to Portugal, would include them in his macabre game. That was a virtual certainty. Gallagher decided it would be safer for them too if he also made a quick departure, though separately from Miranda.

Borodin had once more been studying Gallagher intently. “Some things are falling into place?”

Gallagher nodded. “Yes,” he confirmed heavily. “But go on. Tell me the rest, then I'll tell you what's been happening on this side of the old Curtain.”

They continued their walk.

“With the dissolution of the old Soviet Union,” Borodin resumed, “several factions have come into being. Some are of no consequence: people who in the early, heady days expected Western-style democracy. Reality soon gave them a harsh lesson. The others form a wide spectrum, from liberal-minded intellectuals to varying degrees of hard-liners, the most extreme of whom make one of our late and unlamented party chairmen—he of the shoe-thumping habit—look like a pussycat.

“And then, even beyond those, are the shadowy ones—the ones who, even before Gorbachev became the man the West thought it could do business with”—there was the barest hint of a sneer in Borodin's voice—“have been busy preparing their ground for future action. They are the ones who will give you in the West nightmares.

“My operatives have infiltrated many of these groups, but the shadowy ones are too dangerous even for my own special units, seconded from my Spetsnaz.” Borodin suddenly grinned. “You didn't think, did you, that because we now have a ‘parliament’ and so-called elections every time the president wants to pass a new decree, that my forces would have been disbanded? Have you disbanded your SAS? Or the Americans their various Special Forces units?”

“Don't look at me. I'm free of all that.”

“But are you?” Borodin did not wait for a reply as he went on. “One of the most able of my people, a

Ukrainian—oh yes, my own units still operate the way we always have . . . without this new and ridiculously fashionable need for national and ethnic demarcation. My operative discovered the Queensland file literally by accident. He was in a very privileged and trusted position . . ."

"'Was'? What happened to him? Or her?"

"I'll come to that in due course. He was in a car with a senior Intelligence man who was searching in his briefcase for, of all things, a packet of cigarettes. The driver had to swerve suddenly and the briefcase fell off the seat. My man picked it up, as was expected of him. The case had fallen partially open and a file, highly classified with the name 'Queensland' on it, caught my man's eye. As we later found out, the Intelligence man, responsible for the conduct of the operations in the file itself, though not the authority behind it, should not have been traveling with those documents. It was one of those moments in Intelligence gathering that we all pray for; the moment when after months, sometimes years of patient waiting, chance finally throws something your way. If you do survive this, my friend, you may well owe your life to that packet of cigarettes." Borodin seemed genuinely amused by the irony.

Gallagher said nothing as he waited for Borodin to continue.

"What fascinated my operative was the fact that there was no Cyrillic script on the cover. Nothing at all in Russian. Just that single word, in English. The file's high security grading was denoted by the color of its jacket. He decided then to check it out at the first opportunity, feeling certain I'd be interested. It was one of the most dangerous, and most important, pieces of work he has ever done for me.

"The operation in that file is a trial run for something, I am convinced, far more inimical. The assassin they have chosen is not Russian. That, for the moment, is all I know about his possible identity. He was recruited to carry out a series of apparently random killings, to gauge their effect on the West's law enforcement and Intelligence agencies. But they are not to be restricted to the West. There will be killings throughout the old Soviet Union. Again, the effects will be judged. The real surprise in the package, however, was the hit man's type of payment. He demanded full cooperation and support, full expenses, but . . . no fee."

Gallagher stopped once more. He looked back. They had walked a long way. Above them, the throttled-down roaring whistle of a 737 on finals for Faro Airport intruded. He waited until the aircraft had passed.

"What do you mean no fee?" he asked.

"There is a kind of fee. You. The man they have coded Queensland specifically demanded that they give him all the facilities necessary to find and hunt you down. Then he'll do their killings for free."

"Jesus."

Gallagher felt his mouth go suddenly dry. Who could possibly want him so badly that the forfeit of his life—and surrounding him with others' blood—had been made the fee. Who was cold-bloodedly killing innocent victims, deliberately selected if they had anything to do with him—or, as had been the case with Miranda, were merely standing close to him? It was as if he were being herded by death itself, for a particular purpose.

"In our careers," Borodin said, not unkindly, "there are those whom we have bested but not destroyed, and who unfortunately cannot bear to lose. I have many adversaries, both inside and outside what was the Union, who would do anything for my head." He sounded quite cheerful about it.

"But this is something else," Gallagher remarked quietly. "This feels like a personal grudge."

Already, a subtle transformation was taking place

within him. The organism was under direct threat. Steps had to be taken. There was only one thing to do.

Borodin was peering at Gallagher, knowing something was happening but not quite sure what. Then he saw in Gallagher's eyes the thing that had once so frightened Rhiannon Jameson. Despite the warmth of the day, Borodin found he had to restrain a shiver.

"I wish," Borodin began softly, "I'd had you working for me."

"Not a chance," Gallagher said.

Borodin was unperturbed. "Just a thought. Though we have worked together for mutual benefit and our aims do not necessarily conflict, we do have different loyalties. I can accept that. Greywolf. You are aptly named."

At the mention of his code name, Gallagher felt all his senses go to full alert. He had briefly considered Borodin as the unknown assassin and had equally quickly, and with a degree of shame, discarded the idea. The GRU general would not have come to do such a job himself.

Borodin began to reach into his jacket. He paused, watching Gallagher. "Are you armed?"

Gallagher, in off-white jeans and a pale blue baggy T-shirt with long sleeves drawn up to the elbow, shook his head.

"If you had come to kill me, this is the worst place you could have chosen, unless you intended to escape by boat. And in any case, you can be identified."

Borodin smiled. "The taxi driver at the airport. I knew you had considered all the options once I'd seen where you picked for our meeting. I'm also quite certain you arrived well in time, to wait for me and to prepare your escape route should that be needed. I approve. I am of course armed, just in case." The hand continued to reach for whatever was inside his jacket.

Gallagher had brought Haslam's mini-arsenal, but

had left it secure in a compartment that had long ago been constructed beneath one of the rear seats of the Ford. There was no outward sign of the compartment's existence. It had been put there by the previous owner, who'd explained its presence by saying it had been for the safe transportation of his wife's jewelry. Gallagher had entertained the idea that at times, the compartment had been used to transport rather less innocent cargo, probably the sort of thing that would have greatly interested the likes of Pinheiro.

Borodin handed Gallagher an oversized white envelope. "A present for you; for looking after Irina when she was on Skye, and for not betraying me in Norway when your Intelligence people had hoped to kidnap me."

As Gallagher remembered it, Borodin had well been able to look after himself. And as for Irina, whom he had come to know as Lucinda, she had died on his back on Skye when he'd been desperately trying to get her to safety. It was she who had saved his life.

He slowly opened the envelope, and stared in disbelief. *"A section of my confidential file. Good Christ."*

He read through it quickly, feeling a cold anger begin to simmer within him, then looked up from it at Borodin.

"This is the first time I've seen anything from my file. There's a lot of detail about me in this. My whole life's in there." His eyes were chilling. "The *bastards!* I've long suspected that devious sod Fowler, of course; but it never occurred to me that even he would go as far as getting the doc to draw up a psychological profile to justify his little schemes. What a prime shit! Fowler's going to have some explaining to do when I see him next. And the doc's right: I do hold them bloody responsible for Lauren's death. How the hell did you get your hands on this? Have you read it all? And are there copies?"

Borodin said, "They are very flattering about you, and you're obviously very highly thought of."

"To hell with what they think! How did you get your hands on this?" Gallagher repeated. "And have you read it or made copies?"

Borodin gave a deprecating shrug. "I could hardly not have read it. My operative knew nothing about you and correctly assumed that such detail about a Western agent would be of interest to me. I apologize for the personal sections, but out of my regard for you I have made certain there are no further copies. The people we stole it from had themselves, for obvious reasons, made no copies. Neither did I." Then a somber look came to Borodin's features. "This was found in the Queensland file."

"*What!* You've got to be mistaken . . ."

"I'm afraid I'm not."

"Then how the hell did it . . ."

"That's precisely what I've been asking myself for some time, since I discovered what it was."

"Exactly what are you saying?" Gallagher demanded in a voice that had grown dangerously soft.

"I'm saying that it certainly didn't get there through our efforts. None of my people are responsible."

"Are you telling me it was *given?* By *my* people? To what purpose?"

Borodin merely looked at him.

"Fowler?" Gallagher said disbelievingly. "Fowler wants me dead?" He shook his head, smacking at the envelope. "Not after what I've just read. It wouldn't make sense. Why try to coerce me into working for the Department, then have your lot put an assassin on my trail? I can—"

"Not my lot," Borodin corrected in protest.

Gallagher went on over Borodin's pained comment. "I can believe the devious bastard—and believe me, he's as devious as you are—I can believe he would drag me into one of his crazy operations; but never order a hit on me. No. Not Fowler."

"Loyalty even in extremis," Borodin observed. "He

has got a good man in you. However, I've told you what I know. It is up to you to make your own conclusions. Am I really as devious as Fowler?"

"Fishing for compliments? Of course you are. You're two of a kind. I'm willing to bet that despite all your efforts to get this to me personally—for which I of course thank you—you want something from me too."

Borodin opened his mouth as if to protest further, shut it, and said smoothly, "Of course, should you manage to stop Queensland's activities . . ."

"You mean kill him. Why not just say so?"

" . . . it would seriously affect the current operation, trial run or not . . ."

"And ruin, for the time being, the plans of the group your man's infiltrated."

"Precisely."

"Now I wonder why I *thought* that would be coming."

"You are of course going after Queensland."

"You knew I would."

Borodin appeared uncertain. "One can't always be sure . . ."

Gallagher was not fooled. "Don't pull that one. Of course you were sure. You didn't come all the way out here to go back empty-handed. You were absolutely certain I'd go after him. I've got to go on to the attack. It's my only choice. As well you know. So don't give me that 'one can't always be sure' routine."

My God, Gallagher was thinking. Rhiannon's in there too.

Borodin favored Gallagher with a huge grin, as if Gallagher had just passed some kind of test. "Really . . . you could have been one of my stars."

"In your dreams." Then Gallagher raised the envelope briefly. "But thanks for this. I really do mean it."

"My pleasure."

Gallagher was certain there was more to come. "So what happened to your man?"

"I moved him immediately. But he died in a brawl in the Baltics. Those witnesses who were prepared to talk say he was set upon without warning by Latvian nationalists. I didn't believe they were Latvians."

"What did you do?"

"Some genuine Latvians did get hurt for killing a Soviet citizen . . . or CIS, if you prefer, whatever that means," Borodin replied. "But soon after, we got the real culprits and the Baltic got a little more pollution. And now," he continued, "your turn. Tell me what has been taking place on your side of the fence."

Gallagher told him about the mystery killings, about Miranda, about the men by the safe house, but not about its location or its security systems. He would not have expected Borodin to give details of his own safe house arrangements. He also said nothing about the cigarette stub that had been left in the grass on the hill, and omitted a few other items of information.

Borodin was thoughtful as he listened and did not press Gallagher for omitted details, though Gallagher had no doubt that Borodin knew he was getting only part of the story.

"So you know about the rifle," Borodin remarked when Gallagher had finished. "Remarkable weapon. A sniper's dream—in diverse models, it will revolutionize the assault rifle of the future. Its potential market is vast, and it will rock the world the way the AK-47 did when that weapon first came out . . . if it goes into production."

"If?"

Then Borodin told an astonished Gallagher what the new rifle could really do. "The bullet with your name on it," Borodin went on, "is now a reality, in a very literal sense. For the moment, there are just two of these rifles in existence. The fact that Queensland has been allowed to use one of them should tell you how highly he is regarded, and how important to the group is this particular operation. If the rifle should fall into the wrong hands . . ."

"You mean if the West gets hold of it."

"And other people . . . private individuals with access to technological facilities and funding, criminals ditto, terrorists ditto, governments ditto. In short, no one should get their hands on it."

"So you want me to hand it back to you, after I've got Queensland. And why should I let you continue to develop it? It's my life on the line, with my name on the bullet, as you've so nicely put it. If I do get Queensland, I won't be in a charitable mood. As it is, I'm already itching to wring Fowler's neck for allowing part of my confidential file to get stolen in the first place, whether he knew about it or not, and for what the doc's written in that profile on me."

Borodin's eyes grew hard, wiping out the air of cheerful friendliness as if it had never been, and showing the true persona beneath. This man, Gallagher reminded himself, was a GRU general who could "hurt" people he knew were innocent of the killing of his agent, and then calmly admit to later "polluting" the Baltic with the bodies of the real killers, after his people had caught up with them. The claws were being unsheathed.

"It is," Borodin said, "our property."

"I'll think about it," Gallagher retorted.

The thought that a rifle with an electronic card that could make the weapon lock on to him actually existed had brought more icicles to his spine. If he did manage to get his hands on it, he would destroy the damned thing. *No* one was going to get hold of that piece of kit. Certainly not Fowler, and not Borodin.

The Russian was suddenly friendly once more. "There is no need for this tension between us. We have the same goal. We both want you to remain alive."

"We've got different reasons."

"Of course . . . but we have accepted that. And what is your next move?"

"I'm going to drag him out into the open. Choose my own battleground."

"If I may make a suggestion. A little advice . . ."

Gallagher waited.

Never disregard advice, sir, from whatever quarter. You don't have to take it, but always listen. There may be something you can make use of.

O'Keefe.

"Go to Queensland," Borodin suggested.

"Why go way out there? I can take him in England."

"I doubt it. He's had time to lay his snares, and has been calling the agenda. Take him out-of-area, but on *your* terms."

"Queensland may well *be* his area. Hence the code."

"I don't think you believe it to be that obvious, though it possibly may have to do with Australia."

Gallagher had already considered the possibilities, and felt the shiver of a particular memory. It still didn't make sense. A lipstick mark on a deliberately planted cigarette stub. No. It was impossible.

"I have an idea," he said. As Borodin waited expectantly, he went on, "You used to have a restricted-circulation weekly newssheet for people in your sphere of the business, both at home and abroad. All the various Intelligence services got it. Is it still going?"

The vaguest of smiles. "Yes. It's still in operation."

"I'd like you to arrange for a little block advertisement to be included in the very next issue . . . without compromising yourself, of course. Can you do it?"

Borodin was still looking on with amused expectancy, as if waiting to see what Gallagher would next suggest. "It can be done."

Then Gallagher told him what should be put into the newssheet.

Borodin nodded. "I approve. That should put the cat among the pigeons. Or perhaps I should say wolf."

10

"I would not like to be in their shoes when Queensland finds out the file's gone and he's been compromised," Borodin said as they walked back towards their cars. "It's obvious they haven't told him, or whoever they've allocated as his helpers."

The killer, Gallagher knew, would realize this as soon as he saw the advertisement that Gallagher intended him to read.

"On the other hand," Borodin went on, "I wouldn't like to be in his shoes either."

"Meaning?"

"If they haven't warned him . . ."

"They intend to dump him once he's completed the job."

"There is the distinct possibility. They have no idea who's got the file. When your little message appears, they'll know his cover has been blown, and even though they won't know to what extent, they won't want to take any chances. Once that happens, he'll become a liability with a very precious commodity."

"The rifle."

"Precisely. They'll want to get it back."

"That should be fun."

"You do realize," Borodin continued as they clumped back across the sand, "that Queensland may have other items of information that was not in the file . . ."

"Like knowledge of people I've met over the years. Yes. I've thought about that. If the information was indeed leaked from this side, there's no telling just what might have gone over. There may be nothing further; but there are things I'll have to do, just in case." Gallagher favoured Borodin with a quick glance. "What about you? Last time we met, Fowler knew of you as Borodin."

"I've only used the name with you. As Fowler doesn't know what I look like, it hardly matters."

"There's Kirstin Størvaag of Norwegian Intelligence, from that time in Norway."

"What she saw," Borodin said, "was a Norwegian-American tourist named Thomsen carrying the usual touristy accessories, on a visit to the old country. As I remember, she was exceptionally young—or looked it—and was somewhat out of her depth. I very much doubt that she could identify me, even if you put a photograph in front of her." Borodin chuckled suddenly. "Assuming that any photographs of me are identifiable."

Gallagher had fond memories of Kirstin Størvaag. Not a trained agent, she had indeed looked much too young to be on the job and had been seconded to him as a sort of driver/guide. But she'd handled a confusing situation admirably, taking a bullet meant for him in the process. Fortunately, it had been a graze. Born on one of the islands off Bødø above the Arctic Circle, she had called herself the Arctic Maiden. He could still see in his mind's eye the gleam of her naked body as she'd jumped off the speedboat to swim among the skerries of the Sognefjord.

The memory caused him to smile briefly. He hoped Queensland would not target her.

They had now arrived at the road and as they walked along, their feet crunched upon the thin film of sand that lay upon it. A slight breeze had sprung up, intermittently teasing at the fine grains and whirling them into small, ground-level eddies.

Gallagher stopped at the alleyway.

Borodin looked along it. "Where's your car?"

"There." Gallagher pointed to a shedlike structure a few feet from the mud flats of the estuary. "Behind that."

"I shall come with you. You can drive me to my car."

"As you wish."

They walked down the alley and round the back of the shed.

"Very nice," Borodin commented. "Fast? And alarmed?"

"Yes to both questions," Gallagher replied as he unlocked the car.

"But of course."

Gallagher had been about to say something when he paused suddenly, then leaned quickly into the Ford to grab a pair of binoculars from the glove compartment. He straightened and focused on the road bridge leading to the peninsula.

"What?" Borodin queried, looking in the same direction with narrowed eyes.

"Trouble. The taxi that met you is coming this way. The driver was specifically told not to, just in case he might be followed. There's a local policeman, Pinheiro—I say 'local,' but he's no ordinary copper—who would love to get his nose into this. But Pinheiro's not the only reason . . ." Gallagher's words faded as he tracked the binoculars to the right, scanning the set of traffic lights behind Antonio's taxi.

Nothing. No car waiting, or following.

But there must be trouble. Antonio would never have come otherwise. It was his way of warning Gallagher.

"If it's bad trouble," Gallagher continued, lowering the glasses, "you may well need your gun. Shit. I didn't want this to happen down here."

"What about you?"

"I've got weaponry."

"But I don't see—"

"Take my word for it."

Borodin wasted no time in pointless argument. "Very well. This is your show. How are you going to play it?"

"Let's get you to your car. We'll take it from there."

They entered the Sierra 4 × 4 quickly and Gallagher drove out from behind the shed.

The section of the road they were on had a single but shallow S-bend. Antonio's taxi came into view just as they arrived at the last apex. Antonio stopped immediately and got out of his taxi to hurry across. He glanced briefly at Borodin before turning urgently to Gallagher.

"Two men," he began, "at the airport. I watch for a long time, but they are not passengers. They wait and wait, looking for someone. They look like police, but not police. They are not Portuguese. I think perhaps they are looking for you, *Senhor* Gordon." He glanced once more at Borodin. "Or . . ." He let his words fade.

"Did they see or follow you?"

Antonio shook his head. "No. I am sure."

"Good. Thanks for coming. It may be nothing, but it's best to be certain. Now take a small break from the taxi business. Let your other drivers do the airport pickups until we've sorted this out."

"But—"

"No buts," Gallagher said firmly. "You know my feelings about getting you into trouble. If these men are what you think they may be, take it from me they're very bad trouble indeed. I want to keep this well away from your family. Give me half an hour. If they're okay, it's enough time for me to make sure. If they're not, I'll have them away from the airport before you get back. Now stay here. Please? If not for my sake . . ."

They both knew he meant Estella. Against such stakes Antonio was powerless.

He nodded. "Okay," he agreed reluctantly.

"There must be at least one café open around here. Have some coffee and take it easy."

"Sim."

Antonio returned to his taxi and Gallagher drove on, stopping once more a short while later where Borodin had left the Citroën.

"Irina mentioned this about you," Borodin remarked. "You worry about people. And now?" he added, looking at Gallagher expectantly.

"I'm going to lead them out, if they're really on the prowl. Wait in your car beyond the airport to keep them in a sandwich, and follow my lead. I suppose there's no need for me to tell you to make sure you're not seen or recognized."

"None at all."

Borodin got out and went to his car. Gallagher drove on.

At the airport, it took less than a minute to get the men's attention. Gallagher had merely walked into the concourse, making no attempt to merge with the scenery, when the two, wandering aimlessly and clearly thinking of giving up, could not restrain themselves from a start of recognition.

Gallagher had never seen them before, but it was clear they had been given his description. Antonio had been quite correct in his reading of the situation. Those two were very bad news, and certainly not Portuguese. Both were tall, hard-looking men with cropped hair and identical sunglasses. They wore pale cream suits. Tourists they were not.

"Right," Gallagher muttered to himself as he wandered back out. "Now the fun begins."

The men casually followed.

"I like it," Gallagher said as he led them a meandering route through the parked cars.

They kept their distance, but they were definitely tagging him. After a while, they got worried about being able to get to their car in time and hurried back to where they had left it.

Gallagher strolled to the Ford, then took his time about getting in, still apparently unaware of being followed. When he judged the time to be right, he drove out of the car park and onto the exit road for Faro.

Some distance from the junction with the N125, the main coastal route to the western Algarve, he saw Borodin's Citroën parked at the side of the road, apparently empty. As he passed, however, the Citroën's headlights flashed once. Borodin was on station. Gallagher took a quick look in his mirrors. A white car, as yet unidentifiable, was trailing in his wake.

Gallagher reached the junction and in the far distance behind, he saw the Citroën pull into the traffic coming out of the airport.

The lights at the junction were red and the queue grew. The white car had slotted itself seven cars away.

The lights changed and Gallagher, first in the queue, pulled smartly away, turning left. The white car was balked by traffic turning right for Faro, and Gallagher could almost sense the frustration of the men inside.

He drove at a deliberately fast pace. It would help establish once and for all whether the white car was indeed following him.

He need not have wondered. The car had finally been able to get free and it stormed onto the main road, building speed rapidly. Far back, Gallagher saw that the speck that was Borodin's Citroën had also made it before the lights had changed again.

The road branched right from the Loulé route for a flyover that curved left towards Almansil. This would lead the men away from Antonio's home. Though Gallagher and Miranda had moved out to a small villa at Vale do Lobo, there was no need to take chances.

He knew exactly where he was leading his pursuers.

At Almansil, he turned left off the main road and onto a narrower one that would eventually lead to Vale do Lobo. But he was not going there. Miranda was alone in the villa.

He came to another junction. He turned right for one kilometer before turning left onto what was little more than a paved track. He was now driving through a pine plantation and back towards the sea. Here and there, substantial houses were glimpsed through the trees.

After a while, he came to a partially complete development of more holiday homes. He drove through and onto an unpaved road that headed towards a deserted beach. A plume of dust trailed behind as the road curved and switchbacked past great mounds and gouges of loamy soil left by the mechanical diggers. Then he turned off it. He had found what he'd been looking for.

He hoped Borodin had been able to keep up.

If matters developed the way he was afraid they might, it could be a killing ground. He'd try not to make it so, but you never knew how people would react in a given situation. The men might decide to shoot first and ask questions later, although Gallagher felt that would defeat Queensland's purpose, assuming they *were* Queensland's heavies. The hope, therefore, was that the men would exercise restraint.

He parked the car in full view in a depression created by the digging, then quickly went into the rear to get the SIG P226 out of the compartment. He checked its load and put on the silencer. Taking a spare magazine, he hurried out, locked the car, and ran into a big colony of pine trees that was close by. He followed a rough path through to a small clearing where, unexpectedly, the rust-smeared white hulk of the smaller version of an old-model Ford Transit van was propped forlornly against the trunk of a tree. The battered vehicle was minus all its windows, its sliding side door, and its rear wheels. The deflated carcasses of its front tires were still on, although the wheels would no longer turn.

Gallagher wondered how it had got there.

He positioned himself just beyond the Transit. He was well in cover, and had a clear view of the path that led to the Transit. He had just settled down to wait when he heard the sound of an engine at speed. He could tell by its cadences that the men were driving without due respect for the condition of the road. Every so often, the engine would scream as the car momentarily left the ground after hitting a particularly severe bump in the road.

Then, in a cloud of billowing dust, the white car, a big Peugeot sedan, swept into view to come sliding to a halt as the men saw the gunmetal Sierra. There was the slamming of doors as they got hurriedly out to inspect Gallagher's car.

Gallagher watched them from a good hundred yards away as they stalked warily around it. Neither man touched the Ford, as if afraid it might be booby-trapped. Then one of them paused and looked to the trees. He said something.

Now both had stopped and were in earnest conversation.

Both now looked at the trees. One of them was looking directly at the spot where Gallagher was hiding, and though Gallagher knew he could not be seen, he unconsciously touched the P226 with his free hand, as if to reassure himself it was ready for action if need be. Another part of him listened for the engine sound that might signal the approach of Borodin. But the only noise he heard was the faint banging of a workman somewhere among the distant unfinished houses.

The men began to approach the trees cautiously, fanning out slightly. Just before they reached the edge of the colony, they paused to draw their guns. Both carried pistols. Each reached into a jacket pocket to take a silencer, which each then screwed on. They removed their sunglasses with studied care and put them away.

"Shit," Gallagher muttered. "I was hoping you prats had more sense." He waited, unmoving, as they continued to approach.

There was still no sound of Borodin's car.

The men were well into the trees now, and still approaching. They had fanned out wider, so that Gallagher would have to turn from one to the other to get both, if he were forced to shoot. He'd have to do something about that.

Then they were close enough to hear him clearly, and well within killing range.

"That's it, gentlemen!" he ordered sharply. "Far enough!"

They froze where they were, but very alert. Gallagher knew that the slightest misjudgment on his part and they'd be at him.

"I don't want to kill either of you," he continued, "but if you leave me no choice, I shall. Drop your weapons!"

Nothing. It was as if he had not spoken.

"Drop them!" Whatever language they spoke, he decided, it was impossible to mistake the command, surely.

It still had no effect. They remained in their frozen stances, eyes darting, clearly estimating the odds of getting a killing shot away without getting killed in return. Gallagher felt a despairing anger. This was not the result he wanted.

Gallagher stood up slowly, pointing his gun with two hands. "Easy!" he cautioned as both men tried to move. "I'll say again . . . drop your guns. *Now!*"

Instead, they did all the wrong things. Perhaps they thought that with two against one, they could take him. Perhaps they had only hoped to disable. Or perhaps, totally against what was expected of them by Queensland, they had decided that to survive, they needed to kill Gallagher. Whatever their reasoning, they were suddenly diving in opposite directions, hoping to create confusion by dividing his attention while they took him out at their leisure.

Unfortunately for them, Gallagher was ready for just such a move. He fired once to disable, at the one he considered the most dangerous.

The P226 coughed deeply and the targeted man gave an involuntary scream as he was hit in the shoulder of his gun arm. The weapon flew out of his hand and out of reach as he went down, thrown to the ground by the shock of the big 9-mm bullet hitting home.

But by then Gallagher had whirled, tracking on to his companion. This one had already rolled and was down on one knee, zeroing in on his target. Gallagher knew his next shots would have to be quick and killing; no time for a carefully placed maimer. Hitting the better man had given him all the time needed to sight on the slower companion.

The P226 coughed twice this time. Both shots hit the second man squarely in the chest. Incredibly, already dying, he *rose* to his feet in a reflex action and was pedaled backwards by the momentum of the blows, to slam against the shell of the Transit. The hollow body of the vehicle boomed eerily in response. Then the man was sliding downwards, his cream suit sporting a new and blossoming dark red flower, a bright smear staining the rear of the van.

Gallagher moved swiftly to the wounded man. "Your friend's dead," he snapped. "Who sent you?" He pointed the gun just feet from the man's forehead while remaining out of reach of a sudden lunge. "Well?"

The man lay where he was and glared. He said nothing.

"What bloody language do you speak and understand? *Answer,* you miserable crud! I haven't got all bloody day."

Silence. The glare was defiant, despite the blood that was now staining the shoulder of the man's jacket.

"Svenska?" Gallagher persisted, though he doubted they were Swedes. *"Italiano? Français? Deutsch?"* Former East Germans, perhaps? He went through a gamut of languages before diving into the uncharted waters of his very rusty Serbo-Croatian. "*Srpsko?*" he suggested in desperation, using the shortened term. He had deliberately left out Russian.

Nothing.

"Right," Gallagher said. "I've had it with you. My patience is gone." He swung the P226 to point it at the already-wounded shoulder. "Time's just run out."

"Nyet!" There was high alarm in the voice as the man finally spoke.

"Well, well, well," Gallagher said quietly. "Russian." He stepped back, but still kept the man covered. "So what's it to be? What language do we have our chat in?"

"English is good."

"English it is."

"You are one shit bastard!"

"Believe it," Gallagher said calmly. "So who sent you?"

"I have orders. My shoulder hurts."

"I'm glad your shoulder hurts, and I know you've got bloody orders. I want to know who gave them. Then you can take off to whatever doctor you've got access to. I'm not interested in you. You can save yourself."

The man glanced uncertainly at his dead colleague, then again at Gallagher, clearly wondering whether Gallagher meant it. "We were . . . in North Africa," he began eventually. "We were given an area to search. That is all I know."

"All you know? Or all you're telling?"

"Is same thing."

"No it damned well isn't! But I haven't the time to stand here all day chatting with you, and you know it. So I want you to deliver a message to the person who's given you orders and whom you don't know. Tell him . . . I've gone to Queensland."

Gallagher watched keenly for a reaction. There was nothing. Either the man was very good indeed, despite the pain of the wound, or he genuinely knew nothing of Queensland. It was quite likely. The details of an operation so secret would not have filtered down to the hired help.

Staying on full alert, Gallagher lowered the SIG. "All right," he said. "Get moving. *Don't look for your weapon!* And don't try for a shot from your car if you've got one in there. You wouldn't make it."

"He's right, buddy!" an American voice confirmed from within the trees.

Borodin.

The shock of knowing Gallagher had a backup hidden somewhere showed clearly on the man's face, as did the final acceptance that he'd lost the confrontation. He looked at the body of his companion.

"Better leave him," Gallagher suggested. "You've got enough problems as it is. I don't want a local cop picking you up with a dead body. I want my message delivered. Now move!"

The man stumbled back to his car. Soon, Gallagher heard it start. Then it lurched away in a series of hops. The man was clearly having difficulties with his driving, but Gallagher was sure he would make it. That one had a strong survival instinct.

After the sounds of the white car had faded, Gallagher said, "I know where you are."

"Ah, but do you know when I arrived?"

From his left, Borodin came into view.

Gallagher turned to him. "When I first called out to them."

"*They* didn't hear me."

"That's because they were all eyes and ears, concentrating on me. But I did, and that's what matters. When I didn't hear your car, I assumed you had stopped some way off and would do the rest on foot."

Borodin smiled as he reached Gallagher. "My fellow Russian is right: You are a bastard when you're at work."

"Why didn't you do something?"

"You were so capable, it was more interesting to watch. Quite a revelation. You made every bullet count."

"And if I hadn't been capable?"

"I would not have allowed you to get killed."

"That's a comfort." Gallagher said dryly, turning to look at the body. "Now to take care of him."

"How?"

"Let's put him in the van. Then I'll let Pinheiro know."

"He'll have questions."

"Yes. But he won't get the answers from me. And I've let you off the hook, by the way."

"Oh?"

They picked up the body and placed it with unexpected gentleness in the van. Then Gallagher collected the discarded weapons and gave them to Borodin.

"I'm sure you can dispose of these," he said. "I don't want to have to go into long explanations with Pinheiro. You heard what I said to that man," he continued. "No need now for you to place that ad. Less risk."

"Thinking of my safety?" There was a hint of slyness in the question.

"Let's put it this way: We need each other. I want you to keep digging for as much information on Queensland as you can get to me. Leave messages on the machine. I can beep it from wherever I may be."

"I hate those things," Borodin said with feeling. "They're the personal version of the lying secretary. The one that says the boss is at a meeting, when you know he isn't. Those machines are no longer used for taking all those calls you were afraid of missing, but to keep other people at bay. I hate those things," he repeated.

"A man in your position doesn't normally need to worry about returned calls, surely?"

They were walking back to Gallagher's car.

"You'd be surprised. But one way or the other, I do get my answers." Borodin gave one of his grins.

"I'll bet. Well, you don't have to worry about me. I'll await your calls with great eagerness."

They got into the car. Gallagher put the P226 beneath his seat, then again drove Borodin back to where he'd left his car.

They both got out after Gallagher stopped near the Citroën. Borodin turned to face him, jacket weighted down by the two extra pistols.

Borodin gave Gallagher one of his Russian embraces. "Be very careful, my friend. I'll see what other information I can get to you. I must get back before it is realized I am not in the Baltics."

"And thank you again for coming over."

"As you've said . . . mutual benefit. Be very careful," Borodin repeated before turning away to enter his car.

Gallagher leaned against the gunmetal Sierra and watched him drive away. He didn't trust Borodin totally; but for the time being, it was better than trusting the Department. Much bloody better.

He got back into the car after the Citroën had disappeared, and headed for the villa in Vale do Lobo.

The two-story villa was in a prime spot on high ground and set in moderately spacious grounds among the ubiquitous pine trees. From its roof terrace, there was a clear view of the sea less than 300 meters away.

Gallagher drove up to find another car waiting. Antonio's taxi. He got out and went up to the Mercedes. Antonio was straightening to an upright position behind the wheel. He had clearly been hiding.

"Antonio," Gallagher began, opening the driver's door. "What are you doing here?"

Antonio climbed out and smiled sheepishly. "Ah, *Senhor* Gordon. I did wait for the half hour. Then I was going to the airport and I saw your car and the white car leaving. I saw, also, Mr. Thomsen's car. So, I too follow. No one notices a taxi . . ."

"Don't you believe it. But go on."

"After Almansil, I see you do not go to Vale do Lobo. So I come here to look after Miranda."

"Where is she?"

"In the pool."

Gallagher shook his head slowly and placed a comradely hand upon Antonio's shoulder.

"Antonio, what am I going to do with you? I asked you to keep out of trouble."

"There is no trouble here," Antonio said reasonably.

Gallagher gave a mental sigh of relief that there hadn't been. Had the men who had chased him known enough to come to the villa, Antonio would not have lasted seconds. All the same, it was a brave thing to have done.

"Thanks for coming," Gallagher now said.

"It was nothing."

If only you knew.

"And the two men?" Antonio continued.

"We . . . er, managed to get rid of them. Perhaps it's a good thing you are here, because we're going to the airport and I'm leaving the car. You'll have to drive it back to Loulé later, if you don't mind."

Antonio was both surprised and disappointed. "I will drive the car . . . but you must leave?"

"I'm afraid so. We should get back to London quickly."

"So the men . . . bad trouble?"

"Very. Now I'd better warn Miranda and start packing."

"Shall I help? Or shall I wait to see if anyone comes?"

"Antonio, this is your property. You can come and go as you please."

"No, no. When you are here, it is your house. I shall wait."

Gallagher knew there was little point in trying to dissuade him. "All right. I'll try to be as quick as possible."

Gallagher returned to the Ford, retrieved the P226 from under the seat and, out of view of Antonio, took the weapons case out of the compartment. He removed the silencer from the automatic, placed both items back in the case, and shut it. Taking the case, he then went into the house.

He found Miranda in the pool as Antonio had said, wearing a skimpy bikini that belonged to one of Estella's friends.

She maneuvered herself around the rim of the pool with her good arm across to where he was standing, and supported herself on the edge. She had managed to keep the wound dressing from getting wet.

"Isn't this great?" she said in greeting, smiling up at him. "I can't do much swimming, but I'm getting a good soak. Come on in. No need to wear trunks. And as for these things I've got on, they can come off in a trice, even with one properly working arm. You can hold on to me and if I hang on to the edge of the pool like this, we can . . ." She paused. "I really can get these things off. Look . . ."

She was about to demonstrate.

"Antonio's out there. Wouldn't want to shock him."

"I suppose not," she agreed with great reluctance. "I think he's standing guard. Did you put him up to it?"

"Nope. It was his idea."

"So how was the mystery trip?" She was staring at the case, but resisted asking about it.

"I've got good news and bad news."

"I knew this was going too well." The fear was coming back into her eyes. "I was beginning to relax and have fun. You're not going to tell me they've found us, are you?"

"They have, but that's no longer a problem. That's not really the bad news. We're going back. Today. At first, I thought it would be safer for you that we return separately, but things have changed and it's more practical not to. The good news is that you are not in danger anymore."

She stared at him, trying to take it all in. "Suddenly I'm no longer a target?" Her eyes briefly wandered back to the case.

"No."

"How come?"

"I thought you'd be pleased."

"I'm overjoyed, if it is true. But I still don't see how—"

"It is true, and the 'how' does not matter."

"It does matter. I've been shot at, a policeman's been killed outside my home, I've been hunted in Oxfordshire, then I was whisked over here. Now you tell me everything's all right. What's the real reason, Gordon?"

"What's this? The hard-nosed journo back on the job?" He could see she was trying really hard not to ask whether he'd made use of the weapons in the case.

"Part of her is . . . if you won't tell me more." Miranda began to work her way towards the pool steps.

Gallagher moved across to help her climb out, putting down the case to do so.

"Well?" she said, as she allowed Gallagher to pat her dry with a bath towel. "Are you going to tell me?"

He continued to pat her. Wrapped in the towel, she obediently turned so that he could do her entire body. Unaccountably, she reminded him of a vulnerable child, just out of the bath.

Whether she was out of danger or not, he had to get her back to London as quickly as could be managed. If she remained with him, she would continue to be targeted. Letting "Queensland" know he was now aware of the game might not necessarily keep her safe, especially if the unknown killer believed her continuing presence close to him meant there was a weakness to be probed.

"There's nothing to tell," he said.

She moved to stand away from him, looking at him with uncertain eyes. "Estella says you don't trust easily but that when you do, it's done completely. Am I not to be trusted?"

"What a question!"

"It requires an answer."

Gallagher sighed. "Let me tell you something. When I was a boy . . . a child, really . . . my father took me to a barbecue at the home of one of his colleagues. I was seven. There was a little girl there nearly my age. I think she was six months short. I thought she was the most beautiful person I had ever seen.

"There was this huge table in the garden, loaded with all sorts of goodies, and right in the middle was a big dish of fantastically prepared lobster. I think it was put there deliberately to keep it out of our reach—that is, the kids. The little girl was trying to get at it, but she couldn't do so without falling into all the other stuff on the table. As you can imagine, she'd have been about as popular as a squadron of wasps if that had happened.

"I was quite tall for my age and I knew I could reach it easily. I went over, although I knew the grown-ups wouldn't like it if we got caught and my father would have a few tough things to say to me. But I felt invincible. She gave me the sort of smile that turned me into jelly inside but made me feel very brave. I got her a piece, and she took it graciously and gave me another of those smiles. She seemed to take her time about eating it. Then I heard my father calling. He wanted to show me off to some new colleagues. I told the girl I'd be back. She said okay.

"When I returned she was back at the table. This time, she'd got another boy to do the dirty work. He was not as tall and he fell all over the beautifully prepared food. Scared, covered in mangled food and all sorts of dressings, and hugely embarrassed, he said the girl had put him up to it. I'd watched her when he'd fallen in. She had enjoyed every moment and was secretly laughing at him. She denied ever having told him to get at the lobster. Everyone believed her.

"You see, she'd thrown away the piece I'd got for her, and that boy and I were the only two who didn't know she hated lobster. I looked at her. It was as if she never knew me. I learned a lot about people that day."

Miranda was staring at him. "Is that how you see me? Like some feckless little spoiled brat of a girl?"

"No. That was not why I told you the story. I told it as an example of how not to get yourself involved in someone else's schemes, especially when you don't know what the rules are. You're in one right now. True, you fell into it. But you certainly don't know the rules and I want you safe again. You're out of danger, and it's going to stay that way."

"Estella also said it's the people you trust who make you vulnerable, because you care about them. So you do care about me?" The words came out like a plea.

"Yes," he answered. "But especially, I want you in one piece." He picked up the case. "So let's get packed and out of here."

She looked at him for a long time. There was a redness in her eyes that had nothing to do with having been in the pool.

"All right," she said at last and went inside, still wrapped in the towel.

He thought he'd never seen her so lost, but his mind was already racing ahead, planning a sequence of moves in preparation for the approaching combat with his unknown adversary.

The packing was done quickly and the journey back to the airport made in almost complete silence. When they had climbed out of the taxi and taken their luggage, Gallagher shook hands with his friend, while Miranda surprised Antonio with an unrestrained hug.

"Let's make this quick," Gallagher said. "I don't want anyone who may be watching to link us too closely with you, Antonio. Thanks for all the help and do apologize to Estella for us. It was best not to call her, in case anyone might have been listening."

"Thanks for everything," Miranda said. "Tell Estella I'm sorry we had to leave so suddenly."

"She will understand."

"Look after yourselves," Gallagher said to him. "I don't have to remind you of what I mean."

Antonio nodded. He looked at Miranda. "You must come back."

She glanced at Gallagher. "I'd like to."

Gallagher said, "You'd better get out of here now, Antonio. Just in case."

"*Sim.* And you look after yourself, Gordon."

"I will. You see?" Gallagher went on to Miranda as the taxi pulled away. "He does call me Gordon when he feels like it."

At one of the public phones, Gallagher waited as Haxton's direct number rang out at the other end. It was picked up immediately after the first ring. Haxton must have been waiting right next to the phone.

"Roberto Haxton . . ."

"Roberto, Greywolf."

"How nice to hear from you! Where are you?"

"At the airport."

"The airport! But . . . how . . . I mean why? . . ."

"We're going back to London. But first, I must see you and Captain Pinheiro."

"As a matter of fact," Haxton said after a pause, "he is right here with me."

"How cozy."

"I beg your pardon?"

"Just muttering to myself, Roberto."

"We'll pick you up."

"Good."

"And as for your flight back, you're in luck."

"Oh yes?"

"The Citation is still here."

Gallagher shut his eyes. Jesus. If somehow Queensland had found out about the Citation, given the organization at his disposal, all it needed was for a group of searchers to spot the aircraft at its destination airport. It would have been as easy as that. No wonder those men had been hanging around.

Gallagher felt despair. Who the hell had been so stupid as to leave the aircraft out in the open or, even worse, at Faro? Or had that, too, been deliberate?

"Hello! Hello!" Haxton was beginning to sound frantic. "Are you there?"

"I'm here. We'll be waiting."

He hung up before Haxton could say more, and turned to find Miranda looking anxiously at him.

"Trouble?" she asked as they walked away from the phone.

"No."

"You don't look very happy about something."

"That's my thinking expression. We've got our flight back. We'll be traveling in style again—the Citation's still here."

"And I suppose that girl."

They had stopped by a pillar, away from the general melee of people.

"I suppose so," he said. "I won't know until Haxton gets here. We'll be going to his office first. There are some things I must do."

"I can feel you moving away from me," she said in a quiet voice. "What am I supposed to have done?"

"Oh, Miranda, you've done nothing. Try to understand. Somehow, I seem to lose almost everyone and everything I have cared a lot for. It's as if my enjoyment of people and things are seen as some sort of affront to the gods. At least, that's what I would have said had I been an ancient Greek. They get taken away from me. My one weapon is not to appear to care too much. I learned a long time ago that only nightmares seem to come true. Dreams don't get a look in. I'm setting you free, Miranda, from all that . . ."

Her deep blue eyes filmed over. "But I don't want to be! . . ." A slight tremor had entered the voice.

He placed a gentle hand upon her cheek. "Shh," he said, and kissed her on the corner of her mouth.

Fifteen minutes later, a squeal of tires heralded the arrival of Haxton, with Pinheiro glued to his wake.

"Mr. Gallagher . . . Miss Lacey," Haxton began. "How can we be of service?"

Pinheiro said nothing, but his eyes were lively.

"First . . . your office please, Roberto," Gallagher said. "I'd like to have a word with you and Captain Pinheiro, in private."

"Of course."

"Then back here for the flight to London."

"Of course," Haxton repeated, cooperation personified.

They were driven quickly to Haxton's office in Faro. While Miranda was looked after by one of Haxton's female colleagues, Haxton showed Gallagher into a private room. A very watchful Pinheiro joined them, glancing more than once at the weapons case that Gallagher had brought with him.

Gallagher wasted no time. "Captain Pinheiro, there's a dead man on your patch."

Haxton's eyes seemed to want to pop out as they widened in a mixture of shock, anxiety, and horror. He looked sick. Pinheiro was very still, but his eyes jumped.

"Dead?" He glanced at the case. "How?"

"Shot."

"By you?"

"Yes."

"I see. So you have started your war, Mr. Gallagher." Pinheiro did not look pleased. "Where is this body?"

Gallagher told him.

"And may I have the details of this incident?"

"I'm afraid not. This is where Roberto will have to liaise with you."

"I will?" Haxton asked weakly.

"Yes, Roberto. Talk to London."

"I . . . I see." But Haxton did not see at all.

Pinheiro was looking furious. "Mr. Gallagher!"

"Captain Pinheiro, I know precisely what you're about to say. But let us not forget you were assigned to assist me. You will be assisting me by taking care of that man in the derelict van and, of course, keeping the story out of the media. I am very sorry, but I cannot tell you more. I am certain that my people will liaise with yours."

My people, Gallagher thought. That's a joke.

Pinheiro did not look as if he was happy with that at all, but there was not much he could do about it. His frustration showed. Gallagher thought a little diplomacy might help soothe ruffled feathers.

"Captain Pinheiro . . . Mario. Look, you're a good copper and I know your position is difficult. But if you were in my place, you'd be saying the same thing to me. There must have been instances when you've found yourself in an awkward position with your colleagues in other branches of the police force, when you weren't able to tell them everything you knew. I am in that position now. I really cannot tell you more. If I could, I would."

Pinheiro appeared mollified and felt bound by politeness to respond in kind.

After a while, he nodded slowly. "Very well, Mr. Gallagher . . . Gordon. Yes, I have been in the position you mentioned, and sometimes it has been difficult to keep the traffic police, for instance, out of my hair." He gave a fleeting smile. "But no more bodies, please. At least, invite me next time."

"These are dangerous people, Mario."

"I have come up against dangerous people before."

"I don't doubt it," Gallagher said.

But not like these. For his own sake, Gallagher thought, Pinheiro should hope he never came into contact with them. Fortunately, the chances were that now he never would. The battleground had moved on.

Gallagher turned to Haxton. "Time to go, Roberto. And how come the Citation's still here?" He asked the question almost as a throwaway, wondering about Haxton's part in all this.

But Haxton seemed almost relieved to talk about the aircraft, after the news of the dead man.

He gave a weak smile. "One of those things. Mr. Hammond and the young lady who traveled with him went out for a meal. Mr. Hammond must have eaten a bad prawn. He got sick, very severely, for a day. Today, he feels recovered enough to fly."

Gallagher did not believe it for a second. Too convenient. On the other hand, these things did happen. The best-laid plans . . . even so.

"Lucky for us then," he said.

Unsure of how to respond, Haxton said, "Yes."

They left the room and found Sian waiting with Miranda, who seemed less than pleased to see her.

Sian smiled brightly at him. "So we're taking you back."

"Yes," Gallagher replied. "Aren't we lucky? Bad prawns are very bad for pilots."

The green eyes were speculative. "You know about that."

"Any reason I shouldn't? I suppose the infected prawn was just one of those things."

"Things do happen."

"Don't they just."

"Are you suggesting . . ."

"That you gave Hammond a mild dose of food poisoning? Oh, that I should be so unkind! Problem is, when things 'happen' conveniently, I get twitchy." Gallagher changed tack suddenly. "Enjoyed your stay in the Algarve? Done some driving?"

She actually seemed amused. "I went all the way west, to Portimão and as far as Sagres. Plenty of area to cover, plenty of places to go to ground; but of course I didn't find the one that mattered. Hardly enough time."

"At least you're prepared to admit it. How did you know we were here?"

"Got the news just now when I got back. I don't use car phones or radios, if I can help it. All this technology only makes it easier for people to eavesdrop." She looked as if she wanted to grin. "As a few unlucky people have found out. Car phones are useless without scramblers."

"You could have brought one from London. Why didn't you?"

Sian's eyes were at their most probing. "Like you, I tend to prefer to do things my own way. You're aware of the parameters then; at least, most of the time."

"Like me."

A hint of a smile. "Yes. And now it's time for me to play the stewardess once more. See you aboard." She turned from him then, to enter one of the other offices.

Gallagher watched her walk away, her movements unconsciously sensuous. Probably going to report to Fowler, he thought.

Then he turned to see Miranda staring at him.

II

The Citation was doing its usual effortless cruising at 50,000 feet, on its way back to London. Miranda looked across the aisle at Gallagher, who was fast asleep. Yet she got the impression that he would be instantly awake, should the need arise. She also had the strongest of feelings that he had become very different. The thought confused her. There were not specific differences that she could point to. It was simply that he had somehow *changed.*

The word *changeling* came into her mind. He was still the same Gordon about whom she had come to know more, much more, during the past days than she had learned over all the previous years; and yet, he wasn't. Something had been changing within him ever since the shooting in the churchyard, and now, metamorphosis was complete. He had become someone . . . *something* . . . she could never reach. It seemed to her that there was a common bond between him and Sian which, despite her own intimate moments with him, was quite beyond her.

It was an uncomfortable realization. She was actually jealous of a woman who was not a sexual rival! At least, she hoped she wasn't. But worse, she could not remember ever having been jealous of any woman before. It was usually the other way around. Women were normally jealous and frightened of her when their men were present. Suddenly, women who could shrivel machismo at fifty paces would become clinging.

And now just look at me, she thought. Behaving like a possessive schoolgirl.

She moved her left arm experimentally, testing it for pain. The wound was healing very nicely but she continued to use the sling, though she sometimes allowed the arm to hang free.

She had not asked him about the weapons, but her instincts told her he'd made use of them while he was out. She was no longer a target. He had said that with such certainty, she was now convinced he had taken some kind of action. Someone had died during the afternoon.

She kept her eyes upon his sleeping form. Even in repose, he looked dangerous. She glanced out the window. At this altitude there was bright sunlight, but down below, beneath a wispy cloud cover that was itself several thousand feet below them, the late May twilight was beginning to claim the day.

She turned to look at Gallagher once more.

"You can almost see a sign that says, 'Don't touch, unless you want to lose an arm.'"

Miranda was startled out of her reverie. Sian was standing close by with coffee. She had not even been aware of the aroma, so far had she gone into her own thoughts.

"Nice and hot," Sian said, placing it before her.

"Thanks. Is he really that dangerous?"

Sian glanced at Gallagher, a tiny, almost fond smile hovering about her lips. "We've never worked together so I don't know firsthand. But he has quite a reputation."

"That sounds almost like hero worship."

"Does it? I didn't mean it that way. Don't worry, Miss Lacey. I'm not trying to get into bed with him."

Miranda was taken aback by the directness with which the remark was delivered.

"I didn't . . . I mean I wasn't . . ."

"That's all right then." Sian gave her a smile and went up to the flight deck.

Parson's Green, London.

Haslam was looking forward to a quiet evening before the TV in his three-bedroom mews house when the phone rang. He sighed, debated whether to pick it up, and, after the fifth ring, did so.

"Sorry, George," Fowler said. "You'll have to tape that favorite wildlife program of yours. I'm sending a car round."

"Why?"

"You're getting as bad as Gallagher."

"What do you mean 'bad'? You mean *he's* getting as good as I used to be. Come to think of it, he's in a class of his own."

"Stop being awkward, George. The car's on its way. Our birds are coming back."

"Tonight?"

"Indeed."

"Now that's interesting."

"Thought you might see it that way. Go and welcome them, then bring them here. Separate cars. There have been developments."

"I see. Who's picking me up?"

"Prinknash."

"That's nice," Haslam said crossly and hung up.

The buzzer sounded at the door within ten minutes, which meant Prinknash had been well on his way by the time Fowler had chosen to call.

Prinknash opened his mouth to speak as Haslam climbed into the white Rover 600.

"Just don't say a word," Haslam told him grumpily.

Prinknash shut his mouth quickly and headed for Heathrow, the Citation's destination airport.

Heathrow, 2200 hours.

The two Department Rovers were airside when the Citation touched down and taxied to its slot.

Inside the aircraft, Miranda looked at Gallagher uncertainly as she stood up and began to collect her things. Sian had come down from the flight deck, but Hammond was still engaged in shutting down the Citation's systems.

Sian released the door and stood back for them to make their way out. The sounds of the continuously busy international airport flooded in, despite the time of night.

Gallagher paused, allowing Miranda to leave first.

"I'd like to think you had nothing to do with that prawn that Hammond ate," he told Sian.

The green eyes, seemingly possessed of a special luminance, reminded him of another pair, belonging to someone else. But the person hovering at the faint edges of his memory was long dead.

It could have been the subdued aircraft lighting. It could have been his own heightened state of awareness; all his senses had become so sharply focused, he was operating in what felt like physical, mental, and emotional overdrive. He was primed. The wolf was unleashed.

"It really did happen normally."

"You had the same dish, I believe."

"I've got a very strong constitution."

"Well," Gallagher said, turning to follow Miranda out of the aircraft. "Look after it."

"I will." She, too, paused briefly. "And stay lucky."

"Count on it," he said, and climbed out into the lighted darkness and noise that was Heathrow, knowing her eyes were still upon him.

The first thing to come into close vision was the bulk of Haslam.

"I see you've got my case," Haslam greeted. "Used it too, I gather."

Gallagher indicated the aircraft with a slight movement of his head. "Reported to you, did she?"

"Haven't got the full details yet. Just a brief resumé from Fowler, sent via Prinknash. Fowler's waiting. Miss Lacey comes in my car, while you go with MacDuff."

"Who the hell's MacDuff? That really his name?"

"It is, and he's driving that car over there."

When the Citation had been on finals, Gallagher had found his seething anger over his stolen confidential file returning with a vengeance. He was in no mood to see Fowler as yet. He strode over to the second Rover, followed by Haslam. A man in his late twenties with too much fat waited by the driver's door.

Gallagher opened one of the rear doors and put his things inside, including the case.

"Keeping that, are you?" Haslam asked.

"I might need it," Gallagher replied grimly. To MacDuff, he added, "Oxford."

MacDuff stared helplessly at Haslam.

"Tell Humpty-Dumpty here," Gallagher went on to Haslam, "that I'll crack his shell unless he gets into the bloody car and takes me where I want to go. I'm going to get the Quattro, and I don't want company. That means no tails. MacDuff comes straight back. I'll see Fowler in the morning."

Gallagher was not going only for the purpose of collecting the car; there were other things he wanted to do, and he did not want the Department breathing over his shoulder.

Haslam said nothing, momentarily caught out by Gallagher's vehemence. He seemed in deep thought.

"All right, Bob," he eventually said to MacDuff, "take him where he wants to go. I'll sort it out with Mr. Fowler."

"Yes, sir." MacDuff quickly got in behind the wheel.

Haslam went to his own Rover to have a word with Prinknash and Miranda.

"Gordon?"

Gallagher turned. Miranda was standing a short distance away. He went over to her. Haslam was still with Prinknash.

"I was apparently being taken to see this Fowler person," she began, "but now I'm being taken home instead. He'll meet me there." Her eyes seemed to be searching his. "You know where I am if you want to see me again. Not everyone is like the people who have hurt you. Remember that."

She turned and went back to Haslam's car. Prinknash held the rear door open so she could get in, then shut it firmly after her. The sound of its shutting seemed like a punctuation of her words.

"What's happened between you two?" Haslam was back.

"Nothing."

"And pigs fly. I recognize that honed, relaxed state of yours. I used to get like that once. I called it my pre-combat tension. But there's an extra sharpness in you tonight. Something's got at you."

"You don't know the half of it."

"So tell me."

"Wait till morning."

"I hate it when people say that."

"So do I." Gallagher got into the Rover.

"Please don't say, 'Lead On, MacDuff,' sir," MacDuff begged.

"I wasn't going to. Move it."

"Yes, sir!"

As the Rover set off with a squeal of tires, Gallagher idly wondered whether MacDuff had been taking driving lessons in Portugal. He glanced out of the rear window. Haslam was still standing there.

Then the big figure merged into the airport half-light. The Rover was rushing through the night at 100 miles an hour on the M40 motorway, heading for Oxford. Every so often, the reflected image of MacDuff's eyes in the rearview mirror, lit by the soft glow of the instrument panel, would glance in Gallagher's direction. After a while, curiosity got the better of him.

"Been on a job, have we, sir?" he queried tentatively.

"MacDuff."

"Sir?"

"Do people really say that to you?"

"All the time. Ever since school. And just about everybody gets it wrong. You'd think that if they're going to use their Shakespeare, they'd at least do it correctly."

"Rough."

"I can't even begin to tell you how rough, sir."

"How long have you been with the Department?"

"Six months, sir. Seconded from the Terriers."

Gallagher wondered how someone as obviously overweight as MacDuff had got into the Territorial Army, the nation's reservists.

"What did you do?"

"Drove tanks, sir, and fast scout cars."

What a surprise, Gallagher thought dryly.

"And your civilian job?"

"In the City. Dealing."

"You left a well-paid job to drive for the Department? Isn't that slightly upside-down thinking in the world of the upwardly mobile? Or have the nineties curbed your taste for wheeling and dealing?"

MacDuff took a long time replying. "Well, you see, sir . . . I . . . didn't leave. I was . . . released from contract."

"You mean sacked."

"Yes, sir. One of the victims of the recession."

"So you lost the snazzy pad and the Porsche 911."

"Lost everything, but kept the Porsche. Had to have at least one thing to remind me of the good times."

"Quite. So how did the Terriers come into it?"

"I was already in. Then one day the CO, boss of a friend of mine at a Bank in the City, suggested I might like this job, as it involved driving and I was discreet. I'm a sergeant. He recommended that I receive clearance."

"Discreet," Gallagher repeated. "MacDuff?"

"Sir?"

"There's an unwritten rule in the Department. Everyone takes it very seriously."

"Sir."

"*Never* ask someone you don't know whether he's been on a job. In fact, never ask it of anyone. That is not discreet."

"Sir!"

MacDuff was silent for the rest of the journey.

They made it without incident to the safe house, where Gallagher collected the Quattro. He was pleased to note that it was exactly as he had left it. No one had attempted to interfere with it. Haslam had been as good as his word.

Gallagher waited until MacDuff had driven away before heading for a car park near the small river bridge to wait. He remained there for a good twenty minutes, in case MacDuff had got it into his head to double back to check on him. He then drove slowly on, looking for signs of a lurking Rover. Half an hour later, he was satisfied there were none and headed back to London. But he did not do so by the M40, using instead a series of back roads.

As he drove, he thought of the people whom he believed might be of interest to Queensland. He thought especially of Rhiannon, but had no idea where she was.

He saw the first of the items he was looking for in a sleeping village. It was a card-operated public telephone. He stopped by it and climbed out. No one had been tailing him. He went to the phone, inserted the anonymous card that anyone could buy over the counter, and dialed the first of the numbers he'd be calling that night. Boyd-Callum would have had his own home and family closed down tight since the shooting, but you never knew. The local top bobby, Parring, was probably still in charge.

"Yes?" came the familiar voice.

"Alun, sorry to call you so late but—"

"Gordon! Where are you?"

"Doesn't matter for the moment. Are you all okay?"

"We're fine. Why?"

"Just checking. Go back to sleep."

"If you're wondering whether we've had any further interest since the church, the answer is all quiet. I've taken precautions, of course."

"All I wanted to know. I'll be in touch."

"How's Miranda?"

"She's in good hands."

"Anything you need?"

"No thanks. Go back to sleep," Gallagher repeated, and hung up.

He got back into the car and drove on. The next card phone he found was in a twenty-four-hour filling station thirty miles from his last stop. This time the call was international.

"Von Talheim."

"Freddy . . ."

"*Ja* . . ." Then recognition dawned. "Gordon! You are in Germany?"

"No. Sorry to make it so late . . ."

"No matter. We have just closed."

Von Talheim and his wife had a very lucrative restaurant business in the Altstadt, in Ingolstadt. The fact always amused Gallagher, and they invariably argued over whether going from spook to restaurateur was a more natural progression than from spook to photographer. Somehow, they never seemed to resolve it, but did manage to consume many glasses of von Talheim's excellent wines during the course of the discussion.

"Are you and Eva okay?"

"Yes, we are. Gordon, what is the matter? Ah . . ."

"Yes, yes? What?"

"I have just remembered. Two days ago I thought I was being followed. I made a call to a former colleague. That sorted the problem."

"What happened?"

"Two people were deported. Are you involved in this?"

"Indirectly. They were trying to get to you in order to get to me."

But they hadn't done anything about his own home in Holland Park, which they had to know about from in the file. Strange. Perhaps Queensland had not, after all, been told everything by his bosses just as Borodin suspected. Loss of the file would also have considerably inhibited them.

"Should I remain on alert?" von Talheim was asking.

"No need. They'll know they've failed and won't try again . . ."

"But just in case?"

"Yes."

"Understood. I take such things as part of the old life anyway."

"Give Eva my love."

"But of course. And come and see us soon."

"Will do. Bye, Freddy."

"*Wiedersehen*, Gordon."

The next call, also international to a very private number, was made from an M1 motorway service station many miles north of London. A sleepy voice answered in Hebrew.

"Anat . . ." Gallagher began.

She was instantly alert. "You are never in Israel," she said in English.

"No."

"Okay. I shall change this number and send you the new one in the usual manner."

"Fine."

Anat, a very tough but strikingly attractive big-boned woman with the supple body of an athlete and a rich head of fine golden hair, had been of great help to him in the past. Their paths had first crossed when he'd been hunting Lauren's killers. Mutual interests had led her to put her team, tough specialists working in the shadows of government, at his disposal. He was eternally grateful to her.

"So," she now continued over the phone, "are you responsible for my little adventure yesterday?"

Gallagher felt a tingling in his veins. "What happened?"

"Some idiots tried to snatch me. At first, I thought they were some of our traditional enemies who do not like the peace process . . . and there are many of those. But they were not the ones."

"And . . . ?"

"As you can hear, they failed."

The way she said it confirmed to Gallagher that the failure had been terminal. Going up against Anat, who normally looked as if she belonged at a classy dinner party, was foolish in the extreme.

Though she had never told him directly, he'd also known that for years members of her unit had been making secret and tentative contact with some factions among the "traditional" enemies.

"Some people were trying to get to me through you," he now told her.

"Well, they have lost two. Are you all right?"

"I'm okay."

"Need help?"

"No. But thanks for the offer. Just wanted to make sure you were okay."

"Thank you for the concern. And Gordon . . ."

"Yes."

"It would be nice to see you sometime. Perhaps next time I am in Europe?"

"That's a date."

"Okay. Look after yourself."

"I always do. And you do the same."

"Always."

They hung up together.

In the Park Lane penthouse, a very unhappy Siminiev looked at his watch. It was 2 A.M. The news of the previous day had all been bad, and he had just arrived to deliver the worst. It didn't help that the information was much delayed because of what had occurred prior to its being sent.

"All right," Queensland, dressed in a blue, calf-length bathrobe, began ominously. "Tell me."

"If you'll remember, I did advise that some of these people could be dangerous."

"And *I* remember telling you," came the harsh retort, "that if your people—even those you said I could choose—could not handle themselves, they deserved whatever they got. So spare me your bleatings. Now *tell* me!"

Siminiev took an involuntary step back. "This information came in late from Portugal. One of our men is dead, the other seriously injured. That's why it took so long. Our man had to drive a very long way to reach secure medical attention and then safely communicate. He also had a specific message." Siminiev paused, as if afraid to continue. "This is very serious. Gallagher has somehow found something out."

A silence greeted this.

Siminiev coughed nervously. "The . . . er, message seems addressed to you. Gallagher deliberately left our man alive so that it could be delivered."

"Are you going to tell me what it is? Or shall I have to drag it out of you?"

"Gallagher said he's going to Queensland."

There was a sharp intake of breath, followed by a silence that lasted several minutes. Siminiev became so nervous that he actually began to sway backwards and forwards, as if in preparation for a coming gale.

But there was no gale. Instead, a peal of laughter rang through the penthouse.

At the end of it, the killer said, "Oh, but you are *good*, Mr. Gallagher! You are beginning to understand. But do you know who is on your trail? I very much doubt it. But we'll meet soon. You will give me a good fight and I shall not be disappointed. But it can end only one way. Queensland it is. I look forward to it."

Listening to this, Siminiev felt as if his presence had suddenly become totally irrelevant. The other had spoken as if Gallagher were actually in the room.

"If he knows of the Queensland file . . ." Siminiev began tentatively.

"I care little that he knows. It makes it an even better challenge. He still has no idea of my identity. How could he? It is not in the file."

"But it means someone with access has given him information! This puts our entire operation in jeopardy."

The killer turned upon Siminiev, with eyes that froze the Russian's blood. "You listen to me, little round man! I do not care if your operation, your republics, your ludicrous Commonwealth of Independent States or whatever names you choose to call yourselves disappear up your collective backsides. I care for just *one* thing—*getting Gallagher!* Your people and I made a bargain. I have carried out my part, and will continue to do so, but *nobody,* not you or your whole organization, is going to get in my way. *Do I make myself clear?*"

The chilling eyes were within inches of Siminiev's. He was so scared, he forgot to take a step back and remained petrified at the spot where he stood. The gale had finally arrived.

"Do you hear me?" the killer yelled at him.

"Yes. Yes!" Siminiev replied, trembling.

The killer moved away. The storm had passed.

"Good. Now please go and make the arrangements for my flight to Brisbane. I want to be in place before he gets there. And, Siminiev, you can also tell your bosses I shall be attending to the targets down there, as arranged . . . *after* I have finished with Gallagher."

"I shall see to it." Siminiev made to hurry out.

"Wait."

The killer went over to a writing desk, sat down, and began to write on the pad supplied by the hotel, after first tearing off the hotel logo and address. On completion, the note was handed to Siminiev.

"I want this message sent to South Africa."

Siminiev read the note quickly, then folded it and put it into a jacket pocket. "It might take some time to reach this man."

The killer had left the chair and was once more staring at Siminiev with lifeless eyes.

"I know you'll find a way to do it quickly."

Siminiev nodded with rapid jerks of the head. "Yes."

"And you may as well call off your hounds . . . those that are still alive. Their activities have been marked by failure and mounting casualties. Now that Gallagher has thrown down the gauntlet, he won't be too difficult to find. He has challenged me to the hunt and will lay a trail for me to follow. He will expect me to be wary of it. I shall be."

"You sound almost as if you admire him."

"A worthy prey deserves to be admired."

The killer paused, eyes riveted upon the portly man, who clearly wished they were not.

"You look upon me as dangerous, Siminiev. You're quite right to do so. I am . . . I am; but I'm also in control. And Gallagher, he is also dangerous and, like me, in control of himself. But you, little man, and people like you, are dangerous in another way. You are dangerous and stupid and out of control. People like you use countries and governmental power as if they were your own personal weapons, and will do anything, betray anyone, to protect your interests. That is why I have contempt for your kind.

"I have made a bargain which I shall keep, and I expect the same in return. I expect you to ensure that preparations in Queensland are as I want them. If anything goes wrong, if your people betray me, I shall find those responsible and, Siminiev, you will be my first target. I am betting your life on it. Now go away. I need my sleep."

Siminiev knew this was no idle threat; it was a firm promise. And if he felt resentment about what had been said or that his own sleep had been equally disturbed, he wisely refrained from mentioning it. He took the lift down to the lobby, walked out of the hotel with a relieved expression upon his face, and entered the anonymous sedan that was waiting for him a short distance away in the shadows.

"Anyone watching us?" he asked the driver.

"No one," came the reply.

"I'm glad this is going to be someone else's headache soon," Siminiev muttered with feeling.

The driver said nothing.

It was 4:30 A.M. when Gallagher finally pulled into the carport at his home in Holland Park. From a variety of locations, he had contacted all those he thought might be at risk, using up several of the phone cards in the process. There were some he had been unable to reach, but of those with whom he had succeeded in achieving contact, only one more had reported unusual activity: Lauren's father, in Boston.

But Myron Tanner III had friends on Capitol Hill. One phone call had brought two men and a woman to the attention of a SWAT team. Unfortunately for them, they had tried to shoot it out with the SWAT unit, and in the ensuing gunfight all three were killed. Tanner was baffled by the incident until Gallagher's brief call, which had given an explanation but no details. Gallagher had promised to clarify matters later. Tanner knew when not to press. He offered Gallagher help from powerful friends, but Gallagher had politely refused.

Gallagher already knew what he was going to do and wanted no one getting in his way, no matter how well-intentioned.

The killer, despite being under the pressure of time, had still managed to spread his net wide, with his secret partners in assassination continuing to give him vast organizational facilities.

However, Gallagher felt that now that he'd challenged the killer openly, there was no longer the need to play cat and mouse, nor for the random killing of people either close to or in any way connected to him. Neither, he figured, should it be necessary to send minions out after him via any contacts he might have.

Even so, it would be sheer folly to rely totally upon that being the case. There was always the unexpected.

And there was still Rhiannon.

As she had not been in contact for several months, Gallagher had no idea where she was. He hated having to go to the supercilious man who owned the art gallery where she worked, a nasty item who'd found it difficult to contain his glee at the breakup.

Taking everything out of the car, most importantly the weapons case, Gallagher entered his home. He checked it thoroughly. No one had been near. He checked the answering machine in the hope that either Borodin or Rhiannon might have left a message; in Rhiannon's case, this was a long shot indeed. There was nothing from either of them.

Gallagher listened to the usual crop of business and social calls, ran the tape to the end, and, after resetting the machine, took a quick shower before going to bed.

He cleared his mind of the worries of the day, and instantly fell asleep. By the time he awoke he would be refreshed, sharp, and incisive.

Never let worries sit on the mind, sir. There is no purpose in it and it hinders clear thinking.

O'Keefe.

It was one of those superb English days when even the sun believed that all was right with the world and put on one of its most glorious displays. The sky looked as if it had never known a cloud. The air was still, but there was a freshness to it that seemed to invigorate everyone.

People waiting in long queues for buses that came along when they felt like it seemed more cheerful than usual and even spoke to each other. Drivers and passengers in cars, finding to their relieved surprise that the rush hour had decided not to exist for the time being, played music on their car stereos and looked happy. Even commuters waiting for trains that were inexplicably canceled without warning appeared calm.

Gallagher woke up, listened to the busy chatter of the birds in the branches of the big plane tree outside his window, and decided it was going to be a tough day. There was the gallery to go to, and then it would be Fowler's turn. Neither prospect cheered him, and thinking of Fowler brought with it the unwelcome reminder of his confidential file, effectively ruining the day for him before he'd even started. But there was nothing to be done except to go through with it.

It was possible, Gallagher hoped, that "Queensland" knew nothing of Rhiannon; possible that the killer's bosses, for their own reasons, might have indeed decided not to give him that information. As Borodin had pointed out, the killer was to be betrayed in any case and, hedging their bets, they would have divulged only such information as they thought necessary for the completion of whatever operation they were running, and no more.

He hoped.

12

The Quattro's big double tailpipe gave out a power-ful, muted rumble as Gallagher drove towards Mayfair. He was astonished by the remarkably smooth flow of the traffic and briefly entertained the idea that the day was perhaps was not going to be too bad after all, before reality poured cold water all over that notion. He discovered just how lousy it was going to be after he'd parked the car and made his way to the gallery.

Francis Francke-Maynard possessed a name to savor. In happier days, Rhiannon had told him between fits of giggles that the *e* was silent, as insisted upon by the owner of the august handle. Francke-Maynard was the kind of gallery owner who firmly believed that those who dared enter his hallowed salon knew precious little about art. He gave the impression that he only sold his wares because of the unpleasant necessity of making large sums of money quickly and that he was happy to fleece those with sufficient equity with which to make such purchases.

A man of medium height with a spare frame and a fast-receding hairline, he gave the impression when standing still that he was the work of an incompetent taxidermist of Spartan tendencies. He had a Roman nose along which he tended to sight those lesser orders who dared breach his domain. This meant practically everyone. Mean eyes blatantly telegraphed this disdain and he held his chin so high, it was a wonder he did not have a permanent crick in the neck. Each day, he was smartly attired in a different suit that had seemingly been worn only once. The fleecing business was obviously very good to him.

Gallagher walked in, prepared for a hard time and more than willing to reciprocate. Francke-Maynard was scrutinizing a print by Matisse, in the company of two reverent female assistants.

Gallagher waited close by until Francke-Maynard was forced to stop pretending he hadn't seen him enter.

"Yes?" Francke-Maynard said in reluctant greeting. It sounded like "yiss."

"Good morning, Mr. Francke-Maynard," Gallagher began mildly, deliberately pronouncing the last syllable in Francke the German way. It gave him some pleasure to watch Francke-Maynard's eyebrows shoot up both in recognition and annoyance. "We've spoken on the phone several times. I'm Gordon Gallagher."

"Ahh, yiss. Mr. Gallagher. I do remember. I'm afraid Miss Jameson isn't here."

"I realize she isn't," Gallagher said, keeping a tight rein upon his temper. "I've actually come here to have a word with you. I need your help. Could we do this privately, please?"

The request for help did wonders for Francke-Maynard's ego, though he had no intention of giving any. But he could always pretend. He shooed his assistants away.

"Would you like my office? Or is this suitable?" His tone indicated that going into the office was really more trouble than Gallagher's unimportant request could possibly be worth. The office was for VIP clients only.

"This will be fine. I need to see Rhiannon immediately, or at least talk to her. It's a matter of great importance."

"*Miss* Jameson," Francke-Maynard said, stressing the form of address, "is away on business for the gallery and I'm afraid—"

Gallagher decided to waste no time with the pompous man before him and cut in, "I really haven't got all year to listen to any bullshit from you. This is a matter of life and death. Not yours, unfortunately. Now please tell me how I can get in touch with her."

But Francke-Maynard was perched high upon his dignity. "How *dare* you talk to me like—"

Gallagher's eyes appeared to lose all warmth as he took a step forward. Francke-Maynard gave a little backward hop and looked anxious.

"I've already done so, and I'm going to do it again. I'll ask you once more, and still nicely. How can I contact Rhiannon?"

"Or what will you do? Beat me up?" Francke-Maynard looked defiant. "If you even attempt to touch me, I shall call the police."

"It will be worth it!" Gallagher snarled at him suddenly. "I wonder how much close investigation this little business of yours can stand. There are people I know who could make you wish you'd never looked at a painting in your life. But I don't care how many people you rip off if they're stupid enough to come here in the first place. It really is of no interest to me. Now come on! While you're standing here puffing yourself up she could be in danger!"

"And who brought that risk to her, may I ask?"

Drastic action was called for. Gallagher began to reach forward.

Francke-Maynard shrank involuntarily away as Gallagher took a step closer. "Don't you dare touch me!" It was close to a squeal of fear.

"Gordon!"

Gallagher paused and turned at the sound of the familiar voice. Rhiannon was looking at him, the golden eyes he could not forget surveying him in a confusion of emotions. Surprise, anxiety, pleasure, uncertainty, and a certain degree of guilt all seemed to be in conflict within them.

"What were you going to do to him?" she demanded.

"Nothing. So nice to see you, Gordon," he went on dryly. "How have you been? Been sleeping well since I left?"

"That wasn't funny," she said.

"It wasn't meant to be. I need to talk to you." Gallagher gave the still-cringing Francke-Maynard a contemptuous glance. "Not here."

She was just as he remembered her. At five feet eight inches tall, the gently curved athletic body was as exciting to him as ever. There were no muscled ripples but a smooth, rounded form with softly shaped long legs. She still wore the brown hair with its naturally light tinges the same way: in gentle billows to her shoulders, but clipped back on either side of her face to show off the perfection of her ears.

Her face was saved from being too round by the subtle prominence of her cheekbones, and her mouth from being ordinary by a suffused natural redness of the full lips. There was the slightest suggestion of a point to her chin, and her nose appeared to have been stopped just in time from being too sharp. It was as if her design had been pushed to its very limits and halted at its optimum. The result had captivated him as no one else had since Lauren's death. She wore a smart but simple blue jacket, a white blouse, and a short dark skirt that showed off the beauty of her legs. On her feet were shoes that were open at the heel. Even the smell of her—oh God, that he loved so much—was the same.

She still kept her lightly tanned legs bare, he noted. That always drove him wild. Still trying to come to terms with her departure, he could not believe that this was the same woman with whom he'd made such intoxicating love all those months ago.

But things had changed.

Nothing of these thoughts showed in his expression.

"Where do you want to talk?" The well-remembered voice broke into his reverie.

"Anywhere but here."

"We'll use my office." She didn't wait for Francke-Maynard to give approval.

Gallagher followed her while Francke-Maynard looked on in a deep sulk.

In her luxuriously furnished office, Gallagher went straight to the point.

"I did not come here to make trouble for you. I was worried for your safety."

The golden eyes widened in fear. "*My* safety? What do you mean?"

"I mean someone's after me, and may use people close to me as a form of pressure."

"What do you mean by 'pressure'?" Rhiannon paused. "This is to do with your old life, isn't it?"

No point denying it. "Yes."

She sighed. "Now do you understand why I left?"

"No," he countered vehemently. "I don't. I didn't bring you into my life. You came. Your brother needed help and when he got into more trouble than he could handle, asked me to look after you. And he did that *because* of the work I used to do. So don't tell me it's anything to do with my past life."

"Keep it down, please, Gordon. Francis will—"

"Stuff Francis! I didn't come here to discuss him, nor to have a row with you. I came to see if you were okay, and to get someone to keep an eye on you, just in case." He turned to go. "I can see it was a mistake."

"Gordon, wait. Look. It's been very difficult for me too."

"It always amazes me when people say this. Like the headmaster when he's giving you six of the best, who says it hurts him more than it hurts you. Bullshit."

"Look, Gordon . . . I know you're angry . . ."

"You can't even begin to understand just how angry. But it's not all to do with you."

"That's not much of a comfort." She took a deep breath. "There's no easy way to say this. I . . . I'm seeing someone . . ." She stopped, seeing the look that had come into his eyes, sadness and betrayal rolled into one. "Don't look at me like that, Gordon. Please."

He took a long time before he said anything. "That stuffer's experiment in there?" he began eventually. "I hope you're both very happy. There are not many people in this world that I could turn my back to and know I wouldn't get blown away. You were one of them." He paused, eyes fastened upon her. "I thought you had more backbone." He saw her flinch at the words but continued, caring no more. "So what's next? The new man's baby? Best way to flush me out of your system, I suppose. Buddy Holly sang a song about someone like you. It's about not mattering anymore."

She seemed to reel from the blow, her face paling as she took in the full bitterness of his words. Then her cheeks flamed.

"That . . . that was not fair!"

Protecting himself, he had switched off from her now. All those who had once been close to him, whom he'd since either lost or been betrayed by, were ghosts marching across the landscape of his memory.

Sometimes, they came into his dreams and nightmares. Now Rhiannon, his Welsh princess, had joined them.

"Life," he at last said, with controlled savagery, "is not fair. Welcome to the fucking world."

He walked out, leaving her staring after him. He heard her rush to follow, but he kept moving.

"Gordon! Wait!"

Her cried words switched his mind back into the past, as if turning to a specific page in a book. He saw himself once more as he did so many times in his nightmares, hurrying out of his home with Celia's betrayal in the marital bed upstairs imprinting itself upon his memory. Rhiannon's were the very words that Celia had used; the words that had driven him to take a plane to nowhere and which had ended in his being held hostage with other bewildered victims in an underground prison in the Australian Outback. But that had also brought Lauren to him and a burst of real happiness, if only briefly.

It had brought something else too. There was a killer out there bent upon revenge, and who was after him. All the hijackers from that incident were dead. But there must have been one of their number on the outside; one who was alive and deadly, and waiting for him.

Gallagher did not turn round as he left the gallery, heading to where he'd parked the car. He did not see Rhiannon stop at the gallery entrance, a hand partially raised, tears in her eyes.

The traffic had changed drastically and Gallagher was stuck in it. By the time he was finally able to get out of it and park his car in the sleepy square by the Department offices, his mood was venomous.

He locked the Quattro and without seeming to, instantly spotted the white nose of the clamper's van, a lurking shark waiting in a side street to pounce.

He strode on, turning into an alleyway. Immediately,

he heard the van's engine spin into high revs as the clamping vehicle hastened towards its intended prey.

Gallagher quickly retraced his steps and caught the man, the perfect example of a modern Uriah Heep, hurriedly getting the yellow metallic trunk out of the back of the van. It was not the usual clamping team.

"You touch my car," he began quietly, "or put that thing on its wheel, and I'll rip your fucking heart out and feed it to you in one piece."

The man put the clamp down and drew himself up to his full height, which was considerably less than Gallagher's.

"You can't talk to me like that!" he quavered.

"Funny, you're the second person to say that to me today. Just doing your job, are you?"

"Well . . . yes." The clamper was obviously hoping that perhaps here at last was a motorist who appreciated the problems of the job.

"Obeying orders."

"Er . . . yes." The man now looked totally confused, wondering what was coming next.

"Fifty or so years ago, people like you became Gauleiters."

Gallagher turned away and entered the building.

The man stood irresolutely for some moments until footsteps made him turn. A male traffic warden, his partner on the clamping team, was slowly approaching.

"Where the hell have you been?" the clamper began peevishly. "That crazy bastard threatened to rip my heart out."

"Got one, have you?"

The traffic warden was unsympathetic. He hated the job, and hated all clampers with a vengeance. His own car, driven by someone else one particular day, had once been clamped in a seaside town. That was how he had subsequently discovered that his wife was having an affair . . . with a clamper from London.

"Anyway," he now said, "you can't clamp this one."

"Why not?" The clamper was beginning to feel cheated.

"You just can't, so put your balls back in the van."

The traffic warden looked pleased with himself.

Gallagher was relieved to see that Delphine Arundel was not at her desk. The way he was feeling, it would have been difficult to greet her civilly, and he did not want to take the foulness of his mood out on her. That was all for Fowler, arch-schemer and devious bastard.

He barged, unannounced, into Fowler's Spartan office. Haslam was there, looking expectant and amused at the same time.

Fowler looked up from his desk, and rose carefully.

"Hullo, Gordon," he greeted mildly. "Nice of you to make it. We're all dying to hear your news."

"Cut the crap, Fowler," Gallagher snapped, his eyes cold. He reached into his jacket pocket for the envelope that Borodin had handed him in Portugal and flung it onto Fowler's desk. "A present for you. I want you to tell me what the fuck this is all about." He glanced at Haslam as Fowler cautiously reached for the envelope and began to open it. "George."

Haslam gave a barely perceptible nod in acknowledgment, eyes shifting to Fowler, who was now extracting the contents of the envelope.

Fowler sat down again slowly, and stared at the document. No outward sign betrayed the turmoil that must have hit him, but both Gallagher and Haslam knew him well enough to realize that the presence of the document had given him a shock. Haslam even heaved himself out of the seat where he'd been lounging, to go over to the desk.

For a few seconds, Fowler made absolutely no movement, and then, like a striking snake, his free hand reached for a telephone.

"I want the senior officer-in-charge of Document Security *now!*" he barked into it, then slammed the phone down. For Fowler, this was supreme agitation.

It was the first time Gallagher had witnessed it. And judging by the expression on Haslam's face, it was the first time for him too.

Fowler looked up at Gallagher, eyes expressionless behind the glasses. "Where did you get this?"

"If you look very carefully at the bottom left of the first page," Gallagher began, twisting the knife, "you'll see a small annotation—almost faded enough to miss—in pencil. Someone, who should have known better, was careless with his or her allocation."

Fowler looked for and found the written annotation.

The faint inscription read: КГБ–Куззнсланд.

He was well versed in Cyrillic script, even its many variations, and understood precisely what the letters stood for.

Involuntarily, he gave a sharp intake of breath. "KGB—Queensland. The double *e* is Belorussian," he added pedantically. "Although some Ukrainians have been known to use it."

"That stands for the Queensland file," Gallagher told him in a voice totally lacking in emotion, "not for KGB personnel who might be in Queensland. Queensland is the killer's code name. It's supposedly written on the file cover, in English."

"The *KGB*—or whatever they've decided to call themselves these days—*handed* this, and the information, to you?"

"No," Gallagher replied, watching Fowler closely. "But that's the source. All potential targets are in that particular file, which is where *my* bloody confidential information was found."

"Jesus!" Haslam said quietly. Fowler had passed him the document. He looked at Gallagher after he'd scanned it quickly. "We can take it that this department is not your favorite organization at the moment."

"You have a nice line in understatement, George."

"For my sins." Haslam turned to Fowler as he put the document down gingerly. "I think I'll leave you two to sort this one out. I'm going to find me a cup of tea."

"Deserting the ship?" Fowler asked flatly.

"No. Just going for a cup of tea." Haslam went out.

A deferential knock sounded almost immediately after.

"Come!" Fowler ordered.

A smallish man with cropped hair and tufted silvery eyebrows entered. He had hard, piercing eyes and a proud, sharp nose that gave him the look of a small bird of prey.

"Ah. Slocombe," Fowler began in a voice so calm, it was a distinct warning.

Slocombe obviously realized this, for the bird-of-prey expression became wary. "Sir," he said uneasily.

"There are certain items of confidential material that you're cleared for access to Slocombe. I believe you'll recognize this." Fowler tapped at the document Gallagher had brought. "Take a look." He pushed at it with a finger. "This is not on the computer files."

Slocombe went over and began to read, then paled. He glanced nervously at Gallagher. High-grade docs were never put on the computer, in case of indirect hacking that bypassed the Department's rigorously secured, closed network.

"I . . . I don't understand, sir," he said to Fowler.

"That makes two of us," Fowler retorted coldly.

"But I would have booked it out myself."

"It's going to get even more unpleasant, Slocombe. You haven't yet heard how it got here. How's your Cyrillic?"

"Pretty good, sir."

"Then take a further look. Here . . . bottom left."

Slocombe did as directed, then gave a very good

impression of what a clean white sheet should look like.

"The *KGB? In Queensland?*" He spoke in a disbelieving whisper, but all kinds of emotions had laced through his words. Among them was the full appreciation of the kind of trouble he was in. As the person directly responsible after Fowler for the security of high-level staff documents, the buck was crashing unerringly towards him. "But that's impossible. I don't understand," he repeated.

"So you've already said," Fowler reminded him harshly. "And this is not about a unit in Queensland. It's a file by that name. Can you possibly imagine how this document got to me without your first having booked it out?"

"No, sir!"

Fowler paused deliberately, letting Slocombe stew. "Gallagher brought it in," he said at last, his voice still unnervingly calm. "And it came, Slocombe, from behind what used to be known as the Iron Curtain. It came from that KGB file I just told you about. How long it's been there is anyone's guess. For all we know, there may be other documents belonging to this department still in their hands. Can you throw some light on the proceedings, Slocombe?"

Slocombe had darted Gallagher a look full of anxiety upon Fowler's mention of how the document had arrived. Now, there was a sickly pallor upon his face as the enormity of the implications descended on him. His mouth hung open, making him look less like a bird of prey and more like a gaffed fish.

"N-no, sir," he stuttered, uncertain of what to say or do. "I just can't see how this could have happened. Nothing gets past me."

Fowler's eyes were cold steel behind the glasses. "I do hope that comment was a joke, Slocombe. Unfortunately, I'm not in the mood for jokes. The evidence is staring you in the face, man. *Something did get past you!*"

The sudden raising of Fowler's voice made Slocombe jump. He had nothing to say in his defense and his expression was now one of utter bewilderment.

"Well?" Fowler barked. "How do you explain it?"

"I . . . I can't."

Fowler just looked at him, then said, "An immediate investigation will be carried out. It will be thorough, I can promise you that. Consider yourself relieved until we've got *all* the answers. Hand over to James Gresham, then ask him to hold himself in readiness for my call. It does not mean that Gresham is less culpable than you are. For the time being I hold everyone responsible, until blame is conclusively apportioned. I shall inform General Crombie. How long have you been with this department, Slocombe?"

"Fifteen years, Mr. Fowler."

"Have a good think about that while you're on suspension. All right, Slocombe. Thank you."

"Sir."

Slocombe, after a parting and apologetic look at Gallagher, went slowly out.

Gallagher had been following it all with interest. The fact that Fowler, who normally addressed senior colleagues by their first names, had consistently used only the surname with Slocombe was clear evidence of both his anger and how greatly the incident had disturbed him.

Then again, it could have been yet another masterful display for Gallagher's benefit. Nothing was beyond Fowler. Gallagher was still not convinced that he was totally innocent. The deputy head of department may not necessarily have instigated the passing of the document, but it did not mean he knew nothing of its disappearance.

Fowler was speaking into another phone. "I want a

Sky Blue sent to all our people in the field. Of course immediately! What's the point of a Sky Blue if it's not to have immediate effect?" He put the phone down firmly.

A Sky Blue, Gallagher knew, was the Department's next-to-highest alert to agents in the field. It warned them of imminent war or discovery, and survival procedures were to be made ready. Sky Blue *Alpha* meant the shit had hit the fan and that predetermined actions, either to engage in clandestine warfare or to get out fast the best way available, would be set in motion.

Fowler looked up. "You've certainly brought us a hot potato, Gordon. Don't do things by halves, do you?"

"You created the hot potato. I didn't even know this existed in my files . . ."

"Come, come, Gordon. You're not a green recruit. We all have confidential files, myself and Crombie included. Someone, somewhere, has a file on us. The trick is to make certain it's not in the wrong hands."

"That's a laugh," Gallagher said. He pointed at the desk. "As far as I'm concerned, all that information about me was in the wrong hands, even when it was here."

"You should be flattered. Demonstrates our high regard."

"Isn't that interesting," Gallagher remarked bitterly. "Someone expressed the same opinion the other day."

"The person who passed this to you?"

Gallagher stared at him neutrally.

Fowler raised his glasses just high enough to clear the bridge of his nose, which he pinched at with forefinger and thumb before putting them back in place.

"Look . . . Gordon. There's just one person among our chummies on the other side of the divide with sufficient clout and regard for you who could have got this from a KGB file without making the effort a terminal one. So it must have been your friend Borodin, who, I remember, magically managed to give us the slip in Norway. You didn't help him get away, I suppose?"

"Suppose all you like. Borodin can look after himself."

"I don't doubt it. Pity, though. We might have learned quite a lot."

"Or nothing. He could have fed you anything."

"Granted. He could also have fed *you* this document."

Gallagher had thought that one out several times over. But he believed Borodin, up to a point. He said nothing of this to Fowler.

"Possibly. But that doesn't make it any less genuine, and there *is* a pro hit man on the loose."

"There is indeed," Fowler agreed heavily. "And I suppose you really do think we were responsible for what happened to your fiancée in France?"

"Perhaps not directly, but I have my suspicions. One day, I'll find out the truth."

"And then?" Fowler's eyes were unmoving.

"That's for you to wonder about."

Haslam returned at that moment, carrying a small tray with three mugs on it. Steam was rising out of each.

"See?" he began. "I did go out for the tea. Black coffee, no sugar for you, Adrian. Tea with milk and no sugar for you, Gordon, and black tea with sugar and lemon for me." He handed the mugs out. "And now, tell me you've sorted your differences." He took his seat, placing the empty tray on the floor next to him, and began to sip at the hot tea.

Fowler glared at the offending tray, but said nothing.

Gallagher remained silent, his anger in check but unabated.

"I see," Haslam commented. "Shall I go out again? I promise to make a better entrance—"

"Stay where you are, George," Fowler commanded. "I've had Slocombe in. I've also sent out a Sky Blue, and there's going to be an investigation."

"You have been busy."

"Now it's your turn," Fowler said to Gallagher. "Perhaps you can tell us about Portugal."

After some moments Gallagher told them, leaving out most of the details about Borodin's active involvement, except for the more obvious ones. He left out the description of the car the GRU general had driven, just in case it entered Fowler's head to attempt a trace. He made no mention of the backup Borodin had given during the shoot-out, nor of the fact that Borodin would again be in touch. He also said nothing of the rifle's properties. All things considered, he'd solved a substantial part of the mystery for them. He figured they should be grateful.

"You certainly appear to have made an implacable enemy," Fowler said when Gallagher had finished.

"I'm certain it's linked to what happened in the Outback, and my file was used to give him the trail. It's revenge by someone who was part of the group, but not out there at the time. It must be. That's why I'm going. I'll set my own trap."

"And that other business," Haslam said. "The other killings . . . It's a definite program?"

"Absolutely. But I've no idea to what purpose. I may find out while I'm down there."

"You can take the Citation," Fowler offered.

"Gosh. How you spoil me. What's the catch?"

"You'll need a second pilot to accompany Hammond for the long haul, and of course Sian and George will be going along, for moral support."

"Oh, will I?" Haslam remarked, feigning surprise.

"I'm glad the catch is out in the open," Gallagher said. "Bet the 'second pilot' will have other duties as well. No."

"What do you mean 'no'?"

"Maybe your tame millionaire's quite happy to allow you to use his corporate jet at will—God knows what you've got on him—but I can buy my own passage, thank you. As you can see by my supposedly *confidential* file, I've got the money. So thanks, but no thanks."

Fowler decided to polish his glasses. He took his time.

"Don't make life more difficult than it needs to be, Gordon," he said when he had put them back on. "I could ensure you have a very tough time indeed when trying to leave the airport after your arrival down under. The delays could last for . . . well, who knows?"

"He'd do it," Haslam said cheerfully. "He can be that kind of bastard. Can't you, Adrian?"

"I'd find a better way of putting it."

Gallagher's eyes held Fowler's. "I can get there without your help, and your knowledge."

"I have no doubt you could manage it. I know you have a network, and probably Borodin would help. But it would cost you time, and time, I believe, is not a commodity you can spare at the moment. I can place the Citation at your disposal and you can make your journey in great comfort, without running the risk of alerting your nemesis. Give you time to prepare your ground.

"In stopping him, you'll be stopping the killings and whatever scheme's been hatched on the other side. And of course, when you do kill him, we'll have that rifle." Fowler gave the tiniest of smiles. "You do remember the rifle, don't you?"

"Just find whoever sent my file extract down the line," Gallagher told him.

13

He was not even quite eighteen, but as a car thief, he was a supreme veteran. What was more, he had never been caught. No court had been graced with his name. No police officer had managed to apprehend him. In his hands, cars had miraculously vanished. Items carelessly left on display—radios, briefcases, wallets, even an expensive laptop computer that someone had once foolishly left on a backseat—had all fallen victim to his skilled hands.

As a computer whiz kid, he should have been planning a lucrative career. Including the laptop, he possessed six computers of different make and processing power at his home, none of them acquired legally. But there were a lot of other other whiz kids about, so job competition was fierce. And besides, he enjoyed the risks.

Not for him the insanity of joyriding. Waste of time, too high-profile, and could one day lead to an appointment with the police. Imagine being caught for doing something so stupid. People got killed—sometimes, even, those in the stolen car. He approached his activities with a businesslike degree of seriousness. It was a job.

He walked along the quiet gloom of the alley, having long since checked that no one was about. He was making for the big, pristine, dark Mercedes coupe parked at the end near a mews house, just behind a large sedan. For the moment, they were the only two cars in the narrow street. He could not have asked for a better opportunity.

He reached the Mercedes. It was discreetly marked with warning security stickers. Nevertheless, he tentatively tried the door. He always did that first. It was amazing, despite the number of cars that got stolen every day, how some people still left their cars unlocked, even after having had alarm systems fitted.

The Mercedes was unlocked. He assumed the owner either lived in one of the houses and thought the car was sufficiently safe or had simply forgotten to lock it. Tough.

He wasn't after the car itself. Even though the owner had left it open, the stickers showed there was at least one immobilizer operating. There wasn't going to be time to work at it. He would take that expensive-looking radio instead.

He climbed swiftly in, pulling the door softly shut in order to switch off the courtesy light, and got ready with the bent wire tool to tease the stereo out. From the twilight within the car he could just make out a small sign above the radio.

Beware of Dog, it warned.

He smiled. At least whosever vehicle it was had a sense of humor. He reached for the radio, but as soon as he touched it, it slid inwards.

Well, well, well, he thought. Whatever will they think of next? There were radios with fake covers, radios that were part of the dash, radios that were portable, radios that died as soon as you took them out, turning a pricey item into a lump of useless junk, although if you were lucky you could sometimes revive even those.

But this piece of merchandise was something else entirely.

As soon as he'd relieved the pressure on the radio, it had sprung back into place. He touched it again, and the performance was repeated.

He glanced swiftly about him. The alley was still quiet. No one was looking from the houses. He was not going to be defeated by any radio. This was a challenge.

A quick scrutiny with a tiny pencil torch showed no obvious mounting. He might have to leave it, after all; it was taking too much time. But he was reluctant to admit defeat. One more try. This time he held on to it to see what would happen.

It was a mistake.

The radio kept moving inwards, easily resisting his pull and dragging his hand into the opening slot. As soon as his hand passed the lips of the slot, two steel shutters moved up and down, trapping it.

"Oh, shit!" he exclaimed in sudden panic, and tried to withdraw his hand. But he was clamped neatly at the joint of the wrist, and the pressure was increasing. "Oooh, shit!" he said again as the metal tourniquet began to interrupt the blood flow. *"Oh, shit, my hand!"* He decided it was better to be caught than to lose the hand. He opened his mouth wide to scream for help.

"You like my radio?" a voice queried mildly.

He looked round. He was barely able to focus, through the pain and the level of light in the car, on what appeared to be the coldest eyes in the world. Then he saw the silenced gun.

"Oh my God! Oh God. No, no. Please! I'm sorry about the radio. Just let me go. Please just let me go!"

"I am sorry too. But you have seen my face."

"Oh God, oh God," he whimpered, babbling now. "I can't see you properly. Anyway, I won't tell anyone. I won't tell anyone. I promise I won't!"

"Of course you won't."

The automatic coughed once. The whiz kid was hit in the chest and died instantly. A small remote control attached to the car keys was pressed once and the shutters opened, releasing the dead hand. As yet, no blood from the body had spilled into the car.

"What have you done!" another voice exclaimed softly. "This is right outside one of our safe houses!"

"Don't panic, Siminiev. I didn't ask him to try and steal my radio. Get your driver. Let's move this thief into your car before he starts to bleed on my seat. You chose this place because of its relative isolation. It's just getting dark, and in an alley like this no one can properly see what's happening out here even in full daylight. Anyway, people don't like to get involved even if they do see."

If Siminiev thought he didn't want the blood of the dead car thief leaking into his own car either, he knew from experience to keep his mouth shut. With the help of the driver they moved the body as if dealing with a drunken friend.

"Get your staff to dispose of it," the killer said. "It is time that I leave for the airport. Send a driver you can trust—no, one *I* can trust—to pick up my car with the spare keys I have already given you and take it to the usual place until I return. And remind him not to smoke in my car. Very bad for his health." It was a warning that was not lost on Siminiev. "I'll leave the car park ticket in an envelope to be picked up at the airline information desk. The name on the envelope will be Paul Chandler . . ."

"I still think you should let us fly you out."

"No! I want some time by myself to think about the new battleground. I have been waiting for this for a long time, and I prefer the anonymity of an airline. I'm a first-class passenger; who's going to suspect me of being anything else?"

"No one," Siminiev agreed with some reluctance.

"Here. You'd better keep the pistol. It wouldn't do to

be stopped by airport security. Just make sure," the killer added, "that the rifle and my other weapons will be waiting by the time I arrive. I hate traveling unarmed."

"They will be."

"Good. Now I must go. The traffic should be easy. Get that body disposed of, and you can go back to pretending you're an attaché. I will see you when I return."

"So you'll be staying in this country for some time?"

"Any reason why I shouldn't?" Cold eyes bored into Siminiev's very soul.

"N-no. No."

The killer continued to stare at him for a long moment before entering the car and driving off without another word.

But the assassin code-named Queensland had not been telling the complete truth. In a scanner-proof compartment of the cabin luggage, packed within padding that effectively disguise it in the event of a search, was another pistol with a full load and extra ammunition. The weapon had always been carried and had successfully passed through airport scanners on all flights taken. This one was expected to be no different.

The killer *never* traveled unarmed.

While Gallagher's pursuer was relaxing in the first-class luxury of the Boeing 747-400, he was himself dozing high above the eastern Mediterranean in the Citation. Hammond was indeed accompanied this time by a copilot, but the newcomer—whom Gallagher did not recognize—was a hard-looking individual who somehow managed to look more like a commando than a corporate aviator. He'd introduced himself as Markston.

As there was now no space for her on the flight deck, Sian was spending most of the flight in the cabin, in a seat opposite Gallagher's. Two seats farther back,

Haslam was trying not to snore too loudly, and failing conspicuously.

When Gallagher had boarded the aircraft at Gatwick, Sian had met him with a huge smile, green eyes full of anticipation.

"We meet again," she'd greeted.

"Small world, isn't it?"

"Anyone would think you didn't like flying with us."

"Oh, I like flying with you. Private jet. Way to go. It's just that I have a thing about picking the time when *I* want to go. This, on the other hand, is being shanghaied in style."

"Might as well enjoy it, then."

"Might as well."

Gallagher now opened his eyes slowly and noticed Sian reading. At an altitude of 50,000 feet and a speed of nearly 600 miles an hour, the Citation was smoothly outstripping the much bigger airliners that were crossing the area several thousands of feet below. The cabin was so well kitted out, the subdued hum of the aircraft was a muted lullaby.

"So what are you reading?"

His sudden speech did not startle her. She was good.

She closed the book, smiling. "Just an airport novel."

"A novel about airports? Or one that can be bought there?"

"The second option."

"Any good?"

"It's all right, as these things go. The sexy bits are a little unbelievable. Well . . . I think so, anyway. Apparently, the author tried them out first." She gave a sudden giggle, remembering one example.

"A he, or a she?"

"A she. Some men must have thought it was their lucky day, if only half of this is really based on actual research. The jacket blurb says all of it was."

"Well then. She must have had a good time."

She gave him a look that said she wasn't sure whether he was joking or not. "Need anything to eat, or drink?"

"No thanks. I'm fine for now. You gave us quite a meal after takeoff."

"Long way to go yet. Just let me know."

"Will do."

She fell silent for some minutes, then asked suddenly, "You're not going to try to avoid me again when we land in Queensland, are you? You just might need us, you know."

Gallagher studied her carefully, wondering what was really behind the question.

"Why not wait and see?" he told her.

Gallagher reminded himself that once he'd got away from them after landing, he would beep his answering machine from a public phone to check if Borodin had left any message.

Hammond was an excellent pilot. He flew the Citation judiciously, using an altitude envelope of between 45,000 and 50,000 feet and taking advantage of high-altitude tail winds.

From time to time, he and Markston altered the cruising speed to achieve the best fuel economy with as high a rate of knots as possible. As a result, with a load of three passengers plus crew, they were able to stretch usage to three refueling stops instead of the four it should have taken, while still leaving an emergency fuel safety margin of over one hour's flying time.

Hammond left the controls to Markston and entered the cabin to speak with Gallagher.

"After our stop at Singapore," he began, "we can do the last leg all the way to Brisbane, although we could risk running on air even if we flew at optimum fuel-efficient altitude. I suggest we land first at Cairns, which nudges a thousand miles by air north of

Brisbane, and refuel there, just to be sure. I hope that won't upset your schedule, sir."

Gallagher, who had no desire to risk tumbling out of the sky through lack of fuel, shook his head.

"You're the pilot," he said. "Do what you think is best."

"All right." Hammond nodded, then returned to the flight deck.

Gallagher thought about Cairns. The location of the city, on north Queensland's eastern coast, had given him an idea. He wondered how far it was by road.

At 6 P.M. local time the next day, the Citation made a smooth touchdown at Singapore's Changi Airport. Gallagher had felt a faint twinge of nostalgia as the aircraft had curved over the Johore Straits. He had once been sent on detachment to Singapore, during his Service career.

The passengers left the aircraft just long enough to stretch their legs while it was refueled. They were soon back aboard, and with Markston at the controls, they took off for Cairns.

By the time Queensland's 747 had landed at Singapore, the Citation was already two hours into its flight time as it headed for Cairns.

Two flight attendants—one male, one female—were quietly discussing a female passenger, out of earshot.

"That Mrs. Gordon," the man sighed wistfully. "God . . . she's so beautiful!"

"Must be at least the tenth time you've gone into your routine, Kenny," his companion remarked wearily. "You need a cold shower. We've all seen the way you've been looking at her and being *so* attentive." There was a friendly, teasing edge to her remarks. "But I'm afraid you, and most of the other male passengers in first, can forget it. That's real class out there, with real money and a protective husband, I'll bet—if he's got any brains, knowing you predators are about—waiting for her."

"So? A man can dream."

"If I didn't agree with you that she is beautiful, I'd feel insulted watching that glazed look come into your eyeballs."

"You know you're my number one, Janie."

"In a hundred, perhaps," retorted Janie cheerfully. She knew her colleague very well indeed.

Johannesburg, South Africa, 2:55 P.M. local time, the same day.

A Boeing 747 heaved itself into the air, on its way across the Indian Ocean to Australia. It would first land at Perth in Western Australia, then travel on to Sydney. Those passengers continuing their journey would change aircraft for the flight to Brisbane. Among these were two men who sat in different parts of the airliner, several rows of seats from each other. They were total strangers, but one of them was aware of the other's identity. The unaware one was Piet Villiger, the Afrikaner intelligence man with whom Gallagher had teamed up during the escape from the Outback underground prison. The other man, a Portuguese citizen named Fernando da Silva, was Borodin.

There were another four people aboard, three men and a woman, who were also interested in Villiger's movements. They traveled in pairs, but were not on the same team. The man and the woman had tagged the two others as potential adversaries, but the men themselves knew nothing of this, occupied as they were with keeping tabs on Villiger. None of the four knew of Borodin's presence aboard the aircraft, and had they even noticed him board, would not have recognized him as anything more than just another passenger.

For his part, Borodin knew each for what he or she

really was, and the true reasons for their presence aboard the 747.

Hammond had returned to the Citation's cabin.

"Hope I didn't wake you."

"You didn't." Gallagher had shut his eyes, but had not been dozing.

"We've been over Australia for some time now," Hammond informed him, "and are just crossing the middle of the Gulf of Carpentaria, which at our current cruising speed puts us an hour from Cairns. Normally, there are no aircraft movements at this sort of time, but we've got clearance to land, take on fuel, and take off again for Brisbane."

"Everything's going like clockwork," Gallagher said.

Hammond grinned. "Just the way I like it. This is a beautiful plane. She's singing sweetly. Wish we could keep her for good," he added hopefully.

"You never know."

"Put in a word with Mr. Fowler," Hammond suggested.

"Me?"

"I think he'd listen to you, sir," Hammond said mysteriously, then returned to the flight deck.

Gallagher stared after him for a few moments before turning round in his seat to address Haslam, who was still asleep, or pretending to be. Across the aisle, Sian seemed genuinely so.

Gallagher remembered that despite Haslam's apparent equanimity when he'd arrived in the helicopter at the safe house near Oxford, the big man actually hated flying. Helicopters grabbed first place on Haslam's list of nightmare machines, followed by any small aircraft. Small, twin-engined biz-jets cruising high above vast, shark-infested oceans were a very close third. He coped by falling asleep.

"Are you awake, George?" Gallagher called in a whisper. "Or just pretending?"

"I'm doing what I've done throughout this journey,"

Haslam replied. "I'm imagining I'm still on the ground." In the subdued cabin lighting, his eyes remained shut.

Gallagher gave the benign and mildly superior smile of someone who had flown fast jets as a career. "Cheer up. We'll be landing again soon."

"Yes. I heard what Hammond said."

"Fowler must have sweet-talked somebody if we can land, refuel, and take off again so late, after all aircraft movements have stopped for the night."

Haslam straightened in his seat. "Fowler always looks after his own. You would do well to remember that from time to time, Gordon. Don't get me wrong: I've no illusions about him. Sometimes even *I* get the impression I should count my fingers after shaking hands with him, but . . . despite what you may think, he's always in your corner when things get really tough."

Gallagher was not convinced, but making no further comment, he waved a hand briefly in temporary surrender and settled back in his seat. He glanced across the aisle to see Sian watching him intently. In the cabin, the green eyes were dark.

Exactly one hour later and coming from the north, Hammond entered a right-hand circuit that crossed a mangrove swamp as he banked the Citation steeply over the waters of Trinity Bay, turning on finals for Runway 33 of Cairns International.

The fact that they were about to touch down on Australian soil sent a variety of emotions coursing through Gallagher, bringing with them memories of what had occurred in the Outback.

He glanced out of his window to see the lights of Cairns and the pinpoints of other lights on the islands of the Great Barrier Reef moving past above the right wing, as Hammond went in for a fancy approach. He also glimpsed the neat rows of mooring lights of what seemed like squadrons of small boats at anchor. Beyond the limits of the window, he saw in his mind the immense spread of the island continent, and the great expanses of water surrounding it. It was too much for him to take in all at once, and he concentrated instead on the real purpose behind his journey.

Even as Hammond leveled the aircraft for the touchdown, Gallagher could feel an eerie tingling along his spine. For days, an insistent nagging had been screaming for attention, but he had forced it out of his thoughts as being impossible. Yet, he felt that being shadowed by the code-named killer was at once being hunted and *haunted.* It was as if his subconscious was refusing to allow him to ignore what it already knew. Here in this huge land at the other end of the world, a cycle in his life was about to close and, if he survived it, a new one was about to begin.

He'd hoped Rhiannon would have been part of it. No chance of that now.

In London, Delphine Arundel walked slowly along the Mayfair street, looking at the gleaming shop fronts until she found the one she was looking for.

FRANCKE-MAYNARD FINE ART

She studied the elaborate, gold-bordered writing on the large window with secret amusement, then went in.

Francke-Maynard was on to her like a shark spotting a helpless flounder. She had stopped before a Mondrian and was scrutinizing it with interest.

"I see Madam likes bold strokes and colors," he began eagerly. It was an unfortunate way of putting it, but he had thrown caution to the winds in the hope of selling the expensive Mondrian.

"I like Mondrian," she told him, making him very happy indeed. "Especially this one."

Francke-Maynard was ecstatic. The thought of the

sale had banished his superciliousness to the wilds. Delphine Arundel possessed the sort of class he could only dream about. Here was *serious* money.

"Do you know why I like this one?" she asked mildly.

"No, Madam. But Madam shows great perception." He could not help himself. Years of unctuous patronizing had created a habit he could no longer break.

"The reason I like it so much," Delphine Arundel said, a new edge coming into her voice, "is because I've got it at home."

Francke-Maynard was horrified. "What is Madam *saying?*"

"Madam is saying someone's got a fake . . . and it isn't me."

He looked from Arundel to the painting and back again, mouth working noiselessly.

"It's impossible!" he blustered at last.

"If you say so, but I'd check with the people who sold that to you. I know where mine came from. It was a wedding present from my father, and I know where *he* got it. Now," she went on sweetly, "I'd like a word with Miss Jameson, please."

Francke-Maynard's eyes grew round. "Miss Jameson! Are you . . . are you an investigator?"

"Good heavens, no. I'm here to see Miss Jameson on an entirely personal matter. Could you get her, please?"

"What? Oh. Yes. Yes." Francke-Maynard backed away from the painting as if he half-expected it to grow claws with which to rake at him. "I'll . . . I'll see if . . ." He scuttled away, still staring at the offending piece of art and clearly wondering if he'd been fleeced by whoever had sold it to him.

Rhiannon came out soon after, and looked at Delphine Arundel uncertainly. "I'm Rhiannon Jameson. Can I help?"

"I might have known," Arundel began approvingly. "His choice of women is always good."

"I beg your pardon?"

"Gordon, my dear. I'm Delphine Arundel."

"Oh." Taken completely by surprise, Rhiannon blushed, a sudden streak of pink going from neck to cheek before fading almost as quickly.

"It's all right. I'm not a secret lover come to do battle with you. I've actually come to speak on his behalf. Is there somewhere we can go?" She held out her hand. "I don't think this place is . . ."

They shook hands, then Rhiannon glanced around. Francke-Maynard was not to be seen, but one of his assistants was talking to a customer.

"There's a coffee shop not far from here that I use," she said to Arundel. "Being Sunday, it shouldn't be crowded at this time of day. Eloise," she called softly to the assistant, "I'm going out for a moment. Tell Francis, will you?"

"Yes, Miss Jameson."

"Right," Rhiannon went on to Arundel. "Let's go. We've only just begun to open on Sundays. Francis has decided to *exhibit,* if you get my drift. No money actually changes hands today."

In the coffee shop, Rhiannon seemed to be restraining a giggle. "Whatever did you do to him? He came in looking as if someone had stolen his Ferrari."

"Someone may well have. At least the price of a Ferrari. The Mondrian's a fake."

"What?"

"I hope you didn't acquire it for him."

"No. I remember that acquisition well. He made the deal. He was all hyper-hyper about the purchase. He was certain he'd got a bargain and was looking forward to an enormous profit. The person he said he'd got it from was a City broker who'd been made redundant and who'd had to sell his home and most of its contents, at any price."

"I'm surprised he fell for such an old trick."

"He did a check. Very thorough. At least, he thought so."

"They were better. The sort of people who go in for that kind of con would have done their homework."

"Much as I like the idea of Francis being caught out . . ."

"He's your business partner. Don't you mind?"

"He's certainly not my business partner. I'm there strictly as a consultant on fine prints. Besides, he can take the loss. He'll sell a few pieces at higher prices to make up. It's still a mess, though. That should keep him awake for months."

"And?"

"There's no 'and.'"

"You're not involved?"

Rhiannon gave an uninhibited laugh. *"Francis?"*

"But I thought . . ."

The laughing stopped. "Gordon told you this?"

"Are we talking about the same person?" Arundel countered. "Gordon doesn't tell anyone anything, especially if it's personal. He carries his problems very close to—"

"Don't I know it."

"Bitterness?"

"Yes . . . and no. I don't know. Anyway, how do you know all this? Are you . . ." Rhiannon paused as realization dawned on her. "You're in his line of business. Is that how you know about me? Is there a file on me?"

"Not exactly."

"Exactly what's 'not exactly'?"

"Let's say I'm not in the field. Not my province. And no, there's not a file on you."

"But there are mentions of me . . . in his file."

"Yes. If you've ever filled in any kind of form, there's always a mention of someone else somewhere in your documents. We all have that."

"Perhaps, but not like this."

A silence descended between them as they sipped at their coffee, mentally assessing each other.

Then Arundel said, "Your parents died on Malta under strange circumstances, didn't they?"

"Yes."

"And have you talked to Gordon about one day looking into that for you?"

"How did you . . . Of course, the files."

"No. No files. I'm merely following a train of thought. So you did ask him."

Rhiannon nodded. "Yes."

Arundel looked about her, noting there were three men among the coffee shop clientele. "Would you have asked any of the men in here?"

Rhiannon looked at her, wondering what she was getting at. "Of course not."

"So you asked him because you knew it was the sort of thing he would be capable of handling. He is what he is, Rhiannon, and was like that before you met him. If you walked out on him because of his past, it doesn't make sense. His past brought you to him. You can't have it both ways."

Rhiannon said nothing.

"You've hurt him, you know," Arundel said after a while.

"Yes," Rhiannon admitted softly. "I know. I did something really horrible. I told him I was seeing someone else."

"And are you?"

Rhiannon looked surprised, as if she had never even contemplated the idea. "Of course not," she repeated. "I . . . I wanted time to think. I was feeling angry and I suppose I just lashed out."

Arundel stared at her. "You wanted time to think. Oh, very nicely done. First you walk out on him when he most needs you, then for good measure you rip him apart?"

"Don't make me feel worse than I do already."

"I'm sorry, Rhiannon, but I'm not going to make this easy for you. I don't know what your friends are like, or what kind of nonsense they've been putting into your head. I don't really care. You're either capable of making up your own mind, or you're not. I've seen it happen all too often. What matters . . . the *only* thing that matters . . . is what you and Gordon feel for each other. Ignore those friends, and listen to your own feelings.

"People spend whole lifetimes hoping for the one person that can give them what they're looking for. Most fail. But every so often, some strike it lucky. I'm not going to tell you it's all a perfect fairy tale. It couldn't possibly be. But there's an element of joy in knowing you have come close, even if it's as close as you're ever going to get. And sometimes, if that person's taken from you, you might even get another chance. When that happens, count your blessings over and over. Only idiots throw them away." Arundel paused. "Good heavens. Listen to me."

Rhiannon studied her closely. "You're in love with him."

"Don't be ridiculous! What would Gordon want with an old battle-ax like me?"

"Now *you're* being ridiculous. You're not much older than I am, and you're beautiful and sophisticated—"

"Out of the mouth of babes . . ."

"Don't try to cover up. You know I'm right."

Arundel studied her cup, then said, "I was much younger than my husband, you know . . . twenty when we got married. He was a captain, but already an acting major. Within a short time he was confirmed as a lieutenant colonel, young for the rank. Going places, his brother officers used to tell me. Then he was killed in Northern Ireland . . ."

"Oh, I'm so sorry . . ."

"It's all right. I'm fine. Many years now. I've learned to handle it. Peter and I . . . we had . . ." Arundel looked up at Rhiannon. "What I'm trying to say . . . what I'm trying to get you to understand is this: Don't squander what you've got. You never know when you might lose it. Don't waste the time, no matter how long or short.

"And do remember, you can never tell which it's to be. It's a form of roulette." She stood up. "I must get back. Listen to yourself, Rhiannon. Your *real* self, I mean, not what you imagine. I know people who've lost sight of what was really important, for things that were supposedly just over the horizon. We seduce ourselves with ideas of what we think we want, and by the time we've come to our senses, we've already lost the prize."

Arundel glanced about her, as if searching for answers.

"If you don't believe me," she went on, "take a good look at some of the faces you see in the very next wine bar you go into. You'll see plenty of missed opportunities marked on them. Very easy to spot . . . if you know what to look for. So if he wants to take you to live on some desert island, or in a tent up a bleak mountain . . . for God's sake, go with him. I'm assuming, of course, that you do love him."

Rhiannon put out a hand to touch Arundel. "And you? You love him too, don't you?" she insisted.

"Not the way you think."

"It *is* the way I think."

"No. That would have been very easy."

Rhiannon looked as if she wasn't quite sure whether to believe that. "And where is he now?"

"I can't tell you. But just be there when he gets back. He would have stuck by you."

There was the slightest of pauses. "You don't really like me, do you?" Rhiannon said. It was more of a statement.

Arundel looked down at her neutrally. "The question is not whether I do or not, but whether you like yourself. There's so much said about men causing women pain, but anyone with a bit of a brain knows it's frequently a two-way street. *People* cause each other pain. Now I really must be going. I'll do the coffee."

Arundel paid the bill and went out.

When Rhiannon returned to the art gallery Francke-

Maynard virtually pounced upon her, so great was his agitation.

"Does that woman know what she's talking about?" he asked sharply while she was still at the entrance.

"Do you mind if I come in off the street first, Francis?"

He backed away reluctantly for her to pass fully through the doors, but was at it again almost immediately.

"Well? Does she?" Suppressed rage boiled in his voice.

"Yes," Rhiannon answered, her mind on something else entirely. "She certainly does."

Francke-Maynard turned away, muttering to himself. Suddenly, the rage burst uncontrollably into the open and he began shouting. *"How could I possibly have bought a fake?"*

Fortunately for him, there were no customers present. The assistants, however, were transfixed with astonishment.

"It's all a question of knowing what's genuine," Rhiannon told him calmly, "and what isn't."

He rounded upon her, eyes bloodshot with fury. "Don't you dare presume to tell *me* about art!"

"Actually, Francis, I wasn't thinking of art."

In Gallagher's Holland Park home in London, a message was waiting on the anwering machine. The caller had left no identification.

"He . . . is a *she,*" the caller had said urgently. "I repeat . . . he is a *she!* Will attempt to discover more."

The caller had then hung up. There had been no need for identification.

It was Borodin.

14

Hammond made another of the smooth landings that Gallagher had by now come to expect. The Citation was taxied to a space in the general aviation area, well away from the international and domestic terminals on the far side of the runway, and the engines began to spool down. Sian went to the door and opened it onto the night. A waft of warm air entered the cabin. After Singapore, the night air of tropical Queensland was welcome for its lack of humidity.

"Stretch our legs while Hammond and Markston see to the refueling?" Haslam suggested.

Gallagher left his seat to approach Haslam's. "You just want to get onto terra firma as quickly as possible," he said.

"There is that," Haslam admitted. "But also something I want you to see." A small case was on his lap, about the size of a large medium-format camera. He tapped at it. "Brought this along. Now that it's dark, we need to be outside for it to be demonstrated properly."

Sian was waiting by the door, looking out. "Something coming," she said. Her stance, though apparently relaxed, revealed an alertness that Gallagher fully recognized.

Even as she spoke, lights flashed briefly into the cabin as an approaching vehicle headed towards the aircraft.

"Fuel bowser?" Haslam queried.

"That's coming too, but it's still some distance away. This one's a car."

Haslam put the case down and slid it beneath the seat ahead of him. "Better leave this for the moment."

The car drew to a halt and the headlamps were turned off. Footsteps sounded, then someone climbed up the aircraft steps. Sian moved back to allow in a man of wiry build in shirtsleeves and a tie that hung from an open collar.

He smiled at her before turning to Haslam and Gallagher. "G'day, gentlemen. Or perhaps I should say good evening. Welcome to Cairns, Queensland, and Australia," he greeted expansively. "My name's MacAndless, and I've been instructed to give you every cooperation." He didn't say what organization he belonged to. He held out a hand, first to Gallagher. "You're Mr. Gallagher . . ."

They shook hands.

". . . and you're Mr. Haslam, of course." MacAndless shook hands with Haslam. He then turned to Sian, the hand again outheld. "I promise you I haven't forgotten my manners."

"I'm sure you haven't," Sian told him as they too shook hands. She didn't give her name, and he didn't ask. She remained alert.

MacAndless once more turned to Haslam and Gallagher. "Well, gentlemen? How can I be of service? It's a fair bet you're not here after the black marlin, as it's not the season and you wouldn't be even if we were in the season. So you're after a different kind of game fish, I reckon."

"If you can get us refueled and off again as quickly as possible," Haslam said, giving nothing away, "that would be a great help."

MacAndless took that with good grace. "Being done. The fuel truck is on its way. Anything else?" He was eagerness itself, keen to get in on whatever the action was.

Gallagher was still working on a flexible strategy, in which the Cairns location seemed increasingly likely to play a part.

"Not for the time being, thanks," he now said to MacAndless, "but we might well need you later. We'll know after Brisbane."

MacAndless grinned. "I'll hold you to that. This is just a house call to let you know we're around and ready to help. Now I'll leave you to get on with it." He again shook hands all around. "Nice to have met you." He looked at Gallagher. "Anything at all, just sing out."

"I'll hold *you* to *that.*"

"Hope I don't live to regret it."

You and me both, Gallagher thought as MacAndless, with another quick grin, made his way out of the aircraft.

Gallagher waited until he'd heard the car start and move away. "Know of him?" he asked Haslam.

"I know the name, but he could be anyone, of course."

There was the growing noise of the approaching fuel truck, then the hiss of air brakes as it stopped close to the Citation.

"We've been allowed to land," Gallagher said, "the fuel's here, and we haven't been visited by the Customs people. It's reasonably safe to assume that MacAndless, whoever he's with, at least has some clout."

"Reasonable, but let's not get too complacent."

"I never am," Gallagher said.

Hammond was coming from the flight deck.

Haslam picked up the case. "Time to sample the Queensland night air and leave our pilots to deal with the refueling. Coming, Sian?"

"No. I'll stay aboard, if that's okay."

"Fine by me."

Gallagher followed Haslam out. Hammond came down the steps after them and went up to the fuel truck.

As they moved some distance away from the airplane, Gallagher looked up at the clear, starlit sky. The scent of sea air filled his nostrils. It was strangely peaceful.

He sniffed appreciatively. "Wish I could enjoy this, instead of working out how to trap a killer." Then the bowser began its whine and the fumes of aviation fuel filled the night air.

"I've got a little item that might help," Haslam said. "Being the tropical north of Queensland, this sort of darkness is perfect, even with airport lights." He removed something from the case. "Here."

He handed over a heavy set of goggles which had a one-piece outer lens, rather like a mask intended for snorkeling. Inside, twin inner mirror lenses kept the whole structure shallow so that in use, it would protrude no farther than a real snorkeling mask. A single expandable strap, anchored by forked sidepieces, kept it firmly attached to the wearer.

"Put them on," Haslam prompted. "There's a switch on the right, near the corner of your eye. Press that."

Gallagher put on the strange goggles and discovered they did not feel heavy when worn. He could see nothing but sheer blackness. He felt for and found the flush button, then pressed it as Haslam had directed.

The night was transformed. Suddenly, he could see. In infrared.

He looked about him. Everything was clearly defined on a palest field of red. The Citation, the fuel truck, Hammond, and the driver were all sharply visible. There was good peripheral vision too. Over to his right and eastwards beyond the main 15/33 runway, he could see the terminals and the control tower, parked aircraft, vehicles both moving and stationary, and even tire marks close by, very clearly. Straight ahead to the left of the runway was the airport fire station. The faintest of hums, barely perceptible, came from the goggles.

"Bloody hell," Gallagher exclaimed softly. "Does it see through walls as well?"

"Thought you might appreciate it," Haslam said. "If you remember the infrared camera you used during the Windshear business on Skye, this little kit picks up where it left off. Fowler thought you might need something to give you a bit of an edge against the monster rifle. Those are zoom lenses in there, though obviously the range is nowhere near that of the rifle itself. But it's something your opponent knows nothing about, and that's a tactical advantage. I've got the feeling you intend to operate at night wherever possible."

"Yes," Gallagher admitted, as he continued to discover what the goggles could do. "And this will certainly help. But what if *I'm* being scanned? Is there any bloom that might make it a dead giveaway to a sniper's scope? If there is, you might as well take it back. Someone sighting on this could put his first shot right through my bloody thinkpot."

"No chance of that happening. The beauty of these goggles is that there's no bloom escaping from them. Many night sights, as you know—like starscopes and the like—are image intensifiers, or light gatherers. Some do betray their presence with a faint green glow. This does not. There are no emanations whatsoever that can be picked up."

"What about sound? I can just about hear the faintest of hums. An acoustic scope—"

"Would have to be damned big—which means too heavy to be man-portable—and exceedingly accurate to pick this up. However, it has a built-in upgrade, just in case in the near future some demented but smart boffin who should know better manages to come up with a miniature system that could do the job. That faint hum is the cooling system. The entire unit operates on solar energy and needs only the barest exposure to even weak sunlight to keep it fully powered up. At the corner of the left eye is an identical switch. Press that."

Gallagher did so, and the hum disappeared.

"The noise is gone," he said.

"It's still there, but it's being countered. Result, no *audible* sound and nothing for any detector to pick up, even if one of the necessary sensitivity existed. The button right between your eyeballs is the zoom switch. Press for as long as you want to determine the range, and press again at the limit to reverse the process. Well? Are you pleased?"

"I am. I am!" Gallagher tried all the switches alternately and on zoom, the airport images seemed to come right up to his face. The zoom function was completely silent in operation.

"That's an addition to the weapons case. Don't bloody lose it, for God's sake. Now the rest is up to you. When you get the rifle, we'll have two quite interesting pieces of kit."

Gallagher made no comment about the rifle as he turned the goggles off and removed them. He had to blink several times to get his eyes readjusted to the available light, and didn't like that at all. He put the goggles back on, switched on, then switched off again, this time shutting his eyes briefly. He took the goggles off for a second time and when he'd opened his eyes, found there was no need to adjust. He was relieved.

It would be no fun if for some reason the thing fell off while someone was drawing a bead on you, he mused, making you temporarily as blind as an earthworm, and just as vulnerable.

"So, George," he began as he handed the infrared night-sight back to Haslam, who returned it to its case, "with all the rumors about more openness in your line of business—"

"Yours too . . ."

"Not anymore, old chum. So what's going to happen to the Department? Is Fowler going to come into the full glare of parliamentary light and start giving press conferences?"

"Some hope," was Haslam's reply. "This is where the earthworm principle takes over."

"I was just thinking about those."

"Strange beast, the earthworm. Nature hasn't totally abandoned it to its fate, leaving it defenseless against all predators. Imagine a line three inches long on a piece of paper. Imagine rubbing out an inch, and saying that's a degree of openness. Now you're left with two inches. You may reasonably assume that rubbing out the remainder will signify that total openness has been achieved. But there's a catch. As we both know, there always is.

"Just suppose, after rubbing out the first inch at one end, you were to *add* a new inch at the other. You've got your three inches back, but the position of the line has shifted. That's my earthworm principle."

Gallagher gave a short laugh. "And I thought I was the cynic around here."

"I prefer 'realist,'" Haslam said. "As I told you on that steel tube you call a plane, it's sometimes worth checking to see now and then that all your fingers are still intact." He paused, staring in the direction of the refueling vehicle. "We'd better get back aboard. Looks as if our Pegasus has drunk its fill, and Hammond might panic and think we've been abducted."

As if on cue, the fuel truck began to move away and Hammond appeared by the door. As they approached, they saw that he was indeed looking anxious.

"Thought the Aussies had nabbed you," Hammond remarked as they climbed aboard.

"They're not a republic yet," Haslam told him. "They're on our side. For now," he added portentously.

But the stirrings of Australian republicanism were

not really on his mind. For the moment, there were other matters to concentrate upon.

Like when Gallagher was intending to strike out on his own.

Haslam was certain that Gallagher had already decided to lose them sometime after arrival at their destination. It was simply a question of waiting to see exactly when that would happen.

Within a short time, the Citation was lifting off the runway and heading south for Brisbane.

They were just over thirty minutes from Brisbane when Gallagher turned to Haslam, who had swapped seats with Sian when they'd left Cairns.

"Best if we're not seen together in Brisbane," he began.

Haslam was impassive, waiting for more.

"They're bound to have people watching the airport," Gallagher continued into Haslam's silence, "even at this time of night. In their place I would, and I don't want them to see who's with me. I suggest I leave the airport on my own, openly. I want them to know I've arrived. The rest of you, I'm sure, can find a way of leaving without being seen, sometime after. If they don't know my backup, it will be more of a surprise for them when the time comes."

"Makes sense," Haslam conceded. "But how do we keep in touch? Would you like a radio?"

"No. No radios. I'll keep in touch. Just leave me a contact number."

"Fine." Haslam seemed unperturbed.

Too easy, Gallagher thought. Haslam was planning something. But whatever it was, it wouldn't work.

"Happy with that, are you?" Gallagher asked mildly.

"I'm happy if you are. We're here to assist."

"Oh, good. That makes me feel really secure."

Then the note of the engines changed perceptibly as

Hammond prepared for the descent. Haslam gripped the sides of his seat and began to look anxious.

All landings, for him, were the worst of times.

Haslam need not have worried. Hammond had decided to carry out the landing himself and as a result, the Citation's wheels touched the runway with barely a tremor.

Haslam slowly opened his eyes as the aircraft taxied to its parking space.

Gallagher had been watching him. "If you hate flying so much, George, why did you come on this long trip? You've only got to do it all over again to get back to the UK."

Haslam stifled a groan. "Don't remind me. And I didn't have a choice. I'll be fine once my feet are on solid ground, though the jet lag will probably wreck me," he went on grumpily. He glanced back to where Sian was sitting, looking at ease with herself. "Jet lag doesn't seem to worry you two."

"Some have it, and some don't," Gallagher said.

Haslam frowned at him. "Very witty."

The aircraft had again been directed to the general aviation apron. It came to a stop and Sian released her seat belt to perform her routine with the door. Someone bounded up the steps almost before she'd got it completely open.

A very tall man of indeterminate age, crouching to enter, appeared and stood in the aisle. He was smartly dressed in a lightweight, pale suit. He had to lean against the backs of the seats to give himself head-room, despite the cabin's generous clearance.

"Gentlemen," he began to Haslam and Gallagher, "I'm your welcoming committee. I hear you've met Jock MacAndless. I offer you the same cooperation. My name's Ansen, Patrick. I'm an Australian of Irish-Swede parentage and no, no one calls me Paddy. If we're going to be friendly—which I prefer—it's Jan, which is what I've been called since childhood. 'Jan' with the soft Scandinavian *j.* Challenging for a boy growing up in Oz, but I could look after myself."

As he watched Ansen, Gallagher did not doubt it. Boyhood bullies would have quickly learned prudence.

"If we're going to be formal," Ansen continued, "it's Major Ansen."

The outside air that had come into the cabin, Gallagher noted, was perceptibly lower in temperature than at Cairns. He continued to study Ansen, waiting for Haslam to speak first.

Ansen had a narrow head topped with crisply barbered hair that seemed reddish blond in the cabin lighting. His features were sharp but the nose was shorter than one might have expected, with flared nostrils. His mouth, wide but firm, seemed slightly off center. His eyes gave the impression of being permanently narrowed, as if everything before them was due for inspection. Gallagher decided that Major Ansen's presence at an interrogation would make many a suspect extremely uneasy, not because Ansen appeared to be promising violence but simply because he looked as if nothing that was said would be believed.

This, Gallagher decided, would be a tough man to fool. Given a choice, he would gladly have swapped Ansen for the more easygoing MacAndless. On the other hand, MacAndless's apparent bonhomie could well have been just another smoke screen.

After all, Gallagher thought, I use all sorts of smoke screens myself.

He was planning to use one very soon.

"Let's start with Jan," he heard Haslam saying, "and see how we go from there."

"Agreed," Ansen said.

"I'm George, and the young lad over there—to me he's a young lad—is Gordon, but you'll have had that information already. Our young colleague by the door is

Sian. Up front are Hammond and Markston, our pilots."

They began to shake hands.

Ansen turned the suspicious eyes upon Gallagher when it was Gallagher's turn. "A few years ago, you had that little problem in the Outback." It was not meant as a question. Ansen held on to the hand, as if somehow that would help him detect hidden information.

"You were involved?" Gallagher looked right back at him.

"I was in the team that came in to collect the bodies. You did a thorough job. There were plenty lying around. I was a lieutenant sniffing at my captaincy at the time." Ansen released the hand to give Sian the briefest of handshakes. "Sian." His attention returned to Gallagher. "And so, Gordon, what are your plans? It appears that little episode has come back to haunt."

Gallagher felt a chill go through him, but gave no outward sign. Did Ansen know more than he was prepared to disclose?

You're paranoid, Gallagher. It was just a casual comment.

Gallagher decided to let it pass, but casual or not, the remark had raised the level of his alertness considerably.

"Looks like it," he now said to Ansen. "But my immediate plans are to find me a nice bed and sleep off this jet lag."

If Haslam thought that particular remark—especially after their earlier conversation before the landing—suspicious in the extreme, he gave no sign.

"That goes for all of us," Haslam put in, following Gallagher's lead smoothly. His expression, which was no pretense, still showed the effects of the landing and gave added weight to his words. "Why don't we all meet later during the day? It's been a very long flight and I just want to get off this plane."

Ansen thought about that, and obviously considered it reasonable. He nodded his crisp head. "Righto. I've got transport waiting to take you wherever you'd like to go. There are hotels with which we have arrangements, and there's a house we can use. The choice is yours."

"I'll have one of the hotels," Gallagher said. "The others can have the house, and I'll need a contact number."

Ansen looked at Haslam, who nodded.

"Seems okay," Ansen said. "The hotel for you, the house for your colleagues. Shall I assign someone to you?"

Gallagher shook his head. "No thanks, and for the same reason I gave George: I don't want whoever's out there to know what my backup looks like."

"You're taking a chance."

"Life is one big chance. I'd like to leave the airport normally, and not in one of your cars. I'll take a taxi, if there's one at this time of night."

"I'll drive you over to the domestic terminal," Ansen offered, "staying airside. You can then walk through to the rank. There should be a taxi or two, either still hanging around or early birds waiting for the dawn arrivals. Black and white, or yellow cabs. I can arrange to have one of my men drive it. He'll take you to the hotel. No one need be the wiser. To anyone watching, he'll just be another taxi driver."

"I'm happy with that," Gallagher said.

It was worth giving Ansen something, if only to get away as quickly as possible. He knew Ansen's man would also lurk around afterwards, but for the time being that would not matter.

"Then we'd better get the show on the road," Ansen said.

Fifteen minutes later, Gallagher walked alone towards the cab rank outside the terminal. There were three taxis waiting. Two were black and white, one of which was first in line.

He carried his travel bag and the weapons case. By removing the infrared goggles from its own case, he was just able to find room in the briefcase to fit it in. As he reached the cab rank, he paused to put the travel bag down and looked vaguely about, as if waiting for someone to pick him up. In reality he was scanning the parked cars to check if anyone was on airport watch. Most of the cars were in the long-term car park.

He saw a man leaning against a car, talking to another behind the wheel. The man took no interest in him, but an infinitesimal shiver coursed through Gallagher. The men could easily be airport staff, he knew, but there were already two specifically designated areas on either side of the long-term park, with plenty of spaces. Airport staff would not be where these men were waiting.

"Taxi, sir?"

The driver of the first cab had got out and was approaching, hand reaching for the travel bag, which he picked up. Was this Ansen's man? He was of medium height with dark hair, and had the build of a rugby player.

Gallagher remained primed. "Er . . . yes, please."

He let the driver take the bag, carry it round to the back of the cab, and place it in the trunk.

"And the briefcase?"

"I'll keep that." If the driver turned out to be neither a bona fide taxi driver nor Ansen's man, there'd be a nasty surprise coming out of the case. "Thanks," he added as the driver slammed the trunk shut, then opened a rear door.

Gallagher climbed in and settled in one of the backseats. He snapped on the seat belt. The driver returned behind the wheel and the taxi moved off.

Gallagher did not look back at the men he'd spotted at the parked car. If they had been on station to await his arrival, the surveillance might have been established for days, using rotating shifts. They may well have expected him to spot them, in which case they would remain where they were and simply report his presence, along with the details of the taxi, which another car would follow.

The cabdriver remained silent as they headed out on the thirty-minute drive to the hotel. Gallagher found that odd. A real taxi driver would have at least asked if this had been his first time to Brisbane. Surreptitiously, Gallagher began to open the case.

"I'm John Rapicci," the driver announced abruptly. "You're very still back there. Got a gun?"

"If you're the person I hope you are, you've nothing to worry about."

Rapicci's laugh was nervous. "You don't mess around, do you."

"No."

"Well, I am Major Ansen's man. Ever been to north Queensland?"

No point in saying he'd landed at Cairns. "No."

"Well, my folks come from there. The cane fields."

"My mother came from a family that owned a cane plantation," Gallagher said, to keep the conversation going. If he kept Rapicci talking, he might glean some idea of what the good major was up to. "But on the other side of the world."

"So we've got something in common."

Gallagher would not have gone that far, but he let the remark pass.

"The grandparents were Italian immigrants," Rapicci continued. "My parents named me Gianni, which I'm sure you know is John in English. I'm usually called Johnno by my mates, sometimes Rapi. Someone called me Rapist once. I decked him."

What was this sudden trend with people having problems with their names? Gallagher wondered. First there was MacDuff in London, then Ansen, and now Rapicci. Must be the season for it.

"So what do I call you?"

"Johnno, or Rapi will do."

"Johnno it is." Gallagher shut the case quietly.

Another silence descended within the taxi. Gallagher took a quick look through the rear window. Rapicci noted it.

"Expecting to be followed?"

"I expect the unexpected. Always."

"A man who takes no chances."

"Something like that."

More silence came between them as Gallagher decided he'd definitely have to lose Rapicci. It was as certain as anything could be that Ansen had instructed his man to stay close.

They were now entering the city itself and Gallagher peered out at the elegantly well-separated, tall buildings that gleamed in the lights of the night. Gallagher decided he might as well give Rapicci the bad news. "Johnno," he continued, "I know the major ordered you to stay close to me, but I'm going to have to lose you. I have my own way of doing things . . ."

"The major said you would."

"Did he also tell you to stay close?"

Rapicci shrugged. "I was told to do my best."

"I hate doing it to you, but I've got to."

"Perhaps I can help. An extra gun . . ."

Gallagher shook his head. "I don't want you dying on me. These people are rough. Very rough. Australia needs you alive."

"Whoever they are, they're on *my* soil. That makes it my job. There isn't a choice."

"Then you're going to have to keep up. I won't be waiting around for you. If I set out to lose you, I will."

"No worries. I'll take my chances."

"Well, you've been warned. For now, when we get to the hotel I'm going to sleep."

"I'll be on watch."

Gallagher stared at Rapicci through the mirror. "*You'd* better not go to sleep. You might not wake up."

Gallagher hoped Rapicci took the warning to heart. Because he hadn't spotted a tail didn't necessarily mean they hadn't been shadowed in relays from the airport. Rapicci dozing in the beaconlike black and white taxi would be easy meat.

15

The hotel that Ansen had instructed Rapicci to take Gallagher to overlooked Town Reach on the Brisbane River, and was next to a trendy café that had not long ago shut for the night. However, its white tables and chairs, with their white, opened parasols, were still in place on the pavement, as if awaiting ghostly diners. No lights came from within the café itself, and no staff members were about.

Rapicci had made the journey from the airport in twenty minutes. He now parked the taxi in relative shadow just beyond the tables, so that it faced the hotel entrance. There were noises of the city and the river all about him and some way off, like the cry of a lonely creature in the wilderness seeking its way home, he heard the plaintive sound of a police siren. But generally, the city was having the last of its sleep before rousing itself to greet the new day.

There was no one to be seen in his immediate vicinity, and even the hotel entrance, despite its bright lights, appeared drowsy. After just over an hour of sitting, he began to relax a little.

He was thus taken completely by surprise when someone tried one of the rear doors.

Prudently, Rapicci had locked all the doors from the inside, except his own. As he looked about to check, the man who had tried the door came round to his side of the taxi.

"I'd like to go to a casino," the man said. "Do you know a good one that's still open?" The accent was not Australian.

"Sorry, mate," Rapicci told him pleasantly. "I'm off duty. I'm just having a quiet nod till I go back on." Trust his luck to get a bloody lost tourist.

"Couldn't you do that for me?" the man pleaded. "I can't find another cab . . ."

"No worries, mate. I'll just call one up for you. No extra charge. A few minutes, and he'll be here. You really need casino city down south. Surfer's Paradise. All the casinos you want. If you don't mind, mate, I'd suggest you catch up on some sleep and start the night afresh. Just give me a couple of ticks to call—" Rapicci stopped when he saw the gun. "Shit," he finished softly.

"Shit is right," the man said in a harsh voice, then ordered sharply, "*Open the door!*"

"All right, all right. Don't get your strides in a twist."

"Touch that phone and you're dead."

"I won't even look at it."

Rapicci's mind raced, thinking of ways to get out of his predicament. But the strange man appeared to know exactly what was going on.

"It would be futile," he said in the harsh voice as he got into the back, "to think of doing anything stupid. You'll be dead before you finish."

"Like saying that, do you?"

"Shut up and drive!"

"Yes, sir. Where to?"

"You think this is funny?"

"Nope."

"Then don't give me any smart-ass comments. I'll direct you. You go where I say."

The voice sounded American, but didn't *feel* American, Rapicci thought.

"Fair enough," he said, as calmly as he could.

Rapicci wondered whether he'd get a chance to call the major. He'd have to wait for the right time to make the move. But the man in the back of the taxi didn't look like someone who would give chances easily.

Like a strident alarm bell, Gallagher's earlier warning pealed in his mind.

At 0545, the 747 landed at Brisbane International. As he stood with his female colleague to wish the departing passengers good-bye, the flight attendant received a ravishing smile from the latest object of his lustful desires.

"Oh God!" he groaned softly as he watched her walk away. He had offered to carry her hand baggage, but she'd politely refused him.

There was a small gap in the string of people and Janie, her air hostess smile fixed upon her face, glanced at him.

"You sound as if you're in pain, Kenny."

"What kind of luck does a man need to get a wife like that? That walk of hers is a killer. Mr. Gordon is one fortunate bastard."

"Thanks, Kenny," Janie said coldly. "You know just how to say all the right things."

"Aw, look, Janie. No disrespect intended. We're mates. You know what I mean."

"I know exactly what you mean, you shit."

The smile remained in place for the next passenger.

▪ ▪ ▪

The woman who had traveled as Mrs. Gordon was met by a limousine. She climbed elegantly into the back. A traffic cop was standing a short distance ahead, his parked motorcycle leaning on its rest. He watched the flash of her legs with wistful interest, giving him a good start to his day. He continued to watch idly as the driver loaded the huge trunk and shut it before getting in behind the wheel.

"Is everything arranged?" she asked of the driver as the car moved off.

"All in place and awaiting your instructions."

"And my target list?"

"That has arrived, and is also awaiting you."

"Good. I shall work through it after I've attended to Gallagher."

"Pardon me, but is that really wise? Wouldn't it be better to first eliminate the targets, then concentrate on Gallagher? There would be no distractions . . ."

The frostiness of the silence in the car was so palpable, the man stopped talking as if he'd suddenly been slapped across the face.

Then he tried to redeem himself, which made it much worse. "Er . . . what I really mean—"

"I'm assuming," she began in a voice that raised the hairs on the back of his neck, "that your comment suggests you feel I might not survive the encounter with Gallagher . . ."

"No! I—"

"Don't snivel your way out of it! I have an agenda that has served me well so far. You will not again attempt to tell me what to do. *Is that clear?*" The last words were so softly spoken that, despite the emphasis, he almost didn't hear them.

"Yes. Yes!" Like Siminiev before him, the man had a strong instinct for survival and knew when it was prudent to retreat.

"Now we've got that straightened out, has he arrived?"

"He has, and we've identified his hotel."

"Any problems?"

"None at all," said the man who had taken Rapicci.

The traffic policeman followed with benign eyes the stately progress of the vast stretch Mercedes until it had glided its way out of his line of sight.

The limousine drove on to a secluded house in one of the more exclusive suburbs of Brisbane.

In the specially built, cavernous trunk of the car was Rapicci's still-warm body.

Gallagher had been pleasantly surprised to find that Ansen had selected a very comfortable hotel. His room had a really splendid view of the river, and its furnishings displayed just the right amount of luxury. He'd taken a long shower and immediately after had gratefully climbed into the large, sumptuous bed. He'd decided he'd check his answering machine when he woke up, but wouldn't call from the hotel.

Barely an hour later, it felt like, the phone on the bedside cabinet began to ring. He took his time answering it, hoping whoever it was would give up. But the ringing persisted. Once he'd decided to pick it up, he was sharply alert. He checked the digital display of the clock radio that was itself part of the top half of the bedside cabinet. 0640. He'd actually been down for nearly three hours.

"Yes?" he grumbled unenthusiastically into the phone, pretending to stifle a yawn.

"It's Jan," came Ansen's voice. "We're down in the lobby. We're on our way." Conversation ended.

Gallagher stared at the receiver. "'We'?" He replaced it, then reluctantly began to put some clothes on.

Soon after, Ansen was knocking on the door. "It's Jan."

Gallagher opened the door and found a surprise in

the shape of Haslam, waiting with the tall major.

"What have you done with Rapicci?" Ansen immediately demanded as he strode in.

Haslam followed at a saunter, closing the door quietly behind him. The look he gave Gallagher was neutral.

"I've done nothing with him," Gallagher said to Ansen, making a show of stifling another yawn and talking through it. "He's playing watchdog outside. I tried to dissuade him, but he insisted. Said you'd ordered it. He's parked somewhere in that taxi you gave him."

"He's not outside," Haslam said.

Gallagher became absolutely still. "What?"

"He's supposed to call in every two hours," Ansen said. "He's missed the last two checks. The second was due ten minutes ago. I told him there'd be some leeway if he missed the first, but that he'd better have a bloody good reason. Missing the second . . ."

Gallaghed sighed. "There are times when I despair, and I do wish people would listen sometimes. You offered us cooperation, but did one of the very things I'd hoped you wouldn't: You gave me a minder whose real purpose was to keep tabs on me. Now I think Australia may well have lost herself a valuable son."

"What do you mean by that?" Ansen's narrowed eyes zeroed in on Gallagher.

"I mean you've probably got him killed."

"Now look here . . . !"

"If I may," Haslam interrupted quietly. "Gordon could be right," he continued to Ansen. "Not about your getting Rapicci killed, of course, but that we should seriously consider the possibility that he might indeed be dead."

Haslam's words, though mildly spoken, contained within them a brutality that left Ansen visibly shaken.

"I think we should start looking for him," Haslam suggested in a gentler tone as Ansen stared at him. "The sooner the better, just in case we may be in time." His real feelings were that it was already far too late, but he didn't think it fair to Ansen to say so.

But Ansen was wasting no time. A tall French window in Gallagher's hotel room opened out onto a high-railed balcony. He went up to the window, opened it, and went onto the balcony to issue snapped orders into his closed-net personal radio. He returned soon after, closing the doors behind him.

"I'm coordinating the search," he said to both Gallagher and Haslam. "The boys from Eagle Farm—"

"Eagle Farm?" Gallagher queried.

"The police air wing," Ansen explained. "They've put a chopper at our disposal. Rapicci was also a copper, from a special unit and seconded to me. You may have made your point, Mr. Gallagher—"

"Not the way I wanted to. And first names, please," Gallagher reminded him mildly. "Remember?"

Ansen seemed to swallow his next words, then went on, " . . . Gordon. You may have made your point, but please don't run amok on my territory."

"People are always saying that to me. I wonder why?"

"Just keep me in the picture. This *is* a joint operation."

"I'm not likely to forget," Gallagher assured him. "But in case I have any lapses, George here will kick me back onto the straight and narrow."

Ansen stared at him for the beat of a second, then with a curt nod went out.

Haslam waited until he was certain Ansen was well on the way to street level before he spoke.

"'George here will kick me back onto the straight and narrow,'" he mimicked. "And when is this wonder supposed to happen?"

"You can talk," Gallagher said. "Why did you jump in to save his bacon? If Johnno's dead, it's Ansen's bloody fault. I warned him not to take these people for granted."

"Don't you think the man already knows that? I watched his face when you laid the blame on him. He was already thinking it. I didn't think it was worth the grief of rubbing it in."

"It's my neck on the line, George," Gallagher said uncompromisingly. "When Ansen or someone like him screws up, it *is* more grief . . . for me. Look . . . I'm not saying he's bad at his job. He's probably an ace at storming airplanes or embassies and taking out hijackers, but I doubt if he's dealt with this particular kind of thing before. We're dealing with a type of killer who hires other killers. Ansen may have been on the clear-up team in the Outback, but they were collecting dead bodies. He has no idea what it was really like."

"No one's saying he does," Haslam said placatingly. "I'm only asking you to go easy on him. He's not going to be a happy man when he finally does find Rapicci."

"So you do believe Johnno's dead."

"I've no doubts about it. And I think Ansen already knows that; which is why he was looking so miserable when he went out. So what's your next move?"

"Change hotels, for a start. I wanted them to know I'm here, and they do. Now it's my turn to put the pressure on. I'm not going to let you know where I am, George, until I'm quite ready. So please don't set either Markston or Sian on my trail. I'll call you when the time's right. That's a promise."

"Then you'll need the new number," Haslam said in his calmest voice.

"New? But I thought . . ."

"As soon as Rapicci failed to report for the second time, I decided to split my forces. Sian and Markston are out in the field, so to speak, passing themselves off as a tourist couple. They'll choose their own accommodation, and I've decided to check into an apartment hotel. That will be our headquarters. I'll give you the number. Ansen's got it, of course. Actually, he found the place; so he is doing right by us. But I've got an assurance from him that no one else will know that's where I'll be. It's the apartment's direct line, so there's no receptionist to go through first."

"It's a relief to know you're taking this as seriously as I am."

Haslam gave one of his rare, lugubrious smiles. "I used to be like you once, I've been told. Or perhaps you're the way I used to be. I haven't quite forgotten everything."

Gallagher's own smile was sheepish. "Sorry, George."

"Apology accepted."

Gallagher yawned. This time, it was genuine. "Sorry," he repeated, "but I still need my sleep, so it's back off to bed for me. You ought to do the same. They're not going to pay a second visit. Nothing so clumsy. They'll make mistakes—and I'll see to that—but this won't be one of them. They'll also expect me to move out, which I shall do, at my own choosing. Oh, one more thing. Sian looks as if she has discipline. I'm not so sure about Markston."

Haslam nodded. "She does know her stuff. Markston . . . well, he's not really one of ours, but he's effective heavy muscle. Sian will keep him in check."

"You've got to be joking."

"Don't underestimate that girl. She's tough when she needs to be, and you'd be surprised at how tenacious." Haslam gave Gallagher a searching look. "I suppose I'll just have to await your call."

"I'll be in touch."

"I sincerely hope so," Haslam said, and went out.

A couple of hours later in another part of the city, Sian and Markston booked into an unpretentious little hotel. The room they were given was like any other hotel's of its class, but was spacious.

Markston, wearing a shoulder holster under his lightweight, casual jacket, went immediately across to the bed, sat upon it, and began to bounce.

"Nice this, isn't it?" he said. "Quite good, in fact." He looked at her appraisingly. "This should be a fun assignment."

"I sleep on the bed," Sian told him, "and you take that over there." She pointed at a full-sized sofa bed.

"Hey, come on, Sian. Don't be such a prude. What do you think I'll do to you?"

"Nothing. You won't get the chance. I never mix business with pleasure."

He gave her a sideways look. "Never?"

"Never." It wasn't strictly true. There was one occasion when she . . . But what the hell. It was none of his business.

He thought about that, then a fleeting darkness touched his face. "It's Gallagher, isn't it? You've got the hots for him."

She shut her eyes briefly, and sighed. "Why is it that some men seem to think that if you don't immediately fall at their feet, there's got to be another man involved? I'm quite capable of existing without hanging on to a man, you know? And forget what I know you're thinking. It's not a woman either."

"I still think it's Gallagher."

"Think what you like." The green eyes fastened upon Markston. "Let's establish some ground rules. This job is going to be done properly, and I don't care what or whom you think I'm saving myself for. Neither am I some hard-arsed feminist . . . which is what men like you usually think if you don't get your own way. I'm not a fluff-brain who doesn't know what she wants. This means that if I take my clothes off and get into bed with a man, I'm saying I'm as ready and willing for action as he is, so I'm not going to get up in the morning and scream rape if I think I've made a horrible mistake.

"I actually do like having doors held open for me, having chairs pulled back, and being given a helping hand if I'm wearing a dress that makes climbing stairs awkward. I like wearing short skirts, showing off my legs when the feeling takes me, and I like my body most of the time. I don't think all men are rapists and I will even let a man pay the bill at a restaurant, if the occasion demands it.

"But I'll tell you something else, Markston . . . it's not ever going to happen with you. So if you give me any shit, I'll blow your fucking balls away." She smiled sweetly at him. "Okay?"

Markston stared at her openmouthed. It was not merely the force of her words that generated this reaction from him; the huge snout of a Magnum revolver was also pointing at the region in question, where Markston felt an involuntary, sympathetic twitch of horror. He'd not even seen her draw the weapon. In his mind's eye the Magnum took on the awesome and menacing presence of a cannon.

"*Okay?*" she repeated.

His mouth worked uselessly for fleeting seconds that seemed like years.

"Yes," he finally said. "O-okay. Christ! You're bloody crazy! You wouldn't really do that, would you?"

"If you keep remembering I'm crazy," she told him as she returned the gun to its normal hiding place in a large shoulder bag she'd brought with her, "and you don't cross the line, you can hang on to your balls." Another smile. "Now that's been established and we know exactly where we stand, let's go out and play the tourists we're supposed to be."

"So what are we looking for?" Markston asked with a modicum of civility. "What's all this in aid of?"

It was eleven o'clock, and his ego still smarted. They had been playing the tourist game for the better part of two hours. They'd briefly done the South Bank Cultural Center across the river and now they sauntered up Queen Street Mall, pausing to look at some street entertainers. To Markston's chagrin, Sian had vetoed the idea of hiring a car, electing instead to purchase the all-day passes that for five Australian dollars gave them unlimited travel on the city's public transport system.

"We're supposed to be using our eyes and ears, Markston," she told him with deliberate patience. "Imagine us as spiders waiting for the strands of the web to vibrate. When that happens, we check to see what has caused it. I'm sorry to disappoint you about the car but this really isn't the time to hire one. I don't think the Brisbane police would like us doing chases through their city."

"And what do we do if we see someone we want to track?"

"We tell Mr. Haslam. He'll sort it out with the major, unless the situation requires us to defend ourselves. In which case, he'll still sort it out with the major." She stared at him. "Exercise some patience. You're supposed to be a professional."

"I'm a weapons man," he said tightly. "People call me when they need surgical removals. In and out quickly. That's me. This stooging around is not my province."

"In and out quickly. Sounds like you, all right." She had spoken so neutrally, Markston was not sure whether she was making fun of him. "Impatience," she added, "can get you killed."

They walked on in silence.

"Do you think we could stop for a coffee?" Markston asked abruptly. "Or is that also against the rules?"

Sian bit back a retort, glanced about, and saw a place that gave a good view of the mall.

"How about that coffee shop over there?" she suggested.

Markston looked at the one she had chosen. "It will do."

"I'm so glad you think so."

▪ ▪ ▪

The large detached house in an exclusive enclave about twenty kilometers north of the city, built in the colonial style, gleamed whitely within the high, plant-covered walls of its vast, secluded garden. A spacious verandah went right around the two-story building, and the garden itself, well kept, was ablaze with the colors of subtropical flowering plants. At one end, the deep, clear waters of a large swimming pool, dwarfed by the garden, waited invitingly.

Beyond the pool and the garden walls was an expanse of lush vegetation, as if the house had been constructed within a small forest. Inside this haven could be heard the sounds of birds at ease with their surroundings. From time to time about three or four double-barred finches would swoop onto a section of the verandah, chatter among themselves, then fly off again into the tall trees beyond the garden. To anyone within the grounds, it was difficult to believe the Bruce Highway was barely three kilometers away to the east.

There was no one at the pool, and three loungers were neatly arranged at its edge. One lounger was placed in solitary splendor beneath a large, brightly colored parasol, while the others, some distance away, had to share a smaller, all-white umbrella.

Parked at the front of the house at the end of the gated drive were three cars: the Mercedes limousine that had been at the airport, a big Toyota four-wheel drive, and a dark blue Holden sedan. Just beyond the cars and attached to the verandah was a large building that formed an added wing. Its ground floor was a garage capable of housing five vehicles. The garage doors were closed.

In the large bed in the master bedroom of the main house, Mrs. Gordon opened her eyes, which were of a sea green so vivid in color, they gave the unnerving impression of being lit from within. A rich abundance of long, golden-blonde hair partially covered her face.

One of the eyes looked out at the world through some strands that had fallen across it. The single sheet that covered her body had draped itself about her, creating a voluptuously embossed shape upon the bed. For some moments, she lay absolutely still as she listened to the sounds of the house and the world outside. She then pushed back the sheet and, completely naked, got out of the bed. With feline grace, she walked over to a full-length mirror and studied herself critically.

To say she was beautiful would be to describe her in terms of exceptional understatement, and to anyone observing her as she stood there, it would have been very easy to appreciate why the flight attendant had been so enthralled.

She was a tall woman, with the sort of shape that would be described as Junoesque. Every curve, every indentation upon the full body was an expression of perfection. She slowly raised her arms above her head, joined them by the hands, and stretched on the balls of her feet. With that great mane of hair, it was like watching the postdinner stretch of a great cat, and when she walked—long, slow steps with her feet slightly turned in—the flowing movements were indeed reminiscent of a feline creature.

She pirouetted slowly, inspecting the curve of her back, the firm roundness of her bottom, the flatness of her stomach, the firmness of her full breasts, whose nipples began to swell even as she watched. She patted her stomach approvingly. It was firm without being hard and overtly muscled. Her complexion was flawless, with the barest hint of a tan over her entire body.

She relaxed, bringing her arms down and settling back on her feet as she continued to survey herself in the mirror. This was no narcissistic exercise. There was no preening expression upon her face, and her scrutiny of herself was almost clinical in its detachment.

"Think of what you have missed all these years," she said to the mirror, clearly addressing someone she was thinking about.

There was a powerful Slavic strength to her features. The blonde hair contrasted sharply with thick, dark eyebrows and her proud chin was complemented by a wide, sensuous mouth. As if to further defy expectations, her well-shaped hands were delicate, with long, expressive fingers. Her legs and thighs were long and though too richly full to be considered slim, were beautifully and smoothly sculpted. Radiating from her was a potent and dangerous mix of physical strength, power, and sensuality.

But there was not total perfection. Going closer to the mirror, she raised her left arm and peered at the reflection. Just beneath her left breast was a very faint, jagged scar that descended perpendicularly for about six inches. It had obviously not been acquired recently, and though it would never quite vanish, it was barely noticeable. There was no raised weal. She stroked at it gently, and her eyes darkened as she remembered how it had been given to her. It was a remarkable phenomenon, this darkening, as if the light had gone completely from her eyes.

She again lowered the arm, and turned from the mirror to go to a shelf in the room-width, deep wardrobe at one end of the bedroom. She got out two pieces of black attire that could be hidden in the palm of a hand, and put them on. One strained to hold her breasts in place, the other was virtually a thong with a small triangle and was secured to her lower body. If anything, the scant strips of clothing served to enhance further the sheer scale of the physical magnetism that emanated from her.

Her bedroom overlooked the pool and as with Gallagher's hotel suite, large doors opened onto a spacious balcony, much bigger than Gallagher's and floored with terra-cotta tiles. She went out to lean against the solid white barrier and looked down at the pool. Tall trees within and beyond the garden walls gave her complete privacy. The nearest neighbors were over 350 meters beyond the garden boundaries. She detected movement near the pool but some distance from the balcony, smiled, and went back inside.

The two men were playing chess. The younger one had driven the limousine from the airport. His companion, older and more at ease with himself, was studying the board keenly.

"That was a very rash move," he said.

"I don't think so."

"Are you quite sure? You can try another . . ."

"Don't do me any favors."

The older man shrugged. "I gave you a chance. It's your funeral." He promptly took an exposed, strategically vital rook.

"Shit!" the younger man swore, staring at his now-vulnerable flank. "I thought I had that covered."

"What you don't see always gets you. Remember that."

They were not speaking English.

The accommodation above the garage was more of a guest wing than living quarters for household staff. For the duration of the men's stay, there were two people—a man and a woman in their mid-thirties—who would be looking after the house and its cooking requirements, and who did not live in. They had been specially recruited and there was no fraternization. There was also one other person on the premises.

The men were playing in one of the guest wing's reception rooms, the younger man studying his position with increasing chagrin, not at all liking what he saw. He glanced at his watch.

"When's that plane due?"

"Fifteen-oh-five. We've got plenty of time. Your move."

"And that stiff in the Mercedes, we ought to do something about it before it starts to stink the place out."

"All in due time. Everything's going according to plan. Now play. It's your move."

"Shit," the younger man said.

The snake, nearly two meters long, was black on top with a golden belly. It paused briefly, tongue flicking. A small group of about six double-barred finches had landed near the edge of the pool, pausing just long enough to chatter at each other before taking off again. But one remained, engrossed by an insect it had found at poolside.

The snake chose its moment and reared to strike.

There was a sharp cough and something hard struck the snake, catching it in midlunge. The reptile was flung bodily into the air, furiously coiling and uncoiling about itself, its two-toned body coloring making it seem like a monstrous piece of living candy as it twisted and writhed in its death throes.

It fell to the ground still coiling and uncoiling until gradually, its movements began to slow down. Then, with final, jerky spasms, it at last became still. Its head had been smashed by the bullet, but it had taken a relatively long time to die.

Up on the balcony, the bikinied Mrs. Gordon gave another smile, the silenced pistol she still held two-handedly now pointing upwards by her right cheek. Slowly, she lowered the pistol, turned after a final look at the snake, and reentered the bedroom.

She sat down on the bed and removed the silencer. On a small table she had brought close to the foot of the bed were carefully laid-out cleaning materials. She took the pistol apart and meticulously began to clean it.

Outside, the finch that had narrowly missed being

eaten returned to hunt out more of the insects it had enterprisingly discovered. Its efforts took it close to the dead snake.

It pecked at an insect that had settled on the snake's golden belly.

In the guest wing, the chess players were sitting by an open window and had picked up the eerie, sighing sound of the sharp cough. The balcony was close enough to enable them to hear with sufficient clarity, and they'd immediately identified the familiar noise for what it was.

They now stood at the window, staring at the dead snake and the miraculously fortunate, newly emboldened finch.

"How many more of those things is she going to let that old black turn loose?" the younger man demanded with a shudder of disgust. "I hate those bastard reptiles."

"It only eats small birds and rodents," the older one said cheerfully. "It's not venomous."

"I don't care, and I don't want to be given a demonstration of your knowledge of snakes. They give me the creeps. That old black gives me the creeps as well. Just how many of those things did he bring?" The younger man repeated.

"Six, I think."

"Six!"

"Five now, if you leave out the one by the pool."

"Shit."

As they continued to watch, an old aborigine in stockman's clothes and hat that had seen plenty of wear strode up to the dead snake, and picked it up.

They followed him with their eyes until he had moved out of sight.

"How come she knows these people?" the younger man asked.

The other gave one of his shrugs. "I don't know and I don't care. It's none of my business, nor yours. Come on. Let's continue the game. I've got you on the run."

"I wish she'd use something else instead of those damned snakes for target practice," the young one grumbled.

"They're fast-moving targets," the older one said, "and difficult. It was a hell of a shot. Would you prefer her to practice on you?"

"Your jokes stink."

"Let's get on with our game," the older one said.

When she had cleaned the gun to her satisfaction, she put it and the cleaning materials away; then she walked over to a corner of the room where a large black case stood on one end, leaning into the corner. She inspected it closely for damage that might have been caused during its travels, but there was none. She began to open the case.

They heard the first long, drawn-out note, followed by the characteristic triplets and crotchet of the opening measures of the piece.

"What the hell's that?" the younger one asked.

"A cello."

"I know it's a cello," the young man snapped crossly. "I meant the piece she's playing. It's giving me the creeps."

"This time, I agree with you: It should, though in a quite pleasant way. Your education is lacking. Don't you recognize Schubert when you hear it?"

"I did not have time for such decadent—"

"Decadent! I didn't think anyone said that anymore. The piece is *Death and the Maiden.* It really is quite pleasant. Come on. It's your move again. I'd watch your queen."

The younger man glared at him. "I know what I'm doing!" Then he made his move.

The other took the queen. "You never learn," he said, shaking his head slowly. "You could have saved that queen."

"Shit!" the younger man said, annoyed with himself.

After about half an hour, she stopped playing. The cello, held between her legs, had lain gently against her bare thighs, and as she rose to return it to its case, marks were temporarily left upon her flesh. She rubbed at the marks with slow, sensuous movements and a slight tremor went through her as a haunting memory returned.

She stopped abruptly, locked the instrument away, then stroked the case as if it were a well-loved pet.

"Next time we play together," she told the case, "he'll be finished."

The chess players heard a loud splash and the younger man rose to look. He saw her swimming a length of the pool at great speed. She reached the end, turned with the skill of an Olympic swimmer, and headed back. She swam another two lengths with barely a reduction in speed while he watched in awe.

Then she stopped, and climbed out of the pool to go over to the lounger with the large parasol. There was a jug of iced juice, croissants with butter and a selection of jams, and a pot of coffee on a tray that had been placed upon the circular table, from the middle of which the parasol appeared to be growing.

He watched her pat herself dry, then ease herself onto the lounger with the flowing motion of something perceptibly feline.

"Oh my God!" he uttered slowly in a voice suddenly

hoarse with unrequitable desire. "What a body! That piece of nothing she's wearing is just a string up her backside. Come and have an eyeful! How can anyone look this good? I picked her up at the airport, but I never imagined . . ."

Reluctantly, his older companion approached the window. "You're just trying to get out of another beating." His voice indicated he was not about to be impressed. Then he saw her. "Oh, mother," he said.

The younger one was almost gleeful. "Something gets to you at last. Have you ever seen anything like it . . . ?"

The older one frowned. "A black widow, perhaps."

His younger companion turned to stare at him. "You're strange. You know that? Really strange." He turned again to look at the figure on the lounger. "A woman like that—"

"Is dangerous. Mortally. Despite the sunshine, it can't be all that warm in the pool, but do you see her shivering? You must be suicidal. We've got work to do, and those we're doing it for will not take very kindly to any screwups. You know why she's here, and still you're talking *and* thinking with your dick. If you forget why *you're* here and try something stupid, my friend, you'll end up like that snake. Don't say I didn't warn you. Come to think of it, you won't be saying anything. You'll be dead."

The older man moved away from the window. Ignoring him, the younger one remained staring at the tantalizing body on the lounger.

16

"I'm going into Brisbane to have a look around."

She was standing next to the Toyota Land Cruiser, dressed in a short-sleeved, loose-fitting silken white blouse that only partially hid the fullness of her breasts, and a pair of thin khaki shorts that displayed a great expanse of bare thighs and legs. On her feet were white trainers, and upon her head a wide-brimmed hat. The golden-blonde hair gleamed past her strong shoulders, and the green eyes were concealed by expensively stylish dark glasses.

The day was bright and pleasantly warm, without being hot. Above her the sky, virtually clear save for a few high wisps of translucent cloud, appeared to have been painted on by someone with a preference for vivid blue. She looked clean and fresh, and there was an assuredness of manner about her that bespoke a total control of herself. Completely devoid of makeup, she still managed to look as if she had spent long hours with a dedicated beautician.

She had spoken in English.

The two men were standing before her, like retainers awaiting orders. The one who had driven the limousine was trying hard not to stare at her legs and was not succeeding.

"Is that wise?" he now asked. "You might be seen."

The dark glasses shifted slightly, like a gun turret tracking onto a target. "No one knows who I am." There was a deliberate pause. "Unless you have been talking."

The ensuing silence brought a sharp-edged tenseness that caused both men to stiffen perceptibly.

"I've been talking to no one," the younger man said tightly.

"Good. There are precise arrangements with those who are paying for my services. I have warned you before about trying to dictate to me. You seem to have a short memory."

She opened the driver's door of the Toyota, got in, then shut the door behind her. The young one had avidly studied every movement, savoring the shifting of the muscles in those thighs and legs as she'd climbed in. She was sensuality personified, and he was having a hard time of it.

She turned to look at him, the dark glasses seeming to have an ominous life of their own. "I saw you watching me from the window. I do not like people who leer at me. Perhaps you are the type of man who believes a woman should wear a potato sack all the time, or cover herself totally the way the men of some countries make their women do, if she is not to be accused of deliberate temptation."

She tapped once with an index finger on the rim of the steering wheel. "Do not make the mistake of crossing the boundaries of our professional association. And . . . do not ever dream of putting whatever passes for thought in your mind into practice. Your fate will be very much worse than the snake's. This is not a threat."

She started the engine, and drove away.

They watched as the Toyota went through the opened gates and turned onto the road.

"Not a threat," the older man began, switching languages as the sound of the engine faded, "but a promise. Those are the words she left out. I hope you're wise enough to know when the danger signals have been hoisted. I warned you about thinking with your dick. You'll really never learn, will you?"

His younger companion looked stubborn.

"This woman," the older one continued, "is an expensive, professional killer, and like all of us, as I've told you before, she's here for a purpose. I'm not going to allow you to screw things up because of your suicidal desire to fuck her. You won't get the chance, and I'll lose one of my team in the process. But *she* won't have to shoot you: If you even think of going near her, I'll shoot you myself. That *is* a threat, *and* a promise. Now let's attend to that body."

The younger man glared at him, but complied.

They opened a section of the garage doors, drove the Mercedes in, then shut the door from the inside. They removed Rapicci's body from the trunk and, wrapping it carefully in a blanket, placed it in the trunk of a second Holden sedan. They then opened another section of the doors and drove out and down the drive. The door section closed itself after them.

Once on the road, they took the direction opposite from the one in which the Toyota had gone. They traveled without haste, as if they were simply out on a leisurely drive. Sometime later a police patrol car went past, going the other way. Its occupants did not even glance at them.

In the trunk of the Mercedes, smears of blood remained untouched.

▪ ▪ ▪

Gallagher had slept till 11:30, taken another long shower, then packed all his gear, ready for his move to another hotel. But he had decided to first make his call to his answering machine in London before beginning the hunt for an appropriately low-profile accommodation. The calls would be made from public telephones.

In the bedroom, concealed by a large, solidly framed aerial photograph of Fraser Island, was a combination safe, flush-fitted into a wall. The safe was deep enough to comfortably hold the weapons case until his return. He'd left the Do Not Disturb sign on his door.

Dressed in white jeans, a pale blue denim shirt and soft-soled walking boots, he strolled along Albert Street looking for a telephone. During his walk from the hotel, he had deliberately varied his route in an attempt to flush out anyone who might have been tailing him. So far, he had detected no one on his trail.

He found a card-operated phone that allowed international calls and dialed his home number. He briefly considered the possibility of satellite eavesdropping on his line, thinking that perhaps Fowler had decided on a little clandestine listen-in, but quickly dismissed the idea. If Borodin had left a message, it would be one without clues for an eavesdropper.

He beeped the machine when the connection was made and there among the other messages was Borodin's, clear and concise, but devastating in its implications. Borodin had promised more information. Perhaps a later call would throw further light upon the killer's true identity.

Gallagher replaced the receiver slowly, a tingle running up and down his spine. *He was a she!*

Gallagher again thought of the one "she" who was as

deadly as the unknown killer, and decided it was most unlikely. He had *seen her die.* He'd been there, close enough to touch her. He had placed his fingers upon her opened eyes, to gently shut them. It was just not possible.

He was a she!

A relative? A close friend bent on revenge? Haslam would have to be told, but not just yet.

He would first have to modify his own strategy, Gallagher reasoned, to accommodate this new factor.

Then he would tell Haslam.

Markston was feeling rebellious. After agreeing to a coffee, four coffees later Sian appeared quite happy to continue to sit in the café and watch the world go by. What was she up to?

Markston reluctantly had to admit that some of the female passersby were definitely worth looking at, but it was a sterile pastime. He wanted action.

From where he sat, he had an excellent view of a substantial length of the mall. He was just about to suggest acidly that they might as well have a snack lunch, when a strange noise came out of him.

"You sound as if you're in pain, Markston," Sian remarked unsympathetically. "Tell Doctor Sian."

But Markston was not listening to her. His eyes were riveted on what to him was a vision, approaching the café.

"Oh God," he eventually began softly. "I think I've just died and gone to Heaven. It should be illegal for anyone to have such a pair of legs. Illegal, and unfair to all other women. Tell me I'm not seeing things."

She followed his gaze without enthusiasm, but despite herself was impressed.

"She's certainly got . . . something," she agreed reluctantly and with perhaps more than a twinge of jealousy. She studied the woman interestedly. "I'm amazed there aren't at least ten men escorting her . . . a woman like that."

"Ouch. Ouch! Admit it. You're jealous. Oh Gawd. She's coming in here!"

"Down, Markston. Let's have a little control."

Markston glanced about him. "Look at the faces of all the other guys in here, then tell me again."

She didn't bother. "So? They've all got your problem. That's not news."

Markston did another quick survey. "There's a table over there. Maybe she'll take it."

"Grow up, for God's sake. You men can be such children at times. Come on. Time to move."

"Oh, no you don't. I fancy a snack lunch. You've had me sitting here for ages. Now I want to eat."

Sian decided he had a point. She had indeed kept him in the coffee shop while she had closely studied the many people who had passed by and the customers who had come into the café. The mall was a street that inevitably drew people. She had long ago discovered that sometimes, sitting for a good length of time in any one place could bring unexpected dividends.

The woman entered. Everyone stared, especially the men, young and not so young. She took the table Markston had hoped she would, and removed her hat. She kept on her dark glasses.

Then she removed them, and Sian found herself looking into eyes that were greener than any she might ever have expected to see. Her own eyes, she realized, impressive though they might be to some people, were totally eclipsed. The unknown woman's eyes were, quite simply, spectacular.

Markston could barely contain himself.

Then the astonishingly beautiful woman smiled and Sian felt a chill go through her, without fully understanding why.

One cup of coffee later, the woman left without a backward glance. To Markston, it was as if a bright light had suddenly gone out.

"Why can't I," he complained ruefully, "just once in a lifetime meet someone like that?"

Sian remained silent, staring after the woman as she made her way along the mall at a relaxed pace.

"Ready to leave?" she then asked.

"No." He sounded annoyed. "I still haven't had my snack. Why are you looking so po-faced, anyway?"

"Am I?" She spoke absently.

"Yes. You've got on Thoughtful Expression Number One."

"If you say so. All right. Order your snack. I might as well have one too."

She continued to look along the mall, trying to understand why she had experienced such a sense of foreboding.

The woman had disappeared.

Mrs. Gordon walked along Albert Street. She smiled to herself, pleased that her instincts had led her to make the trip to the city. She had sensed something odd about the couple as soon as she'd spotted them in the café. They had not even been behaving like friends. In the course of her career, she had seen a sufficient number of paired police and security people to know a surveillance team when she saw one.

But they'd had no idea who she was. That much had been obvious. The man, like the others in there, had been too influenced by his loins to have done any coherent thinking.

But the young woman, whom she suspected of being the smarter of the two, had felt uneasy. That, also, had been obvious, just as had the fact that she didn't understand why.

Feeling pleased that she had spotted at least one team, Mrs. Gordon continued her leisurely walk.

Gallagher turned a corner and saw a flash of legs that brought on a sudden rush of memories he had thought deeply buried. By the time he'd turned to check, they were gone in the throng of people.

I'd know those legs anywhere, he thought in consternation.

"Bloody hell," he muttered to himself. "Now I'm beginning to see things that aren't there."

It was the message from Borodin. Clearly, it had brought those memories to the surface and they were causing his mind to play tricks on him. He'd probably simply glimpsed one of Brisbane's more specially blessed daughters and his mind, going into overdrive, had done the rest.

"She can't possibly be alive," he said, again speaking to himself.

A passerby, close enough to hear, glanced at him warily.

Mrs. Gordon paused suddenly, causing someone to narrowly miss bumping into her. As the person walked past with a hurried apology Mrs. Gordon turned to look behind her, a slight frown creasing her forehead. She turned slowly, a full 360 degrees.

No one was following her.

As she walked on, she felt a slight shiver.

"Gordon?" she said, only partly to herself.

The men had driven northwards to Gympie along the back roads until they were some thirty kilometers from where they'd started. They now turned off the road they were on, drove a while longer along a bumpy track bordered by tall bushes, and stopped by a creek that bled itself from a small lake.

They got out, went round to the trunk of the Holden, lifted Rapicci's body out of it, and rolled it unceremoniously out of the blanket and into the creek. It paused briefly, faceup, then rolled over and lay facedown in the creek.

"That's one problem taken care of," the older man said dispassionately. Wearing gloves, he folded the blood-spattered blanket neatly, then stuffed it into a large waxed paper bag which he put into the trunk. He shut and locked the trunk, and handed the keys over.

The younger one took them, stared at the body without emotion, then got back behind the wheel.

"I still think she shouldn't have gone out," he said as his companion joined him in the car. He started the engine. "She's hardly unmistakable. She could put everything at risk."

"On the contrary. I think it's all going rather well. And let's not forget we'll be having guests this evening. One of them's rather special, and should be on a flight to Brisbane even as we speak. Now let's find our next stop."

The Holden moved off.

They found what they were looking for, fifteen minutes later and five kilometers from where they had left the body. It was an old shed, practically overgrown, that had once been used to house farm machinery. A narrow concrete path, wide enough to take a car the size of the Holden, led up to it. The floor was also concrete. It was well hidden from casual view and was perfect for their needs.

They drove right in, stopped, and got out quickly.

One by one they jacked up the wheels, deflated them slightly, and removed what looked like an outer skin, from each tire. These were in fact false treads that had been slipped on like rings, and which had been kept in place by the then properly inflated tires. Careful driving had ensured no slippage during the required period. They put the tire rings in the trunk after attending to the last wheel. They reinflated all the tires with a foot pump and then set off back for the house.

They left nothing to betray their brief presence, and the dry, bare concrete betrayed no tire tracks, either coming in or going out. There were plenty of the false tracks, however, in the slightly damp soil by the creek.

At about the time that the men were returning from dumping Rapicci's body, Mrs. Gordon parked the Toyota in the domestic terminal's short-term car park at the airport. She went up to an airline information desk with an envelope marked "private."

She smiled at the young woman behind the desk. "You've got a passenger arriving on the fifteen-oh-five; could I leave this for him, please? It's an urgent message. He has a meeting scheduled and is expecting the information in there. He knows the message is being left."

In addition to her linguistic abilities, she was also a flawless mimic when she needed to be. Her Australian accent was impeccable. She did not remove the sunglasses.

"Certainly." The ground hostess looked at the name on the envelope. "Mr. Villiger. I'll just check to make certain he is aboard." She tapped at her computer keyboard and waited for the information to come onscreen. "Ah, yes. He did make the flight."

Mrs. Gordon described Villiger in detail. "Just so there's no mistake. He really mustn't miss the meeting."

"Don't worry. We'll see to it that he gets it as soon as he comes through."

"Thank you very much."

"You're welcome."

The hostess watched her leave.

The domestic flight from Sydney landed on time and Villiger went straight to the information desk. The urgent message he'd first received in South Africa had been quite specific.

"My name's Villiger," he said to the hostess. "I believe you have a message for me."

She looked at him with the usual smile of welcome, but her eyes studied him swiftly, matching his appearance with the description she had been given.

"Ah, yes, Mr. Villiger. We were given a good description of you." She brought the envelope out.

"Were you?" Villiger smiled at her. "Just like him. He's always careful."

"Wasn't a 'him,' sir," she said, "but a very beautiful lady."

Villiger's eyebrows moved upwards briefly. "A lady. That's like him too. A few seconds in Australia, and already he's got one of you beautiful ladies in tow." He grinned at her.

She smiled, pleased by the compliment. "South Africa, sir?"

"It shows, does it?" He opened his passport so she could see his picture. "Just so you're quite satisfied I am the person in question."

She passed him the envelope. "There's no need, sir. The description was enough."

"Thank you very much," he said as he took the envelope.

"My pleasure, sir. Enjoy your stay in Queensland."

"Thank you. I will."

He waited until he was in a taxi and heading out of the airport before opening the envelope. The message gave the address of the hotel he should book into. They would meet there at eight o'clock in the evening. It was signed *G.*

He gave the taxi driver the name of the hotel, carefully folded the single sheet of paper, and put it back in the envelope, which he slipped into a jacket pocket.

"So, Gordon, man," he said quietly. "You dragged me halfway round the world. What do you need from me?"

"Did you say something, mate?" the driver asked.

"No, no. Thinking aloud."

"Know what they say about talking to yourself."

"First sign of madness," Villiger replied dutifully.

"Exactly."

Taxi drivers, Villiger thought dryly. The world's comedians on hot wheels.

Villiger's taxi was being followed at different distances by a small convoy of three cars. One was a prebooked rental that had been collected on arrival, the second had been waiting with a driver for its passenger, and the third was a parked, private car in the long-term section. One of the couples had brought their own keys.

The cavalcade, mingling with other traffic, followed the taxi to a small, unpretentious, but quite comfortable hotel not far from the Botanical Gardens. None of the cars stopped when Villiger's taxi came to a halt, but two of the three eventually stopped some distance away, at a point from which the hotel could be discreetly observed, and the occupants of one of those cars also kept an eye on the other car that had stopped.

The car that had picked up a single passenger kept going. The passenger looked back for the briefest of moments, checking the position of the cars that had stopped.

"They're in place," Borodin said to his companion. "Now we've got some preparations to discuss, and I've got a phone call to make."

Villiger entered the hotel, checked into his room, and was handed another envelope by the manager. The meeting was to be at the Botanical Gardens. The message specified the meeting point.

Villiger went up to his room, which, as a matter of routine, he promptly checked for bugging or hidden cameras. He didn't suspect the hotel management. Hotel rooms could be bugged and wired on-site for cameras and then cleaned up without the management ever being the wiser. He should know; he'd done it himself on occasion. He checked his window views to see if the room was overlooked. Long-range rifle mikes and telephoto lenses were a possibility, but he could not see anywhere that would serve as a suitable vantage point. Satisfied as much as could be expected under the circumstances, he decided that the room was clean.

He locked the door and undressed to his underwear. Then, setting his watch alarm, he gratefully lay down to sleep.

While Villiger was taking his nap, Gallagher walked onto the balcony of his new hotel suite. He'd changed his decision to book into a small establishment in the suburbs, and had opted instead for another big international hotel overlooking the river. He was still looking out on Town Reach, but this time from the north bank. There was a certain degree of anonymity in a big hotel, and this suited his current purposes.

He'd also hired himself a Range Rover Vogue with all the mod conveniences, including air-conditioning. It was not as fast, nor as accelerative, as his Quattro. It was, however, exactly the right vehicle for what he had in mind.

Gallagher smiled as he remembered the comments of the young woman who'd been processing the rental documents.

"With or without roo bars, sir?" she'd asked, as if offering a meal. What she'd really meant was the stout grid of metal tubing that had been solidly fixed to the front of the Range Rover, and which was intended to nudge suicidal kangaroos out of the way without damage to the vehicle's nose.

"With," he'd said.

"A wise precaution. You never know what you might come up against on the road, especially at night."

"That's certainly true," he'd agreed. But he hadn't been thinking of kangaroos.

The Range Rover, though a different model, had also brought back memories, reminding him of the ones that had been used during the escape in the Outback. That had inevitably brought back the other, more recent memory of the legs he had thought he'd seen, and the person to whom the originals belonged. However, he still believed his mind to be playing tricks, despite his inner condition of heightened alert. There was just no way she could still be alive.

Gallagher went back inside, sliding shut the door to the balcony. He'd been pleased to find that this suite also possessed a combination safe. Its hiding place was behind a mirror, and the weapons case was once more in secure storage.

He put on his lightweight jacket, then went out. It

was time to check his answering machine to see if there were any new messages from Borodin.

He found a public telephone not far from the hotel and called his number in London. There were five new messages since his last call, but none from Borodin. Then came a longish pause. Gallagher waited. The termination beeps had not sounded, which meant another message was on the tape.

"South Bank. Park. Nineteen hundred." *Borodin.*

The termination beeps came.

Gallagher hung up slowly. *South Bank. Park.* A car park at the South Bank? Or was that *South Bank Park?* What was Borodin on about? The South Bank complex on the Thames in London? On what date was this meant to be? And where the hell was the park? There was no park . . . Then he paused.

Borodin was in Queensland and probably already in Brisbane.

South Bank Park.

Gallagher remembered one of the many maps he'd bought, and the café area near his previous hotel. South Bank *Parkland.* Borodin had deliberately left out part of the name in case of eavesdroppers, purposely making it sound as if he'd meant London's own South Bank.

Borodin in Queensland. He certainly got around.

Gallagher returned to his hotel, taking another roundabout route in order to flush out any possible tails. Once, he thought he spotted a man who looked like a candidate, but lost him well before the hotel.

He went back to his suite and began to prepare for what might lay ahead.

At the neocolonial house, two more snakes had been coughed to death by the silenced automatic.

At the front, the Toyota was again parked next to

the Mercedes and one of the Holdens. The one that had been used to dispose of the body had been thoroughly cleaned and was back in its place in the garage, while the Mercedes had been brought out. The bloodstains were still in the trunk. The two men, in dark clothing, were standing by the Holden getting ready to leave.

"Two more gone," the younger said. "How many left now?"

"Three," the other replied irritably. "Can't you count?"

"I'll be glad when she's got rid of them all. It's six-thirty now. She's not really going to let more of those things loose tonight, is she?"

"You've been here long enough now to know she always does what she says she's going to. She'll be tracking them with the rifle when it gets dark."

The younger man shuddered. "I thought snakes were cold-blooded."

"They've been sunning themselves all day. There'll be enough residual heat for the rifle to detect. Besides, infrared's not the only sensor in its systems."

"Well, you're not going to get me out in that garden tonight. When we've done the pickup I'm going inside as soon as we return, and I'm staying there."

The older man smiled thinly. "What makes you think the snakes will stay in the garden? She might miss."

His companion stared at him in disgust. "You've got a sick mind."

"There speaks a man who carries one of the most vicious-looking daggers I've ever seen, and who has used it recently."

The other ignored the comment. "Anyway, you're always telling me what a great shot she is. She never misses."

"You never know. Maybe I lied. There's always a first time for everything."

The younger man glared at his colleague.

▪ ▪ ▪

Gallagher drove across Victoria Bridge towards his rendezvous with Borodin. He parked the Range Rover and began sauntering past the cafés, keeping a sharp lookout for both Borodin and any people who might be shadowing him. So far, he was clean.

But there was no sign of Borodin.

Had he misunderstood the message after all? Had Borodin indeed meant London? But there had been no date.

Gallagher glanced quickly at his watch. Still some minutes to go. He had deliberately come early to check out the area, and now came to a café with tables set on a wide, plant-decorated verandah. He decided to go in, choosing a table that left his back secure while allowing him a wide field of vision. He ordered a coffee and settled down to wait.

Less than a minute later he saw Borodin approaching, wearing what appeared to be the same suit he'd worn in Portugal.

Borodin ordered a coffee from the waitress, who had arrived at the table almost simultaneously, then turned to Gallagher with outstretched hand.

"My message was easily understood, of course."

"Of course. You do get around, don't you."

They shook hands and Borodin sat down with an amused smile.

"You are going to have an interesting time," Borodin went on. "Some old friends are here."

"Old friends?"

Borodin nodded, watching Gallagher carefully. He noted the constant, unhurried sweep of Gallagher's eyes.

"Do not worry," he said. "My people are watching our backs. But I don't think we are the focus of attention from . . . er . . . our adversaries for the moment.

They will be engaged elsewhere. But we should know exactly which area when it happens. I have people watching them too."

They paused as Borodin's coffee was brought.

"Would you mind telling me what you're talking about?" Gallagher demanded after the waitress had gone. "What old friends? Who's engaged elsewhere?"

Borodin took a sip of the hot coffee, eyes surveying Gallagher over the rim of the cup. "The big South African arrived this afternoon."

Gallagher stared at him. "What? You must be mistaken."

Borodin just looked at him.

"All right. So you're not mistaken. Why is he here?"

"Same reason that you are. He's a target, and I think they'll be going for him soon. He's booked into a small hotel on the other side of the river. One of my people will follow if he leaves. We're also checking to see if anyone visits him."

"If what you say is true, how could they possibly have got him to come way over to Queensland . . ." Gallagher's voice faltered, then faded as the thought hit him.

Borodin waited, looking smug, his expression suggesting that Gallagher was getting warm.

"Queensland," Gallagher repeated softly. "They sent him a message, possibly from me . . ."

Borodin was nodding approvingly, still waiting.

". . . and whoever sent it," Gallagher continued, "would know that he'd respond . . ."

"I think it's now safe to assume you know the identity of the sender," Borodin interjected, a sly edge to his voice. "The first of my new messages on your machine must have set you thinking."

"But that's impossible! She's dead."

"It is not impossible. She is very much alive, and she is here."

Breaking his own rules, Gallagher still did not want to believe what his instincts had been telling him.

"You've got proof?" he now asked Borodin.

Again, the Russian nodded. "Documentary, and visual. We found some other papers, originally deeply hidden, that cross-refers to the code name Queensland. It mentions her by her real name. That was when I realized the assassin was a woman. There's even a photograph."

Borodin gave a grim chuckle. "Be thankful for bureaucracy; it is its own worst enemy. Without that cross-reference, we may well have never found out. There are still no clues to how part of your confidential documents got into the file. I'll keep trying to find out. We've left the papers in place, but took photographs."

Gallagher, in a kind of shock, said nothing.

"Then we had visual confirmation today," Borodin continued. "One of my people saw her at the airport. She was bold enough to leave a message at an information desk for the South African. I arrived on the same flight. We saw him collect it."

Marika was alive!

"My God," Gallagher whispered. "I really did see her."

It was Borodin's turn to stare. "And you did not recognize her? Surely . . ."

"I did. I just didn't want to believe it."

Gallagher explained the fleeting encounter on Albert Street.

"But she did not see you."

"I'm quite certain," Gallagher said. "She clearly knows I'm here in the city. It was what I intended, although at the time I obviously didn't know she was really the person behind all this. But I've since changed hotels. That should at least keep me a couple of jumps ahead."

"A good move. And the South African? Do you consider him a friend?"

Gallagher nodded. "Yes."

"Then drink your coffee. He will be needing you tonight."

17

"We've got about fifteen minutes," Villiger said to the taxi driver. "Take me the scenic route."

"You've got it," the driver said, quite happy to extend the fare. "I'll get you to the Gardens in time."

But Villiger was not looking at the nightscape. Without seeming to, he was continually checking the other cars. None aroused suspicion; but he did not therefore rest easy. Like Gallagher, he didn't accept the belief that seeing was believing. It was always what you didn't see that brought you the most grief.

London, 9:45 A.M., the same day.

Fowler leafed through the draft report, then looked up at the man who had brought it in.

"Are you quite mad?"

The security officer leading the inquiry into the

missing section of Gallagher's confidential file stood his ground. "Not the last time I looked."

"Don't be flippant with me!" Fowler snapped. "You were given wide powers of inquiry, not freedom to be insubordinate."

The security officer still held his ground. "I've put down my conclusions in this draft. While you may, if you so wish, disagree with what's in there, Mr. Fowler, my state of mind does not come into it."

Fowler jabbed at the pages of the report with a prodding index finger. "Your chief suspect is Sir John Winterbourne, the former head of this department. For God's sake, man. *Sir John Winterbourne.* Is this a joke?"

Fowler had always thought Winterbourne an incompetent fool who should never have been let near the Department; but that didn't mean he considered the erstwhile head as someone who would traffic in highly restricted material. Winterbourne could be mean and nasty, and even at times treacherous on a personal level. But communicating sensitive information to a foreign power was a very different ball game.

The security officer, a beanpole of a man called Greaves—which he pronounced "Graves"—with soft eyes that belied an incisive mind, was not in the least bit intimidated by Fowler's piercing stare.

Greaves chose his words carefully, aware that Fowler was in a dangerous mood. "It's not a joke. I checked very thoroughly before making the report. Three years ago, the document was signed out to Sir John. He signed it back in. As we now know, it was never returned."

"Someone had to countersign as having logged it back in."

Greaves cleared his throat. "It's Slocombe's signature."

"There you are."

Greaves again cleared his throat. "I'm afraid not, sir. Slocombe does not remember signing it back in."

Fowler's eyes were cold behind the glasses. "Does Slocombe remember every item he's booked in, or out?"

"He says he does."

"You're not now going to tell me that Sir John forged Slocombe's signature, I hope?"

"Not exactly."

"What do you mean by 'not exactly'?"

"We did a forensic check on the logbook. Slocombe's signature had not been written as original script on the paper. It had first been *traced,* then the grooves filled in. The most likely method would have been transparent paper placed over his genuine signature, a tracing made, then that trace used as a template and, finally, carefully inked in. It points at Sir John, who must have had some specific reason for doing this."

Fowler's mouth had tightened while Greaves had been speaking. "You had better be very, very certain, Greaves. The Soviet Union was still in existence when that section of file went missing. This is an extremely serious accusation, not to say offensive, if you're proven wrong. If Sir John is hauled back from wherever he is to answer these charges and is shown to be innocent of them, he'll want your head. And he'll get it."

"I was well aware of that before I made this report."

Fowler took some time before making further comment. Then he closed the file containing the report with a snap, and handed it back to Greaves.

"Very well. Put it into formal shape."

Greaves took the file and went out.

Fowler slowly removed his glasses and pinched at his nose. He laid the glasses on his desk, rubbing his eyes wearily as he did so. He'd had very little respect for Winterbourne's ability to run the Department. But this, if true, would leave a very nasty smell indeed. It would also give an excuse to all the mad axmen of the budgeting departments, whose sole reason for existence was to balance the books, irrespective of the damage to the nation's security they might cause.

He sighed and replaced the glasses. The Department would not be allowed to come under such a threat, no matter what.

Brisbane, 7:55 P.M.

"So what name are you traveling under now?" Gallagher asked as he walked back with Borodin to their vehicles.

The Russian gave a short laugh. "I am da Silva, a Portuguese citizen."

"Now why didn't I think of that?" Gallagher remarked.

They went first to where Borodin's car was parked, out of reach of the streetlights. A young woman with shortish hair, eyes hooded by the gloom, seemed to materialize out of nowhere; but Gallagher had noted her approach.

"They are in place," she said to Borodin, "and the South African's taxi is on its way." She was attired in what looked like a sort of dark-colored overall that a mechanic would wear, but of snugger fit.

Borodin gave a sharp nod. He did not introduce the newcomer.

"An ambush is being set for your friend," he said to Gallagher as the young woman went to wait by the car, "and we're about to stop it. I believe they intend to snatch him at the Botanical Gardens. My Spetsnaz are in position, and one is also following."

"You've got some Spetsnaz over here?"

Borodin appeared to be smiling. "I had to pull a couple in from Africa, and others from Indonesia. The Pacific Rim and Africa are going to be areas of great interest in the very near future, when the dust settles in my homeland. Years ago, we conducted a study—one of our scenarios similar in a general sense to your own exercises, I'm certain, to include the disintegration of the Soviet Union—and one of the results was that Africa and the Pacific Rim countries would become very high-value spheres. Current trends seem to confirm those results."

"Why are you telling me this?"

"Why not? We have the same interests. We don't want the idiots to blow up this planet, or destroy our respective countries. Our job—"

"Your job . . ."

"Our job is to hold the line, whoever is in power. In my own country, I sometimes frustrate these excesses. It will never mean that I work against my country, only against those who would destroy it from within . . . or from without."

Gallagher said nothing.

"Are you armed?" Borodin asked him.

Gallagher shook his head.

"No matter," Borodin said. "I can give you a weapon."

"No. I don't want to put a load of dead bodies on Brisbane's streets."

"Neither do I. Some of these people are Russian, or former Soviet citizens. If, unfortunately, one or two are killed, we shall dispose of them. We'll try to neutralize instead of kill; but I won't put my own people at risk."

Gallagher nodded. "I can understand that." He glanced at his clothes. "These will show up."

"I've got the answer. In my car." They went to the car and the young woman took another pair of dark overalls from the trunk. "Take off your jacket and put these on," Borodin added.

Gallagher did so, and Borodin grinned.

"Now you are Spetsnaz," he said. "Ironic."

"It's something," Gallagher said.

Gallagher went back to the Range Rover, dumped

his jacket in the back, then climbed in to follow Borodin's car.

Villiger got out of the taxi, then paid the driver.

"Want me to wait?" the driver suggested, pleased by the generous fare.

"No, thank you. This will do."

"Okay. Have a good evening." The taxi accelerated away.

"I hope so," he murmured to himself, senses twitching as he looked about him.

The Gardens were closed. He began walking along a cycle path that bordered the river, as he'd been directed. Beyond his line of sight, the path curved to the right and beneath the intersection of the Riverside Expressway, where it formed the start of the Captain Cook Bridge. A low stone barrier ran the length of its outer edge, along the riverbank. There was no one about. No cyclists came his way. Where, then, was Gallagher?

The Gardens seemed strangely quiet, as if waiting for something to happen. Out on the river, a modern paddle wheeler with diners aboard made its way along the reach, and on the opposite bank a string of lights seemed to be perpetually renewing itself.

Having spent many a month out in the field in Africa and knowing how to assess the approach of a possible threat by listening to the noises or lack of them coming from his immediate environs, Villiger stood still, his eyes scanning the shadows. Despite the fact that he had come to meet Gallagher, he found himself wishing he had brought a gun. You just never knew, sometimes.

"Mr. Villiger."

Villiger whirled at the sound of his softly spoken name. A man was approaching from one end of the path. Then another soft footfall made him turn to look. A second man, coming from the opposite direction.

Ambush!

This would not have been Gallagher's doing. Villiger felt an anger within himself. Why hadn't he brought a gun?

Almost immediately he relaxed and stood where he was, watching the first man approach, assessing his own chances. Then he saw the gun pointing at him. He didn't believe they intended to kill him here. They could have done so from the shadows. *They were going to snatch him.*

Who could want him so badly, he wondered, to take the trouble to lure him all the way to Australia? He thought of possible factions in South Africa. There were certainly a few that would want him out of circulation permanently, but only if they first knew certain things about him. To all intents and purposes, he was a die-hard Afrikaner Intelligence man. So who outside the country could know enough to want to dispose of him?

The last time he'd come under such a threat, Gallagher had helped him neutralize it. None but his most trusted allies—a group that included Gallagher—knew he also worked clandestinely against the Afrikaners. He didn't want a bloodbath in South Africa, and was doing his best to ensure that matters over there didn't get any worse than they already were.

Which led him back to the original question: What organization would know enough to mount this snatch?

Then he saw another figure, indistinct, following the man with the pointing gun. He did not react, waiting to see what this new development would bring. The new figure appeared to be stalking the man pointing the gun. Across the river life went on as normal, giving an eerie feeling to the events taking place on the cycle path.

Something in Villiger's manner must have warned the one with the gun, for he spun round, the pistol searching for a target.

There was a sudden, spiteful cough that Villiger instantly recognized and the man with the gun gave a sharp cry and jerked upright, arms flung outwards, gun spinning away into the darker shadows out of dying hands.

Villiger dived forwards, groping for the fallen weapon, hoping it had not fallen over the stone barrier and onto the bank, or into the river itself. He'd not heard a splash and assumed it had not. Then his searching hand got hold of it and he rolled, looking for the man who'd been approaching from the opposite direction. Running footsteps made him turn. The man was trying to get away.

As Villiger watched, his second kidnapper fired with his own silenced pistol at someone else in shadow. Another spiteful cough followed and the running man halted in midstride, as if jerked by a rope, then collapsed upon himself silently, sitting loosely upon his heels before pitching forwards with a thud that was clearly audible. In the distance a car started suddenly and revved away, clearly in a great hurry to escape. It kept going. Then all was quiet once more.

"Hullo, Piet," a voice said.

Villiger, still on the ground, looked up. "Jesus, man! Is this your idea of a welcome? I thought I would be going for a swim." He stood up and held out his hand. "It's always good to see you, but what was that all about?" He brushed fastidiously at his suit. "And how did these jokers know I'd be here?"

"They knew. I didn't."

Villiger peered at him. "What? You didn't send for me?"

"Nope," Gallagher replied.

"Then how . . ."

"We'll talk in a while, but first let me introduce you to your guardian angel."

Gallagher turned to look for Borodin. Instead, he saw the young woman. She appeared to be smiling shyly at him.

"He asked me to give you this," she said, handing a card to Gallagher. "There is a number. You can reach him there. I will take the oversuit, and perhaps your friend will give me the gun. We shall clean up."

Villiger stared at her interestedly.

"Go on, Piet," Gallagher said, removing the overall. It had done its job, keeping him camouflaged during the crucial moments. "Give her the gun. They'll dispose of it."

"Thank you," she said politely as a silent Villiger handed her the weapon. She took the overall from Gallagher, nodding her thanks. Another shy smile. "Good night," she added, and walked quickly away.

Villiger stared at the retreating figure. "Was she one of those doing the shooting?" he asked.

"She took out the one holding the gun on you."

"Very neat." He turned to Gallagher. "I saw her coming up behind him. She's good. The guardian angel's team?"

"Something like that. Now let's get out of here before people come looking."

"You've a lot of explaining to do."

"Let's get to the Range Rover first."

"Range Rover. That brings back memories."

"You don't know the half of it," Gallagher told him grimly.

"Marika *alive,*" Villiger said in an astonished whisper. "But, man, I shot her. I saw her die."

Gallagher had driven the Range Rover to Kangaroo Point and had parked at the end of Mackenzie Street, nose pointing towards the river. He had given Villiger most of the story, but had left Borodin's identity out of it. It was obvious that Borodin did not want Villiger to know of his real function, nor to allow the South African to see his face. Gallagher also made no mention of the true capabilities of the rifle. Even so, there was enough to leave Villiger stunned.

"So all this," Villiger now said, "is revenge?"

Gallagher nodded. "You shot to kill, and we both thought you'd succeeded. That makes you a target, but," he went on with a short laugh that held no humor, "I'm the prime target. The real game in the hunt. By her rules, I've committed the greatest betrayal. In a strange way, I don't even believe she cares anymore that we destroyed her organization. She's after me because of *personal* betrayal."

Villiger was shaking his head. "I don't see how I could have missed."

"I saw the blood. You didn't miss."

"Then she can't be alive. Man, I'm a good shot."

"I know. But you were on a dune and running, and it was in the middle of one of those Outback deluges. You had all that rain in your face. You did hit her. We both saw the blood coming out of her mouth. It looked as if you'd got her in the lungs. I touched her. I closed her eyes. But she is alive, and don't ask me how. All I can tell you is that those legs belong to just one person. There's not another pair like them. She's here. Count on it."

"So what do you intend to do?" Villiger, still in a state of shock at the news, was attempting to come to terms with what Gallagher had just told him.

"What I've planned. I'm going to lure her onto my own battleground. She tried for you tonight. I think her decision to kidnap you instead of going for a quick kill was to stake you out as bait for me. She'd still have killed you in the end, if she survived her little encounter with me. Tonight's failure will drive her crazy. That makes her vulnerable. I'll use it to my advantage."

"Tell me what you want and I'm in."

"What I want . . . is for you not to come in with me. I'll take her on alone, but I'll need you as backup to keep the others busy."

"What others? Her people?"

"More than that. It's a zoo out there. God knows how many groups are involved. There's my lot, and I say that advisedly. Then there's Marika's. There's Ansen's crowd. There's the group that saved your bacon tonight. And then, beyond that, there's an as yet unidentifiable bunch for whom she's working on a separate agenda."

"And their function?"

"To take out Marika when she's finished what she's doing for them. They may not even wait, and may just decide to cut their losses. It was bound to happen. She's no longer of use now that her cover's blown."

Villiger nodded slowly. "That would explain the Spetsnaz interest in whatever operation she's involved in."

"How do you know they're Spetsnaz?"

Villiger gave him a sideways look. "What do you think, I just walked in from the veld? The young woman who smiled oh-so-sweetly at you, who could kill so professionally, and who speaks English like an American but with just that edge of Russian in it . . . was on the plane from Jo'burg."

"You spotted her?"

"Come on . . ."

"Yes, yes. I know, Piet: You didn't just walk in from the veld." Gallagher chuckled. "That wouldn't please someone I know. He thought you'd missed it all."

Villiger grinned sheepishly. "To be honest, I only noticed her on the plane because of her looks, and if I hadn't seen her again tonight I wouldn't have made the connection. She's got that mildly Asiatic face you get in certain areas of Russia. A hint of Siberia. Beautiful. Were there others on the plane?"

"Luckily for you, yes. But for them, you would have been a guest of Marika's tonight."

"That would have been a wild time."

▪ ▪ ▪

Marika was livid.

She showed her anger not by ranting and raving at anyone, but by having two of the snakes released into the garden and then hunting them down with the rifle. It was not an easy task, for despite the advanced sensors, the snakes were able to find many places in the mature shrubbery of the large garden in which to hide and hunt, moving swiftly from place to place. It took her nearly two hours to get one.

She was still hunting the second, a very dangerous northern tiger snake. She hunted barefoot, moving carefully, varying her speed, sometimes remaining absolutely still for several minutes at a time. When she moved, she held the rifle at the port, but could swiftly bring it to bear at any time. She was using the rifle with its silencing system activated. Though this cost some power, it was still much more powerful in that mode than any unsilenced modern assault rifle.

She paused and brought the rifle up. She'd heard something. The faintest of rustles. She was now well beyond the pool, and had been moving over open ground. Though there was no moon, the clear sky allowed illumination that was sufficient for her purposes. To cut down any residual lighting from the house, she had ordered that all lights on the side facing the garden be turned off, including the pool's.

The image-intensifiers of the rifle brought up the garden into pale green relief as she panned it across in an arc. Nothing. But she knew she'd heard something.

Remaining where she was, she lowered herself slowly to one knee, rifle back at the port, and waited.

Presently, she heard the softest of rustles again. It was *close.* She remained perfectly still. Then something was slithering over the bare toes of her left foot, and stopped.

The reptile was an unusually big example. Two and a half meters of irritable tiger snake was having a rest on her foot.

Snake and human waited for the other to move first.

At last, the snake began to move. Marika waited until its entire length had passed over her foot. And still she waited, her body attuned to the night, listening to the snake's progress, making no move that might cause a vibration for it to home upon. Then the faint sounds faded.

She still did not move.

Two minutes later, she did. With infinite slowness, she brought the rifle up. She was using the acoustic sensors and in the sights, she saw the target-box hunting until it remained fixed to one spot. She zoomed in. There was the snake, moving away from her.

Then something small scuttled across its path. The snake reversed itself with incredible speed and gave chase. Marika breathed deeply and held still. *Hunter and terrified prey were coming directly towards her.*

She did not move, keeping the target in the intensifier in lock. There was not going to be much time. Her hand caressed the trigger.

Now! She fired.

The rifle made a noise that was both a cough and a snarl. The swiftly moving snake was lifted off the ground, ripped into two pieces by the shock of the blow, instinctively leaking its venom as it went. She knew it would still be very dangerous when it came back to earth, for the head was very much alive. She followed its trajectory with the sight, locking on to the head while it was still airborne, following as it began to fall.

She fired a second time. The head of the snake shattered in a dark starburst.

She stood up and walked away from the dead reptile. It had been a good hunt. She was now ready for the real one.

▪ ▪ ▪

"So tell me, Piet," Gallagher said, "are you still playing your dangerous game of riding two horses in midstream?"

They were driving to a meeting with Haslam. Gallagher had made contact, but had not said he was bringing Villiger.

"One way to get your crotch ripped open," Villiger replied in a deadpan done-it-all, seen-it-all voice. "I'm still running with the hare and hunting with the hounds. In a strange way, just as the end of the old Soviet Union has made the world a far more dangerous place, so has the beginning of the dismantling of apartheid brought everything to the knife edge. If we're not very careful, we could lose it all over there and Bosnia will look like a children's picnic. So yes, I'm still playing. In fact, for a moment back at the Gardens, I thought I'd been set up by a faction from back home."

In the gloom of the Range Rover, Gallagher studied Villiger briefly, remembering the first time he'd seen the Afrikaner in that underground prison in the Outback, where they had been taken by Marika and her murderous friends.

A big, solid body with a mean-looking face and almost black, piggy eyes that were now and then reflected sparkling pinpoints of lights from the passing city; blond hair cut so short that under certain conditions he appeared bald; and an accent that was the perfect stereotype of South African English. Gallagher had once been told about Villiger that in his guise as an Intelligence man, in the bad old days that were only marginally worse than current times, he had once helped people experience the principles of flight from high buildings.

Gallagher restrained a smile as he remembered Villiger's reply when challenged about it.

"Man," Villiger had replied, "sure I knocked a few

about, and I've killed in the field. But the torture I left to the bastards who enjoyed it."

He had since learned a lot about the real Villiger. The man who, as a seventeen-year-old reared on Afrikanerdom, had secretly fallen in love with a so-called Cape colored teenager, with whom he had subsequently fathered a daughter. The man who for years had been totally ignorant of the existence of this offspring. The man who, because of the warped restrictions of the laws of the period, had been forced to endure the marriage of his teenaged love to a colored man to satisfy such laws, unaware she had been carrying his child. The man who, letting no one know the true reason, had himself never married.

But on the day of that first meeting with Gallagher, Villiger had been on a mission to assassinate a known African National Congress sympathizer, when Marika's people had taken them all hostage. The Afrikaner's damascene conversion had begun during the escape when, teamed with Gallagher and the other escapees, among whom was the very man he'd been sent to kill, they had fought their way to safety. The targeted man, an African called Nbwale, had fought side by side with him against their pursuers. Villiger had gained respect for his erstwhile quarry, but Nbwale had died during the final battle by the water hole in the desert.

The next time Gallagher had seen Villiger, it was with a remarkably beautiful, blonde, young woman who had subsequently turned out to be the daughter of Villiger's teens. By then, Villiger had been questioning the tenets of his own beliefs for some time and had begun to clandestinely work towards the dismantling of the hated system, while still remaining in his old job.

One day, the blonde young woman had confronted him with the news of his teenage paternity. Though she had looked completely white, the laws of the land then still in force had designated her colored. Faced with the true obscenity of the system's effect upon his own flesh and blood, very little had been further required to complete his conversion.

But Villiger was no longer a father. The briefly known daughter had been killed on a mission they had undertaken together, and in which Gallagher had been involved.

"How do you feel about Lorraine now?" Gallagher asked gently as he remembered what had occurred.

"Oh, man," Villiger said, a sad heaviness in his voice, "I still feel so guilty. She grew into a woman and I never knew her until it was too late. We had such a short time together. How could a boy of seventeen, in those times, have known?"

Villiger's heartfelt cry of regret seemed to be an echo of South Africa's own torment.

Gallagher was also nursing his own guilt about Lorraine's death, for Villiger had entrusted her safety to him.

"Look," Villiger went on, correctly understanding what was going on in Gallagher's mind, "I know you're still blaming yourself for what happened. Forget it. She knew the risks, and in any case, there was nothing you could have done. I told you that at the time. Better to have gone the way she did than to have been shot down like a dog in the street by some panicky soldier one bad day. We did a good job. All three of us. We stopped a big shipment of arms. I'll always be proud of her." Villiger peered out as Gallagher brought the Range Rover to a stop. "This looks more like an exclusive club than a hotel."

"It is. A club, I mean. Sure you don't mind meeting him?"

"Quite sure," Villiger said.

18

The building was a gentlemen's club reminiscent of a colonial past, and was not far from the Gardens. Haslam had raised an eyebrow on seeing Villiger, but made no further comment until he'd shown them into a room where they could have privacy.

"Places like this always make me feel like an NCO invited to the officers' mess," Haslam said, indicating the entire club with a wave of his hand.

Haslam's modesty was, as usual, misleading. Haslam was about as "NCO" as a diocesan bishop. In military terms, his rank would have been a senior lieutenant colonel at the very least, to Fowler's one-star general.

Haslam was holding out a hand to Villiger. "Mr. Villiger, I presume." He gave the tiniest of smiles.

They shook hands.

"You don't seem particularly surprised to see me here," Villiger said.

"I've been in this game far too long to be surprised

by anything, especially where Gordon is involved. After all, you did work together on that little incident in the Outback."

"Aren't you curious to know why I'm here?"

"No. I'm certain there's a good reason. I'm more interested in knowing whether you two had anything to do with the excitement at the Gardens tonight."

Neither Gallagher nor Villiger reacted.

"Is that innocent silence a yes? Or a no?"

Finally, Gallagher said, "Someone tried to snatch Piet."

"As they quite clearly did not succeed, I'm assuming you took care of those who attempted it. Ansen's hopping mad, of course."

"How did he get to know? It was over very quickly."

"He doesn't know. He's hopping mad because he doesn't know where you are. He's asked me, and I've said I didn't know. I'm not sure he believes me. There's another reason he's hopping mad. Rapicci's still not been found. For my money, the man's been long dead, but Ansen's hoping against hope."

Gallagher nodded. "For my money too. And how did *you* get to know?"

"It can't have escaped your notice that this place overlooks a boundary of the Gardens, which is across the street. Another boundary is bordered by Parliament House and the University. There are always people about. But the ambush was well planned, for no one gave the alarm. Now that you've told me a snatch was intended, they clearly expected it to be over quickly and with no fuss.

"It was Sian who discovered something was happening. She had been to see me with Markston, and afterwards managed to persuade him to accompany her on a walk. He reluctantly agreed, not thinking much of any hunch she might have had. A car racing away about eight o'clock or thereabouts nearly ran her down when it mounted the pavement as it came round a corner. Pity a police car was not cruising by at the time. It would have been interesting to discover who that driver was.

"Sian felt this warranted further checking and decided to retrace the direction the car had come from. They eventually found themselves near the cycle path by the river. After some further argument, Markston agreed to walk down it with her. He'd assumed, you see, that it was probably just a bad driver who'd had one too many. Not very intuitive, Markston. Good with the rough stuff, but that's about it. But movement at the far end of the path caught Sian's eye. So she stayed in cover and alerted Markston. Guess what they saw."

"You tell me."

"A very inert body being carried away. Those involved tried to make it look as if the person was a drunk once they'd got it upright; but of course she'd seen enough. She waited until well after she'd heard a car being driven away before continuing farther along to check with Markston—at last, now ready for anything—in tow. She searched the general area, testing the path surface with her fingers. It was damp.

"She sniffed at the tips, expecting the smell of blood. Instead, she got the sharp pong of some disinfectant cleansing fluid. A cleanup job had been very efficiently done. In the morning, there'll be no sign that anything untoward took place during the night. She didn't see either of you, so I'm assuming you had some help."

Gallagher said nothing. There was a long silence.

"Are you running another team, Gordon?" Haslam at last inquired mildly. "Or if not you . . ." He deliberately left the words hanging.

Gallagher took his time before replying. "Sorry, George," he said. "I can't tell you about that."

"Let me hazard a guess. It's the other lot, then. The

ones who gave you the file extract. They're here too."

Again, Gallagher said nothing.

"Ansen's not going to be most pleased," Haslam warned.

"There's more than one 'other lot,'" Gallagher eventually said. "They may well end up fighting each other. Best if we stay out of it."

"Easier said than done. Ansen's not going to like rival teams taking each other out on his patch, especially as someone's already drawn blood from him."

"I have a suggestion," Gallagher said.

Haslam looked at him neutrally. "Which is?"

"I want Piet to team up with Sian and Markston to watch my back, and I want him to be in command."

Haslam gave that some thought. "Do you agree to this?" he asked Villiger.

The South African nodded. "Yes."

"There'll be no problem with Sian. Markston might—"

"Markston will lump it," Gallagher interrupted firmly, "or stay out. I haven't got the time to deal with prima donna weapons men. I've worked something out with Piet, and he's happy to go along with the idea."

Haslam looked at Villiger. "If anything happens to you, I sincerely hope we're not going to get any flak from your people in Johannesburg."

Villiger smiled thinly.

"And as for the good Major Ansen," Haslam continued, "God knows what he'll say. We're just about straining his hospitality as it is."

"Tell him this concerns Piet as well." Then Gallagher hit Haslam with the bombshell. "Marika's alive and well, and is somewhere in, or near, Brisbane tonight. Ansen's people would suffer a lot of casualties."

Haslam stared at him. "But she's supposed to be dead. You got her in the Outback." He looked at Villiger.

"It's true," Villiger said. "Somehow, she managed to survive my shot."

Haslam returned his attention to Gallagher. "So all this is for revenge, Gordon? Just as you thought?"

"Now that I know it is Marika," Gallagher replied, "it's very much more than that. Her other agenda still stands. She intends to go back to it when she's disposed of us. I'm going to lure her to Fraser Island," he continued. "She'll be coming under my rules, to my chosen battleground. But I don't want the backup team there. I'll do this alone. If I'm not back by the time I'll set, you can come looking."

"Won't it be too late by then?"

"Not necessarily."

"We'll still have to let Ansen in on this. He'll blow a fuse if we try to go it alone. Besides, we'll need his help for some firepower, and perhaps a chopper."

"I'll leave you to handle him, George."

"Thanks for nothing."

"I can't have the place crowded with people. She's very, very good. If she sniffs I've got whole teams saturating the area, she'll simply pick another time and place, and I'll have lost the initiative. She'll disappear. Then we'll be back to wondering where she'll strike next, until her next target is found wearing one of her bullets. Impress that on the major. I know what I'm doing. I understand her."

"What if she brings her own team?"

Gallagher shook his head slowly. "They'll be a defensive screen, much the same as Piet, Sian, and Markston will be for me." He said nothing about Borodin, nor of the strong possibility that hit teams might be after Marika as well. He wasn't certain, but felt a warning to Villiger might be prudent.

"She's doing this as a lone hunter," he went on, "just like me. She won't want to share her kill with anyone. Those are the terms she's set, and I'm going to abide by them. She missed Piet tonight. That's going to make her very cross indeed, so it gives me an edge. But watch out for her team, and any others, Piet," he added to Villiger. "There may be more than one."

"I can handle it," Villiger said.

Gallagher knew he'd done the right thing in giving Villiger command of the backup. Otherwise, all sorts of people would be stomping all over the place, getting in the way, and getting killed. He needed someone with a cool head watching his back. Haslam would have been good, but while Haslam's age had not curbed his expertise, he was nowhere as fast as Villiger.

Against Marika and whoever she had chosen for her team, it could mean the difference between life, and death. Gallagher had no intention of putting Haslam into such a perilous situation.

As if knowing precisely what Gallagher was thinking, Haslam looked at him steadily. The eyes said it all.

Haslam understood.

Marika had cleaned out the rifle barrel and had put the weapon away in its case. In a short, thin nightdress, she now sat before a mirror slowly brushing her hair with long, deliberate strokes. The green eyes stared back at her, apparently unblinking. The daughter of a blonde Rumanian mother and a northern Greek father, the turbulent history of the Balkans seemed reflected deep within those eyes. There was a dark, haunting look in them, and something else too. She had given the hair so many strokes, it gleamed as if on fire; and still she continued with the brushing.

She had not eaten dinner, electing instead to remain in her room after she had finished off the second snake. She knew that Giraud, the younger man, had expected her to summon him to give vent to her anger after the failure of the attempt to kidnap the South African and the deaths of two of their colleagues. But she had decided not to. Letting him wait and wonder was much more effective. It would keep him on his toes.

She had not gone with them. That had not been part of the plan. Having herself carefully prepared the operation for months, it should have been easy enough for them to carry it out. Instead, they had failed. Disposing of Giraud in a fit of anger, she'd decided, would have been counterproductive. This was not the right time.

Gallagher had somehow found out and had been waiting. It could only have been Gallagher. Despite the quietly simmering anger she felt, she was still impressed. He was not letting her down. He would fight and was, she knew, more dangerous than any of the snakes she'd been hunting. It was fitting that the Taipan would be the last, to celebrate his defeat.

She stared at the reflection of her body beneath the nightdress as she thought of him, and saw that her nipples had begun to swell. She put down the brush, placed a hand upon her right breast, closed her eyes, and breathed deeply. Her mouth opened slightly and a low moan came out of her. She remained like that for long moments.

In his room, Giraud, the car driver who had nearly run over Sian, was polishing a strange, vicious-looking dagger of extraordinary beauty. The quality of its manufacture was such that it looked like a precious antique, making it seem an unlikely weapon to be in his possession.

Made in eighteenth-century India, it had two seven-inch blades of immensely strong, watered steel. These were of diamond section, with deep radiating grooves on each face, and fixed to a twin-barred horizontal hilt with gold incrustations. Twin elongated and slightly curving shafts rose from each end of the hilt, as protection for the forearm.

Giraud had come by it in a very odd way. Originally

a gift to a British naval officer, it had been taken to Afghanistan in the nineteenth century by a descendant who was himself an army officer. This officer had subsequently been killed on a mountain pass, and his body robbed. The dagger had then become the possession of the robber, in whose family it had remained for generations.

Came the Soviet Union's war in Afghanistan and an army colonel, a Russian, had found the dagger on the dead body of a guerrilla. He had promptly acquired it. Before the disintegration of the Soviet Union, Giraud had shot the colonel in his barracks. It had been a sanctioned kill. The dagger, on display on the colonel's desk, had been stolen by Giraud.

Since its acquisition he had killed with it four times, Rapicci being the most recent victim.

The next day, Haslam got the shock of his life. He had made friends with a silver-haired, moneyed club member about his own age named Digger Moran.

"It's my real name," Moran had told him.

Moran was now coming briskly towards him in the club lounge, a big grin on his face.

"There you are!" Moran greeted. "You lucky devil."

A puzzled expression appeared on Haslam's face. "Why am I supposed to be lucky?"

Moran still looked as if he'd just discovered several new ways of making even more money. "As if you didn't know!"

"You've got the advantage of me, Digger."

Moran gave him a knowing wink. "She's waiting, and you definitely are a lucky old devil. What have you got that I haven't? If you try to tell me she's your daughter, I won't believe it."

"Digger, what on earth are you talking about?"

He couldn't have meant Sian, Haslam reasoned.

Moran had seen Sian, if only briefly, and would have said so.

Moran looked uncertain. "All right with me if you want to keep it a secret. One of the staff told me a young lady was in the foyer asking for you. I went to have a look and perceived a vision. Some of the other members are in risk of cardiac arrest, and the younger ones are probably even now working on their chat-up lines. Now I'm a nice, mature gentleman who's made his fortune . . ."

"Perhaps she likes them poor like me," Haslam said as he heaved himself up from the very comfortable, dark brown leather armchair.

He began making his way towards the foyer. Moran followed.

Haslam paused. "Digger."

"I want an introduction."

"Shame on you. At your age too."

Moran gave an exaggerated sigh. "The messenger always loses. Shot if he brings bad news, and nothing if it's good."

Haslam smiled at him, shaking his head as he went out to the foyer. What he saw was indeed a vision.

She was wearing a calf-length floral dress that was just thin enough to show the shape of the body beneath it. Her legs were bare and on her feet were expensive, medium-heeled shoes with open toes. Her fingernails and toenails, neatly trimmed, were unpainted. Her lips were also unpainted, but were suffused with their own natural color. She wore a plain white muslin hat with a broad brim, which gave rise to the illusion that her gleaming curtain of hair was cascading from beneath it. She carried a shoulder bag and held dark glasses in one hand.

Moran, Haslam saw, had not exaggerated. He'd been right about the club members as well: Anyone near the foyer was looking at her, and some of the younger men indeed looked as if they were drumming up the courage to pounce.

She gave him one of her most ravishing smiles as he reached her. "Mr. Haslam."

"You have the advantage . . ."

"Can we go somewhere"—she glanced about her—"more private?" She sounded Australian, but with something else tagged on. "I get the feeling everyone will jump to all the wrong conclusions."

"They already have, and it will be even more so if we go to a private room."

Another smile lit her face. "I won't mind, if you don't."

"Well, I . . ."

"I am Marika," she told him softly, watching the shock spread across his face, "very much alive, and I've got a gun in my bag. Now I'm certain you don't want any of those nice gentlemen or their ladies to get hurt." She kept smiling. "Shall we go?"

Haslam was calmness personified, after the initial surprise. "But of course."

He took her to the same room where he'd met Gallagher and Villiger. "What do you want of me?" he demanded after he had shut the door.

"Nothing," she said. Her hand was now deep within the bag.

Haslam stared at it, as if already seeing the gun. "I understand. Having failed with Villiger . . ."

"So . . . he told you. But you do not understand at all. I am not going to kidnap you. I have no score to settle with you. Villiger shot to kill me, and Gordon . . ." She paused, falling curiously silent.

"Then you intend to kill me," Haslam said.

"Wrong again, Mr. Haslam. I merely wanted to show you how easy it would have been."

"How do you know who I am, and how did you know I was here?"

"Who you are is a matter of record to the people I'm working for. And finding out where you are was easy. The young girl with the green eyes, and her partner who thinks so much of himself."

Haslam let out his breath slowly, never taking his eyes off her. "You had them followed. It really was as easy as that?"

"They came here this morning. Don't be too hard on them. They don't know what they're looking for. Although I believe she's better than the man. I first saw them in a café. The man wanted to get into my pants. But she was . . . using her brain. My presence disturbed her, but she could not understand why. It will be interesting to see her in action."

"You could obviously have killed them both. Why didn't you? It would have been a simple thing, given your opportunities."

Haslam was still trying to come to terms with the fact that this was the person who had created such havoc, and who was responsible for bringing him all the way round the world. Her beauty was so astonishing, his eyes insisted on telling him it couldn't be. But he knew it could. In his younger days, during the war, he'd once known a beautiful killer while he was a liaison officer with the maquis.

Marika's beauty surpassed hers by far. Nevertheless, she had wrought her own devastation upon the hearts of men. But the greatest devastation had been wrought upon the enemy, whom she had killed without compunction. On being told she had once been a novice at a convent, Haslam, with the naïveté of youth, had at first refused to believe it. But it had been true. He had also fallen in love. Looking now at Marika, his eyes reluctantly agreed with his mind.

"Oh, Mr. Haslam," she said, as if to a slow but fond uncle. "You really do not understand. Why would I kill them? They were of no threat to me."

"You had no such qualms about the security man you killed."

"What security man?"

Haslam frowned. She seemed genuinely surprised. Gallagher had said there were other teams involved. Had one of them done the killing? He studied her expression closely, and found himself believing she really hadn't known about Rapicci. She appeared to be giving the matter serious thought. She also seemed annoyed. He wondered why.

"You are surprised that I don't know about this . . . person," she now said.

"Am I?"

Unexpectedly, the ravishing smile came back. "I shall leave now, Mr. Haslam. Nice to have met you."

"I could call the police."

She shook her head. "You would not be so stupid."

He sighed. "You're right. I don't want a massacre in here. But of course, you knew that even before you entered this club."

"Of course." Before he realized what she intended, she had leaned forward to kiss him on the cheek and was at the door before he had recovered. "Good-bye."

She closed the door quietly behind her.

"Remarkable woman," was all Haslam found he could say.

He touched the cheek she had kissed. He would remember those astonishing green eyes for a very, very long time.

"She came *here?*" Gallagher stared at him.

Haslam nodded. "Even gave me a kiss before she left. On this cheek," he added, touching the spot briefly with a forefinger.

"She's got more balls than many men I know," Villiger commented. "I can almost admire her. A bold woman."

"And confident," Gallagher said. "It's her way of telling us she's not walking away from this fight. She's accepted my challenge. From now on, the real stuff begins. The gloves are off. She's not going to be predictable, and I've got to be more than one step ahead of her."

It was afternoon, and having completed their preparations, they had returned to meet Haslam at the club. Haslam had given them the details of Marika's visit, including the discovery that she had appeared to know nothing of Rapicci's disappearance. They were sitting in the private room, having coffee. Despite the fact that his own hotel was not far away, Gallagher had decided not to tell Haslam. That way, Haslam could truthfully continue to claim to Ansen he had no idea where Gallagher was.

"Beautiful woman," Haslam said thoughtfully. "Such a shame. The club members were quite beside themselves with admiration."

"She has that effect on people," Gallagher said, giving nothing away.

Haslam gave him an inquiring look. "Sure you want to do this?"

"There isn't a choice."

After a while, Haslam nodded. "You're right, of course. More coffee? I can have some brought . . ."

Both Gallagher and Villiger shook their heads.

"Do you really believe she knew nothing about Rapicci?" Gallagher asked him.

"I've given the possibility some serious thought. She seemed genuinely puzzled. Unless she's a consummate actress . . ."

"Which she can be when the situation demands it."

"Even so. Sometimes, even the best can't hide everything. She was taken off guard when I mentioned Rapicci. Her eyes were puzzled, almost as if something unsanctioned by her had occurred. Some of her crew working independently, perhaps?"

It was just possible, Gallagher thought, that the people Borodin had mentioned had also infiltrated Marika's team and were waiting, under instruction, for the right moment to betray her. He said nothing of this to Haslam.

"Have you told Markston about the arrangements?" he asked instead.

"That joy still awaits him," Haslam replied, with distinct relish. "As a matter of fact, he and Sian are due here"—he glanced at his watch—"any moment now."

"This should be interesting."

Villiger said nothing and remained expressionless.

"When are you setting off?" Haslam asked Gallagher.

"Tonight. I'll make certain I'm seen." Gallagher stood up. "I've got a few more things to attend to before then."

"And when do we come looking for you?"

"Two days after I've reached Fraser Island."

"Leaving it a bit long," Villiger said.

"I'll need the time. Besides, Piet, you'll have your work cut out making sure her people don't join in, and trying to get Markston to obey orders while keeping Major Ansen happy."

"Just what I need for Christmas. *Two* days," Villiger went on, emphasizing the time limit. "Forty-eight hours, man. Then we're coming to look for you. Let's hope we'll not be searching for a body."

"Nice to know someone cares," Gallagher said dryly. "Piet, I'll see you about six this evening, where we had our little chat last night, for a final check. Just you. After that, we won't see each other again until I've come off the island . . ."

"Or until we come looking."

"Let's hope that won't be necessary. See you later, George," Gallagher said to Haslam, and went out.

Haslam stared at the closing door. "Think he'll make it?" he asked Villiger. "She may not go alone."

"That's why we're his backup."

"Yes. But will he make it?"

"Man, if anyone can . . ."

"Quite. I'm fond of that lad. I'd like to see him again. And if you tell him I said so . . ."

"Did you say something?" Villiger asked.

They both grinned.

"Have another coffee, Mr. Villiger."

"Thank you, Mr. Haslam. I will."

Then the door opened and Markston, followed by Sian, entered.

Markston was furious and was making a poor job of hiding it. He clearly resented being under Villiger's command. Sian appeared unconcerned, and favored Markston with a neutral glance that could have meant anything.

"You do have a choice, Markston," Haslam was saying in a hard voice. "You can opt out. I'll go in your place."

Markston would not have been able to live that down, which Haslam knew perfectly well. To be replaced in action by someone of Haslam's age would be very difficult to explain to his peers when the news reached them. Haslam had left him no choice, and he knew it.

"Well?" Haslam demanded.

"I'm okay for it, Mr. Haslam."

"Good. We won't discuss it further."

"We saw Gallagher on the way out," Sian now said.

"Did he say anything?"

"He said hello. Nothing more."

"That's a surprise," Haslam remarked, suppressing a smile. "Sit down, you two. It's crunch time, and we've got some final matters to discuss. Have you both eaten?" They nodded. "I'll order some more coffee—or tea, if anyone would prefer." He glanced at each in turn.

"Coffee, please," Sian said.

"Tea," said Markston.

Haslam glared at him.

As soon as he'd left the club, Gallagher had taken a taxi along the Riverside Expressway to Coronation Drive, where he got out near a public telephone. He had deliberately chosen the multilane road so as to flush out any followers. He was certain he'd spotted at least two cars. Making no effort to evade, he walked to the first phone and called the number Borodin's young colleague had given him.

Borodin answered immediately. "I wondered if you'd call."

"How did you know it was me?" Gallagher countered.

"You're the only person meant to use this number. So, you are ready?"

"Yes. I'm going tonight." He briefly told Borodin about Marika's visit to Haslam, and about Rapicci.

Borodin laughed softly when he'd heard about Haslam's reaction to Marika. "You have got to admit she is very daring. A pity she works for others. I could use someone like her. The two of you . . ."

"Forget it."

Borodin laughed softly once more. "I am having my little joke with you. I am sorry about that policeman," he went on gravely. "I believe you are right about her people being infiltrated. One of them has intructions to eliminate her at a prescribed juncture. There may be more, plus some on the outside. My own people have identified a number of them. Some familiar faces."

"How many?"

"There are at least two within Marika's team, I think. Also, there's an extra team keeping in the shadows. At least eight."

"Jesus!"

"These are serious people, my friend. They are playing for high stakes, of which my own country is one. We hope to capture one or two. They may have valuable information."

"Why not pull in a few of those you've identified?"

"They don't know we're here. If we did that, it would warn their principals. We must wait until you have begun your own business. With the number of people who will be involved, they'll think they're fighting Marika's people, or the security forces. We'll be involved, but keeping a very low profile. We should end this conversation. You're on a public phone, but as we both know, interceptions are a matter of routine these days."

"Yes."

"Good luck, my friend. We'll be watching for you."

"Thanks."

They hung up together.

As Gallagher walked away from the phone, he noticed a car parked across the street. It was one of those he'd seen on the expressway, a dark green sedan with fancy wheels. He pretended to have missed it, and hailed another taxi.

The car followed him at a discreet distance all the way to his hotel. He didn't mind. After tonight, it wouldn't matter.

He paid off the taxi, then entered the plush foyer of the hotel. At the reception desk, he collected a parcel and went up to his room. He already knew what was in it. He put the Do Not Disturb sign on the door, then went onto the balcony and looked down upon the river. The car that had followed him, he was certain, would be parked somewhere near the hotel, waiting to see what he'd do next. Whoever was in it would have a long wait.

Leaving the balcony doors open, he went back inside

and got out the weapons case. He checked, cleaned, and reloaded each firearm with precise care. He also checked the spare magazines. He had plenty of ammunition for the job at hand, even if he came up against Marika's people as well. Provided Villiger handled the backup as expected, there should be no need for more. He hoped.

He returned the case to the safe. He then went to the bed and, setting his watch alarm, removed his shoes and lay down upon it. He had prepared everything he'd considered necessary for the task at hand, and all the required equipment was already in the Range Rover, which was itself enclosed in a secure area of the hotel car park.

But he was still not taking any chances. The vehicle itself had an electronic locking system whose special key possessed a billion combinations, of which only one was the correct code. When he was ready to leave, he would again check it thoroughly for hostile devices.

He did not open the parcel.

He allowed himself to relax totally, feeling his senses become acute. After a while, he fell asleep; but it was the sleep of an organism at the peak of alertness, and which would come awake fleeting seconds before the alarm went off.

The wolf was ready.

19

At precisely 5:05 P.M., Gallagher woke up. The alarm beeped seconds later. He removed the sign from the door, then took off his clothes and went into the bathroom for a quick shower. After a change of clothing for the trip, he opened the parcel he'd picked up from reception. Inside was a pair of brand-new, calf-length olive green canvas boots with thick, pliable soles and cross-laced all the way to the top. He'd bought them at a military surplus shop and had left the parcel at the desk to be collected on his return.

Gallagher was well familiar with the type of boot, having worn similar footwear on missions in Southeast Asia. He was not going to wear the boots immediately. Instead, he closed the box and secured it, then put on a pair of loafers of soft leather that were secured by single overstrips with Velcro fastenings. Next, he retrieved the weapons case and took out the big SIG Sauer P226, with its holster. He strapped it on and shut the case. Five minutes later, a knock sounded on the door.

Gallagher put on a lightweight, aircrew-style zipped jacket made of fabric over an olive green T-shirt to hide the weapon, then went to open the door cautiously, ready to move swiftly if need be. Being careless cost more than being careful. Before going out to see Haslam, he'd ordered a light meal, and this was the time he'd designated that it be sent up. It could be the order; or it could be something else.

It was room service. A young woman pushing a trolley laden with appetizing seafood snacks smiled at him.

"Your order, Mr. Gallagher. I hope this is to your liking."

"It most certainly is," he said appreciatively. "I'm spoilt for choice."

"We aim to please."

"You're certainly doing that," he told her pleasantly. "Thank you very much. I'll take it from here." He pulled the trolley into the room.

"Thank *you*, sir. Just leave it outside the door when you're finished."

"I will."

"Enjoy your meal."

"That I shall."

Another smile, and she headed back for the lift. He watched her leave, waiting to see if anyone had come up with her. But the richly carpeted corridor was empty. He waited a full thirty seconds before shutting the door.

He ate quickly, then put the trolley outside, moving it a short distance away from the room. There was still no one in the corridor. He reentered, collected the weapons case and the box containing the boots, and went out. He pulled at the door until he heard it click shut behind him.

He saw no one suspicious on the way down. He handed in his keys at the desk. Still no one.

"I'm going up to Fraser Island for a few days," he said to the receptionist, loud enough for anyone interested enough to hear. "Two, or possibly three. Fancied driving up instead of taking a plane. I'll call you when I'm on my way back."

"No problem, sir," she said. "It's beautiful on the island. You'll want to stay longer. I've been there. The lakes are gorgeous. Have a good trip."

"On that recommendation, I will. Thank you."

"My pleasure."

As he walked out, Gallagher thought he saw a man watching him interestedly.

Now they knew.

Gallagher went to the Range Rover and checked it thoroughly. It was clean. He put in the box and the case and climbed in. This time, he intended to shake off any pursuers until after he'd met with Villiger. No point in leading them to his backup. The more surprises in store for them, the better.

Gallagher drove slowly away from the hotel, turned left, and followed the Edward Street one-way system before turning right into Alice Street. The route took him past Haslam's club. He continued along Alice Street until that led onto the expressway and across Captain Cook Bridge, which spanned the river at the Botanical Gardens spur.

He glanced in his mirror. The green sedan was following. He then checked his watch. It was exactly 5:30. Time for fun.

As he crossed the bridge over the Brisbane, heading southeast, he unobtrusively increased his speed. His followers would be wondering about his route. Fraser Island was northwards.

The road had now become the South East Freeway, but Gallagher had no intention of going much farther along it. He waited until the sedan, clearly afraid of losing him, drew too close. His intended exit was just before the Vulture Street flyover and he wanted to take it before his pursuers realized what was happening. They would then be forced to continue for some distance before they found another exit, by which time he'd be long gone.

The exit signs came up. Gallagher maintained his speed. There was no other traffic close enough in his lane to either balk his intended maneuver, or for him to obstruct. The sedan was probably modified and very fast, but it did not matter. As the exit approached, he speeded up in the inside lane. Bearing down in the outside lane, the sedan matched his speed. The exit was now almost too close to take.

Gallagher braked suddenly. The car shot past, now desperately trying to stop in time and balking other cars, which blared their horns furiously, forcing it to continue.

Gallagher took the exit, curved left to join Vulture Street, but came off again almost soon after, turning left onto a narrow side street. A few more corners saw him heading north on Kangaroo Point, towards where he would be meeting Villiger. After leaving Villiger, all he'd have to do would be to join the nearby Bradfield Highway northwards out of the city, towards Fraser Island.

At six o'clock, Gallagher drew to a halt behind Villiger's all-black Toyota Land Cruiser. Another brilliant sunset was in the making, gleaming off the river. He got out and went up to the other vehicle. Villiger was looking at him from the driver's seat. He climbed into the passenger seat.

Villiger was still studying him, inspecting his clothes. "Jungle greens."

"Not quite, but it'll do."

"And where are the boots?"

"In the Rover. I'll put them on before I leave. I didn't fancy stomping out of the hotel looking like a refugee from a paramilitary outfit. Surprising what a pair of boots can make you look like."

Villiger grinned without humor. "It's like that every day back home. I take it you're armed?"

"Yes. Had a tussle with a green job with fancy

wheels. Probably souped-up. Two men." Gallagher gave Villiger a full description of the car that had been following him.

"We'll tag them," Villiger promised. "Sian and that jackass will be in another Range Rover. Metallic blue. A deep color, almost black. Don't shoot at it. Well, as long as you don't hit Sian."

"I see you like our Mr. Markston very much. So much, you won't travel with him."

Villiger stretched his lips in what looked like a snarl. "The girl's good; I like her manner. But that idiot . . . we must be careful he doesn't go off at half cock."

"From your glowing enthusiasm," Gallagher began, "I gather he was not pleased when he heard."

"Let's just say that a big cat from the veld with a boil on its balls would have been in a better mood."

"Happy families."

Villiger glared at the water, thinking of Markston. "But Haslam insists he's pretty damn good with weapons. Man, I hope Haslam's not mistaken. We've got some kit from Major Ansen, by the way. Good stuff, too. Not a bad bloke if you handle him right. The major, I mean. Got all the firepower we need. Here . . ." Villiger was reaching into the back and was pulling at something from beneath what looked like a car rug. "Present for you."

It was a Beretta M3P semiautomatic 12-gauge shotgun, with a 5-round magazine and folding stock.

"Plenty of ammo, too," Villiger added. "Or how about this?"

He pulled out another weapon. This time Gallagher saw the 40-mm snout of a grenade launcher.

Gallagher shook his head. "I'm okay. Enough for my needs. I'm not going after an army."

"You may find yourself facing one."

"That's why I've got you to watch my back. To make sure there isn't one."

Villiger slid the weapons back under the rug. "That's nice to know," he said. "More presents. This time, you can't refuse. Some things you asked for."

Villiger handed him four slim, olive green cylinders about a foot long each, and bound tightly together with broad green tape. They were spiked at one end and flat-topped at the other, with a dark red band just beneath the edge. They were no bigger than candles. Another item, about the size of a large remote control for a TV, was also handed over. It came in a canvas pouch.

"I thought they were such a good idea," Villiger added, "I asked for an extra set. The major was happy to oblige. Well . . . I *think* he was."

"Ah . . ." Gallagher said, taking them. "My sensors. Great. Oh, did Haslam get that permit for me?"

Normally, access to Fraser Island was by a minimal-fee national parks permit.

"Coming up," Villiger said, offering a slip of official-looking paper, "again courtesy of the major. Haslam's really been doing a good job on him. You are hereby exempt."

Gallagher took the permit and put it in a zipped inside pocket of his jacket. "Thanks, Piet."

"Some news," Villiger went on in a voice that warned Gallagher it was going to be bad. "They've found their man. Rap . . . Rap . . ."

"Rapicci."

"Yes. Dead."

Gallagher was saddened to hear of it, but not really surprised.

"Damn it. Where?" he asked Villiger.

"In a creek north of here. There were two deep puncture marks in his chest."

"Not a snake, surely?"

"No. Some strange weapon. They were big and deep bloody holes, man. Diamond-shaped."

"But what kind of weapon would do that?"

Villiger shrugged. "Perhaps a type of two-bladed

spear, or sword, or dagger . . . not modern. That's what Ansen said the forensic people told him. One of them's a weapons historian."

"The bastard responsible enjoys what he does," Gallagher said quietly. "I hope we get him. Poor old Johnno," he continued. "What a way to go."

"They killed him, then dumped him. Watch yourself, Gordon."

"Count on it. Just you keep an eye on green sedans and their mates."

"You can count on *that.*" Villiger's pebble eyes stared at Gallagher. "See you at Rainbow Beach . . . in one piece. I still think we two should travel in loose convoy."

"Not a good idea. But I appreciate the thought." Gallagher began to climb out. "Rainbow Beach then."

"I won't shake hands," Villiger said.

"Save that for later."

Villiger nodded as Gallagher climbed out. "And watch out for snakes in your suspension!" he called, grinning. He started the Toyota and drove away, heading back to meet with Sian and Markston. He did not look round.

Gallagher felt a strange sense of loneliness as the Land Cruiser moved off. He waited until it had disappeared round a corner before going back to his own vehicle. He changed his loafers for the boots, then got in to commence his journey northwards, for his deadlier rendezvous with Marika.

Snakes in the suspension. He knew about that. If you pulled off the road, especially near a cane field that had been burnt for clearing, irate snakes tended to like coiling round the suspension, so the story went. Nasty surprise if you had to change a wheel at night. He wondered how many snakes had been transported hundreds of kilometers that way.

But he had more dangerous things to worry about.

He found an early access to the Bradfield Highway going north, which took him back over the river across the Story Bridge at Kangaroo Point. This was part of National Route 1, which would eventually lead him onto the Bruce Highway for the journey to Fraser Island.

As he crossed the river, he checked his mirrors. There was no green car lurking there. It didn't mean they weren't using radios, probably scrambled to avoid interception, or that they hadn't even by now alerted another car.

But he felt no tingling of the senses. They were certainly out there, but as yet, apart from the sedan with the flashy wheels, they had not made contact.

The equipment fit of the Range Rover included an excellent stereo system. Gallagher had bought a selection of CDs for the journey, and he now programmed one. It was an old favorite. He was on his own as night approached.

The headlights pierced the darkness, illuminating the dark ribbon of empty road as the blue Toyota sped along. Markston was driving.

"I'd suggest slowing down," Sian told him calmly. Every so often, she checked behind for tags. The road was empty, but far in the distance, she thought she could see the glow of fast-traveling lights. "If we hit a kangaroo at this speed . . ."

She inclined her head briefly to glance at the speedometer. She said nothing about it, but noted on the odometer that they were now passing the ninety-kilometer mark since leaving Brisbane. Just over fifty-six miles.

"I don't see any warning signs . . ." Markston was saying.

"You expect the fucking animals to read?" she said irritably. It was going to be a long night. Markston was at last bringing out the worst in her. She should remain calm, but it was going to be tough.

"Why didn't we just take the bitch out in Brisbane?" Markston griped. "Why drag us all the way up to some crappy island?"

Sian gave him a hard stare. "It's not a crappy island. It's supposed to be quite beautiful."

"So fucking what?" His face, etched by the glow of the lights, was uncompromising.

"You're a real dickhead," she said bluntly. "You don't really understand anything, do you? Didn't you hear *anything* Mr. Haslam said? For a start, we had no idea who she was when we saw her in the café. And even if we had known, do you seriously believe we could have taken her? If she is as fast and as dangerous as we've been told, she would have taken *us* out, and God knows how many other innocent people as well.

"That's why Gallagher's enticing her up there, where no bystanders are likely to get in the way. You also seem to forget there's more to it than just taking her out. There's a bigger operation running. Our job is to do as instructed. Gallagher can handle her."

"Gallagher, Gallagher, Gallagher . . . !"

"Don't look at me, Markston. Look at the bloody road."

Markston was negotiating a bend just after Tanawha.

"*Jesus!* You'd think the sun shines out of his . . . *shit!*" Markston was braking hard. A kangaroo was in the middle of the road, transfixed by the lights. It was making absolutely no effort to avoid the oncoming vehicle.

Sian stared at it. Something was wrong.

"*Don't stop!*" she screamed. "*Drive on!*" She'd pulled out the big Magnum revolver.

"What? You just told me to slow down—"

"Drive on, you stupid . . . ! *It's an ambush!*"

She had lowered her window and was leaning out, firing at the kangaroo.

Markston, while clearly believing she had taken leave of her senses, speeded up after a moment's hesitation as the weapon roared massively within the confines of the vehicle, bringing with it the sharp stench of the discharge.

Then, even before he hit it, the kangaroo was falling and, unbelievably, a pair of human legs was crumpling beneath the tottering marsupial. Then everything seemed to collapse into a mass of rapid, disconnected images. A pole shot from beneath the tumbling animal to catapult across the road and into the surrounding darkness beyond the dancing lights, as the Land Cruiser bucked and heaved. It clambered over the obstruction of kangaroo and man as the stout nudge bars at the front slammed them sideways and partially beneath the nearside wheels.

"Don't bloody stop!" Sian was yelling. "Go! Go! *Go on!*"

She had emptied the weapon, and was now swiftly reloading with a snap loader which contained six replacement rounds. She swiveled round as they roared past, preparing to fire to the rear of the Land Cruiser.

By now, the night had become peppered with what seemed like fireflies, but the solid, spattering thuds hitting the vehicle told them these were rather more inimical. Then they were out of range. There was no need for her to fire the reload. No bullets had come near them.

"Are you all right?" she demanded sharply, ducking back in as the Toyota hurtled along the highway. She turned in her seat to look back. There were a few desultory flashes, but the serious firing was already over. "Are you okay?" she repeated, turning round again to look at him. She held the Magnum ready, in case there was another ambush farther on.

"Yes. Yes. I'm fine." Markston checked the instruments. "Nothing vital seems to have been hit. Fuel's okay too. Christ. That was a lucky escape. How did you . . ."

"First time I've seen a kangaroo in jeans and boots. They hadn't positioned it properly. The man who was propping it up with that pole didn't do a good job of hiding his feet. They must have deliberately killed it, then stuck it in the middle of the road to wait for us."

"So we've been tagged, after all."

"She must have described us to her people and had someone watching back in Brisbane. She left us alone before because then, we weren't seen as a threat. It's all different now."

"I knew we should have taken out the bitch."

She relaxed in her seat, leaned her head back against the headrest, and sighed. Markston was fixated. It was no use trying to reason with him. She said nothing and they traveled on in silence, the revolver still ready for quick use.

Markston kept giving her surreptitious glances.

"That was pretty good," he said after a while.

It must have cost him, she thought. But it wouldn't last. One incident would not change his attitude. Still, she did not want a night of bickering if she could help it. After what had just happened, they were clearly going to have their work cut out just to stay alive. It would be stupid to diminish their effectiveness. She'd just have to be the more disciplined; she could expect little help from him on that score.

"Thanks," she said.

When they were sure no one had as yet given chase, they stopped just long enough to inspect the Toyota with low-light torches. There were a few holes, but none were near anything vital. Their unexpected response to the roadblock had obviously taken their intended ambushers by such surprise, they had managed to bolt out of range before accurate fire could be brought to bear. It had been a very lucky escape indeed, thanks to Sian's quick reactions.

Thirty seconds later they were back aboard and quickly on their way again. They hadn't used their radios because even with a scrambler, a frequency hopper trying to eavesdrop could get a lucky break. The idea was not to give any positions away with a transmission unless the situation had become so desperate, immediate backup and rescue were needed. Ansen's people had choppers with armed teams standing by on alert should help become necessary.

"They could have zapped us with a grenade launcher," Markston said. "That would have been effective."

"Not everyone believes in thud and blunder, Markston," she said wearily, not bothering to raise her head. "A blown-up Toyota is more difficult to move from the public highway than one that's had its passenger and driver killed. They're not some of your lot playing action men for the cameras. *I* wouldn't like a high profile in my job, and *they* want to be practically invisible. A grenade launcher is hardly the mark of subtlety."

The sarcasm in her voice made him shut up. More silence followed, disturbed only by the sound of the Land Cruiser hurrying through the night.

"I know you think I'm a shit," Markston suddenly began, "a boneheaded macho man. You've made that plain enough. But what do you know about me? I mean, *really* know. It's not what you imagine, based on the brief time you've spent with me."

She remained silent. If he wanted to talk, she reasoned, it was best to let him. It was better than arguing.

"There are two kinds of people in the world—the shits, and the shat on."

Sian still remained silent, but now she turned her head slightly to watch him. His hands appeared to be gripping, rather than firmly holding, the steering wheel.

"When I was a boy," he continued, speaking in a tightly controlled voice, "we had a large house, two cars, and a small motor cruiser when such accessories were still a big deal, and a huge garden for me and my friends to play in. My father was chairman of his own firm. I looked up to him. He was my hero. Then one day, it all began to go wrong.

"The money mysteriously started to run out. Demands in brown envelopes began to come to the house. Then people with smug faces started entering our home, assessing our things, digging into our privacy. My mother's jewels went. The cars went. The cruiser went. People who used to call my father 'sir' and meant it began asking for cash before allowing him even an order for milk. Then they stopped delivering the papers.

"Valuable pieces of antique furniture and a few paintings that my father had collected after working for years were taken away. He was quite poor when he started, you know. He'd never been to university." Markston paused briefly, then went on. "The house grew emptier, and my friends stopped coming. My mother couldn't give dinner parties anymore, so my friends' parents stopped inviting them in turn. It was a really awful time. I watched my father shrink, his dignity crushed.

"One day, he sat next to me on the grass in the garden and put his arm around me. That warned me that something terrible was going to happen. You see, my father never did that. He was always so . . . strong. He used to give me a little punch on the shoulder and I'd tap him back and we'd laugh. We'd been doing that routine ever since I was . . . I suppose about three."

Markston paused again, staring into the night. Sian kept looking at him but continued to say nothing, allowing him to speak uninterrupted. It was probably the first time he'd said so much about his past to anyone. Perhaps the ambush had turned some kind of key within him.

"I'll always remember the last thing he ever said to me that day. 'Spike,' he said—he always called me Spike when he had something really special to say to me . . . I was spiky-haired when I was born, apparently . . . Stuff from the afterbirth gave that impression; I had plenty of hair, you see—'Spike,' he said, 'there was once a man, a mass murderer who lived in a seaside town. When it was discovered what he'd done, someone made a remark that I find most memorable, even today. The person said he was such a nice man, he always paid his bills on time. So you see, Spike, you can commit any horrors you like, and as long as you pay your bills on time, you'll be a nice man.' One hour later, he shot himself. I was twelve."

Markston drew a deep breath, as if what he'd just said had been a supreme effort for him.

"I'm sorry about your father," Sian told him in the uncomfortable silence that followed. It was a genuine sentiment.

"Don't be."

"How can you—"

"My father was a fool!" Markston responded savagely.

"I can't believe you're saying that after what you've just told me."

"He was weak. Yes. *Weak.* I didn't discover what had really happened until I was in my late teens. My father had played by the rules and his colleagues ripped him off. He believed in an aggressive, but honest, way of doing business. They simply looked upon him as an idealistic moron. They ran rings around him, and when he thought he was in control, they really had him where they wanted. Add envy and greed to that, and it was only a matter of time before the bastards ruined him. I despise him for letting that happen. This is a world of savages, and you've got to be the biggest savage on the block."

She was staring at him. "You really do believe that, don't you? I was beginning to feel some sympathy, Markston, but all you've done now is make me understand even more why I don't like your attitude. You should be proud of your father. He was a very brave man . . ."

Markston was uncompromising. "He failed. There's no bravery in failure."

"You had a father," she said. "For a while you knew him, and admired him. Or was that only for as long as he fitted your own ideal? I never knew my father. As far as I know, he could be anywhere, or nowhere." She stopped suddenly, not wanting to say more about it.

"Your precious Gallagher," Markston said after another long silence, "is a little like my father was. He likes to play fair. That's a weakness, and it will cost him."

"From what I've heard, it doesn't seem to have prevented him from succeeding on some very dangerous missions. He's alive, while many others are dead—people who'd thought they were very tough. People like you. You wouldn't last very long against him, whatever you might think.

"He has a very impressive record; which means it's been bad news for anyone coming up against him. They were the ones who wound up dead after the encounter. That's a pretty powerful message. Mr. Haslam says he's devastating when he gets going. Even frightening."

Markston chose to ignore her remarks. "He's got a vulnerable side. That woman will take him. But if I get her in my sights, I won't give her the time to blink."

Sian wondered whether some part of Markston, knowing he would never get the chance to have sex with Marika, was determined to destroy what he couldn't have. He'd never see it like that, she knew, and would probably vehemently deny the connection. But he was still carrying the poisonous hatred of the people who had ruined his father and had stolen his childhood, and must have spent years taking it out on anyone conveniently available.

He was still doing it, and Marika was the handy new target. His frustrated desire for her body was giving the whole thing an added and very dangerous quality, and as such could put their own lives unnecessarily at risk.

She began to wish Haslam had not paired him with her. She didn't care how good he was with weapons, or how adept he was at flying the Citation. All she really knew about him was that he had gone into military service very young, taken a degree through his particular branch of the Services and, being ambitious, eventually received a commission.

His secondment to the Department had been carried out by policymakers who were far above her in status, and who were probably quite unaware of the ticking bomb within him. However, as far as she was concerned he was dangerously unstable, and she intended to mention the fact to Haslam after this little operation was over. Meanwhile, she'd have to watch him very closely indeed.

She took a look behind. No one seemed to be following.

She didn't put the gun away.

Behind them, the people who had laid the unsuccessful ambush had dragged the crumpled bodies of the man and the kangaroo off the road, and hauled them about a hundred meters into the bush. There was swampy ground nearby and, stripping the man's body of anything that might have identified him, they left him there, with the kangaroo for company.

They hurried back to their vehicle, which was parked well off the road along a short, secluded track that went nowhere. Using a low-watt map-reading light attached to the cigarette lighter socket, a man in the passenger seat was tapping at the keyboard of what bore a passing resemblance to a laptop computer. The device was wired to a hidden communications unit. There was a display panel in the opened lid, but instead of graphics it showed a series of rapidly moving pulses. They appeared to be hunting. Beneath them, a twenty-figure sequence of numbers was continuously changing.

"Nothing," the operator said in disgust. "They can't be transmitting." He tapped furiously at the keys.

"Or they've got an effective block," one of those who had disposed of the bodies suggested.

"Even a block should leave some evidence of transmission. But there's nothing. All I've got is dead space."

"Perhaps you're right," another commented. "The simplest answer is sometimes the true one. As a deliberate policy, they've maintained radio silence."

"After a firefight? I'd have thought they'd warn their colleagues."

"Not necessarily. Come on. Turn that thing off. Someone might zero in on *us*. Let's get going. We've been here long enough as it is." It was the voice of authority.

The operator swiftly obeyed.

There were three of them now where previously there had been four, and they were extremely annoyed at having failed in their ambush and taken casualties so soon.

Their vehicle was not the green sedan, and they had not conversed in English.

They were also not Marika's people.

On a hill that overlooked the bend, two figures propped themselves against a tall tree, after having first checked its upper reaches with their light-intensifying binoculars for any denizens that might drop down on them. Satisfied, they then concentrated on the spot where the ambush had failed so disastrously.

They watched as the remaining three ambushers got into their vehicle and took off in belated pursuit. They had been following at some distance, and had noted the sudden dipping of the headlights when Markston had braked. Then had come the momentary skyward lurch as the Toyota had bounded over the dead kangaroo.

They'd driven up quickly, stopping off the road well away from the bend, then had got out to hurry to their vantage point. They had arrived just in time to catch the last of the firing, though they'd heard much of it as they had approached.

"Gallagher's people have drawn first blood tonight," a male voice commented. Borodin. He had spoken in his native tongue.

"The man was driving," his female companion said in the same language. She was the young woman who had spoken to Gallagher at the Gardens. "So it's the woman who spoiled their little ambush."

"You sound pleased," Borodin said. There was a smile in his voice. "Do you consider she may be as good as you? If the world situation had not changed, you might well have come up against her one day."

"That would have been sad. I like her."

"She might have bested you."

She gave a shrug in the darkness. "She could have tried to."

This time, Borodin's face was creased in an unseen smile. "Come on, my little warrior, we've got plenty to do."

Marika was driving alone.

She had left the house after everyone else had gone, with the exception of the staff and the old aborigine, who'd remained to look after the last snake. His presence also helped to reassure the house staff, who had been extremely unhappy with the idea of being left to share the house with a Taipan that was by now in the foulest of tempers. No one had seen her leave.

None of those who had seen her earlier would have recognized her at first glance, and it was doubtful whether further glances would have helped. Subtle alteration of her appearance had transformed her. Her golden hair had been woven into a single plait which she had coiled and fixed to the back of her head. She had then put a bush hat a size too big over it, causing much of her face to be hidden. Though she hated normal use of makeup, for disguise purposes it was necessary. Careful use of shading made her look older, with skin that seemed less than perfect.

She wore baggy trousers and a safari-style jacket with unobtrusive internal padding, to give her waist the appearance of being much thicker than it really was. She had put on lipstick that was much too bright, and her luminous green eyes were hidden behind contact lenses that made them seem muddy and undistinguished.

The impression given was of a middle-aged, antiseptic matron who liked nothing more than to spend her time on nature rambles, who looked as if romance had fled from her at first sighting, and who would give a bone-crusher handshake when introduced. She had even changed the way she normally walked, splaying her feet slightly to give her a clumsy, asexual gait.

Her appearance could not have been further from the bold, sensuous presence of the true Marika.

Her only luggage was a large backpack. Among its contents were the dismantled rifle, two pistols, and plenty of ammunition for each.

She was two hours behind Borodin and his young Spetsnaz subordinate. The route she chose made only partial use of the Bruce Highway, and completely bypassed the spot where the ambush had been attempted.

20

Gallagher made it to his destination for the night without incident. He'd found a deserted track on high ground that overlooked the ocean, about two kilometers away from Rainbow Beach. He reversed into a small clearing off the track, then continued into shrub vegetation among tall trees until the Range Rover was hidden from view.

He shut down the engine and as it cooled, a silence that felt palpable greeted him. The creatures of the night, startled by his arrival, had retreated and become quiet, and would resume their scurryings only when his presence among them became a familiar thing.

He picked up the sensors he'd received from Villiger and, using the infrared goggles to guide him, began to plant them at the four points of an imaginary compass, with the Range Rover at its center. The distance to each from the central point was about sixty meters. The goggles gave him their startlingly clear window on the night.

"Hope I don't step on any bloody snake," he muttered to himself as he worked. "Not what I need right now." But there was not even a rustle. No sinuous movement caught his eye. Even so, he trod very carefully.

When he got back to the vehicle, he actually looked beneath it to check the suspension. No snakes had hitched a ride. He climbed back in, removed and put away the goggles, then took the controller out of its pouch. There were several buttons positioned beneath a small screen. He switched it on and pressed one of the buttons. The screen showed a yellow compass rose, with black radiating lines that marked off the degrees in units of ten. At each quarter, though not at the cardinal points of the compass, a red dot pulsed. His watchdogs were active.

They were close-quarter sensors and operated in three modes simultaneously: radar, infrared, and acoustic. The acoustic mode was so sensitive, breathing and whispered speech could be easily identified. The sensors' coverage pattern was dome-shaped and began at ground level, reaching up to fifty feet. Gallagher had positioned them so that each area of cover overlapped the next. There was no way for an intruder to come through undetected.

With the combined alarm set, he placed the unit on the passenger seat, then reclined the driver's to a prone position. He got out the P226 and lay back on the reclined seat, the pistol at hand. The woods about him were still silent, as if the night's creatures did not yet quite trust him.

He closed his eyes for some moments, then opened them once more. As he'd observed on so many night missions, the human eye, depending on its state of health, could sometimes be a reasonably effective light gatherer. He was blessed with good night vision, and while not up to the standards of the nocturnal hunters of the animal world, it had always come to his aid when most needed.

In the gloom of the Range Rover, he could now see through gaps in the foliage outside that the clear sky had been made relatively bright by the starlight. Through the trees, he could see the dark, vast expanse of the South Pacific Ocean.

Again closing his eyes, within seconds he was asleep. Yet part of him was very much alert, and a breach of his security zone would have him instantly awake and ready to act.

After a while, the woodland came alive once more and something screamed briefly as an unseen predator made a kill.

Sian and Markston made it to their stop without further incident. They had taken a right turn off the Bruce Highway to head for the coast, eventually found a small motel that overlooked the Noosa River near Tewantin, and booked into separate rooms. They had brought in all weapons—packed to look like ordinary luggage—from their Land Cruiser. Sian's window gave her a clear view of the car park and from her room she could see their Toyota, parked directly in the glare of one of the motel's floodlights.

She was looking at it, checking to see if anyone had shown interest, when there was a knock on her door. It was Markston.

"Just saying good night," he told her.

"Good night."

He looked at her closely, then without another word turned away to go to his room. She shut her door slowly.

When she eventually got into bed she kept the Magnum within easy reach, for rapid access.

The motel was fifty-five kilometers south of Gallagher's position.

▪ ▪ ▪

Villiger had stopped off a track on the way to Rainbow Beach six kilometers south of Gallagher, and had similarly staked out his own sensors for the night. Their rendezvous was not due until Gallagher had returned from Fraser Island, or until the deadline was passed and a rescue mission mounted.

"Just watch yourself in there, Gordon," he said into the night as he settled down. "If you're one minute late, we're coming in after you."

The men who had set the ambush drove all the way to Hervey Bay, 125 kilometers north of where Sian and Markston had stopped for the night. They became short-tempered as realization dawned reluctantly: They had lost their quarry.

But the men had themselves been followed.

Borodin's people had kept track of them, and would continue to do so. The men never knew, as they began to painstakingly retrace their route, losing patience with each other and thus reducing their effectiveness, that they were being closely tagged.

Borodin was quite happy with the situation.

Giraud had followed Marika's instructions and was waiting with his new partner in a small clearing near Tin Can Bay, ten kilometers west of Rainbow Beach.

Giraud stood patiently by his car, listening to the lapping waters of Tin Can inlet, a fjordlike gouge that was nearly twenty kilometers in length. His colleague had remained behind the wheel. A short distance from the car, a Bell Jetranger helicopter was waiting.

The pilot approached and stopped before Giraud.

"She'd better get here soon." He spoke to Giraud in a language that was neither French nor English.

Giraud turned his head slightly, not quite facing the dark shape standing next to him. "You can always complain to her when she does get here. I'd really like to watch what happens then. It should be entertaining."

The pilot made a pacifying motion with his hands. "Look . . . I'm not out to make a fuss . . ."

"Then don't." A new sound intruded. "Here she comes. You can bawl her out for being late."

"Look," the pilot repeated hastily. "Forget I said anything. Okay?"

Giraud grinned without humor in the dark. Then headlights cut the gloom suddenly as Marika's Land Cruiser came bouncing towards them. It stopped just short of the car. The darkness returned thickly as the lights died and it took Giraud some time to get his eyes accustomed once more.

The person who climbed out of the Toyota was not the middle-aged matron. Marika had again transformed herself. A kilometer or so from the clearing she had stopped to change into different clothing. She now wore a close-fitting jumpsuit, its camouflage pattern hidden by the night. Her head was bare, though the single plait remained coiled upon its crown. She was carrying the backpack. The ugly clothes were in it.

"You all know what to do," she told them.

They nodded and she began walking towards the helicopter. There was nothing more to be said.

In the morning, Giraud's partner would drive the Toyota to a vehicle ferry and cross over to Fraser Island. He would leave it at a designated spot, then they'd walk a short distance away from it to be picked up by the helicopter. Neither Giraud nor his partner was to remain on the island.

Marika strapped herself into the left-hand seat and

put on the headphones. She watched as the pilot climbed in and put on a helmet with night-vision goggles. "Let's get going."

"There's a military training area close by," his voice said in her ear. "We must keep out of it and go out very low, just in case."

She nodded curtly, not looking at him.

The pilot tightened his lips and went through his takeoff routine, then lifted the Jetranger cleanly off and headed for the inlet. Keeping very low, he banked steeply into a turn that took him eastwards as he sent the aircraft skimming over the waters of the inlet, making for the southern tip of Fraser Island. He kept a sharp lookout along the route for the warning lights of the various pleasure boats that might be moored in the area. It wouldn't do to go crashing into an unseen mast.

Gallagher's eyes came open suddenly, but he remained perfectly still, listening intently for whatever it was that had brought him awake. Slowly, he shifted his eyes to check the sensor control unit. Nothing had excited it.

Then he heard a familiar sound.

Helicopter. Traveling low and fast. It sounded some distance away but the night, like an amplifier, had brought the noise closer than it really was.

Ansen doing a check? he wondered. A military training flight?

Then the faint, characteristic beat of the helicopter gradually died away.

Gallagher lay still, pondering the reason for its passage. What went out, he decided, might come back. After a while, after no new sounds of blade-whipped air beating upon the night had come to him, he closed his eyes and went back to sleep.

▪ ▪ ▪

The Jetranger hovered over a great spread of sand that gleamed whitely in the starlight, near the edge of a forest. The pilot looked out at the swirling cloud that seemed to grow by the second as it was whipped up by the blades.

"We'd better do this quickly," he said to her anxiously. "Sand clogging the filters could ground us here."

But she was already moving, releasing the seat harness and getting ready to jump the six feet to the ground. She tossed out her backpack. It landed relatively softly on the cushion of sand. Then she removed the headphones.

"Stay lucky!" the pilot said above the noise. He was looking at her, the goggles raised.

She favored him with a brief stare, eyes like dark lenses in the glow of the instrument panel. "Luck has nothing to do with it!" she shouted back.

Then she jumped.

"Suit yourself," the pilot muttered. He snapped the goggles back into place, then lifted the helicopter out of the abrasive clutches of his man-made sandstorm and headed back.

Gallagher came awake for a second time. The helicopter was returning, still fast and low. He judged the distance to be the same as before and was certain it was on a reciprocal course.

A guest with influence arriving late for the resort on the west coast of the island? He doubted it. The resort he was thinking of was a good sixty-five kilometers farther north and midway along the coast. It was also much closer to Hervey Bay, a short hop by chopper.

Who, or what, had prompted the flight?

He decided there was little point in worrying about it for now. If it concerned him, he would eventually find out, one way or the other.

Borodin's people had tagged the ambushers for several kilometers until at last, their quarry gave up their own chase and pulled off a road to sleep off the rest of the night.

From a safe distance, Borodin's Spetsnaz kept surveillance on their targets with nightscopes. They made no move towards the sleeping men. The time for that had not yet arrived.

After the helicopter had gone, Marika picked up her backpack and made for the edge of the forest. She had chosen this particular area deliberately. As soon as the news had come that Gallagher was making for Fraser Island, she'd had a large-scale map brought to her and had studied it closely.

She understood what Gallagher was up to and was certain he would pick somewhere isolated. It was what she herself would have done. She understood also that he would be calculating her possible moves, just as she was his. He had led her to Fraser Island. Well, she had come. It would be interesting to see whose tactics proved the most successful.

She wondered now how he had felt when he'd discovered she was still alive. She would've loved to have seen his face. Yet that time in Brisbane, when she had felt the strange premonition, she was certain they had passed within a short distance of each other. It was as if he'd actually been watching her.

"We are close, Gordon," she murmured softly into the empty night. "Much closer than you think. We are alike."

There was no wind and the sky was totally clear as she trudged across the white sand towards the tall, looming mass of the forest. It seemed even darker than the night against the great spread of sand made almost silver by the starlight.

Eurydice, she thought, was going into the underworld and Orpheus would follow. But it was Orpheus who was responsible for bringing her here.

She stopped at a point which she decided would do for the night and dropped the backpack. With her back towards the forest line, she looked about her.

She was at the shore of a big lake that glinted in the starlight. The lake was itself perched atop a massive dune landscape that was a good 700 feet above sea level, and which seemed to stretch forever in three directions. At her back, the forest blocked the fourth.

The beauty of the landscape did not elude her, but she knew that her presence was not for the purpose of admiration. In this arena which could easily have belonged to the dawn of creation, she had come to do battle. She would have to kill Gallagher, or be killed by him.

It was an appropriate place to spend the night.

She reached into a deep pocket of the backpack and pulled out a cylindrical shape that resembled the sort of tube used for storing tennis balls. She removed the cover, then turned the tube over until something dropped softly into her waiting hand. She shook it once. Immediately, it began to glow, giving off a soft light which she shaded with her body. There were five more in the tube.

The light unit was solar-powered. It had a dark concave base topped by a shallow translucent dome. The base contained the solar energy cell and would fit neatly onto the dome of another unit for packing.

She shook it again, and the light went out. She would not be needing it. Her night vision was excellent, and there was enough natural light for her to work by. Even though there was apparently no one around, she did not intend to risk use of the light for any longer than it had just taken to do the check.

She replaced the tube, then from another section of her pack removed a one-person tent that was tightly rolled about its collapsible frame. The entire package formed another small cylinder barely a foot long. Working swiftly, she erected the low structure, then crawled in, hauling the pack after her. She closed the tent flap and, using one end of the pack as a pillow, went to sleep.

There was a flap pocket on the pack, close at hand. In it was a fully loaded automatic pistol.

She woke up with the dawn.

It had been a peaceful night, as if nature had needed the silence in order to prepare for the day to come. She'd expected to have to spend the night shooing dingoes from her tent, but not one had come near her, and none were within sight.

Marika crawled out with a towel, which she dropped onto the tent. She rose to her toes, raising her arms above her head and bringing her body to full stretch as she luxuriated in the arrival of the new day. She did this a few times, unhurriedly, like a big cat priming its muscles in anticipation of a good hunt.

Eventually she relaxed, and began uncoiling and unplaiting her hair. She took her time about this, as if each movement required particular care. Finally, the curtain of golden hair billowed about her head as she shook it from side to side. Then she removed her boots and socks and began to pull at the Velcro fastenings of the jumpsuit. She was naked beneath the suit, save for the small triangle of silken fabric that served as her knickers. She stepped out of the suit and removed the one item of underwear.

For a moment, she remained still, a vision of astonishing beauty in the primeval landscape of another time; then she ran across the white sand towards the deep blue of the lake.

She entered the water at a run, disturbing its stillness with great splashes, like a creature of legend about to take off, only to dive instead into its cold embrace. She stayed down for long moments, then surfaced in a cascade of water and whirling hair. She remained in the lake for about a minute, until invigorated, then left the water and began to dry herself with the towel she'd left on the tent.

Five minutes later, she was again dressed as before and, leaving her hair loose to enable it to dry, began to eat a breakfast of fruit. She also took a couple of high-energy, organic tablets and washed the lot down with a hot drink from a small flask.

She tidied up, took down the tent, and folded it as before to place it in the backpack. By then, her hair was sufficiently dry to enable her to plait and coil it. From one of the pack's many pouches she pulled out a soft bush hat of jungle green, and put that on.

She then got out the rifle and began to put it together. She loaded it with infrared guided rounds, placed what looked like a tiny stethoscope to her ears, and plugged the single probe at the other end into the rifle sight.

Not wanting to place the rifle on the ground, she propped the backpack into the sand with one hand, got down on her knees, and, shifting the weapon from one hand to the other, was able to slip the pack onto her back.

She stood up and, rifle ready, went into the forest. On her hip was strapped the automatic pistol.

The hunt had begun.

▪ ▪ ▪

Many people interested in Marika's activities were also getting up early. Gallagher had himself come awake with the dawn, having had an undisturbed sleep after the second passage of the mystery helicopter. The sensors had been quiet all night and, picking up the controller unit, he left the Range Rover to retrieve them. He also took the P226 with him, just in case.

Finding the well-camouflaged sensors was easy with the controller. Without it, the task would have been time-consuming, if not virtually impossible. He simply needed to move the controller until one of the red dots pulsed straight ahead, while a readout counted down the distance to the target sensor.

He collected all four, returned to the Rover, and stowed them. He then took out a jerry can of water, poured just enough over a cloth to soak it, and used that to wipe at his face and neck. Breakfast was an apple and a pear. He brushed his teeth, rinsed with a mouthwash, and was ready. He started the Range Rover and moved out of his hiding place. From his moment of waking to setting off, six minutes had passed.

As he got back onto the track and turned left to go northwards, he paused for a moment and looked about. His first impression was of the vividness with which nature had colored the new day. The vegetation seemed greener than usual. From his position, he could see the long crescent shape of Rainbow Beach curving away beneath him. The stunning blue of the ocean, mirroring the sky, reached for the white border of sand, whose steep buttress of high ground took fifteen kilometers to drop in a gradual incline until, in the far distance, it appeared to become almost one with the water. Gallagher realized his stop for the night had been within a few kilometers of Double Island Point, and wondered where Villiger had made his stop.

He drove on, heading for the road that would take him down to Rainbow Beach and the ferry for the two-kilometer crossing at Inskip Point. He would be making no attempt to do this surreptitiously. He wanted to be seen by whoever was checking on his movements.

Once on Fraser Island itself, it would be a different matter altogether. Then the fun would begin. Someone in a map shop had told him that viewed from Indian Head, the northern tip of the island, the sunsets were purple.

He was not going for the sunsets.

Villiger was having an interesting morning. Having set off for Rainbow Beach, but like Sian and Markston assigned to remain on the mainland to act as a defensive screen for Gallagher, he spotted a car coming up the narrow winding track towards him. It was the green sedan that Gallagher had warned him to look out for. Must be four-wheel drive, he mused. But it seemed a little short of ground clearance for such terrain; that marked whoever was in the car as non-Australian. Australians would not have made such a fundamental mistake when traveling in the bush. On the other hand, he'd known Afrikaners who'd gone into the veld totally unprepared and had needed rescue. People could at times be exceedingly stupid. Maybe these were such.

There was no other traffic.

Villiger felt certain they had not tagged him in Brisbane. So what were they doing up here? Perhaps in attempting to follow Gallagher they had blundered and were lost. But that was not his problem. He already knew what he was going to do.

He had stopped quickly when he'd first seen the car. Now he turned the Toyota broadside on, blocking the track completely; then, taking the grenade launcher, he climbed swiftly out and ran to position himself in some bushes on one side of the unmade road. That would give him the best field of fire. He waited, listening to the high revving of the engine as the car negotiated the sharp bends. The driver was making quite a meal of it.

At the last bend that led to Villiger's roadblock, the car came round at speed, billowing dust and barely under control. But soon it was scrabbling into a panic stop, wheels locked, as the driver saw the Toyota looming before him. The green sedan finally managed to come to a halt before hitting the other vehicle, engine at a fast tickover as the driver and his passengers wondered what to do next. The dust of its passage hung like freeze-framed plume above it in the still air; then, with infinitesimal slowness, the plume began to settle, an ochre-colored net curtain that descended to shroud the car.

Soon, Villiger knew, they'd be coming out of shock and would act. They were not going to have the time.

"*That's it, gentlemen!*" he called sharply from cover. "Make no move to startle me. I've got a grenade launcher."

The driver paled visibly, while his three companions remained absolutely still.

Whether English was their first language or not, they'd certainly understood his command, Villiger thought with some amusement.

He came out of hiding and walked up to the driver's door, the snout of the launcher pointing menacingly. The driver looked at the weapon in surprise, and went paler.

"Thought I was bluffing, did you?" Villiger queried mildly. "I never bluff."

"W-who are you? And what do you want?"

Villiger looked at each in turn. They sat as if glued to their seats. "Are you the only one who can speak?" he asked the driver.

The others remained silent.

"Who are you?" the driver asked again.

Villiger thought about that. "I come," he eventually replied, "from the land of anger. I hate being followed."

"We weren't following you."

"Strange. I'm here, and you're here. I call that following. Don't you?"

"Listen. This isn't what you think . . ."

"Out! And leave your weapons."

"We don't have—"

"I also hate being taken for a fool. Leave your weapons in the car. Do it!"

Reluctantly, all four complied. One of them had been concealing a sawed-off shotgun.

Villiger stared briefly at it. "Very nice. Just the sort of thing you take with you on an innocent drive. Out of the car! The three passengers first. Driver, you take it off the road, then join your companions. And don't try anything, unless you all fancy becoming toasted breakfast for the animals in the area. I don't think you'd like what the grenade round would do to you. Now move it!"

They obeyed. The driver took the green car as far off the track as the bushes would allow, then went to join his colleagues as Villiger had ordered.

"Thank you, gentlemen," Villiger said. "You see? I can be quite reasonable."

"You're making a big mistake." It was the one with the shotgun. He had nasty eyes.

Villiger stared at him. "I'm terrified. Now take off your clothes. All of them."

"What!" they chorused, outraged.

"*Off!* I haven't got all day. And the shoes. Don't forget those." When they had stripped, he ordered them to put it all in a heap. "Now start walking."

"From here?" The driver was appalled. *"Like this?"*

"I'll drop your clothes some kilometers down the road. I don't know who you are, and I don't want to; but if I see you anywhere in my vicinity in the future, you're dead meat. You now have a choice. You can die here, or you can walk naked."

After giving him poisonous stares, they began walking.

"See how simple life can be when you compromise?" Villiger called after them cheerfully.

He waited until they had gone out of sight before picking up their clothes and dumping the lot in the Land Cruiser. He then hurried to the green car, picked up their weapons, and tossed them far into the bushes. He doubted very much that they would choose to walk back several kilometers to try and find them, and risk disturbing venomous reptiles during the search. Besides, chances were they'd never find those guns again even if they tried.

He swiftly checked the car for some kind of identification of its occupants, but there was nothing. He also knew there would be nothing in the clothes. Such people traveled anonymously. He'd done so himself on occasion.

He went back to the Toyota, put the launcher away, and took out the Beretta shotgun. He went over to the car once more and put a round into each of the tires, shredding them.

Down the road, the naked men paused as they heard the blasts and knew that their car had now been disabled. They continued walking.

Villiger climbed back into the Land Cruiser and headed downhill, forcing the men to hurry off the road and out of his way. He waved cheerfully as he passed, and could see them cursing him. One of them searched desperately for something to throw, found a loamy chunk of rock, and threw it. He missed, and the porous material shattered with the force of the throw, discharging fragments in all directions.

Villiger laughed and drove on. Seven kilometers later, he dumped the clothes by the side of the track, just before he turned onto a paved road.

It should take them all day, he thought. He doubted they would want to be seen like that. Four neutralized. Four less for Gallagher to worry about.

He laughed again. Then the laughter faded.

"Hope that helps lessen the odds, Gordon," he commented softly.

Sian and Markston left their motel early, after just one cup of coffee.

"I could have done with some breakfast," Markston complained. "We had the time."

"We can eat on the move," she said uncompromisingly. This time, she was doing the driving. "We're not on holiday, Markston."

He stared at her. "Leave the iron knickers behind just for once, for God's sake. It's not against the rules to eat, is it?"

But she was not rising to the bait. She glanced at the automatic pistol he loosely carried. "Just make sure you're ready to use that if those jokers from last night try again."

"Don't worry about me," he snapped. "I know my job."

She gave him another glance, but said nothing.

They stopped very briefly at a petrol station to buy snacks, which didn't please Markston because, as he kept insisting, he wanted to eat "properly." But Sian ignored his complaining, which intensified when she left the paved road and headed coastwards.

"What do you think you're doing?" he demanded.

"Going to Rainbow Beach."

"*This* way? By which road?" he added sarcastically.

"A very natural one. We're going along the ocean."

He stared at her. "You're fucking crazy."

"We'll use the beach," she told him calmly. "It's twenty-eight miles north of here to Rainbow Beach, and if you use your brains, you realize anyone hoping to follow us will be on the roads. If we're lucky, we'll probably not see another vehicle for the entire journey."

Markston said nothing after that, until they hit the

creamy sands of the long beach as she turned northwards. Along the way, sand slopes, topped by rocky outcrops that seemed to belong to another planet, appeared to be clothed in many colors within a spectrum of red and beige.

He stared apprehensively at the vast Pacific, which seemed far too close for comfort. "Just what are the tidal movements in this area?"

"Relax, Markston. We've got several hours of dry sand to play with before high tide; I checked while you were still getting ready. Two hours would have been pushing it, because it may take us all of that to get there. You'll notice this is not exactly a motorway."

He pointedly fell silent once more, every now and then looking behind to check whether any other vehicle had appeared on their tail. Sometime later the rusting, pockmarked hulk of a ship appeared, apparently growing out of the sand.

"Christ," he said softly. "Look at that." He stared at it as they drew closer, then passed on its port side.

"We can always take shelter in it."

He glared at her. "Very funny."

Sian gave a tiny smile as she drove cautiously over the undulating surface, picking her way with care. Four-wheel drive or not, she had no intention of being stuck when the tide came in. Being stuck in a *moving* vehicle with Markston was bad enough. But her choice of route so far seemed a good one.

No tail had appeared behind them. It was going to be okay.

Giraud intended to disobey Marika. Later in the day, *he* would take the Land Cruiser across to the island; and he would not be returning to the mainland as expected.

21

Gallagher shared his ferry with only two other 4WD vehicles, but there was a spattering of backpackers, mainly young and female, traveling in pairs and carrying their homes for the night with them. He hoped they would not blunder into his contest with Marika. They might get hurt.

The people with the off-roaders gave him no cause for alarm: a youngish couple patently looking forward to sexual adventures in the wild, if the eagerness on their faces was anything to go by, and a party of seekers after a different kind of adventure, traveling in a multicolored vehicle that sported the tour firm's logo.

"Isn't this just beautiful?" a female voice said next to him over the drone of the ferry. "Especially at this time of day?" It was an American voice.

He turned to look at her. One of the backpackers and very, very pretty. Denim shirt and shorts, walking boots, and bright blue laughing eyes. A good seven inches shorter than he was, with wisps of brownish hair showing beneath a soft white sun hat.

He nodded. The water seemed impossibly clear, and rich in color. The island beckoned mysteriously.

"Are you American?" she asked.

"No. English." Not forgetting the Irish father and the Scottish-Jamaican mother, he thought with some irony.

"You're a long way from home."

"And you."

"Yeah, but I've only had to hop across the Pacific." She pointed briefly at another young woman with a pack, who looked as vaguely Oriental as had Borodin's young Spetsnaz colleague. "That's Mary-Ann. I'm Naira . . ."

"Naira. That's a very beautiful name."

"Thanks." She gave him her best smile, which was quite something to behold. It seemed to light up her entire face, the sparkle reaching the eyes. "My dad gave it to me. It was his grandmother's. Mary-Ann's traveling with me," she continued. "I live on the Islands now. Oahu."

She meant the Hawaiian Islands, Gallagher realized. "And before that?"

"California."

It did not surprise him. He knew she was probably hoping for a lift. Traveling alone in the spacious Range Rover, it was inevitable that he would be approached; but he dare not offer. He could be putting them in considerable danger. Besides, he had all his stuff in there, including the weaponry.

"I'm navy," she informed him. "Well, my dad is. Carriers. I'm kinda old to be traveling around with my parents, but what the hell. I'm recovering from a bad marriage." She was quite philosophical about it, and didn't look a day over twenty-two. Then the dreaded question came. "Are you going to the north of the island?"

He shook his head. "No. I'm cutting inland."

She seemed genuinely disappointed, and not just because she would not be getting a lift. "Hell. Looks like it's a long walk for us. We're hoping to see the whales up there, and the sunsets."

"You'll get the sunsets, but as for the whales I'm not sure this is the season. Is it?"

"I'm not sure myself. We might get lucky. We've been told that Hervey Bay, farther up the mainland coast, is best, but we prefer Indian Head. It's wilder."

"It's certainly that. I do hope you're lucky with a lift."

"We'll find something."

"Just be careful."

Her eyes widened briefly as she realized his concern was genuine. "We'll be okay. You're nice," she added. "Pity."

"Story of my life."

"Oh, I don't think so," she said, smiling. Then she returned to her friend.

He wondered if she really was a genuine backpacker, or someone making a positive identification for later use. But he could feel no alarm. The entire ferry felt clean.

That did not necessarily mean it was.

Fraser Island.

At 127 kilometers long and with an area of some 1,850 square kilometers, it was the largest sand island in the world, the people at the map shop had told him, complete with its own eco system. Millions of years of eroded mountains and fluvial silt had been borne along the coast by the mighty Pacific, piling its deposits until a landmass bigger than many an island nation had been created. They had also warned him to treat it with respect. It was a conservation area, they'd said. Look after it.

He would try to avoid mayhem. He hoped Marika would feel the same, though he thought that most unlikely. The last thing on her mind would be ecological respect.

As soon as he drove off the ferry and onto the east coast beach, he realized that nothing the map sellers had told him could have prepared him for actually being there. What greeted him was a natural wonder: a beach that went on forever; towering sand dunes; and in the distance, a fully working rain forest. Up above, the bluest of skies for the warming day. They'd told him about the lakes, too, perched high in the dunes, but they hadn't done them justice.

There seemed to be a lot of stray dogs around. Then he remembered they were island dingoes. They hung around the backpackers, but didn't come near the Range Rover.

He drove a few yards from the landing area and stopped. It was time to put his strategy into play. He picked up the large-scale map of the island.

A knocking on the door of the Range Rover made him look. The divorced navy backpacker and her traveling companion were smiling at him. He still felt no alarm.

He opened the door.

"Something you ought to know," Naira said. "Some guy back on the mainland asked me to talk to you."

Now the alarm bells began their pealing.

"Why?"

She shrugged. "He just said to talk to you as the ferry left. I thought it sort of weird, so I asked Mary-Ann to have a look while we talked. He had binoculars stuck to his face, and they were pointed at us. Weird, huh?"

"Can you describe him?"

"Sure." She did, in fine detail.

It was no one he recognized, but perhaps the knowledge would be of some use later. Even the smallest item of information could be turned to advantage, if used effectively.

She was studying him closely. "No one you know. Right?"

"Right. But thanks for telling me."

"He said he was a cop." The blue eyes looked at him steadly.

"And?"

"I think he was lying."

"But you don't know me."

"He was lying," she repeated. "Like I said . . . I'm navy. My dad taught me how to be careful and how to spot a flake . . ." She grinned suddenly. "Didn't spot my ex-husband, though. So," she went on briskly, "a guy lies to me about being a cop . . . that makes you the good guy."

"Well, thanks for the vote of confidence."

"You meant it when you told me to be careful, and you didn't know me. That puts you with the angels."

"I really wish I could give you a lift."

"That guy back there a reason why you can't?"

"One of the reasons."

"It's okay. We'll make out. We'll find something at Eurong. Give him a bad day," she went on, "whoever he is. And when it's all over come north, up to Indian Head. We'll still be there. It'd be nice to see you."

"How do you know I've got to give him a bad day?"

She gave him a knowing look. "Hey, c'mon. I've seen guys like you with my dad since I was so high. Different faces, same type. It's in the manner."

"It shows?"

"Only to those who know." She held out a hand. "Hope I was of some help."

They shook hands.

"You were."

"And don't worry about Mary-Ann. She's navy too."

"I should have guessed."

They both gave him a parting smile and with a last wave began walking along the beach. He hoped they would eventually get their lift north. They stood a fair chance of managing it. Eurong was the closest of the three resorts farther up the island's east coast. Supplies could he had there, including petrol. There were bound to be a few vehicles heading north.

He checked his own fuel supplies. Plenty still in the tank, and there was also a reserve of ten gallons in two of the three jerry cans he'd brought with him. Fuel was not going to be one of his worries. He would tank up before leaving the island.

As he watched Naira and Mary-Ann leave, he realized the ferry was already on its way back and the other vehicles had all but disappeared. A few other backpackers were up ahead, and they hurried to catch up. Safety in numbers.

Despite the fact that they'd said at the map shop that the island was popular, it was already beginning to feel as if he were all alone in this beautiful landscape. For Gallagher, his own safety lay in reliance upon his skills and his use of them. It was his only chance.

He checked the map, surveying possible routes and options. The man Naira had described might have been someone sent by Borodin to keep a benign watch; but he doubted it. Borodin would not have telegraphed the presence of his group so openly. Gallagher decided to assume the man was hostile unless events proved otherwise. He folded the map carefully and put it away. He knew how he was going to play out the game.

He began to drive on. The dogs followed halfheartedly, then dropped back. Shortly afterwards, he came to what appeared to be the bed of a dried-out watercourse, between two shrub-tufted dunes that sloped onto the beach. He turned left along it and began to head into dune country.

The watercourse meandered its way between the dunes, climbing steadily, but at the same time seemed to be going correspondingly deeper as the crests of the dunes went higher. The shrubs all but disappeared, and great banks of sand greeted his eyes. The Range Rover worked its way along the dried bed, unperturbed by terrain that would have wrecked the suspension of an ordinary vehicle.

Gallagher peered upwards and on either side. A natural funnel. Not the best of places to be if a flash flood decided strike. It would be like trying to drive upriver against a torrent. But this was not the season of sudden downpours and the sky remained bright and cloud-free. After about half an hour, the dried bed crested a tall dune and Gallagher found himself looking upon a piece of natural magic. The turquoise of a large, perched lake lay before him.

He drove out of the watercourse and stopped. Here was true beauty, he thought. A natural paradise.

But there was something else in this paradise: an implacable adversary. He drove on, to lay the trap for his nemesis.

Back at Inskip Point, Borodin, in shorts, stout boots, a tartan shirt and sun hat, had watched the man speak to Naira and had continued to watch as the same man had trained his binoculars upon the departing ferry.

He'd then turned casually round, as if looking about him. The young Spetsnaz woman, dressed like a tourist, was standing a short distance away. Without pausing, Borodin's eyes had met hers briefly and, barely perceptibly, he'd nodded.

There had been no need for him to do more. The man with the binoculars was now targeted.

▪ ▪ ▪

Marika stood perfectly still within the rain forest, the rifle held across her chest. Since she had left the lake she had neither seen nor heard anyone. She'd heard many of the creatures of the forest, but they always became completely silent upon her approach. They would then start up again after she'd passed, as if satisfied this was one predator which had no interest in them.

But now, she remained where she was, listening. She could hear nothing, yet she'd felt a sudden warming of her body.

"So, Gordon," she remarked softly. "You are here."

She continued on her way. There was something quite specific she was looking for.

Gallagher had spent the entire day traversing the area of the dunes, sometimes stopping at one of the many smaller lakes for a light snack from his rations. He'd seen no one. It was as if that part of the island had been forsaken for the duration by all the island visitors. He knew there were also permanent islanders; but none had appeared upon the dune landscape.

Finally, just as the sky was beginning to show its first signs of red, he came to another lake. Even before he had stopped at its edge his senses, sweeping like radar before him, gave him the kind of jolt that made him turn off the engine to climb out and take heed of the sudden tenseness within him.

Treat your natural sensors with the greatest of respect, sir, even when your intellect tries to tell you otherwise. Modern man, believing himself "civilized," has forgotten how to use them. But a very special few have not. Successful politicians, businessmen, combat pilots . . . they have not forgotten how. You are one of those people. Those sensors are important. They're your guides to survival. They're your stealth systems. Listen to them, and win.

O'Keefe.

He stood by the Rover and looked slowly about him. The silence was overwhelming. The forest, a crescent-shaped border on one side of the lake, was separated from the water's edge by a broad strip of white, sandy beach. At widely spaced intervals, as if they had been planted by a drunken gardener, little colonies of stunted trees with gleaming white bark pockmarked the area in ragged groups of three and four. It was almost as if they were on a long march towards the lake itself, and had paused for breath.

There should be, Gallagher felt, a cacophony of sounds coming out of the forest. But all was still. There wasn't even a breeze. Up above, the red in the sky had deepened. There was, however, still plenty of light to see by.

He took the P226 out of its holster and began to walk away from the vehicle, eyes searching the ground. During the course of the day he'd removed his jacket. There was now little need to hide the fact that he was carrying a weapon. It was going to be a warm night and he decided to leave the jacket off. He was not sure what he was looking for, but the light would soon begin to fade and he wanted to check the area before darkness fell.

Gallagher carried the pistol ready for use. There was no telling how many people he might have to deal with. The man at the ferry station may have been a lookout, placed there to radio his arrival on the island. By now, others might have come over, if they'd got past Villiger's screen.

He had moved some distance from the vehicle, when he came to a sudden halt. He'd come across a line of footprints. The toes were very slightly turned in and though they could have belonged to anyone, he felt certain they were Marika's.

She had arrived before him.

Had that been the reason for the helicopter he'd heard during the night?

He turned slowly, eyes scanning the edge of the forest, now bathed in a golden glow from the approaching sunset. It wasn't purple, but it was still spectacular.

Was she even now watching him down the rifle sights, from in there? If that were the case and she'd wanted to, she could have shot him by now, just as she could have by the little village church in Kent. She was either not there or for her own reasons was not yet quite ready to take him out.

Still feeling as if under observation, Gallagher continued to cautiously follow the tracks. Soon, he came to the spot where she had pitched her tent, and saw the barefoot tracks that led in and out of the water.

He smiled grimly. She'd had all the time she'd needed for a swim. Instead of walking into his trap she had leapfrogged, coming on ahead to set one of her own. She'd also read him well, knowing the sort of terrain he'd have chosen. It was what he'd have expected of her. He moved on until he came to the spot where the sand had been blown in radiating circles, and knew it for what it was. She had wanted him to discover it all, and had deliberately made no effort to remove signs of her presence. Neatly done.

He returned quickly to the Range Rover, every now and then giving the forest a rapid scan as he walked. When he'd reached it, he put the SIG back in its holster, then took out the goggles and put them on, leaving them perched for the moment upon his forehead. Next was the Uzi, with its own spare ammo. He hung that across his chest by its sling. The silencer for the P226 and the spare ammunition clips for both weapons were hooked onto a belt that he snapped about his waist. He screwed on the Department's own special silencer for the Uzi. He then picked up the sensors and the controller, and locked the vehicle.

Describing a wide circle, he planted the sensors to give the Range Rover fully secure and overlapping cover. Leaving them deactivated for the time being, he went back to the Rover, lowered himself to the sand, and sat down, leaning against a front wheel to wait for full darkness.

About 180 kilometers northwest of Fraser Island, a luxury oceangoing motor yacht lay off Heron Island. It looked like the accessory of just another multimillionaire on a cruise, complete with a pair of cocktail-drinking, bikini-clad beauties on the sun deck, their open beach robes of transparent material casually draping their pampered bodies. Belowdecks, however, it was a very different story. There, in air-conditioned comfort, a group of eight men waited. They were busy cleaning and checking an assortment of personal weapons.

At one end of the spacious lounge was a bank of very expensive communications equipment. An operator with headphones sat at its console. Suddenly he stiffened, then his hands began working swiftly at the console. A VDU came brightly alive to display a brief burst of what looked like an alphabet soup of letters. Almost immediately, the coded message was deciphered and appeared on-screen. It was not in English.

The operator turned to the waiting men, who had paused in their activities to watch him.

"We're on our way!" His remark was in the language that had been displayed on the VDU.

The men began to get ready. Their movements were controlled and unhurried. At about the same time the yacht, which had been keeping station by judicious use of small amounts of power, began to throb mutedly as the powerful engines were opened to full max. At a dash speed of fifty knots, it would reach Fraser Island in just under two hours.

▪ ▪ ▪

In its past life, Fraser Island had once been the ancestral home of a tribe of aborigines. Then had come the late nineteenth-century loggers to harvest its precious woods. But aborigines and timber-cutters were now both moments of the island's past, although evidence of their presence remained. The loggers had left harsher marks, rapidly reclaimed by the forest, upon the landscape. They had built huts, and tram rails to carry the timber down to the coast. Vegetation now grew over the long-unused tramrails; and those huts that had not long ago been dismantled had succumbed to nature.

Marika was convinced that at least one hut had survived intact. Throughout history, something or someone always survived the harshest of experiences. She was determined to find the last remaining hut before the forest lost all the light of the day. There was still much more to do.

Giraud had preceded intent with early action.

When the helicopter had gone to take Marika to the island, he'd turned to his companion—a man who called himself Moelner—and said he'd be taking the Land Cruiser over instead.

"But that's not what—" Moelner had begun to protest.

"Forget it. There's a change of plan."

"But—"

"Just follow me in the Holden," Giraud had interrupted. "We'll find ourselves a hotel and I'll tell you all about it."

Reluctantly, Moelner had agreed.

On an isolated stretch of road, Giraud had stopped. There was a steep drop into a ravine on one side. Moelner had pulled up behind, puzzled, as Giraud climbed out of the Toyota. Giraud had come up to the car, which Moelner had been driving with his window down.

"Why are we stopping?" Moelner had asked.

"Good question."

Giraud had moved swiftly. Before Moelner realized what was happening, Giraud had struck. The twin-bladed dagger had come out of the darkness to plunge deeply to the hilt into Moelner's chest. A strange wheeze of pain and surprise had come out of him as he died.

Giraud had then maneuvered the Holden until he'd pushed it off the road and down the slope, where it had burst into flames as it had slammed and bounced on its way, spewing fuel and roasting Moelner's body before plunging into the ravine far below. A few scraps of shrubbery had caught alight, but these had soon died down after being consumed. Soon, the only glows punctuating the gloom and marking the passing of Moelner and his car had been the bloodshot eyes of strange nighttime animals. Finally, the water at the bottom of the ravine had put out Moelner's pyre.

It was again approaching darkness, and Giraud was on the island. Before leaving the house near Brisbane he'd sneaked a look at the map, and knew where Marika was likely to be.

Gallagher eased himself off the Range Rover and stood up. It was time. It had now become quite dark, and nothing to cause alarm had so far occurred. The forest was alive with sounds that came upon the night, its creatures having become accustomed to his presence. He'd expected dingoes to come sniffing around, or the odd, inquisitive wallaby; but none had. Perhaps they knew.

He brought the goggles down over his eyes and

pressed the power button. The night within the infrared window was again transformed. He began walking towards the forest. When he was beyond the sensor field, he paused just long enough to activate the system and continued walking.

As soon as he entered the first reach of the forest, all noise stopped.

Just before the last light of the day had faded, Marika found the hut. It was less overgrown than she'd expected, and was quite intact. The door opened and shut properly, but its single window was unglazed and gaped onto the world outside. Within the rudimentary building, there was less dampness than would have been imagined and though there were scurryings as she entered, there were fewer small forest inhabitants than expected.

She wondered whether people had used it in emergencies; but there was no evidence of recent occupation. It was as if the hut had been waiting for her. A rough table, looking the worse for wear, stood in the middle of the hut, with a single, plain wooden chair at its head. Dinner for one. Both, however, looked sufficiently sturdy.

There was nothing else.

She tested each briefly, then disconnected herself from the rifle and put it down on the table. Next, she removed her pack and placed that beside the rifle. She did not unstrap the pistol. She opened the pouch that contained the solar-powered lights, took one out, and shook it into life. There were more scurryings as the remaining creatures fled outside at this further intrusion. She walked around and inspected the hut minutely with the light. Satisfied, she then placed it on the table.

The hut was perfect for her needs.

She went into the pack again and took several tools out of it, and a few short lengths of thin but very strong nylon rope. The rope was within a bonded sleeve and was tough enough to support a climber dangling off a mountain.

Leaving everything on the table, she went up to one of the sides of the hut and tested it for strength. Solid planks were fitted upright with chunky crossbeams for added rigidity, and had lasted well. It would do.

She went back to the table, laid out the tools and the rope, then took some more items out of the pack. She carried those and a selection of tools over to the area she'd inspected. She tested the wood again, then began to work.

"When this is finished," she said softly, "I'll be coming for you, Gordon, my love."

Gallagher had worked his way deeper into the forest, his progress alert and quiet. Even so, the creatures of the night were aware of his alien presence and fell silent at his passage, only to start up again as soon as they were certain the danger had overlooked them. It was, he reflected grimly, a sure way for others to pinpoint his position.

And for him to pinpoint theirs.

What works against you can also work against a potential adversary. Use it, sir.

O'Keefe.

Gallagher decided on a change of tactic. Every so often, he would remain perfectly still, until the forest noises started up once more. When he eventually moved, there was a lessening of the sounds, but not the sudden, complete silence that had occurred previously. Progress was slower, but less obvious.

He was on one such pause by the buttress roots of one of the island's many giant fig trees, when he felt movement upon one of his booted feet. Very slowly, so as not to transmit the slightest vibration, he looked down. The infrared image of a huge snake was crawling over his instep, undulating as it went over the trunk. It seemed to go on forever.

At last, the tail of the snake slid over and down. Gallagher remained where he was, watching as the reptile vanished into the red-tinged undergrowth. He waited for another five minutes before moving on, the silenced Uzi held ready for action.

Marika stood back to admire her handiwork. All was ready. It was time to go and find Gallagher. She was certain he was already in the forest, looking for her. He would not have to wait much longer.

She'd put everything not immediately needed back into the pack and placed it on the floor in a far corner. She then reconnected herself to the rifle and went out of the hut, shutting the door behind her. She had left the single solar light glowing on the table.

When she had gone a short distance, she turned to look back at the hut. It was, she'd discovered, barely a kilometer from the spot where she had pitched her tent the night before. The soft glow from the light, giving the impression of a dying lantern, was just sufficient to pinpoint the small building. Within the confines of the nighttime forest, it was easy to believe that something unworldly resided in there.

Marika smiled in the darkness. It was also the flame to trap a moth. She turned slowly away, a feline creature of the night, on the prowl.

Giraud had made it to the lake. The night sky was again free of cloud and in the almost moonlit brightness of the starlight, the white sand gleamed. Gallagher's Range Rover stood out clearly.

Giraud paused while still some distance away, studying the vehicle, and as he continued to look his eyes picked out a tiny pinpoint of red.

An animal? He wondered. But if that was an eye, where was the second one?

He swore irritably. He should have brought night glasses.

But he was carrying a rifle with a nightscope. He raised that and sighted on the pinpoint, and knew it for what it was. With his eye to the scope he swung the rifle, pausing each time he found another.

He lowered the rifle and cautiously moved towards the first pinpoint, giving it a wide berth.

Then, without aid of the scope, he saw the second pinpoint of red. Giving that an equally wide berth, he took a curving route past it, heading for the forest just as the third and fourth red lights came into view.

"Very clever," he muttered. "A security zone."

He wondered whether Marika had already taken Gallagher, or whether it had been the other way round. Whatever the outcome, it was time to find out.

Continuing to give the sensors a wide berth, Giraud headed into the forest.

Gallagher felt his trunk touch something hard. He looked down. He was standing next to a pair of rails that appeared to come straight out of a low mound. He looked along the twin tracks and saw that they carried on for a short distance, sometimes obscured by bushes, before disappearing once more into the overgrown forest floor. Another giant fig tree stood where the rails seemed to vanish.

Over to his right and some distance beyond the tree, he thought he could see a faint blooming that suggested an area of artificial light. He wondered what it was. He had no intention of going near it until he'd checked it out from a safe distance. He'd take his time about it, too; it could well be a trap.

He went up to the tree and stopped, the toe of one boot touching a rail as he froze into immobility. He'd heard something, and he'd seen movement. The sound was behind, the movement up ahead. Two of them? Was Marika using helpers, after all? He found that hard to believe. It was not like her. Not when she'd gone to so much trouble to make it personal.

So who else was out there? Villiger would not have come in before the specified time. Borodin moving in early?

Gallagher doubted that as well.

So who?

Perhaps it was a big animal. A brumby. One of those horses he'd heard about that had been introduced and left on the island by loggers, and which had subsequently gone wild. He had no idea how brumbies behaved, except that they could be aggressive.

But this was no brumby.

He waited. The forest had become quiet, as if holding its breath in the knowledge that a burst of sudden, violent activity was about to occur.

He heard the sound again. Very faint, but definite. Someone trying not to make a noise. The worst animal of all: another human being. Long minutes passed. Gallagher still did not move, not even looking behind him.

It came a third time. A mistake. Whoever it was had stumbled on the rail. Gallagher felt the vibration through his trunk. And then he again saw movement ahead of him.

Moving with infinite care, he brought a hand up to touch the zoom switch on the infrared goggles. Silently, the image grew close. A head and upper body, the back facing him. Then the head turned slightly, clearly listening.

Unconsciously, he drew in his breath.

Marika!

Gallagher remained exactly where he was. He had a clear shot at her, but did nothing. He still had no idea what, or who, was behind him. Firing now would only give away his position. There was little point in taking out one target if the other would then get you.

But even as he continued to watch Marika, conflicting emotions went through him. He was reluctant to shoot, and would have been even if there had been no one at the other end of the rails. But he had to do something. She would not remain there forever. Already, it seemed as if they'd both been waiting to catch the unwary sound for hours, though in fact only minutes had passed.

The decision was taken out of his hands. In a brief and violent moment, several things seemed to happen at once.

The person at the other end of the rails was again careless, perhaps overeager and thinking rashly. There was another stumble in the dark of the forest and this time, the noise on the rail was loud enough to be heard with startling clarity.

Marika turned swiftly, rose, and brought her rifle to bear, all in one motion. Through the goggles, Gallagher saw with astonishment that she was aiming at him!

She had zeroed upon him without hesitation, as if she'd known his position all along.

Then she fired.

Gallagher actually saw a streak of light tracering its way towards him and instinctively he ducked, knowing he was already too late. But he didn't die. Instead, he heard a choked-off scream, and the clear sound of something heavy falling.

She had not aimed at him. Perhaps she hadn't seen him after all. She had deliberately shot at the other person. Not a helper, then. But who?

Gallagher rose cautiously to peer round the tree to check Marika's last position. Unsurprisingly, she was no longer there. He carefully made his way back to where he thought the body had fallen. It was not difficult to find the man Marika had shot. The rapid breathing was loud enough to betray the position. The man was still alive, and therefore dangerous. Gallagher decided he had to check to see exactly how dangerous.

When Gallagher eventually came upon him the man was groping in the dark, trying desperately to reach the rifle he had dropped. Gallagher could see everything with infrared clarity.

Covering him with the Uzi, Gallagher slowly lowered himself to carefully move the weapon out of the way. But the man must have thought he'd been shot by Gallagher. Despite his wound, he made one last desperate lunge, catching Gallagher by a leg and hanging on.

Gallagher stumbled and fell.

Shit, he thought. That's all I need.

Off balance, he landed heavily, angry with himself for allowing it to have happened. He grabbed the Uzi by barrel and butt in both hands to slam it against the grunting man's head. But the intended blow was blocked by a vicious-looking weapon. In the infrared light, Gallagher saw the twin blades of the dagger being forced against the barrel of the Uzi.

This was the bastard who'd stabbed Johnno.

The realization enraged Gallagher. He let go of the Uzi suddenly and half-rolled out of the way. The abrupt lack of resistance made Giraud lunge forward helplessly, propelled by his own momentum and unable to move rapidly enough to counter the move he knew was coming. He tried in despair to retrieve the situation but, hampered by his wound, was far too slow.

Gallagher had rolled completely away now, the freed Uzi swinging against his chest. He pounced upon Giraud, swiftly placed a knee against his exposed back and a forearm beneath his chin, and yanked backwards. The other hand grabbed at Giraud's weapon hand and turned it inwards. He shoved downwards with his knee.

Giraud made the same sound that had come out of Moelner only hours before, as his own dagger now entered his chest inexorably. He fought vainly to get the terrible weight off his back and to stop the tearing pain in his chest. Gallagher kept pressing implacably, until the struggles finally ceased.

He moved away from the body and sat back on his heels.

"That's for Johnno, you bastard," he told it savagely.

Then soft, warm lips were kissing his ear. "Hello, Gordon, darling. Good as ever, I see."

There was just enough time for a moment of astonishment before something very sharp entered his body.

The motor yacht had arrived at its destination. The armed men, all in black, disembarked into waterjet-powered rubber dinghies and headed for the shore on muted sound.

Once at the beach, they climbed out swiftly to make their way inland. The rubber dinghies returned to the yacht.

22

The beach seemed to go on forever. He walked *towards the shore, cupped some water in his hands, and ran back to the hole. He did that several times, but the hole kept drinking and wouldn't fill up. Then he was in the hole, and the water was coming down. He was drowning! Then a face appeared above the hole, looking down upon him. His own face!*

He screamed.

Another face appeared, soft and warm. Soft lips kissing him . . .

"Gordon . . . ?"

"Gordon! Gordon!" The face was close to his. He could feel its warmth. It was real. The lips were real. "You were having that nightmare of yours."

A dream, and he was not in the hole after all. He

knew that voice, with its slightest of accents that made it so sensuous to the ear. A searing pain was ripping at his head. He groaned.

"The headache will soon pass," she said.

Gallagher opened his eyes slowly and looked groggily about him. He was not in the hole, but metaphorically speaking he was definitely in a hole.

He was in a hut, and naked. His feet, spread about a meter apart, were encircled at the ankles by metal bands that were in turn attached by nylon ropes to small hoops fastened into the wooden wall at his back. His arms, outspread, were similarly trapped. There was just enough slack to enable him to shift position. At his feet, six small lights were arranged in a semicircle. A sacrifice at a shrine. Not a situation to feel good about. Definitely not.

He pulled at his bonds.

"I would not try this," she advised, stepping back, "unless you want to rip your wrists and ankles off. The hoops have barbed fastenings. Once they are clear of the wood, they spring open and clamp themselves to the surface. The more you pull, the more secure you make them."

In the strange light given off by the half-domes, she was as beautiful as he remembered her.

"Marika," he began hoarsely. "Why?"

"You are not surprised that I am alive?"

"I'm very surprised. I didn't want to believe it when I found out. Then I saw you."

"Where?"

"Brisbane."

"Ah. I felt your presence."

"I only saw your legs."

"Ah," she said again, and seemed pleased. "So you still like my legs."

"They are very beautiful and . . . exciting." He meant it.

"Your voice is getting stronger. The headache is fading. Once," she continued, "you enjoyed feeling them about you."

"Yes."

Gallagher looked about him some more, and saw the single table and chair. Upon the table was Marika's rifle, the goggles, and a pistol. He recognized the P226. In a far corner, beyond full reach of the lights, he could make out his pile of clothes, a backpack, and his Uzi.

Marika had moved farther away. She took the chair and swung it round so that its back faced Gallagher, and sat down spread-legged, arms leaning on the back as she watched him. She'd caught her prey. Now she was studying it, the great feline toying with its victim before the kill.

"How . . . how did I get . . . here?" he asked her warily. The grogginess was virtually gone. Whatever she'd injected into him had been fast-acting, but at least the effects also wore off quickly. He had to think of a way to get out of his predicament. "Fireman's lift," she replied. "I'm a woman, Gordon," she went on, at once coy and defiant, "not a fragile china doll. I can be very strong when I want to be, if you remember. It was not too difficult to carry you, even with my rifle and your Uzi. The goggles that make you see in the dark were still on your head."

She was certainly capable enough to do it, he thought with grudging respect. It helped to know she had not brought in helpers. Trouble was, he could not as yet see how he could employ that to his advantage.

"Would you like to know how I survived?" she continued, as if they were in the most normal of situations. The question seemed to tease.

"Yes," he repeated. His interest was genuine.

"I know you are thinking of ways to get out of my little trap. There are no ways. And if you are wondering about the man I shot and you killed, he was not meant to be there. He was one of my associates. I did not need his help. I had told him to stay away, and he didn't listen. Who is Johnno?"

"Someone you killed, or had killed. A policeman."

"I have killed no one since I've come here to Australia." The surprise in her voice was not faked.

Gallagher thought of what Borodin had said about Marika's principals getting ready to betray her, and said nothing.

But she was doing some of her own thinking. A frown appeared briefly. "How do you know he has killed this Johnno?"

"The dagger. Johnno had two puncture marks in his chest."

She looked puzzled. "But why would he not tell me?"

"Think about it."

"I shall. But first, I will attend to you, my dear Gordon." The green eyes, dark in the light, were fastened upon him. There was no anger in them, but a strange mixture of warmth and a chilling presence that was much more unnerving than the open rage he had expected.

"When your people came to collect the bodies," she went on, "they didn't find me. I was seriously wounded, but not dead. The blood you saw coming out of my mouth was from a capsule. I have used the trick on a few occasions. In the rain, I crawled away until I got to the water hole. I was not going to die. I refused. By the time the rain had stopped, I was inside the hole. There was a narrow ledge. I stood on it and dug my hands into the earth above me to keep me from falling to the bottom.

"I heard Alex Harding's helicopter crash to the ground, then I passed out. Somehow, I did not let go. When I was conscious again, there was silence. I did not move. It was night. I stayed where I was, becoming weaker; but I refused to let go. I was not going to die!

There were many reasons why I should not. One of those was that I would come to get you one day."

She paused, never once taking her eyes off him.

"I stayed that way all night," she continued in a voice that betrayed no emotion. "In the morning, I heard voices. Aborigine voices. It was obvious they were wondering what had happened. I began to call out. I was very weak by now, and I thought they would not hear.

"But an old man did. He came to the water hole and saw me. They pulled me out. I told them no police, even supposing they could have found one in time to get me to hospital in a place like the Outback. They looked after me. They healed me with medicines I have no knowledge about. The scar I'd suffered was still ugly and needed surgery. But there would be time for that. They fed me and eventually, when I was well enough, took me to another community which drove me to a town in one of their trucks.

"I was unrecognizable. My skin had become darker in the sun and I dressed to look like a half-aborigine from one of the communities. I made contact with some people I knew, and was taken out of the country. I went to eastern Europe. When I was fully recovered other things occupied my time, but not this kind of job.

"Then one day, I was offered a very special contract. These people had long-term plans. I told them my price and demanded certain arrangements. I would work for expenses and they would help me to get to you. I am very rich, you see; I don't need the money. I have all the money from Harding for the last job I did for him. You destroyed my people, so there is no one to share it with. But I have a good use for it."

She did not explain.

"A surgeon worked on my scar," she told him, finishing her tale, "and now you cannot see it properly unless you look very hard for it." She stood up. "Before

I kill you, I want you to remember what you have betrayed."

As he stared, she began to slowly remove her overall, tantalizingly opening it up so that the richness of her body came into teasing view a bit at a time. In the eerie light of the solar lamps, her naked body gleamed at him. "Look," she said. "Do you remember? Do I still look good?"

He could not deny it, even if he'd wanted to. She looked magnificent.

"I can see by your eyes that I do," she said. She came towards him. "You could have shot me tonight. You had the chance. Why didn't you?"

"I don't want to kill you."

She stared at him with wonder. "Then why are you here?"

"I want to stop you killing those people."

"How can you do that without first killing me?"

"I'll think of a way," Gallagher heard himself say.

She shook her head slowly, again in wonder. "You are my prey. I've caught you. You are at my mercy."

He could not take his eyes off her. She was so breathtaking, the wild danger of her intoxicated him. Despite himself, he knew he was getting aroused.

"You could have killed me in Kent," he said. "But you didn't. Instead, you tried to kill—"

"That woman who was standing so close to you?" She spoke of Miranda with contempt. "I did not try to kill her. I would have, had I wanted to."

"Then why . . ."

"The bitch moved. I was about to fire a warning shot, just to frighten, and to put pressure on you. She moved into my line of fire. I could have shot all those other people if I was what you think me to be."

"And the policeman in London?"

"That was a mistake by another overzealous associate like Giraud out there."

Again, Gallagher thought about Borodin's words. Marika was herself being set up. Again, he said nothing. He had to wait for the right moment.

Without warning, she brought her body against his and began moving sensuously. After a very short while, Gallagher felt his own body beginning to respond. She experienced a sharp intake of breath as she became aware of this, and began to kiss him.

"Ummmm," she said, pulling him a little away from the wall to put her arms about him. "You have not forgotten."

Gallagher realized his own arms were trying to reach for her, but there was not enough slack to do so.

She paused, holding her head back slightly to look at him. "Would you strangle me if your hands could reach?"

"No," he said, the hoarseness back in his voice.

"I know," she said, and began kissing him again. This time, she raised one of the magnificent legs and, balancing herself on the other, wrapped it about him. A strong desire to enter her took hold of him, but his bonds made it awkward.

He felt frustration, but there was something worrying him, too.

"Wait, wait," she said softly, and slowly brought her leg down, rubbing it against his along the way. She released him from her embrace and stood back. The nipples on her full breasts were so erect they appeared to be trying to burst from their areolas. She was breathing hard, eyes glowing with an intense light. "This way."

She turned, and moved backwards towards him. She bent her knees slightly, placed her hands upon them to brace herself, and continued to move back, until she was right up against him once more. The heat of her body was overwhelming. It was like being next to a furnace.

"This way," she said again. She moved against him

slowly. "This way." Her voice, thick with her own desire, had almost faded into the faintest whisper.

Gallagher found she had positioned herself perfectly, but anxiety killed his response.

She turned her head to look back at him over a lowered shoulder. "You are afraid? You think I have a disease?" She sounded outraged and her entire body became rigid for a brief instant. "Do you think I have so little regard for my body? No man has been with me since we last . . ." She said nothing more, but there was a nascent anger in her voice.

Gallagher found he actually believed her. He remembered Harding once telling him that no one picked Marika; she did the choosing.

Yet she did not move away. It was as if her own desires would not allow her to. She again rubbed herself against him, persistent, determined to conquer his fears. Again, he began to respond, but this time there was eagerness. When at last he entered her, it was with a power that made her squeal sharply and caused her to stagger briefly forwards. Then she gave a long sigh of pleasure as her warmth enveloped him. She pressed hard against him, so that he was deeply within her.

"Aah, *oui,*" she cried in a shuddering voice, thumping against him. "Ah, *oui, oui, oui!* I have waited, my Gordon. I have waited, I have waited! Ooh . . . I have such a taste for you!" she went on in a high voice that was both squeal and agonized wail. "Why did you betray me? Why? Why?" With each query she slammed her body hard into him, impaling herself as if in a form of punishment.

The hut was beginning to shake with their pounding. Marika's wails reached out into the forest. The creatures of the night did not pause in their own cacophony, understanding that this was not the noise of danger.

Inside the hut, Marika was going wild. She was pounding up and down, back and forth, her body now stretching, now crouching, but always locked into him. A thin film of moisture covered her entire body, so that she glistened in the half-light. The pounding grew in intensity. She worked so hard against him that Gallagher thought they'd burst through the wood and out into the night.

Then finally, their noises combined into a hoarse and wailing crescendo. Feet drumming uncontrollably, she shuddered violently against him, mingling with his tremors as their bodies strained for long, delicious moments before slowly relaxing from their exertions. But she did not stop there. Gently at first, then with increasing urgency, she began a second round. Once more, her wails pierced the night. Then a third time.

At last, reluctantly pulling away from him, she gave a little sigh of pleasure and regret. She staggered away towards the chair and slowly put her clothes back on. She sat down, legs tightly together, as if retaining the memory of what had just taken place. Several minutes passed. Suddenly, her shoulders began to shake. Gallagher could not believe it when she turned a tearful face towards him.

What was going on?

She began to reach for the P226. She picked it up and got to her feet. She pointed the weapon at Gallagher.

"Your own gun," she said. "Did you think that just because you fucked me, I would forget? You betrayed me! You know about betrayal. I thought you would understand."

Christ, he thought. She's really going to do it.

Then, behind her, he saw a fleeting movement at the window. He knew it would be no one he wanted to meet.

"Marika!" he said urgently. "Behind you!"

Amazingly, she believed him. The injured, betrayed woman vanished instantly and the superb professional, now under threat, was fighting for survival. She whirled and fired almost in the same instant. The noise of the P226 filled the small hut, but it did not drown out the choking cry beyond the window.

Jesus. She was good.

"Free me!" he urged. "You need my help!"

She did not hesitate. She had considered the odds and had made her decision. She dropped down swiftly, then scrabbled across to her pack to get something out of it. She hurried back towards him and pointed a dark object at the metal bands. They sprang open.

"Radio signal," she said, as he dropped swiftly to the floor. She put the object into a pocket, and her eyes held his for the briefest of instants as she handed him the gun. "You'll have to get dressed in the dark." She hurried to shake all the lights out.

Just then a burst of firing raked the hut.

Gallagher flattened himself to the floor. "Marika!" he hissed sharply. "Are you all right?"

"You are worried about me?" She sounded strangely pleased. "Yes, I am all right. Get dressed and get your weapons. We cannot stay in here. They will fire again soon."

He rolled over to where she'd left his clothes and felt his way into them as quickly as he could. He put on the holster, then clipped the ammunition belt about his waist. He picked up the Uzi, reached on the table for the goggles, put them on, and instantly located her.

She held the rifle, attached to it by its umbilical. She looked ready for action.

She came towards him. "Can you see me?"

"Very clearly. These people are out to get you, as well as me." He told her briefly about what Borodin had said, without identifying the source of his information.

She looked grim. "I suspected something like this.

Giraud did not come to help me. He came to finish me off if you did not succeed."

"He killed Johnno to implicate you if that plan failed. You were never meant to survive this mission. That's why they're out there. I'll go first. I've got the goggles, so I'll spot them faster than you. Once I've started firing, come out fast."

She nodded.

"Why did you trust me just then?" he asked. "You believed me when I called out."

"I knew you were doing this on your own. You left your people behind, just as I have. Therefore those out there had to be my enemies."

He nodded, understanding her reasoning. "It's been quiet for too long," he said. "They'll be creeping up on us. Just remember what I said."

"I'll be quick."

He moved towards the door and opened it slowly. It moved silently. Nothing happened. He didn't believe it for a moment. The bastards would have nightsights. Through the goggles, he could see a head in a dark beret peering through some bushes.

"Marika!" he whispered.

"Yes?"

"Straight ahead from my position, there's someone. Just his head. Can you get a lock on him?"

There was a soft noise as she shifted position. "I have him. Yes. I have a good lock."

"Take the bastard. I'll be out while they try to work out what happened."

"They must know I've got the rifle."

"Not necessarily. That weapon is not something your principals want to publicize, even among their own people."

"Go!" she said, and fired. There was a harsh cough. She was using the silencer.

The infrared round streaked towards the hapless

man in the bushes. Gallagher rolled out just as the man screamed in shock and thrashed about in his death throes.

There was a moment's uncertainty, then another burst of fire raked the hut before dying down once more. They were clearly not in a hurry to rush it. All the better.

Gallagher found himself some cover and looked around. With his window on the night, he felt almost invincible. He spotted another man, and deliberately removed the Uzi's silencer. He fired a single shot. It echoed loudly in the darkness. The man made no sound as he died, but his colleagues immediately concentrated heavy fire on the area where they thought the shot had come from.

But Gallagher was well out of the way by then. He'd kept an eye on the hut and had seen Marika roll out as they fired at him. Then she'd vanished into the forest.

The men out there didn't know it, but they were now in serious trouble. The feline and the wolf were on the prowl. It was nightmare time.

Gallagher replaced the silencer on the Uzi and also put one on the SIG. From now on, the killing was going to be quiet. The trick was to remain out of the scrutiny of the nightsights.

He heard a sudden, harsh cough and saw a brief light. Another wild thrashing in the undergrowth told him Marika had struck again. Yet another burst of wild firing followed, and the hut was raked once more. But this would not help his foes at all.

Gallagher moved on, and found himself behind a man with a rifle. The gun carried a nightsight, and the man was swinging it in a slow arc, looking for a target. The rifleman stiffened. Gallagher looked in the direction the gun was pointing and zoomed on the spot. Very briefly, he caught glimpse of a swift movement.

Marika. But she had moved again into cover. He

could see the bloom of her body heat, although the man with the rifle would not. Gallagher moved closer to him.

"Hi," Gallagher said softly.

The man, startled, whirled. Gallagher shot him as he tried to bring the rifle to bear. As the man fell, Gallagher took the rifle from the dying hands and swiftly removed the nightsight, which he threw far into the bushes. The noise caused another burst of firing, which brought a loud scream, followed by an equally loud remonstration from another quarter in a language that was not English.

Gallagher smiled. They'd just shot one of their own.

For the next half hour, Gallagher and Marika stalked and disposed of the remnants of the assault team. Then for another hour they painstakingly checked out the area, until satisfied they had got all of the men. They met again at the hut.

"We work well together," he said to her. "But we'd better not remain here. Just in case."

"No," she agreed, and pointed the rifle at him.

He simply looked at her, and waited.

Expect the unexpected, sir! How many times do I have to say it?

You would not have liked this, Warrant Officer O'Keefe.

After tense moments, she slowly lowered the weapon. "I . . . I cannot do it," she said at last.

She had spoken with such emotion, it baffled him. He remembered her tears, and was again puzzled by what was happening. But she offered no explanation. She went over to her backpack and began to make ready for leaving.

"We'll go to my Range Rover," he said. "No one can come close without setting off the alarms. We'll be safe there till morning."

"And in the morning?"

"I'll think of something."

"You will not turn me in?"

"Would you let me?"

"No."

"There's your answer."

They made it back to the Range Rover without incident. They put their gear away, but left the weapons out. Gallagher reclined the seats, and they lay down to sleep off what was left of the night.

After a while, she said, "Please make love to me."

So he did, but it was a surprisingly gentle affair, at the end of which he again felt wetness upon her cheeks.

She fell asleep in his arms.

In the morning, she was bright and cheerful. She kissed him, then climbed out of the Rover to run naked into the lake. He picked up her rifle as she swam strongly out.

It was a truly superb piece of weaponry. He had already decided that neither Fowler nor Marika's contractors would have it. Nor, for that matter, would Borodin. He would destroy it.

He watched the magnificent body in the lake and wondered what to do about her. He had no intention of harming her, nor could he bring himself to turn her in.

She was swimming back to shore and soon, had stood up like a goddess rising out of the deep and was walking back towards him. She glistened in the light of the new day as the droplets ran in tiny twinkling streams down her glorious body.

"Wasn't it cold out there?" he asked as she picked up her towel.

"A little. Do we have coffee?"

"In the red flask."

She found it and poured herself a cup. "So, Gordon? What do we do?" The green eyes held his unwaveringly.

"First the rifle."

"I have already thought about that. You shall have it."

He shook his head. "No one gets it. Let's destroy it."

She nodded approvingly. "Good. I am retiring," she went on calmly. "I have finished. Your South African friend . . . I no longer wish to kill him. There are other . . . more important things for me to do. No more guns. Those people I have shot—they were all dangerous. The man at the castle in Nottingham was selling nuclear triggers. He was set up. No one was to meet him that day."

"Were all your targets such people?"

"No. Some were criminals. Cocaine for weapons. Others . . ."

"So why would those who were paying you now want to kill you?"

"I have a list of people who are not criminals. Important international politicians."

"Jesus! You were going to kill them?"

She shook her head. "I used my contractors' organization to get help in getting to you. After I got you, I intended to disappear."

"And of course, they'd let you," Gallagher said disbelievingly.

"I have my own contacts."

"Assuming you'd managed to survive last night."

"Yes," she admitted slowly. "It was good you were with me."

"Still alive."

She smiled. "Yes. I shall give the list to your people."

"A bargain?"

"No. They can still have it. I shall stay here in the forest. I can make my own way off this island." She smiled, almost shyly. "You can come with me. I know you do not like your own people very much. It is they who betrayed you. Someone gave the information that was passed to me. But you have your own sources on the other side. Perhaps they can tell you who. So? Will you come with me? I am very rich."

"I have my own money."

"I know. Then we would not be with each other only for money."

"Put some clothes on," he said. "You're tempting me."

"No," she said, and took the towel to spread it by the water's edge. Then she lay down upon it. "Look by the trigger guard," she called. "There is a panel. Lift it and you will see a red button. Press that. It destroys all the electronics and the weapon will be useless. They do not know I know this."

Gallagher found the outline of the panel. It was so well fitted, it was easily missed. He prised it open with a knife and saw the red button. He took the rifle out of the vehicle, placed it some distance away on the sand, pressed the button, and stood back.

Nothing happened.

Then he saw thin wisps of smoke rising from the weapon. The wisps became a plume that soon turned black. There was barely any smell. In seconds, most of the rifle had become charred. The smoke drifted away.

She had come up to watch. "That is it," she said. "Now it is finished. There is not another, as far as I know. We can throw this thing into the lake, or the forest. It is biodegradable."

"Great," he said. "A biodegradable killing machine. Not the lake," he went on. "The forest. Best place. Now please put some clothes on. I can't stand this temptation for much longer."

"No," she said, and went back to the towel. "Have we got enough food?"

"I should think so."

"Then let's stay here for the day, and you can make love to me by the lake."

▪ ▪ ▪

London, the previous night, 2200 hours.

The security man Greaves had contacted Fowler with startling and frightening news. Fowler had hurried back to the office.

"Are you quite certain?" Fowler now asked him.

"There's no doubt whatsoever."

"My God. Get Haslam in Brisbane. He must have this."

"Yes, sir."

"Let's hope we're not too late."

"I'm going to chuck this thing into the forest," Gallagher said just after midday. "We can't just leave it there all day."

"Must it be now?" Marika complained languidly. "Do it tonight."

She had remained naked in the sun for most of the time, rising only to dip into the lake every so often after bouts of lovemaking. She was fortunate in having the type of skin that was not vulnerable to exposure.

"Five minutes."

"I'll be here," she told him, giving in cheerfully. "Then more love at the edge of the water."

"You're greedy," he said.

"I have waited a long time. I have a right to be greedy."

He shook his head in resignation, picked up the rifle, and walked to the forest.

"My God. Just look at that!"

Markston was sighting with his rifle, the crosshairs of the scope right on target.

Villiger was looking through binoculars. "It's Marika!" He felt a strange sensation as he watched her. She was supposed to be dead. He had killed her.

"And naked as the day she was born!" Markston was virtually salivating. "One right between those breasts . . ."

"Take your mind out of the sewer!" Sian snapped at him. She raised her binoculars to her eyes.

"I don't see Gordon," Villiger said worriedly. "The Range Rover's there. So where is he?"

"Dead," Markston said bluntly. "I told you he had a weak spot," he went on to Sian with undisguised smugness. "She's here, bold as brass, and he's copped it. Dead," he repeated. "Your wonderful Gallagher's been topped by a bird with big boobs."

"Jesus Christ, Markston!" Sian retorted disgustedly. "Shut it! We have no proof that Gallagher's dead."

"That's why she's sunning herself, is it?" He kept the rifle on the distant body. "Any moment now he's going to come out of hiding, doing cartwheels—"

"Shut it, I said!" Sian snarled. "There has to be an explanation," she added to Villiger. "I don't believe he's dead."

"I don't want to believe it either . . . but she is out there, apparently without a care in the world. She's not expecting anyone to come looking. Look at this place. It's perfect. Out of the way . . ."

"Well, I'm not taking any chances," Markston said.

"You don't fire that rifle until I tell you," Villiger said firmly.

"Who says?"

"I do. You'd better believe it."

"I don't take orders from any fucking Afrikaner . . ."

Villiger said nothing.

Markston began to put his smug expression upon his face, believing he had won the contest of wills.

"You really would not like to get me angry," Villiger

said coldly. The hard eyes bored into Markston, who visibly flinched. "Remember that."

Markston appeared to relax.

Sian allowed her binoculars to hang from her neck as she looked at him, not trusting his seeming acquiescence. She had drawn the .357 Magnum.

"Sod it," he said abruptly, sighted, and fired.

Sian was half-expecting him to do that, and she lashed out at him with the revolver. It slammed into the side of his head.

The shot seemed to echo to the heavens.

"You made me miss, you lesbian bitch!" he snarled at her in pain and rage.

"Oh, I get it," she said contemptuously. "I won't let you into my knickers, so I'm either saving it for Gallagher or I'm a lesbian bitch. Very original."

But Markston appeared to have lost control. The side of his face was beginning to swell and an ugly expression had appeared on his face.

"You think you're so fucking clever!" he yelled at her, and turned again to aim the rifle. "This time I won't miss."

Villiger had watched Markston's display with foreboding, knowing it would end badly. Then distant movement caught his eye. Urgently, he brought the binoculars up.

"It's Gallagher! He's alive! Put down that rifle, Markston! Put it down, I said!"

"Fuck off, Boer!" Markston said nastily, setting himself up for a second shot.

Sian hit him again. He ducked, not getting a shot off, but the Magnum still caught him. Even as a glancing blow, its force caused a great deal of pain.

"That's it, bitch!" he shouted. "I've had it with you!" And he turned the rifle upon her, clearly intending to shoot.

But she was ready for him. The Magnum roared once.

Markston was nearly lifted cleanly by the force of the heavy bullet striking home at such close range. He gave a peculiar whimper as he rolled twice across the sand to finally lay still upon his back. His enraged eyes stared up at the sky.

"He's dead," she said simply, not bothering to look. "You'll have to report it."

"Will I?" Villiger said mildly. "We ran into a firefight . . ."

"My bullet's in him."

Villiger went over to Markston's body and calmly rolled it over. There were two holes, one on either side. The exit wound was messy.

"Went right through," Villiger commented flatly, as if already making his report. "At that range it was inevitable. No one's going to find your bullet in him."

His portable phone buzzed with insistent urgency. "Our master's voice," he said as he snapped it off his belt. He listened, growing tense. He looked at Markston's body.

"Too late for that now," he said into the phone. He listened some more. "Where are you? We'll wait. We'll be here for a while."

"Haslam," he said as he broke connection. "He's on his way in Ansen's helicopter. Interesting developments. Seems Markston was dirty. Just how much is not yet known. But it looks as if you did your department a favor." He looked towards the far side of the lake. "We'd better get over there. Something's not quite right, and that worries me."

End Moves

Markston had not missed.

Gallagher had been on his way back when he'd heard the echoing shot, knowing it to be the sound of a rifle. Immediately, with dread in his mind, he'd broken into a run. As he came out of the forest, he saw Marika, off the towel and trying to crawl to the cover of the Range Rover.

"Oh God!" he cried softly, horrified. "Not again."

He ran towards her and got down on the white sand to hold her gently against his chest. He grabbed the towel to place it against the terrible wound in her side. It was in almost the same spot where Villiger had shot her all those years before.

"Marika!" he said helplessly. "Take it easy. I'll—"

She raised a hand to his face. "No use," she said, grimacing with the pain. "This time your friend . . . has succeeded."

"Not my friend," he said fiercely. "Not my friend. He would not have done this."

"Then . . . then who?"

"I don't know," he said in a choked voice that surprised him with its intensity. "Oh God, Marika. I don't know! Hang on. Please hang on. I'll call . . ."

He looked beyond the lake and saw two hurrying figures. They were still some distance away. No matter. He would know who they were soon enough.

"No," she said. "It will be too late. This . . . this time, I am not so . . . lucky."

"Jesus, Marika. I didn't want this to happen."

She was grabbing tightly at him. "Not your . . . fault. I . . . I must tell you something so . . . so you can understand . . ." She gave a long-drawn-out sigh and fell silent.

He was afraid she had died, but she moved slightly, trying to speak.

"Don't talk," he said. "I'll call for help. Just let me get the phone in the Rover—"

"Must. Can't wait." The voice faded so quickly, he had to place an ear to her mouth.

Whatever she said made his eyes widen and his mouth hang open. He seemed to be in shock; then he closed his mouth slowly and swallowed. He turned to stare across the lake, a strange look of pain in his eyes. The people were closer, but he didn't seem to care. Then he recognized Villiger and Sian. Where was Markston?

He looked down at Marika. The beautiful body was still.

"Oh God, Marika," he began in anguish. "How could I have known? All these years . . ."

He held her to him tightly, her blood smearing itself against his chest. He stroked her hair gently, moving some strands that had fallen across her face. The beautiful green eyes had closed forever. He licked at a finger to wipe some sand away from her cheek.

▪ ▪ ▪

Villiger and Sian looked at him curiously as they came up. It was clearly not what they had expected to see. Gallagher was still holding on to Marika, but he'd used the large, now-bloodstained towel to cover her nakedness more completely.

He stared at them emptily. "Who did this?"

"Markston . . ." Villiger began.

"Markston! And where's the bastard?"

"Dead," Sian answered. "I shot him."

Gallagher stared at her. "What?"

"He tried to shoot me."

"What are you saying?" He looked from one to the other.

"Markston was dirty," Villiger told him awkwardly. "We literally just found out. Haslam called. He only got to know just before he passed it on to us. But by then it was of course too late."

"That's just great."

They stood irresolutely for some moments, looking at him.

"It was very odd," Sian said. "He seemed determined to kill . . . her." She stared with fascination at Marika's body.

"Markston," Gallagher said softly. "The bastards covered every possibility."

Their eyes were questioning.

"What do you mean?" Villiger asked.

"They planted Markston to kill her. He was one of many."

"But I thought . . ." Sian began.

"I'll tell you all about it later," Gallagher said wearily. "There are a lot of bodies back there in the forest. First help me get her into the Range Rover and out of the sun. Then I've got to clean her up."

"I'll clean her for you," Sian said.

"No. It's something I must do. Thanks all the same."

It was ironic, he thought. It was almost as if he were back on the snowbound slopes of Courchevel, with Lauren's dead body in his arms. The person who had killed Lauren had been one of Marika's own people.

They helped him to place Marika gently into the Range Rover. Then they heard the sound of the approaching helicopters.

There were armed response teams all over the place. Three helicopters had landed. One had carried Haslam, Ansen, and MacAndless, who'd come down from Cairns. The others, bigger Hueys, had brought the response teams. MacAndless had gone into the forest with one of the teams while Ansen stayed with Haslam.

Haslam looked at Marika's body in the Range Rover. "Sorry it finished like this, lad. You can't keep her here for very long. One of the choppers can take her back."

"And just where is that to be?"

Haslam sighed. "Look. I know how you feel."

"No. You have no idea how I feel."

Haslam looked round at Sian, Villiger, and Ansen, and finally back to Gallagher.

"I . . ." he began, pausing as MacAndless hurried towards them.

"Jesus," MacAndless said to Gallagher. "There are bodies everywhere. Those guys look like special forces to me, Major," he went on to Ansen. "Not ours. Definitely off that yacht." Then it was back to Gallagher. "How did you manage to take them out? They had enough gear to start a war. And there's some bloke back there with a nasty piece of weaponry with a double blade that's gone into his chest, right through to his back. You did that?"

Gallagher nodded, and saw that Ansen understood.

"Christ," MacAndless said. "What are you?"

"Those bodies are not all my own work," Gallagher said, dodging the question. He pointed to Marika. "We did it. Together. She was the best."

MacAndless stared at him, not really understanding at all.

Haslam said, "Thank you, Mr. MacAndless."

MacAndless glanced at Ansen, who nodded slightly. MacAndless went back to his team.

"What yacht?" Gallagher asked.

"MacAndless spotted a large motor yacht off Cairns some weeks ago during a routine chopper patrol. There were two women on the sun deck, but he could see very few crew or guests, which he thought was odd for such a big luxury boat. He didn't give it much more thought, but the strangeness of it stayed in his mind. He decided to have it tagged—unobtrusively, of course, in case it turned out to be some perfectly legitimate bigwig who might take strong exception to being . . ."

"Spied on."

"Yes," Ansen said flatly. "Two days ago, he got news it was off Heron Island. The two women were the only ones who showed themselves during the day, plus one or two supposed crew members. Then this morning, it was seen heading off at speed from this area, making for international waters. It had obviously dropped off those men in the forest. When they didn't return, those still aboard decided to get away as quickly as possible."

"Are you searching?"

"We are, and we've found it . . . or, rather, what remains of it. We believe those left on board were picked up by a sub, after which charges left on the yacht blew it to pieces. It's been done before, in the Pacific."

Gallagher turned away to look at Marika's body. All those people sent to get her, and the one to succeed had been a shit like Markston.

"She had a list," he now said to Haslam. "International politicians being set up for hits. She was going to tell me." His eyes were lifeless. "Now you lot have got a job on your hands. She can't very well tell you, can she? Who these people are, and when those hits are likely to take place, is your guess as well as mine."

"Someone should have checked Markston out, for God's sake!" he yelled suddenly, startling them all.

He took a deep breath, then said, "She's not going anywhere. I'll bury her in the forest."

"You can't," Ansen objected. "First you'd need permission, which you're unlikely to get. And—"

"What do you think she'll do? Pollute the place?" He gave an odd laugh. "She's biodegradable."

Haslam led Ansen aside and talked to him with quiet urgency. "Look," Ansen began, when they had returned. "Perhaps I can arrange something."

"Fine."

They buried Marika near the little hut. It was fitting, Gallagher felt. If anyone had any curiosity about the hoops and lengths of nylon rope in the wooden wall, none voiced them as they were taken down for disposal.

Later, Gallagher stood by the Range Rover, ready to leave.

"You won't change your mind about coming back with us to the UK?" Haslam asked. He said nothing about the rifle.

Gallagher shook his head. "Fowler can wait. I want to stay for a while." He turned to Villiger. "Piet. Thanks for watching my back." He held out his hand. Instead, Villiger embraced him.

"Hey, man," Villiger said gruffly. "We'll have that drink on Table Mountain. Things are changing back home. No one can stop it now. They can try, but they won't succeed."

"I'll count on it." Then they shook hands.

Gallagher turned to Sian. "And thank *you,* Sian.

You're a good backup." He held out his hand, took hers, and shook it.

She reached forward impulsively to kiss him on the corner of his mouth. "Anytime." Green eyes smiled sadly at him. "I look forward to working with you again. Mr. Haslam, or Mr. Fowler, will tell me when you need me. It will be a privilege."

Then it was the turn of Ansen, and MacAndless.

"Glad you got Johnno's killer," Ansen said.

"I'm glad I got the chance," Gallagher said. "I wanted that bastard. And . . . sorry I messed up your patch."

Ansen's smile was so fleeting as they shook hands, it might not have existed. "I'll survive. But don't give me a repeat too soon. Please."

"I'll try not to. Jock."

"Take care, mate," MacAndless said. "Come down next marlin season, and I'll show you how to hook a big fish."

"I might take you up on that."

Gallagher climbed into the Rover and set off without a backward glance.

He stopped at one of the resorts and made a call from a public phone. Two hours later, Borodin came into the restaurant where they had arranged to meet.

Borodin's help had been invaluable, and he wished Marika were alive to provide the information that the Russian needed. But Markston had seen to that. They spoke for about an hour. Borodin had not had an entirely fruitless time. His Spetsnaz had a captive who had proved very cooperative. The information was incomplete, but it was a start.

Then Gallagher asked Borodin to do something for him, something that needed great sensitivity and caution. Borodin agreed to help.

Like Haslam, Borodin made no mention of the rifle.

Gallagher was certain both men had expected him to destroy it. They had read him accurately, and he wasn't so sure he liked that idea.

After Borodin left, he called his machine in London. Among the messages were two very personal ones.

One was from Rhiannon. "It's me . . . I'm . . . I'm sorry about our . . . I want to come back. For good. Let's talk. Please?"

The other was from Miranda. "Still away? Don't forget where I live, will you? Or my phone number. Call me. I'd like that."

He drove up to Indian Head and found Naira. She was astonished, and pleasantly surprised, to see him.

"So you made it."

"I made it."

"I'm glad. This is going to be one hell of a sunset," she continued. "Isn't the world just beautiful?"

"Yes," he said. "Beautiful."

Somewhere in eastern Europe, he had a little daughter called Elena.

At the house near Brisbane, the old aborigine stood in the garden and looked up at the night sky. He knew she would not be coming back. He went to get the last snake and left the house for good.

A day later, in a forest, he set the Taipan free.

About The Author

Born in Dominica, Julian Jay Savarin was educated in Britain and took a degree in history before serving in the Royal Air Force. Mr Savarin lives in England and is the author of several previous novels from Severn House.